Embracing the Darkness

Book 1 in the Black Rose Series

LAURA MORGAN

Copyright © 2013 Laura Morgan
All rights reserved.

Second edition
Produced 2016 by Laura Morgan

For paper copies:
ISBN: 1499139950
ISBN-13: 978-1499139952

An important message from the author.

Before you read this book, please be ready to delve into a dark and taboo world of demons and angels who can and will do as they please. This series, especially the first novel, will immerse you in a world filled with dark places and even darker beings. They are not human, and do not act the way you and I act, or think the way you and I think. Please be ready for some controversial themes and for me to push the boundaries.
I tell you this not just because there are adult scenes or a few taboo subjects, but because I mean it, and would hate to give you any false expectations about happy endings and softly, softly romance. This series is not for everyone, and I know that, so please decide if you're ready before diving in.

If you're on the fence, or have heard the rumours of the depravities and darkness that await you, please assume they are all true. I can understand how some readers were upset and discouraged by the thought of some of the darker themes, but urge you to trust me…
If you're interested, I explain these points further on my blog, and would urge you to take a look before starting this book. Please be aware there are spoilers in the post, but that it might put your mind at ease before you dive in.

PLEASE NOTE

This story depicts explicit sexual relationships between consenting adults, including elements of coerced consent and intimidation, which may be a trigger for some readers.

This novel is absolutely not suitable for those under the age of 18. No part of this publication may be reproduced, stored in a retrieval system or transmitted in any form or by any means without the prior written permission of the publisher.

This is a work of fiction. Names, characters, places, and incidents are the products of the author's imagination or are used fictitiously. Any resemblance to actual events, locales, or persons, living or dead, is entirely coincidental.

Cover art design by Laura Morgan.
Cover photograph © Lucky Luke/Shutterstock

Praise for the Embracing the Darkness...

This book has an amazing dark edge to it and personally I just can't get enough. I am so glad I took the chance and read these books as I was hooked from the beginning and found it overtaking my life.
--Jodie for Queens of the Darkside Book Blog

The story is full of twists and plots that keep you on the edge of your seat and blow your mind! I was warped into this world and felt that I never wanted to leave! The book had me thinking constantly and had inner battles of what is right and wrong but you have to overcome this as the author states at the beginning of the book. Once this happens she warps you in....so much so that I couldn't put it down and read this in 24 hours!!!
--Sarah

Wow what can I say I've read 100s of books and so many are very good but forgettable, this is a book you have to read with an open mind as its dark and twisted but it's absolutely fantastic, after getting over the taboo subjects and accepting the direction of the story, I was pulled into the story so much happens its full of adventure, challenges and different emotions, it's a story that's unpredictable with just the right amount of suspense and twists! I will be reading the next book cannot wait to see what can happen next...
--Karen James

Dedication

I would like to thank my husband Brian and our two lovely children. Without their support and patience Cate and her dark story might never have made it from my mind onto the page.

I cannot thank my amazing street team enough for all the wonderful support and encouragement along the way. Please continue to stick with me, and together I know we can do plenty more wonderful things.

Secondly, thank you to all my close family and friends who encouraged my creativity and read the first few copies of my final manuscript, you helped me to stop being afraid and just go for it, without your support I might never have sent my words out into the world.

CHAPTER ONE

Dark eyes had watched Cate's every move since the day she was born. She had no idea of her fate, or of her father's impatience at having to wait for her. But, he waited. Waited for the day that she would be ready, able and most importantly, willing, to join him. Only then could Cate's true nature be revealed, and only then could she possess the power and the ability to really be a part of his world. Only then could she begin embracing the darkness within and reach her full potential at last.

***

"What the hell am I doing here?" Cate whispered into the cold night air. She'd woken to find herself hidden in the shadows of a tall, dark, sinister looking building in the centre of town that she'd never even seen before, and this was not the first time. She had no idea how or why she'd suddenly begun sleepwalking, but for the third night in a row, she had gone to bed and jolted awake, standing in the middle of town dressed only in her pyjamas, and shivering violently as she came to.

Cate pressed herself into the wall, panicking and feeling desperate to be back home in her bed. She looked around, but found nothing familiar in the shadows, and no sign of home, so she just began running in the same direction she had the previous nights'—heading towards the closest light she could see on the horizon. She took a peek back towards the shadows, and Cate felt as though there were eyes on her. It had to be her mind playing tricks, but she was sure she could even make out the dark figure of a person standing not far from where she'd awoken. The shadow soon disappeared and she pressed on, making her way towards the main road and back to her home without so much as another glance back.

Everything about those episodes freaked her out, but Cate refused to speak about them to anyone, not even her mother. She was in denial. Talking about them would just make it real, and even more terrifying. At just eighteen years old, Cate Rose's life so far had been otherwise uneventful. Well, until the strange sleepwalking sessions had begun a few nights' before.

Her mother, Ella Rose, hadn't heard a thing each time, but Cate wondered if her regular nightcap helped her remain oblivious to the comings and goings after lights-out in the Rose household. They had a close relationship, being just the two of them, and Ella had always tried hard to provide for her daughter. Cate knew her mother was very much alone, but had remained strong when it came to their quiet and sometimes lonely life just the two of them. The salary and bonuses she received from her job as an insurance saleswoman were more than enough to keep the two of them comfortable, but Cate was just as strong and independent. She enjoyed having her freedom, and so earned her own money on the side by working shifts at the local pub.

She looked a lot like her mother, strikingly so. Her long dark brown curls and bright green eyes were exactly the same. Everyone had always commented how she was the image of Ella, and Cate had always been able to see it herself, too. She was the same height, slim build, and even had the exact same curvy, hourglass figure as her. Cate often wondered what traits or looks she might've gotten from her father, but she couldn't see anyone else in herself at all. Ella hardly ever spoke of the mysterious sperm-donor, but when Cate had finally pushed her one night, she seemed ashamed to admit that it'd been a one-night-stand with a boy she'd met during her slightly rebellious younger years. He'd reportedly been at a party she'd gone to on Halloween, and the pair of them had met whilst dancing in the sea of goths and punks. Luke, or so he'd told her his name was, had literally crashed into Ella as they both danced with their friends, sending her flying. He'd then supposedly apologised and offered her a hand to dance, and she had been smitten with him instantly. Ella had then told Cate how it wasn't long until they sneaked off to an upstairs room to be alone together.

"He was just so gorgeous, a real life bad-boy," she'd said, her eyes glazing over at the memory. "One word and I was putty in his hands. We only went up to talk in privacy, honestly, but one thing led to another, and I ended up sleeping with him. The next day, I woke up and he was gone, and I never saw him again. I tried to find him, but have never managed to track him down. A few weeks later I realised I'd skipped my period, and voila!" she had then said, giving her daughter a hug before eagerly changing the subject.

Cate wanted to understand it, but hadn't been able to. In fact, she'd never been interested in boys so couldn't understand the appeal of a one-night-stand. There was just no spark, no lust, or desire for them. If anything, she was so utterly bored by their fixations on computer games, cars, and sports, and so she just switched off whenever she was around them. Her indifference to the opposite sex seemed quite clear, and she'd often found herself wondering if she might be gay.

During her mid-teens, Cate had started hanging around with a small group of girls her age, and most of them seemed uninterested in the boys at their school as well, so it'd suited her perfectly. At eighteen, Cate had put her theory to the test and finally had her first kiss with her best friend, a girl named Dylan. They'd met at school and gotten closer over the years until finally sharing a drunken kiss, and while it'd been nice, Cate still couldn't find that passion within that others described. For some reason, it was as though an unspoken voice deep inside of her chimed in resistance to her ever getting close to anyone—as though she was holding out for someone life changing. She and Dylan were close, but Cate knew things would never go any further. She trusted Dylan completely, so it wasn't that she was shy, but for some reason Cate would always back off if things turned into more than mere flirtation. Nothing had ever felt completely right, and she worried she might never figure it out. Cate had quickly realised that even her relationship with Dylan was nothing more than a deep and lasting friendship. She enjoyed their closeness, but wondered if perhaps she was just struggling so much with her sexuality that she had misinterpreted her feelings for her friend. Deep down, she knew Dylan was no fool. She knew that Cate wasn't serious about experimenting with her, but seemed to be enjoying having that closeness to someone, anyone. Rather than put a stop to their intimate connection, she kept up the pretence as well.

The night after her third strange awakening in the shadows, their group of friends all decided to camp out in an old field close to town. Cate wasn't sure at first. If she were honest, she was worried about finding herself outside the strange building again after another sleepwalking episode, but couldn't bring herself to tell any of her friends about her nightly strolls, or her fears as to why they were happening. She'd even tried to find her own way to confront those fears, but couldn't find the creepy old church during the day, no matter how hard she'd tried.

After being badgered by her best friend all day, she eventually went along with the camping idea. Dylan had fluttered her eyelashes and pleaded with her, and in the end, she couldn't say no. They always had a blast, and Cate had no doubt that night would be any different. Their group of friends would regularly hang out together at each other's houses, or at the local beach where they could enjoy their privacy once the sun went down. Even in the winter months, they'd build a fire or huddle between the wooden huts that straddled the beachfront. Nothing stopped them from having their fun. In their small hometown on the southeast coast of England, the rest of the world would fall away when their group got together. Cate felt at peace with Dylan and the others. She was light and carefree, as though nothing else existed or mattered, and knew she'd needed it.

She often watched her friends and wondered about them, who they were in the recesses of their souls, or what surprises they might be hiding. Cate wondered about a lot of things, mostly their secrets and which lies they'd told throughout their lives. She wanted to get inside their heads and learn their truths, and while Dylan was Cate's best friend and her closest ally, she still wondered what went on beneath the everyday façade she instinctively knew everyone wore—even her.

Cate watched Dylan as she tended to the campfire, and for some reason felt compelled to really take her in. She was a curvaceous girl, and her short height accentuated those curves effortlessly. Dylan always wore her ash-blonde, shoulder length hair up in a constant ponytail and had her hazel eyes hidden behind thickly rimmed, stylish glasses—even though she didn't actually need them. She had a prowess about her every move that made almost everyone stop and take notice. Although not conventionally gorgeous, she radiated mischievousness, and knew how to use her sexuality to her advantage.

Dylan was warm and kind as well, and Cate had been drawn to her from the first moment they'd met at school years ago. She'd been having a hard time with the dreaded long distance running, and one day had decided to skip their PE class, opting instead for hiding out in the girls' toilets to wait for the bell that signalled the next lesson. There she'd found Dylan, hiding out as well. They'd got chatting to pass the time, and had liked one another instantly. From that day on they'd become the best of friends, and she'd been there for Cate in ways no one else had ever been.

It didn't matter if she hid secrets from her or wanted her in ways Cate couldn't reciprocate, she felt it in their bones that they were connected, and would be forever.

CHAPTER TWO

The group of girls pitched their tents in the field and sat around a fire in the centre. They then chatted long into the night and shared a few bottles of a vodka-based fruit drink Angelica—the diva, and without question the leader of their group—had picked up on her way over. The others were giggling loudly without a care in the world, but for some reason Cate couldn't relax. She was tired and wanted to get some rest, but was worried about the sleepwalking, and the whole thing made her feel uneasy. To top it all off, the entire time they were sat around the fire, she was convinced someone was watching her. Memories of the figure in the shadows were now haunting her, and she just couldn't shake it. There was also a strange feeling in the pit of Cate's stomach, almost like something was calling to her, telling her to follow its beacon. It was strange, as though she was needed elsewhere, and the whole thing scared her. Her whole life she'd struggled with peculiar urges she couldn't explain, ones that sometimes scared her. Night terrors had plagued her childhood, and then for years she'd sworn to having seen shadows moving in the periphery of her vision. She'd given up on channelling the urges via art or by trying to pen stories based on her experiences, as all she seemed able to create were sick and disturbing images or scenarios. Since meeting Dylan and the other girls they nightmares had eased dramatically. It was as though the distraction somehow kept her innermost oddities at bay; at least until her sleepwalking sessions had started a few weeks after her eighteenth birthday of course. Still uneasy, Cate grabbed her mobile phone and sent a text message to her mother, checking in with her. She was panicking in case the strange feeling was some kind of omen that things weren't right back at home, but thankfully she got back a quick reply within a few minutes.

I'm fine, have fun with your friends xxx

It was a short response, but probably just meant Ella was pre-occupied or chilled out at home with a glass of wine. Cate imagined her curled up on the sofa watching one of her favourite soap operas, and smiled before sending back a smiley-faced emoticon return.

Hours later, the other girls were all fast asleep, but Cate still couldn't shake her strange urge to leave. She just lay in her tent, wide-awake, listening to the sounds of the night all around them. Their small town was more than safe, so she knew not to be afraid, but still she couldn't settle. Just after two o'clock in the morning, she'd had enough. Cate dressed as quietly as possible in her jeans and hoodie jumper, matched with her black boots and scarf, and then she left the small tent. Her roomie for the night stirred, but didn't wake up, and Cate was glad. She didn't want Dylan to worry, but also needed some time alone, and so headed off towards the nearby town for a walk and to try and clear her head.

As soon as she left the field, she felt different almost immediately. It was as though something really was pulling her towards the outskirts of the small town. There was a powerful urge that compelled her onwards despite the dark, cold night, and it was one that could not be ignored. Cate headed through the empty streets, taking in the shadows around her, and she wondered if the strange urge was the same thing that'd pulled her out of her bed the past three nights as well. This time though, she was fully awake and aware of her surroundings, and the adrenaline kept her pushing on towards the strange beacon. The rational part of her brain thought it was odd that she wasn't scared, but her urge to follow the calling spurred her on. She eventually headed off the street and down a back alley, and was completely unsure where she was even going, but somehow knew she had to go there. Something inside her yearned for the answers she sensed she'd get once she arrived at her destination. Cate had no idea how she knew that, but every fibre of her being told her she had to trust it and follow her impulses.

She soon found herself at a run-down building that looked almost like an old church. Cate soon realised it was the same building she had found herself outside three times previous, and was absolutely sure of it when she found what appeared to be the same spot she'd woken in the night before. The windows of the old building were smashed, and the brickwork was battered and covered in graffiti, but there was a hint of light inside. She couldn't help but go in, curiosity getting the better of her. It was where she needed to be, where her body had been trying to drag her night after night, she just knew it. As she got closer to the source of the light, the feelings inside her intensified and her whole body tingled with anticipation. Her thoughts were running wild, and she forced herself to stop and take a breath.

"How could I just leave my friends and wander off like this?" she wondered aloud, speaking in just a quiet whisper to herself as she leaned against the dusty wall amongst the shadows. It was so dangerous to be out in the middle of the night all alone, and she almost turned back. Her inner struggle was beginning to overwhelm her, yet everything inside implored her to carry on. She knew she was so close to learning the truth. The how's and why's behind her nightly jaunts. Her body was urging her to continue with her pursuit of the strange beacon, and her mind eventually obeyed. She knew she had to find answers, even if she didn't like what she found.

The sound of women chatting quietly greeted her ears as Cate rounded a corner, and inside she discovered a group of four women sitting huddled around a small lantern in the centre of a large, dark room. It was mostly empty inside, apart from an old altar in one corner, but it'd clearly seen better days. The women all looked up at her and smiled as she entered, beckoning her to join them when she came further into the large room. She went to speak, but one of the women, a petite lady Cate guessed to be around forty years old with black hair styled in a bob, held her index finger to her lips in order to shush her.

"Welcome, Cate," she said as her eyes skimmed over the girl standing before her. "We've been trying to reach you for days. It took us a while to get through their protective circle tonight, but I'm glad we managed it in the end." The woman positively beamed, eyeing her warmly and with clear affection in her dark brown eyes. She then shuffled sideways so their new guest could join her and the other women around the small bit of heat that came from the lantern.

Cate was shocked and confused by what she'd found, and yet she stepped closer still. The women all grinned at her as though they really had been expecting her, but she couldn't understand what the woman had meant by her comment. She sat down in the now vacant spot on the floor and looked at her in obvious bemusement.

"How do you know me?" she eventually asked, and took a wary look around.

"I'm afraid I've gotten this all the wrong way around. You see, we haven't had to do this before," the woman replied with an almost shy laugh. "Let me explain, my name is Alma. I'm a dark witch, and these ladies all form part of my coven." She looked around the circle and Cate followed her gaze. Despite thinking they were clearly all insane, she smiled politely and leaned forward to shake hands with each of the women as they introduced themselves. Opposite Alma there was a woman named Sara, a muscularly built woman with long blonde hair and dark blue eyes that twinkled warmly in the dark light as she greeted her. Next to her was another black haired girl called Amy. She had light blue eyes that somehow shone in the dark church, but she seemed colder, more distant than the other two. Cate found herself eager to move on from her intimidating gaze, and quickly greeted the fourth and final woman, a red haired and seemingly much younger girl called Nancy.

After the introductions, Cate was still none the wiser. With the formalities over, she looked back at the woman beside her, and was unsure how best to ask her for clarification on the one word she'd spoken that was still at the forefront of her mind—*witch*. "You must be wondering what the hell I'm talking about?" Alma asked after a few moments, and laughed at what seemed to be an inside joke, but then carried on before Cate could answer. "We were sent here to get you so that your progenitor can come and take you home, my dear."

Cate gasped, and felt incredibly confused. After all, she'd never heard of such old-fashioned words being used in everyday life, nor had her mother said a word about Cate's father being more sperm-donor than long lost relative. Ella had always maintained that she hadn't seen him since the night she was conceived, so had never been able to tell him that his daughter even existed, but never in a way that spoke of such distant overseeing.

She opened her mouth to tell Alma that she must be mistaken, but no words seemed to find her lips, so the strange woman continued with her even weirder story. "You see, he can only visit your world when the moon is in the right phases with the Earth. He's been trying to sire an heir for quite some time, and you're his first and only successful progeny at present. Your father has waited eighteen years for you to come of age so that he can take you home and teach you all about your powers and true heritage, Cate. Today is that day, and it's a truly wonderful occasion, for all of us."

Cate's mind went into overdrive; it was all just too much. She couldn't even fathom what crazy games these women were playing with her, or why. She wanted to get out of there, but found herself rooted to her spot, unable to move her body for some bizarre reason, and soon began to panic.

"What the hell?" Cate blurted out, making the other witches laugh, but Alma remained straight-faced. "This doesn't make any sense at all! Who exactly are you talking about? I don't get it. And what's all this stuff about the moons and siring heirs? Yuk. Who exactly is this guy?"

"That would be me," a deep voice from the other side of the room called over to them, and its ominous sound silenced her rambled speech in an instant. There was power behind that voice. Scary and intimidating power. Cate tried to see through the darkness, but could only just about make out an outline of a tall man over in the shadows. He moved slowly towards them, and as he came closer the witches bowed their heads to him and she heard them mutter the word, *majesty*, in greeting.

Cate felt her body release from its strange paralysing hold, and she eventually stood to greet him, hoping to get some answers at last. As she watched the man approach, she quickly realised just how utterly scared she was of him—terrified to her very core, in fact. Cate could feel the air around her buzz with some kind of omnipotent power, and she felt him drawing her in. It was as if she was opening up to him on some otherworldly level, and the sensation freaked her out. As he reached her, the man outstretched his hand, and Cate instinctively took it. They shook formally, and her whole body went crazy with that same invading sensation. It was as if her senses all came alive at once. His touch was both intense and powerful, and it overwhelmed her.

"I'm your father—your creator—and I'm pleased to meet you at long last." The man smiled and stared down into Cate's eyes, seemingly taking her in easily despite the darkness that enveloped them. "I know that you are known here as Cate, but the name I had wanted you to be given was actually Hecate, in homage to the fabled dark goddess. In Greek mythology she was associated with being the goddess of fire, witchcraft and the moon. It would've been perfect for you. But, despite my attempts to sway her, it seems your mother wasn't too keen on it in the end," he informed her with a small laugh, and then he suddenly pulled Cate into a tight hug.

In his arms, she still felt scared, yet somehow safe. She could sense his power, but still didn't understand any part of the situation at all. Either it was all some crazy and elaborate hoax, or it was for real, but one thing was for sure, Cate knew things were never going to be the same again.

"You're truly my father?" she asked, feeling as though the rest of the world had fallen away around them. He was all that mattered. His power and presence the only thing she needed.

"Yes," the peculiar man told her, smiling down at her affectionately.

"What does that mean? And, who exactly *are* you?" she then added hesitantly.

He pulled away from their embrace and cupped Cate's face in his hands, drawing her gaze to his as he contemplated his response. She had a moment to really look at him then, to take him in as he stared down at her. He was handsome. Cate guessed he was in his mid-forties, with dark blond hair and deep blue eyes that were somehow almost black in the dark church. He had a rugged look about him, sporting a short beard while wearing dark chinos and a utility jacket. But, there was also a softness to him. Cate saw it when he looked into her eyes, but he soon hid it away again behind his stoic features when he opened his mouth to speak.

"I'm the being that gave you life, just like you must imagine, and yet so much more. You belong to me, Cate. I own you," he whispered, and seemed to revel in her surprised gasp. "Oh, and I'm the Devil," he finally added with a sinister grin.

CHAPTER THREE

Cate's head was spinning and the witch's words were almost starting to make sense, but she couldn't bring herself to believe them. She was still incredibly confused and wondered what on Earth he was playing at telling her such an outrageous story. Cate thought about her friends back at the campsite, and wondered what Alma had meant when she'd referred to them and their circle that she'd been inside in that field.

That was the moment she realised that her father could read her mind. He spoke to her as though she'd asked the questions aloud, and didn't even offer a flicker of an apologetic expression that he'd been caught eavesdropping on her private thoughts.

"I know you think you can trust them, but don't. They're a coven of white witches, Cate. They've been keeping tabs on you for a while now, just like Alma and her dark coven. They've tried to hide you from me for years, and used their power to try to keep you away tonight so that I couldn't call you to my side. That's why Dylan befriended you in the first place," he told her, without a care for her pain at finding out the truth about her supposed best friend. Cate's breath caught in her throat, and a small sob forced its way out of her. Had Dylan had been lying to her all along? Cate had to wonder if she'd really been serious about her friendship at all, or had their entire relationship all been simply to keep her under their scrutiny?

"I don't believe so," he answered her thoughts again, and his words pulled Cate out of her sad reverie. "By all accounts she was only ever meant to be your friend, to get close to you and gain your trust. But I think she got too close and started developing a real friendship with you, just as you did with her. I know you'll miss your friends, but the life you have waiting for you at my side will be so much more plentiful than you could've ever imagined. You won't even think about that white witch once you're home with me, where you truly belong," he informed her with a grin. "And besides, we don't consort with white witches anyway. You'll soon forget all about her, my love," he seemed to add as an afterthought.

The dark witches then rose from their places on the floor and encircled the two of them.

"It's time, your majesty," Alma said quietly, and he nodded.

"Will you come with me, Cate?" her master asked, while staring into her eyes and holding her close again. She couldn't truly fathom where it was he meant, but she assumed he was talking of Hell and despite being terrified, Cate knew she had to go with him. Her strange past suddenly all made sense, and she wanted a piece of what he was so willing to offer her. They'd only just met, but she knew then that the strange beacon and urges she'd felt the past few nights were all thanks to him. She was drawn to him entirely and had to know if what he and the witches had told her could possibly be true. Curiosity got the better of her. The promise of a life by his side stretched out before her, and Cate quickly made up her mind.

"Yes," she replied, and she drank in her master's smile. She then relished in the warmth he shared as he held her tight, pulling her to him. Cate had never known a father's affection, and knew she might truly be going crazy, but that this might also be the closest she'd get to it if his words were true. She knew he was powerful and scary, but already trusted that he'd take care of her like he'd promised. He watched her for a moment, and then leaned in close to speak softly in her ear, evidently pleased with her so easily obtained compliance.

"This is going to feel weird at first. You'll feel as if you cannot breathe, but you just need to remember that you're an almighty being—far more powerful than any human. Your power is there for the taking; you only need to open yourself up to embody it. There's no need to take a single breath to survive in Hell, and in fact there's no oxygen at all down there. You are my heiress, and will be henceforth known as the Dark Princess. There's such greatness and potential within you, and I cannot wait to spend eternity with you by my side," he told her, and with that, the world around them whizzed away. She felt like she was being squeezed for a second or two, all the while being pulled downwards, and the odd sensation made her want to cry out, but Cate kept her cool. It only lasted a few seconds, and then it was thankfully over.

She felt the floor solidify again beneath her feet, and as he'd warned her, Cate's chest suddenly tightened. She began to panic, and felt as though she was being suffocated. The heat was intense all around, and her vision blurred for a few seconds, making her panic even more, and yet her conscious mind reined her back in. She slowed her frenzied thoughts and remembered what he had told her, all the while coming to terms with the realisation that it really was no hoax or crazy and elaborate lie. They really had just teleported into Hell.

Cate closed her eyes and thought about the breath in her lungs, telling herself that somehow she needn't do it to survive. She slowed her body's cries for air and focussed instead on regaining her composure. After just a few minutes, she stood tall and stared in awe as the full reality of what'd just happened dawned on her. She even wondered if it could really be real or if she was dreaming, lying beside Dylan in that cold tent while her mind was somehow vividly dreaming away.

"Yes my darling, it's all very real. Welcome home," he said, responding to her thoughts again.

Cate looked up at their ruler, and was finally able to see him fully in the red-tinged light. He took her aback. The Devil was so commanding and had so much power and presence, but of course he did. The almighty master of Hell was everything he had ever been portrayed to be—powerful and fierce, yet alluring and seductive. Cate knew she had a lot to learn before she would truly feel a part of this world, but honestly, she couldn't wait to get started.

It wasn't long until she was given a tour of the nether-kingdom that was to become her home. She had no idea of her place in it as yet, and didn't feel comfortable taking on her title of Dark Princess until she felt she deserved it. He might not have been a father to her during her life, but she was certain there were expectations of how their relationship would go now that she'd come down into the fiery depths with him as his one and only heiress, and Cate wanted to do Satan proud.

She tried not to look lost as Alma led the way. In many ways, Hell reminded her very much of Earth, apart from the red skies and intense heat, and she took it all in with a smile. She even thought to herself how the portrayals in books and on television back up on Earth was actually pretty close to the truth, and she was full of admiration at how they'd created an entire civilization there. In the centre of the gigantic city stood a huge castle overlooking the entire realm. It was vast, oppressive and gothic, yet beautiful, and was surrounded by many buildings and gardens that opened out onto walkways. The setup was similar to a human city and its streets, but without the cars or lights to provide a backdrop.

She was informed that many different beings lived in the city and walked those streets, although she suspected none of them were mortal. Cate let her mind wander and began to imagine where the human souls might be kept. She thought of torture dungeons and fiery pits somewhere in the depths below, but knew those things were most likely very real, and didn't want to ask the question aloud in fear she might be right. She didn't need to know about those things in too greater detail just yet, and she certainly didn't want to see them.

Inside the dark castle itself, Cate was given a tour. After seeing the lavish palace in all its glory, she was shown around her family's private chambers last of all. They were huge, and the living area took up an entire wing in the fortress that loomed over the city. Their wing was her master's main residence and evidently hers now, too. It was spacious, comfortable and private, with access only granted to their dark minions via direct order from Satan himself. She found it odd at first that he wanted her to live with him there, and offered to take a room in the opposite wing where the level one demons lived, but he wouldn't hear of it. The Devil told her how he'd lived alone for thousands of years, but was ready to share his world with another at last. Despite his many underlings, he seemed lonely. Cate took his desire for her to remain close by as nothing more than his need to fill that void in some way, and so took his offer with a gracious smile, and said nothing more about living elsewhere in the castle.

She adored her new home, and there was absolutely nothing old-fashioned about the way the palace was inside. It was smartly furnished with heavy, wooden units and beds, while dark, sultry art covered the walls. In Cate's bedroom, ornate mirrors covered the entire wall on one side, and it made her already huge room look even larger. She also had a huge window that looked out over the black and red hazed skyline, and wondered how it was this had all come to be. Her questions went unanswered for now though, and she embraced the changes with an open mind, rather than dwell on the details.

Cate was given many gorgeous clothes and jewels to wear, and she was informed to let Alma know if there was anything else she wanted. Nothing was too much, and would be procured for her without question. But, there wasn't a single possession she was missing, just one thing. Cate missed her mother. She knew she'd chosen a life with her father over a human existence with Ella that night in the church, but she hadn't realised at the time that she would be expected to stay away indefinitely. Time would tell, but she hoped she might be able to go and see her soon.

As time went by, Cate soon settled into the strange new world she was apparently heiress to, and had the space to roam freely once she found her bearings there. Everyone she came across addressed her as the Dark Princess, and they seemed fearful of saying or doing the wrong thing with her, regardless of her insisting they needn't worry. The witches were so eager to please her that she wanted for nothing, and it was an odd transition from being an everyday human girl to a privileged princess being waited on hand and foot. The only exception was that she couldn't have any food, as for some reason it was impossible to make or teleport down. It would rot within seconds, and was hardly appetising in that state. She didn't really want to think about the reasons why anything full of life perished in seconds, but found that she didn't get hungry anyway. It was just a force of habit to have a cup of tea or a snack as she studied or chatted with her new friends, and it was one she endeavoured to kick.

There were the darkest of beings around Satan all the time, and she couldn't deny it took her a while to grow comfortable in their presence. Witches, demons, and other such things she had yet to learn about surrounded them, and many still terrified the naïve young woman. Cate could tell that each demon or creature was different, as if it was a sense rather than a physical element that gave them away, and she soon learned many things about herself and her master, thanks to his eagerness for her to truly be a part of his reign.

Satan told her about how the underworld came to be, and that he was once an angel up in Heaven. He and the others were brothers-of-sorts, only without a mother or father. They were created by a higher power, and then left to fend for themselves. He told her how they'd quickly put together a hierarchy of angels similar to the demonic structure he'd created in Hell, in which the strongest reigned supreme. A group of the oldest and most powerful upper level angels quickly emerged, and they now made up the High Council of Angels, rather than Heaven having one ruler.

The concept of God, according to Satan, was actually quite unlike the one almighty presence that many humans chose to believe in. There was not one divine being, but the combined say-so of the High Council of Angels, who overlooked mankind from their light realm. They made decisions and commandments for the humans' wellbeing, and the continuance of their heavenly decrees, and grew stronger with every passing year. He eventually sat Cate down and told her how it was he'd come to be ruler of Hell, and she listened enthralled by his gloomy tale.

"One day millennia ago, I had disagreed with their plans for one time too many. My outspokenness that day had come after a spree of disrespectful behaviour, all because I'd found my own mind and wanted to make my own decisions. The council accused me of trying to take over, and they made the unanimous decision to cast me out of Heaven. But, they hadn't wanted to send me to their newly created Earth, so the angels fashioned another realm," Satan told her, and his eyes turned black as they often did when he was angry or tense. "It was a place where nothing thrived, and was truly a hellish pit for me to be banished to. I lived here alone for hundreds of years, and hated the imposed solace at first. I saw it as a prison, but then over time I grew to love it, and felt at home in the darkness and the decay. I created the dark castle using summoning powers I drew from the realm itself, and before long I was commanding my own desolate world with ease. Then, the people of Earth started to evolve, and commit sin. Their souls were thus unwelcome in Heaven, and needed to go somewhere, so Hell was the obvious choice. I quickly found myself accompanied in my exile by the decrepit souls of sinners, each of whom later became either my allies or our playthings."

Cate sat and with him for hours, utterly engrossed in his story. Before long, she learned how two more angels had also fallen from Heaven, too. They'd been cast out thanks to their supposedly sinful deeds, and they'd joined Sataniel's side in the darkness. They were Leviathan and Beelzebub, his closest friends, and still like brothers to him. The pair had readily joined him and quickly became his two most trusted and powerful demons, and the first to be ranked in his highest level of the demonic class system. Those others along the way that were deemed to be of strong enough character or high calibre were then chosen by the Devil to join his ranks, and he'd given the chosen few a higher command in his armies, which began the hierarchy of Hell. That very system then became the chain of command that still held up the pillars of his reign today, and Cate was fascinated to hear all about it. She knew he was reading her thoughts while he spoke, listening in on her inner reactions to the tales he wove, but didn't care. Being around her almighty creator and having him lavish attention on her was wondrous, and she didn't regret her decision to leave her human life behind.

To finish off her lengthy lesson, Satan told her how he'd wanted a child for many years. He'd seen how the High Council of Angels could do it with the child, Jesus, and tried for nearly two millennia without success. It was only when he changed tact that his plan had worked, and eventually his first heir was created, Cate.

"Neither demon or human, but my progeny nonetheless, you were finally born. You're truly a precious gem to me, Cate. I'll never let anything happen to you," he said, and she lapped up his adoring words. It was strange, but she trusted that his words were true. She felt his power and presence flowing through her in her every waking moment now that she had come of age and accepted him as her ruler, and it seemed to empower her more and more as the darkness consumed her willing soul.

It wasn't long until she was happy and comfortable in Hell with her new and unusual band of demonic friends. She soon felt every inch the Dark Princess in her new home and before long she barely even thought of her old life, or those she'd left behind. The weeks, months, and eventually years whizzed by, but Cate didn't age at all, and she knew she wouldn't grow older either. She realised very quickly that this was what her father had meant all that time ago in the old church, and that once she came of age she would stay that way forever.

CHAPTER FOUR

It took Cate a while to get used to her new life, but even after she was familiar with her new world, and the changes she'd made to be part of it, she still had little desire for more than friendship in others. She guessed that her father wouldn't allow anything to happen anyway, and had quickly realised his protectiveness knew no bounds when it came to her safety and care. There were times he'd more than scared her with the forceful delivery of his orders regarding her care, and he'd made it perfectly clear that whatever happened would be his decision, rather than hers. Satan had told her early on that she was not to lose her virginity until he had given her permission to do so, and that it would be with a partner he'd deemed worthy. She hated the very idea of giving that part of herself away at his command, and found it a strange concept to get her head around. Still not wanting to rock the boat, she didn't argue out of fear he might punish her the way she'd seen him discipline the various other beings she'd witnessed at his mercy— or rather lack of it. Cate quickly decided she'd rather remain untouched and in their almighty master's good graces, than begging him for sympathy she already knew he was incapable of having. She just hoped that when the time came, she'd be able to come to terms with a possible forced marriage at the behest of her dark master.

At times Hell could be lonely, though. Many years had passed since she'd accepted her fate, and Cate missed her friends and family on Earth. She'd grown close with one of the witches, Sara, over the years, and was glad to have a true friend in her new life. Sara was a kind witch, and had a fun-loving nature that Cate couldn't help but be drawn to. She reminded her of Dylan in many ways. Sara had been one of the witches that'd welcomed her that night in the church, and Cate had liked her immediately. She had a wicked sense of humour and eyes that twinkled as she played jokes and lured Cate in on her pranks and games, reminding her to have fun and act her age sometimes. Sara was Cate's new best friend, and she was so glad to have someone she could confide her fears and worries to. She still thought about Dylan, but knew that her days as her best friend were well and truly over. She even resented her for not telling her about the white coven and their intentions. Cate could've handled the truth, she was sure of it, but guessed she still would've chosen the other team regardless. Their friendship was evidently doomed from the start, and Cate had to admit it was better she left all thoughts of Dylan in the past where they belonged.

Despite those few regrets and the pain she felt if she let herself think of her mother, she flourished. Cate mastered her demonic powers well. One of which allowed her to teleport and move quickly from place to place, and eventually she even managed to pass from Hell to Earth and back again with relative ease. She was not restricted like her master, being equal part human and darkness. The combination meant she could go between the two worlds any time she wanted to, well, whenever *he* allowed her to.

She enjoyed going to Earth, and was eventually allowed to visit Ella. First though, she had to master another one of her powers—to alter her appearance and age herself physically at will. Cate could make herself look older or younger as she wanted, which allowed her to look the part when she finally visited her mother eight years after disappearing that night in the church. She fed Ella elaborate lies about running off with a boy she'd met and fallen madly in love with. She spun lie after lie, telling her how they'd married and moved to London, where she was now happy and successful. Her mother seemed to believe the story, but Cate knew she was still hurting from her disappearing the way she had. Ella simply couldn't hide her disappointment, even though she seemed happy to know that her daughter was okay.

Cate had learned another power during her time away that meant she could heal her body's ailments almost instantly, but it didn't help ease her guilty conscience that day. In fact, she still hadn't had to use it yet, but she guessed that power might well come in handy in the future.

***

When she was officially thirty years old, Satan succeeded in creating another heir, a boy this time named Devin. The baby was watched over just as Cate had been, by the witches and warlocks working for their dark master, and the news brought with it a wondrous sense of pride for them all. All they had to do was wait until he came of age, and then he would be invited to join them in Hell, just as she had. Cate was so excited that she had someone else to share her world with, and held no jealousy towards him at all. She knew that when the time came, they would both revel in the powerful lives Satan had provided for them, and knew she'd enjoy having else someone around to spend eternity alongside.

When Devin turned fifteen years old, their master came to Cate and told her what he expected her to do.

"I want you to go to Earth and watch over him. Befriend him. Mould him so that when the time comes, he's ready to join us," he ordered her, and Cate had to hide her surprise at being sent away. Her initial instinct was to imagine she must've done something wrong. Part of her wanted to beg him for mercy, guessing she'd displeased him in some way, but his demeanour towards her was no different than usual, and she had a hard time understanding his motives. She went to express her uncertainty, but saw her master's eyes start to darken in his anger, and halted her foolish thoughts before they could become a spoken question. He seemed furious at her hesitation, and she was too terrified to speak against his decision to send her away. Cate forced herself to recover, and agreed to his follow his order, despite the fear still niggling in her gut.

"Of course, but he won't come of age for a few more years," she finally replied, hoping to buy herself more time. It was odd. Now that her freedom was in her grasp, she didn't want to go, and couldn't be sure how she would manage being away from home again.

He was clearly reading her thoughts, and frowned, but didn't address her fears.

"No, not until he's eighteen, but you're to go now, Cate. I want you to alter yourself to look fifteen years old, and you will join his school. You're not to tell him anything of our realm, or his place in it, but you can be his confidant in many other ways," he went on. "Do you remember how you had nightmares and were plagued with dark thoughts that terrified you? Wouldn't it have been nice to have someone to confide those fears in, someone who understood? You can be that person for him; you can let him know that it's okay to let the darkness in." He was right, and Cate knew it. She would've given anything to have a trusted ally back then. Satan smiled to himself, as though already pleased by her receding reluctance. He looked down at her and grinned, taking her face in his hands, just like he had the night she'd first met him. Cate smiled back, silently accepting the order via her thoughts.

Plans were made the next day, and Alma and the other witches were in charge of putting everything together promptly, while also ensuring that it was safe for Cate to live on Earth again. The wise high priestess also tried to raise her concerns with the Dark Prince that it was too soon for her to leave, but he wouldn't hear of it.

"It's for her sake, and mine," he said quietly, before dismissing the witch and returning to his chambers. She didn't have the guts to ask him why, and respected him too much to dwell on it, so she simply strengthened her vow to serve him as best she could. Alma adored her infernal majesty—in ways she couldn't even begin to express—and showed him through service and unyielding loyalty. She wasn't about to stop now.

Cate was sent straight up to Earth just a few days later, and, looking like a fresh-faced teenager again, was enrolled at Highgate Senior School in Devin's home town just down from where she too had grown up.

"Here we go again," she whispered to her coven of comrades as they walked into the school and headed off to her first class.

CHAPTER FIVE

Alma and Sara enrolled at the school alongside Cate, both having used their magic to alter their appearance to look younger as well, of course. They immediately took their places by Cate's side and helped her to become popular at the school. She didn't want to be the queen-bee type, but a well-rounded student who was liked and respected, and quickly became the head-girl type that other girls looked up to and aspired to. Cate guessed there must be some kind of allure to her new power, as for some reason the boys suddenly wanted to know her too. Some went as far to proclaim their affection for her on the first day, and she was shocked at how candid they were about wanting to be with her. Times certainly had changed since she was a teenager. Some of the boys stared, some downright babbled incoherently, and others simply whispered about the new girl while waiting patiently for the gossip. She figured it was safe to say, her arrival had caused quite a stir.

There were no white witches around Satan's offspring this time around, thanks to the dark watchers' having remained extra vigilant during Devin's upbringing, and the girls soon relaxed into their new identities with ease. They dressed casually, acting their supposed ages, but always wore skater-style black dresses with biker jackets, or skinny jeans with boots and slogan t-shirts—pulling off the preppy yet gothic styled look they all looked gorgeous in.

Like everyone else, Devin noticed Cate on the first day, but unlike some, he played it cool. He too was one of the popular boys, and their paths crossed pretty quickly when their groups of friends began mingling in the lunchroom. Cate had to smile at Sara as she snuggled up to Devin's best friend, Jonah, who was already her new boyfriend. He also happened to be the chief warlock of the dark coven that'd surrounded Devin for many years, so they all knew it was just a ploy to get his group of friends closer to Cate's. She and Alma giggled together in their seats, having perfected their teenage girly routine well, but they also knew how to play on the boys' softer sides and capture their attention.

Cate caught Devin's eye across the busy table and shot him a cute grin that she made sure wasn't flirtatious, but friendly. She couldn't deny though that he was gorgeous, and was the first boy she'd found even remotely attractive in years. Devin was tall, and he was dressed casually in jeans and a band logo t-shirt, but what surprised her most was that even at a young age, he oozed desirability. Cate could feel herself being drawn to him, and had to fight the flush beginning to form in her cheeks. Within seconds of meeting his gaze, she'd forgotten all about her indifference to men, and realised at once what all the fuss was about. It terrified her to feel this way about Devin, though, as they all knew he was the next begotten heir of Hell and not her betrothed lover. Could she even go as far to call him her brother, given their shared bloodline? In a world where demons were her friends and the Devil was the closest thing she had to family, Cate couldn't bring herself to care whether Devin was or wasn't considered kin. What she kept coming back to was the fact that Satan hadn't actually given her permission to be more than a friend to him, and she knew she had to fight her feelings until he commanded her otherwise. She reminded herself that she was only there to gain his trust so that when the time came, he'd be sure to follow her back to Hell with their sire.

Cate then, accidentally-on-purpose, reached for a ketchup bottle on the table top at the same time as Devin so that their hands touched, just for a split second. All she'd wanted to do was get his attention on her for a moment longer, but the spark that travelled between them severed any doubts she'd had about her renewed attraction to the opposite sex. Cate wanted him, and bad. Those feelings she hadn't experienced all her life about boys kicked in all at once, and judging by the heat behind Devin's eyes, he'd reacted the exact same way towards her as well. Cate smiled and sat back, doing her best to pretend she hadn't noticed the spine tingling sparks that'd just transferred between them. It had permeated every inch of her being, and she suddenly felt more alive than ever before. The trip to Earth wasn't turning out as bad as she'd once thought, or so it seemed.

Devin sat back in his chair with a sigh, all thoughts of ketchup seemingly gone, and Cate hoped he might be feeling the same way she was. The intensity of their connection was amazing, yet terrifying, and she looked to Alma for some advice, but got nothing other than a shrug from her magical friend.

After their first meeting, Cate couldn't take her eyes off him. Their groups hung around together most days, thanks to Sara and Jonah's blossoming fake romance, and Cate continued to play it cool. She decided to let Devin come to her rather than making the first move, just in case he thought she was coming onto him, and also because she was terrified he might actually like her back.

The next few weeks then went by in a blur, but Cate kept a close eye on her charge and slowly but surely edged her way into his life. She was so focussed on Devin that she had to rely on the witches' help to ensure she kept up her grades and got to her classes on time. They worked their magic and ensured she received good marks, as well as always being on time for classes and her other commitments at school. The pretence was just as important as their mission to watch over Devin alongside Jonah's coven, and together they made sure that he remained under their watchful eyes at all times.

One weekend a couple of weeks into the new term, a girl in their class, Brandy, threw a party while her parents were out of town. Unlike Cate, she really was the queen-bee type, and loved throwing parties and being the centre of attention wherever possible. She'd evidently had her eye on Devin for a long time, but had been heard moaning about he didn't even seem interested in girls, and Cate had to force herself not to laugh. Brandy took offence that he'd never looked her way, and according to her everybody looked Brandy's way, so she bragged to everyone how she was determined to get his attention that night at her party.

As soon as Devin walked into the house, though, he went off in search for Cate. He just couldn't seem to stay away, despite having been too shy to make a move yet. Devin couldn't figure it out, but he just had to get close to her. A deep yearning within pulled him in her direction wherever she was, and it'd happened whilst at school as well. Something about her just screamed to him, and he knew she had to be his. Brandy tried to intercept him a few times, but Devin just ignored her as he wandered around, catching glimpses of Cate and her friends from afar, but he was unable to get near enough to talk to her. He'd decided tonight was the night though. He had to get closer. Devin knew he had to figure out his attraction to her at last, and most importantly, make her his.

Cate also sensed every time Devin was in the same room as her, but she kept up with her friends as they floated back and forth between the spiked bowl of punch in the kitchen and the makeshift dance floor in the living room. Each one of them were playing their parts, enjoying themselves and getting drunk quickly on the strong alcohol, however Alma had disappeared on her, which was unlike the usually so cautious overseer. When she reappeared, she had a smile on her face the likes Cate hadn't seen in a long time, and she had to wonder if their infernal master had put it there.

"He's given you his permission," Alma whispered in her ear, and Cate grabbed her by the shoulders, peering into her face intently.

"What?" she demanded and Alma's smile widened.

"He hoped your connection would lead you both to something more, but there was no way of knowing until after the pair of you met. He said for you to detach yourself from all sordid fears and simply follow your heart. Do not give in to human misconceptions regarding the right or wrong, but go with what you feel is right for you. The pair of you have his blessing, and as long as you don't tell him the truth about his place beside you at Satan's table, you can stay here until Devin comes of age." Cate shrieked with happiness and hugged Alma. This was wonderful news, and while they were far from anything remotely serious, it was wonderful to discover that she had their master's permission to at least give a relationship a try.

With the help of Jonah, Devin finally found his way over the rest of the group. The warlock had torn through the crowd, practically running across the room to grab Sara in his arms and deliver her a passionate kiss. Devin was pushed in closer by the busy throng, and he ended up so close behind Cate that she had to calm her hurried breath. His presence was so intense she trembled with desire the likes she'd never known before. He played it cool and leaned past her to grab a drink, but having his torso spread across her arm and side was almost too much for Cate to handle. The sparks were flying again, and it was enough to make her shudder in sweet anticipation there and then. She turned to look at him, and their faces were so close she could feel his panting breath on her face, and knew he felt it, too.

"Hey," she managed, desperate to move things along, but had to force herself to be patient.

"Oh, hey. Cate right?" he replied nonchalantly, but she could tell he was trying far too hard to keep calm. She could see through the façade, and wondered for a moment if her desperate attempts to fool him were so obvious to him as well.

"Yeah," she replied, aiming for casualness as well, but she ended up sounding more like a shy girl. She mentally kicked herself up the arse and spurred herself on. "And you're Devin, right?" she added with a smile, and had said it more as a statement than a question.

"The one and only. Hey, you want to go get some air?" he then asked, and she nodded, smiling wider. He mirrored her smile, and his light blue eyes sparkled as it reached them. Cate was already head over heels for this boy, and mentally thanked their master for allowing her the opportunity to act on her new and all-consuming impulses.

She then followed Devin towards the back garden where it was quieter, and was grateful for the few moments of comfortable silence they shared as the pair of them filtered through the crowd. It gave her the chance to take a breath and plan her next move. She hoped for privacy, and was glad when they discovered that the only other people out the garden were other couples that were making out and groping each other on the deck chairs or the flattened sun loungers.

The still nervous pair found a spot on the low wall and perched on it side-by-side. She leaned in and they stared into each other's eyes for a long time, neither seeming able to speak. Devin's eyes were the colour of the sea in the summertime, and they made Cate think of her old home with nostalgia and fond memories. She couldn't help but smile to herself, thinking back to all the fun times she'd had there with her friends and family, regardless of how things had ended so abruptly between them.

Eventually, she knew she would have to make the first move. Knowledge and age were on her side, even if he wasn't aware of it yet. She chatted about everything and nothing, and then asked Devin about his family. He was, of course, an only child with just a mother around. There was also the long lost father who'd never been in the picture. Cate wondered how Satan had managed to finally do it, but couldn't figure out the logistics behind it all, so gave up trying. She focussed back on the boy sitting next to her, and truly felt as though they were kindred spirits—the same and yet different in their own ways.

"My mum never really speaks about my dad, but I think it's because she's ashamed. I get the impression he was a one night stand," he told her, and shrugged. Cate knew that story all too well, and put her hand on his thigh in comfort.

"One day you'll know the truth, I'm sure," she replied, and he seemed genuinely eased by her kind words. Cate liked spending time with Devin, and enjoyed getting to know him better, even in the short timeframe. She then decided that enough was enough, and she did what she thought most teenage girls would do—she asked him out.

"Would you like to be my boyfriend, Devin?" she asked, confidently yet with a hesitant approach that wasn't her pretending at all. She really was afraid he might say no and humiliate her. He seemed taken aback by her forwardness, but smiled and nodded.

"Yeah, sure," he said with a shrug, trying to keep his cool demeanour in place, but she could tell he was jumping for joy inside.

After that night, the pair of them couldn't keep away from one another and they spent every day getting to know each other better. Even just walking down the street hand-in-hand left the two of them feeling like the only two people in the world that mattered, and it was wonderful after spending her entire life without that kind of connection before. Cate quickly knew she loved Devin. She adored him with every inch of herself, and their first kiss a while later was an explosive combination of hormones, desire, and insistent need for one another. It was perfect, and she was happier than she could've ever hoped for.

It wasn't long until they were the most popular couple at

school. All the others wanted to be like them, and their single classmates strived to find their own version of that amazing connection they both oozed with. They were powerful in their union, and spurred on others to follow their lead without even realising what they were doing. It was an unexpected new ability Cate hadn't counted on, yet she could feel her dominance seeping into those around them, and she relished the power it gave her.

To be adored by all her friends and peers, as well as their teachers, gave her strength, confidence, and a prowess Alma and Sara told Cate was befitting of her high status as Satan's eldest heiress. She could feel her power growing every day, and cherished it. Devin seemed to bring out the best in her, and he also helped her to realise that beneath her layers of uncertainty and guilt, she also had the strength to lead. Cate discovered that with Devin at her side, she could encourage everyone around her to want to follow her example, and they didn't seem to know they were doing it. She and the witches could sense her influence affecting their human schoolmates, making them confident and in turn, her more powerful. She had a new dark prowess emanating from her now that somehow infected those around her that seemed susceptible to it, and Cate revelled in having a following of sorts for her own.

The formidable couple were also stronger together, and made each other more powerful with each passing day. Devin's power hadn't come to him yet, but it would, and when that happened, Cate was certain he'd be a formidable heir to Satan's throne just like her.

Cate was open with him about her past as much as she could, and in return Devin shared his insecurities and lack of past sexual experience. It didn't matter to her as she had a similar story, though. The details were inconsequential, and all that mattered was that someday they'd be each other's firsts. She would wait as long as it took for him to feel ready, even if it was another decade. Time meant nothing when you had an infinite future ahead, but she refused to take a single day of it for granted.

Much to Cate's happiness, she was given a message via Alma a while later. Her master was pleased with her progress, and urged her to carry on with her chosen course. The dark witch had been summoned back to Hell to give him an update, and had returned again to obey to his command. Strangely, Cate missed him, and hoped he might visit her during the next full moon. She knew Satan had to sense her desire for his company, but for some reason he stayed away, but the messages relayed via Alma were always positive so she didn't take it to heart. He'd left Cate and the witches to carry out their mission without much more input from him, and while she didn't know why, she guessed he needed the time alone.

***

When Cate and Devin were older, they decided to make love for the first time. Both of them had waited as long as they could bear. Kissing and fondling each other, while amazing and climactic, were just not enough for either one of them anymore. He was old enough to know what he wanted, and Cate knew with absolute certainty that she was finally ready for more. Devin's mum was rather strict but, of course, Cate's fake parents—a witch and warlock named Carrie and Jude—were more than happy for them to spend the night at their house in secret. And so, Devin lied to his mother, and said he was staying at Jonah's house, while Cate ensured they had the place to themselves.

When Devin came to her home a little later that night, he and Cate were both nervous at first. They knew what they wanted to happen, but their inexperience quickly showed.

"Are you sure you want this, Devin?" she asked, and knew she needed him to tell her yes before they could go any further. The ancient laws had to be followed, or at least that was what Alma had drilled into her before letting her pursue an initial night of passion with her new beau.

"Yes, I want you. I need you so much," he replied and then led her up to the bedroom. They kissed and warmed each other up, and together they explored each other in ways no one had ever done before. "You're so beautiful, Cate. I love you," he murmured between his kisses.

"I love you, too," she moaned, and gave him everything she'd kept locked away for what felt like forever.

They were insatiable for each other. Every touch was like a

drug, leaving both of them needing the high over and over again. Their bodies were a perfect fit for each other, and she didn't regret a moment of their first night together. They both knew for sure what they'd wondered all along—they were meant for each other, now and always.

CHAPTER SIX

After their first night together, Cate and Devin couldn't keep their hands off each other. Every spare moment they had, the pair of them could be found making out or sneaking off to be alone together. They were quickly the centre of each other's world, and with the help of the witches and warlocks, somehow managed to continue their perfect record of attendance and grades. The pair remained the school's hottest and most popular couple, and always had their groups of friends in tow, before then graduating as head boy and girl. Throughout all of it, Devin still couldn't believe how strongly he felt for Cate after his aversion to girls before. His urge to love and worship her was like nothing he'd ever felt before, and it scared him just how much he needed her. He was honest and told her all about how she'd break his heart if she ever left, and Cate always gave him the same heartfelt answer—that she wouldn't leave his side.

One night, she took him to a concert to see one of her favourite rock bands perform, Forever Darkness. Devin loved seeing her so excited, and the thrill and energy of the crowd permeated them both, heightening their desire for one another even as the warm-up band performed. The pair then pushed to the front of the crowd, where a bouncer immediately escorted them around the back to meet the headliners before they started their performance. What Devin didn't know was that the entire band and their entourage were demons, and they could sense Cate and Devin's true forms beneath their human exteriors. They all knew, of course, not to say anything to Devin and give the game away, but each greeted the two of them warmly, seeming grateful that they'd taken an interest in their music.

The lead singer, a demon named Berith, gave Cate a tight hug. He then took the opportunity to whisper in her ear what a huge honour it was that they'd come to his gig, and she knew he meant it. They were royalty after all, and the title she hadn't felt all that comfortable with before was suddenly a welcome addition to her rapidly expanding prowess. She grinned back and revelled in the demon's attention, while Devin's jaw dropped at the sight of them chatting away like old friends.

It was already a fantastic night out for the young couple, but was made even better when they then watched the rest of the gig from the side of the stage as personal guests of the band. Cate loved the attention and soaked up the energy from the crowd as she danced with Devin amidst the spare guitars and roadie equipment. Berith looked over and give her the odd wink as he sang, and she lapped up his attention as much as their demonic onlookers. The ancient demon was alluring in his own way, and had long dark hair and a thick beard that very much suited his rock and roll look, while his soulful voice wooed the crowd. Cate watched in awe as his mesmerising words encouraged sin and tempted the humans in the crowd to blaspheme and fight, and it was abundantly clear they had absolutely no idea that he was doing anything.

***

As more time passed, the powerful couple continued to excel at everything they put their minds to, and breezed through their final college exams with their friends at their sides. As they approached Devin's eighteenth birthday, Cate knew the time would soon come that their father would reveal his true identity to him, and she was both excited and scared for when the day finally came. She worried that he wouldn't understand or accept her once he knew the truth, or that he might say no to going back to Hell with their sire. Devin didn't seem plagued with nightmares or vivid imagery like she'd been at his age, and apart from their affection, she wasn't sure she'd become enough of a confidant to him. She guessed only time would tell, but truly hoped he'd see sense just like she'd done all those years before.

Cate was officially now nearly fifty years old, but had aged herself to keep in tow with Devin, and knew she would most likely choose to keep up a similar appearance when they returned to Hell. He would soon come of age, then could be taught to master his powers like she'd been, and she didn't doubt that he'd be more than capable.

One month after his birthday, Devin woke suddenly in the middle of the night and shook Cate awake.

"Something isn't right. It feels like I'm needed somewhere, but I can't explain it," he told her with a wide-eyed expression. She knew straight away what it was, and that she had to encourage him to follow those urges.

"It's fine, let's just take a walk and see where we end up, okay?" she replied, and despite the late hour, Devin nodded. He seemed to trust her implicitly, and she hoped he would continue to do so even after he'd discovered where it was she was luring him to.

They left Cate's house and walked silently beneath the full moon, hand-in-hand. She considered taking him via his house so he could say goodbye to his mother, but knew it wasn't possible without giving away what was waiting for them at the source of his inner beacon, and stayed quiet. They followed Devin's lead until they came upon an old church, just like Cate had done before. She urged him to keep going, and only stopped to kiss him quickly before they went inside—one last time, just in case. She pinned Devin to the wall, deepening their kiss and relishing in his touch before forcing herself to pull away and silently usher him inside. He grinned, drawing her back to him for more kisses, but Cate pulled away. She shook her head. She couldn't push her luck or keep their master waiting.

They then made their way inside and wandered through the maze of dark corridors. She could hardly see through the intense darkness, but knew the way as if by heart. When they eventually found their way into the large main room, Devin was surprised to find his friends there waiting for him, all sat in a circle around a small fire.

Déjà-vu, Cate thought with a sly grin.

"Hey. What's going on guys?" Devin asked, and each of his friends offered him kind smiles, but let Jonah greet him with an answer.

"Hey pal, come and sit down. We've got a surprise for you, but you just have to wait a few minutes," he said, and grinned at them both excitedly. Jonah indicated for the two of them to join the group on the floor, and slid sideways to make room. Devin was confused, but did as he was asked and sat in the circle with Cate by his side. No one spoke again, but it didn't matter, because it wasn't long before their almighty master appeared in the doorway.

Satan approached and smiled down at Cate, but said nothing to her. She felt her heart and mind flood with both anticipation and fear in his presence, but she tried her best to hide it from Devin who just looked puzzled and slightly scared of their new arrival. He still couldn't understand why no one was saying anything to him, and she knew he'd be able to sense Satan's strange power, just as she had done.

He peered intently at Devin, who quickly stood to greet the stranger following a nudge from Jonah, and he offered him a hand to shake. The shrouded man shook it, but neither spoke as they took each other in for a few seconds. Devin had no idea that his master was reading every thought and memory in that small touch, or that he was impressed by what he saw.

"May I have a moment?" was all he said after a few seconds, and off they went to a dark corner of the old church. Devin wasn't sure to make of it all, and he rested a hip against the old altar when the pair of them came to a stop. Despite the changes in his confidence over the last few years, he was unsure of himself in the strange man's presence, and fidgeted with his jacket as he waited for him to speak.

Cate and the others stayed in the centre of the room, sat around the fire in wait for their leader's next order. The group talked quietly while their master and his youngest heir had their discussion in the corner, and the small group was eager to get the formalities over with so they could return home. Cate just hoped Devin would embrace his new life in Hell alongside his dark friends and family. She was nervous, and had to stop herself from looking over at them while they talked just out of earshot.

After what felt like forever, the two men came back over. Devin barely even looked at her as she rose to greet them, but their father came straight to her. He gathered Cate in a strong hug and then whispered in her ear, having read her thoughts and sensed her worry.

"Devin's fine. Don't worry. We're going home momentarily,"

he told her. "I'm so proud of you." Satan pulled back from their embrace slightly to lock eyes with hers, and Cate shuddered as the power she'd almost forgotten could be so immense coursed through her at his request. She was pleased to hear him say the words, and felt amazing thanks to his few choice words that lifted her spirits tremendously.

Satan held her gaze for a long while, and she knew he was looking deep into her soul, luring out her innermost thoughts and desires. He took in all the memories she had to offer of her time with Devin, and she could sense him digging around inside her mind and soul. Cate opened herself up to her scary master, and he sent a wave of affection and love back to her in return, randomly allowing himself a rare and wonderful sharing of his own emotion he hadn't ever done before. When he finally shut it off and pulled away, Cate gasped. Their exchange had been wonderful. She'd never felt such a connection with her masterful leader before, or with anyone else, and she wanted more, but it seemed he was done with the affectionate pleasantries.

Satan then took Devin's hand in his while the rest prepared themselves to teleport back home. After a quick speech about Hell, which sounded just like the same explanation he'd given Cate before taking her the first time, she felt the familiar whooshing, pulling feeling she'd become accustomed to after her teleportation training. When they reached their destination—the gates that led into the dark city and up to their large castle home—Cate caught her breath instantly, and then helped Devin to steady himself.

"You don't need it," she told him as he gasped for air and choked on his empty lungs. It took him a few minutes, but it wasn't long until he eventually grasped the concept and stopped his body's desperate attempts to take a breath. Devin slowed his panicked panting, and steadied himself. He stood tall at last, and she was immensely pleased with him. Once he was level-headed again, Cate finally had a much-needed opportunity to figure him and his mood out. She was very aware they'd not had the chance to talk since their father's big reveal, but hesitated when it came to asking him if he was okay. The Dark Princess peered up at her lover affectionately, and knew her worry had to be etched clearly on her face. Devin reached out and put one palm on her cheek, his thumb gently stroking up and down over her red lips and chin as he stared into her eyes. The little moment of tender connection was enough to re-assure Cate, and she smiled up at him.

"I'll be fine. But, I guess I'm gonna have to get used to being in love with my..." he gulped—"sister?" he asked her, and then chuckled to himself.

"Never, ever say that word," she replied with a smile. "We're as bonded by blood as any other demon or dark being. Two heirs together as one." Cate had to wonder what Satan had told him in that corner, and hoped he hadn't changed his mind about who was his rightful heir. Devin could tell she was fretting, and held her close before linking his hand in hers.

"We're to share everything, Cate. Together, as King and queen, man and wife..." he added, and then followed their entourage up through the city steps to the castle while all she could do was gape at him in awe.

The entire kingdom would soon be given the opportunity to welcome Devin to his new home, but first their Cate was allowed to give him the grand tour, starting with her bedroom.

In the months that followed their return to Hell, Devin learned all about his place beneath His Infernal Majesty, and about their powers. He'd laughed hard when Cate told him how old she actually was, and then referred to himself as her toy-boy for a while, until a threat of celibacy from her let him know she was not to one be messed with. She even withheld her affection him for a while until she calmed down and relinquished her stubborn mood, but knew she couldn't stay mad at him for long. The pair were still perfectly comfortable together and desired one another incredibly, now more than ever. They got to know each other inside and out during their free time, and Cate found it was freeing to finally be able to open up to Devin about her real self.

Their almighty ruler was always busy, and seemed content to leave them alone to explore themselves and each other as much as they wanted, much to the smitten couple's delight. He seemed delighted that they'd formed such a formidable duo on Earth, and encouraged that love to blossom now that they were back in their true home. Devin and Cate made love for hours during their alone time, and let their sexual curiosities and fantasies flow freely, while revelling in each other's willing openness. Cate confided everything to him, and even told him all about her lesbian dabbling's during her youth, but that it was never real, and she knew that now thanks to him. He had to admit, he found it extremely sexy, and begged her to bring a playmate into their bed for just a little bit of fun, but Cate didn't want to share him, and pouted playfully in response.

"You wish. And anyway, you wouldn't even know how to handle two of us," she teased him one night. A cheeky grin then curled at her lips before she jumped off the bed and ran for the bathroom in a bid to get away from the slap he tried to administer to her naked bum cheek, and she giggled uncontrollably every step of the way.

***

Many years soon passed by in the blink of an eye. The power-couple spent every day together and made love for hours between Devin's on-going lessons in power control and enhancement. The pair never aged physically, but gained more and more understanding of themselves and each other as the time passed. They truly were the ultimate duo, and even in Hell everyone around them admired, respected, and followed their lead without question. It was empowering to be continually proving their father right, and being rewarded with more power was a prize worth working hard for. Cate did everything she could to serve her dark overlord, and never once shied away from her prestigious role beneath him like she once had. Nowadays she downright demanded their evil minions addressed her as such, and she was sure she made Satan smile on many an occasion as he watched her bloom.

One night, Cate was summoned to his chambers alone. She was still a little nervous around her powerful sire, but she would never disobey, and followed the summoning without question. She wanted to please him and make him proud, but also remained aware to keep herself in check and to ensure she didn't to let him down or disrespect him in any way while vying for more power of her own.

Somehow, Devin had seemingly developed a far more relaxed relationship with their ruler than she had, and Cate wasn't sure how he'd managed it. He seemed to effortlessly be able to carry out his orders without batting an eye, and even addressed him more casually than she ever seemed comfortable enough to. The two powerful men seemed a lot surer of themselves and their relationship than Cate had ever felt, and she often panicked that deep down she might be weaker than her new beau.

When Cate followed her father through an open door into one of his private chambers, she gasped when she saw who was kneeling at his feet.

"Dylan?" she called out, and panic flared in her gut. She started to go to her old friend, but was stopped in her tracks by Satan's stern expression. He was regarding her with apparent interest, and she knew he must have been reading her every thought and reaction to finding Dylan there in Hell with them. He was testing her.

"This white witch was discovered trying to sneak into our realm," he told Cate with a dark look that told her she wasn't there for a social visit. "She claims she wanted to see you. She's here to save you from my evil clutches."

Cate's face dropped. She knew Dylan would be punished severely for coming to Hell, and would beg for death following what he would no doubt put her through for having dared try. Despite those fears for her safety, she still felt glad to see her old friend after all the years since she'd left her behind in that field, and it was good to know she cared after all. Cate could tell her master was waiting to see what she'd made of the remarks Dylan had made about his 'evil clutches,' and she tried to put together a suitable answer. She hesitated for a moment, and was unsure how best to proceed, but then quickly composed herself. Deep down, she knew exactly what he expected of her. Although seeing Dylan again after all their years apart was a welcome sight, Cate knew she had to do what he demanded. She had to give him some recompense. Satan wanted vengeance. It was time to choose sides, once and for all, and while she felt bad for Dylan, she'd known what a risk it was coming here, and so had to have known what might happen if she was caught.

"Well, witch," she said maliciously. "You can see there's no need for your concern. You're not welcome here, or needed. I know how you tried to keep me from my true fate when I was younger, and that you were never really my friend," Cate added, with as much indifference as she could muster. She knew her father could read her inner turmoil, but that he'd also see she was trying to overcome her doubts. Part of her even began to worry if perhaps she was trying too hard. Was she fooling him? She couldn't even be sure she was fooling herself.

"What do you propose we do with her?" he asked, beckoning Cate to come closer, and she went over and stood by his side, where she finally had the chance to take in the awful sight before her. Dylan was chained down, kneeling before him by force, and every inch of skin Cate could see was bloody and bruised. Her shirt and jeans were tattered and streaked with blood, but she was conscious and still fighting the hold he had on her. Dylan tried to look up at Cate, but a flick of Satan's hand sent an invisible blow down onto her head, forcing her even lower in the crouch. Cate couldn't help but flinch.

"We could throw her in a fiery pit?" she suggested, but a disappointed look told her he expected a far more elaborate choice of punishment. "Or, how about we beat the crap out of her and send her back up to Earth, as a lesson to the other white witches?" she tried, and he seemed a little more impressed with that suggestion, but not much.

"Almost there, my dear," he said, and in a surprising show of affection, he stroked her face gently. A snap of his fingers then transported the three of them to one of his torture chambers. Another click, and Dylan's chains were released.

She stood and stared him right in the eye. Hatred and fear mashed her features into an almost unrecognisable guise that Cate could hardly bear to see. Her eyes were puffy, and her darker than usual blonde hair stuck to her bloody cheek lankly. She stood her ground despite his ominous glare, however she shook uncontrollably, which gave away her terror. "You choose first," he commanded Cate, and looked over at the table of weapons and other terrible implements that ran along one wall. She walked over to it, looking the awful items over for a moment, before she eventually grabbed a pair of handcuffs. She didn't want to be the first one to inflict pain on her old friend, and took Dylan by the arm. She dragged her over to a lonely cot that was on the other side of the room and shackled her with her arms up over her head on the bare mattress.

"Please don't do this, Cate," Dylan begged. "You know what they'll do to me."

Cate felt her stomach drop, and guilt welled up inside of her, but her own fear pushed it away again. If she didn't do it, she had the sneaking suspicion she'd be the next one shackled to that bed, and she had to put her own safety first. She stared the witch right in the eye and stifled a sorry sob, but spoke her response without so much as flinching.

"I never asked you for anything, Dylan. Especially this. I don't know what you were thinking of in coming here. But, you underestimate me if you think for a second I'm that same naïve little girl you once knew. The girl you once had so fooled. I won't do you any favours," she told her. Without another word to her old friend, Cate stood back up and walked back over to join her master again.

She caught his eye, and felt his pleasure with her creep under her skin. He'd opened up that strange link between them again, and it pleased her to sense his emotions through the bond she couldn't believe she'd ever questioned. Her body sang with his approval, and she wanted more. It made her ready and willing to commit more sin for him, and she guessed it was perhaps his point. This was still so new, and Cate couldn't understand it, but she felt as though their bond was getting stronger and stronger. Things were finally falling into place, and she wasn't going to let anything come between them.

"You may leave us now," he suddenly said, suddenly releasing her from his hold, and it left her empty. He snapped his fingers again, and in a second Cate was back in her room. She hated that she hadn't had the chance to question his decision to dismiss her, or do more to earn further chances to bask in his emotive affection. In a way she somehow both despised and adored, she hated how unsatisfying her part to play in Dylan's torture had been.

Devin was asleep on the bed, and her frustration quickly turned to desire, so she decided to let him know. She stripped quickly and jumped on the bed, waking him up with a start. One look at her naked body was enough of an invitation for him, and rather than question her, he threw the covers off and tossed his briefs to the floor. Cate pounced. She threw herself onto her lover's stiff cock with such urgency she came after just a few strokes of him inside her, but it wasn't nearly enough. Her body needed her releases more than even she understood, and Devin answered her desperate call without breaking a sweat. The strange energy Satan had shared with her still resonated inside, and it somehow spurred her on in search of satisfaction that was always just out of reach. Devin knew something was up, but she didn't give him the opportunity to ask what, as she kept him busy in bed for days.

When the pair finished the last of their climaxes, they lay exhausted on the bed, revelling in their shared afterglow. Satan then chose to teleport into their chambers at that very moment. Devin jumped up in surprise and grabbed the nearest bed sheet to cover himself, but Cate couldn't reach anything in time. She felt brazen and improper, but didn't rush to get dressed—her naked, just-fucked body completely on show. She could feel his gaze all over her and despite not needing the attention, she lapped it up. Devin noticed, but didn't dare say anything despite his confusion, and she had to wonder if their relationship was really as strong as she'd thought if he wasn't willing to tell her off or demand another man take his eyes off her, even if it was their all-powerful ruler and master.

"Now that the pair of you are finished," Satan said, and she blushed with the realisation that he knew exactly what they'd been up to. "Hecate, I thought you might like to see how well we got on with the witch?" Devin looked at each of them, and was clearly baffled to hear that something had gone on he wasn't aware of.

"What witch?" he asked, but she didn't get the chance to answer him. Cate caught their master's expectant stare and knew he was quickly growing impatient at having to wait for her.

"Later, gorgeous," she said quickly, giving him a wink. Cate grabbed her shirt and buttoned it as she went over to their father and took his hand.

A blink of an eye later and they were back in the dungeon with Dylan, and her previous high was replaced by a vat of hot guilt that almost brought her to her knees. The witch was still handcuffed to the cot, and her body was severely beaten and disfigured. Cate pitied her, and stifled a gag at the sight of Dylan's dirty body. Two demons stood over her, both of whom seemed utterly pleased with themselves and their work. She guessed what they must've been doing to her, and looked away. Her master wouldn't be happy with her for showing her distaste, but she simply couldn't look at Dylan any longer.

"I think she's had enough now, don't you?" she asked him, not meeting his gaze. "I'm sure she and the other witches will get the message when she goes back like that," she added, and continued to stare at the ground. He wasn't impressed, Cate knew, but nodded and ordered the demons to take Dylan back to Earth and dump her outside a white church.

Cate hoped she'd be discovered quickly, and that she'd get some help there. It was common knowledge though, that their demonic minions wouldn't be able to take her directly to her coven. Whenever demons or any other beings from Hell were on Earth, they couldn't cross over into a white church's protective barrier. It was as if an invisible line was drawn around the holy place and they could not cross over it. The same, of course, went for the Satanic churches with the angels or white witches. They couldn't cross over into their hallowed ground either. Cate then wondered what Dylan had done to get through the barrier, and still didn't understand why she'd even wanted to try and get to her after all this time.

"She committed a sin," Satan answered her silent query. Cate was still shocked every time he read her like that, and constantly kicked herself for forgetting that no thought was ever truly safe from his prying. "Nothing too juicy. She convinced a married man to commit adultery with her and then performed a dark spell. It tarred her just enough to cross our threshold and sneak in through our portals, which I shall endeavour to strengthen. So silly the things *they* deem so evil," he added, and pointed upwards with one finger.

She paled at how far Dylan had gone to find her, and yet all she'd done in return was leave her to be tortured and beaten while she got her kicks with her new boyfriend. She hated how much she'd failed her old friend, and wanted desperately to be alone. Satan chuckled to himself, as though he found her guilt amusing, and then he led Cate away without a word.

CHAPTER SEVEN

"I want you both to go up to Earth and oversee one of my companies," Satan informed Cate and Devin later that same day. "It's based in the centre of London, where you will remain until further notice. You will use Black Rose Industries to take over smaller ones and help them grow, but only if the owners sign their lives away for the privilege, so to speak. The basic principal is expansion of our ideas, commandments, and unholy decrees, etcetera," he waved his hand as if he couldn't be bothered to go on, but knew they both understood him clearly. Cate nodded and was surprised that he'd used their surnames to create the business title, and Satan gave her a knowing smile. He'd clearly been reading her thoughts again.

"World domination and all that?" Devin said, chuckling to himself, and Cate giggled.

"Absolutely, my boy. One little bit at a time." He smiled and nodded his head. In a blink, they felt the familiar pull as they were dismissed and sent to Earth at their master's command.

The pair were quickly delivered to a huge penthouse flat overlooking the centre of the vast city, where a tall demon named Belias welcomed them. He bowed and addressed them with their formal titles as Dark Prince and Princess, and Cate still couldn't get enough of it when they did that. Devin was even newer to that sort of treatment, and actually looked quite uncomfortable when being greeted that way, whereas she was coming around to it more and more as time went on.

"Welcome to your new home," Belias continued. "Let me give you the tour." They followed him around the huge home, and found room after room all fully decorated and furnished in dark reds and blacks. *Of course,* Cate thought with a smile. The place had their father's influence all over it, and she wondered if he'd used it as a base the times he'd come to Earth. She imagined wild parties full of sinners and depraved sexual acts, and very much doubted her musings were far from the truth at all.

"I'm gonna like it here," she whispered to Devin with a sly grin as they both took it all in. He beamed back and nodded, taking her hand in his. Devin swung her around, dancing their way through the penthouse as they finished with their tour, and the pair were excited to get started with their next Earthly adventure.

The next few days were completely taken up with shopping for new clothes and getting everything they'd need to look the part in the hectic business world. They both aged themselves up to around thirty years old so they could fit their roles better, and also did it so they'd be more respected than if they stayed at the comfortable early-twenties look they both usually maintained. The business had evidently been run from afar until their arrival, which helped them to slide right into their chosen positions once the day came. They were to assume the identities of Mr and Mrs Black— young entrepreneurs and successful business moguls that'd thus far run the business from Düsseldorf in Germany. They were to say they'd decided to move back home to London so they could expand the business, which would explain the numerous takeovers they had lined up ahead of them. There were no board of directors or shareholders to answer to. The business was their baby to take control of and run as they wanted, and Cate loved having been given the opportunity to show their Dark Prince what they could do in his name. If they did encounter any trouble, almost all of the senior staff were demons, warlocks, or witches, and would help the pair out as per their duty, but they hoped it wouldn't come to that. Both heirs of Satan were looking forward to getting their teeth into the challenges that awaited them, and were more than ready to get started.

Each morning, Cate had a demonic assistant who came to choose her clothes and do her hair and makeup. She wanted to look good every day and, as per her father's orders, she was now the face of the company so needed to look the part. The Dark Princess was perfect at it, and went from strength to strength in her new role. She wooed clients and oversaw all meetings and take-overs effortlessly, while luring in other prospective clients at every available opportunity. They were easy targets, and seemed to revel in her warm, tender allure. To many it felt like she was doing them a kindness, as otherwise they'd undoubtedly try and fail in this cutthroat world, so she made it an easy decision to sign away their businesses, and souls, in order to take their places in her promised favour.

She was used to being sought after by their clients, but was new to running a business, and relied on her employees to ensure things went smoothly. All those she supervised in the Black Rose head office seemed to adore Cate, whether male or female, and did anything she wanted, no matter what that might be. She loved it, and lapped up the attention while growing in confidence and prowess every day.

On the other half of the power-couple, sat a tycoon more commanding than she'd ever known. Devin was the decision maker and firm hand of the company, and he charmed their clientele in other ways. He maintained a strong and powerful presence, and the human staff members were always scared, yet highly respectful to him. He soon discovered how whenever he asked any of them to do something, they all jumped to it right away. They were eager to please him, and he revelled in his new-found power alongside his pretend wife. The women were seemingly drawn to his driven demeanour, and many of them swooned over Devin constantly. They delighted in his powerful, bad-boy attitude, and he played on it effortlessly while lapping up the attention without a care in the world.

The couple later decided to start holding elaborate parties at their penthouse, which of course were invitation-only events. The employees and clients working with them were known to fall at their feet if they thought it would get them an invitation to the highly sought after affairs, and both Cate and Devin enjoyed having such control over their personal minions.

Often it was nothing but a cocktail party, and sometimes they took the themes a little darker and decided on orgies or BDSM themed masquerades. Cate had also been known to arrange for ancient rituals and spells to be carried out at a secret rendezvous, and they were never empty despite their dark premise. The parties almost always involved depravities and luring innocent humans into committing sin. It was in their nature, and neither denied their calling. The humans involved were let in only if they took a vow of secrecy beforehand, and then they could relish in their rewards for signing their lives away to the dark couple, or the attending upper level demons. So very many men and women ended up selling their souls for fame and fortune, and it wasn't long until business was booming. She and Devin enjoyed every second of their new lives, and it felt good being in control and so commanding at last.

The dark pair's love affair knew no bounds. They were so in love and in sync with each other that nothing came between them or made either of their eyes wander. They both enjoyed being back up on Earth together again, and liked having some time away from the stifling reign of their dark overlord. Their master visited Earth many times when the moons were right and he was allowed to come up from Hell, however he usually went off in search of women for him to have some fun with first, but afterwards would head to the penthouse. They'd often throw a party in his honour, to which only upper level demons, witches, and warlocks could attend, along with their choice of human partner. If the time was right, Satan could sometimes stay for two or three days, and the party often went on the entire time of his visit.

One night during his annual Halloween visit, he instigated an orgy. With his loyal demons' help, they lured an entire crowd of women to the penthouse, and the vast living room was transformed into a huge area full of soft black cushions and red sheets. It reminded Cate of a gigantic bed for them all to share, and was grander than any sexually themed soirée she'd thrown in the past. There were no holds barred, but their master was guest of honour, and he climbed in first. The human women were on him in a heartbeat, and the mood was quickly fuelled by the sight and sounds of their arousal. Next, the high-ranking demons brought their human playthings onto the huge bed, while Cate and Devin watched on from the sidelines. They joined the group soon after, and were more than ready for it after having felt the sexual ambiance fill the room, as well as understanding their master's expectations of them.

The pair stripped and began their pursuit of each other's climax as the whole room vibrated with a frenzied energy around them. It was amazing. Cate could hear the women climaxing loudly at Satan's touch, but rather than distract her, the sound fuelled her on. Devin sat before her, and his amazing body was beautiful. His cock was so hard for her, but as he lay back onto the huge silky floor, she chose not to jump right on.

"Mine," she said, and smiled up at him before she sucked the tip of his hardness into her mouth. He groaned and grabbed her hair, urging her down further onto his throbbing length with a cheeky grin, but she didn't fight his hold. When in the throes of passion they were limitless, and afforded each other many opportunities to dominate one another equally. She obliged him, and licked and sucked until he came into her mouth. Once finished, he sat up and pulled her round and onto her back with one swift move. Devin wasted no time. He yanked Cate's hips towards him and spread her thighs with his strong hands, peering down at his prize while she writhed unashamedly.

"Mine," he said, and licked his lips as he leaned down to devour her. Cate groaned with intense pleasure as he slipped two fingers inside her already soaked core and pushed down on her g-spot, and then cried out as an orgasm quickly rippled through her. That was when she sensed someone's gaze on her. It wasn't unusual during an orgy to have the odd voyeur, but this felt different somehow. Opening her own eyes instinctively at the feeling, her gaze suddenly locked with a set of intense blue eyes that didn't belong to Devin. They belonged to their master. He held it just for a second, but the electricity in his stare was enough to make her senses stir. She instinctually knew he'd been watching her, and the grin on his lips made Cate blush.

Devin kept going between her trembling thighs, but Cate couldn't concentrate on anything other than what Satan was doing in the opposite corner. He looked back across at her, and it felt as if he was silently commanded her to keep the eye contact, because she was suddenly unable to look away. He then winked as another climax coursed through her, and she throbbed beneath Devin's amazing touch. Her back arched and she cried out with pleasure, and the intense pulse that flowed through her rendered her powerless for a few seconds while she regained her strength. By the time she could compose herself and get back up into a sitting position, a quick glance at their master showed her he was already busy with another human lover. He was thrusting into her as she cried out in pleasure for him, but he wasn't paying attention to the woman on her knees before him, Satan looked over at his Dark Princess again. His eyes looked black and he was smiling to himself, clearly amused, and Cate tried to convince herself it was because of the concubine beneath him rather their accidental interaction.

It was only another second before Devin leaned over and broke Cate's concentration with a kiss on her shoulder. She turned to face him and kissed him back, before guiding his hard cock inside her. She needed the distraction from the strange feelings that were now corrupting her thoughts, and he innocently gave her it, not knowing how preoccupied her thoughts were.

The lovers moved in time with each other, and Cate welcomed Devin's powerful thrusts. She needed him to take all coherent thought away, and urged him to bury himself even deeper inside of her. The years they'd had to perfect these moves did nothing to take away from their passion or desire for each other, and she stared into his eyes as they came together. She didn't risk another look at Satan and his horde of conquests, but focussed instead on Devin and the way he'd made her feel. Cate loved him with everything she had, and tried to convince herself she'd imagined the strange back and forth with their sire from before. She guessed he'd used every one of his omnipotent tricks to keep the women in his throng ready and willing to please him, and was sure she must've sensed his magnetism as well. That had to be it.

When the party was over and the sun began to rise, their master took a moment to talk with them before he headed back home to Hell. He looked his usual calm and powerful self, and was remarkably kempt, despite having made his way through a few dozen women that night. He'd kept his short beard and had shaved his hair this time, making him look even younger than Cate had ever seen him before. His deep blue eyes took them both in for a moment before he spoke, and she knew he was reading them. She couldn't hide her desire-driven angst, and Satan barely hid his dark grin as he read Cate's thoughts on the strange subject that had her emotions so fraught.

"I've another child on the way," he told them with a smile.

"The mother's due to deliver in the next few weeks," he added, and Cate wasn't sure whether to congratulate him or be worried that he'd chosen to create yet another heir. As it stood, she and Devin weren't vying for his throne, but if there were more of them, she was sure things could get ugly pretty quickly if they decided it ought to go to one of them instead.

"That's great, where are they?" Cate asked, and she tried to be excited about it.

"The USA, New York City," their master replied, seemingly ignoring her uncertainty. "She won't know of me, or the pair of you, until she comes of age, just the same as before. But, she will be watched over by the witches until that time comes, of course."

"She?" Devin murmured, and Satan nodded. Not another word was spoken aloud, and Cate guessed their master didn't feel the need to explain himself. He simply kissed her on the cheek, patted Devin's shoulder, and disappeared down into the darkness below.

***

The business continued to be a success, and as the time passed, Cate and Devin's wealth and power grew immeasurably. They had to alter their look to ensure they'd aged a little more, but of course they both kept looking as good as possible. When the time came around again that their father decided to come and see the pair of them on Earth, his next heiress, named Serena, was six months old. Alma had given the pair regular updates, but like he'd warned, they hadn't been allowed to see her. When the moon was full, Satan went to see the child, and was gone just a few hours rather than for the majority of his Earthly visit like normal. He returned to the penthouse and took his two eldest heirs to one side.

"Things are going to change," he said, watching them both intently. "For all of us."

Neither of them was sure what change he meant, but didn't get much chance to ask before Devin was ushered away by Sara, and Cate was left alone with their master. "I've decided that you're no longer going to be with Devin. He will now marry Serena when she comes of age," he informed her, without any care or compassion at the gut-wrenching loss she felt at his words.

Cate's stomach dropped at the thought of being taken away

from the life she'd loved and the future she'd planned by Devin's side. It terrified her to imagine him with another, and in that moment, she despised the baby girl across the world for having taken him from her. They'd been together for fifteen years. She'd never been with anyone else but him, and loved him with all her heart. Cate stared back at Satan in shock, and didn't understand how it could be over because he'd said so. She opened her mouth to ask him, but then felt the familiar pull that told her they were teleporting away—back to Hell, and without Devin.

When they arrived, she was still speechless, but so many questions filled her head and she couldn't hide them from Satan's prying power. She felt scared, and had to wonder if this meant he was displeased with her, or whether he was planning on giving her to someone else. The sheer thought of being handed over like some prize or bargaining tool sickened her. Cate had to know the truth behind her master's change of heart.

"Please tell me why," she pleaded, but he wasn't interested in her pleas. He'd seen and heard it all before, and she gripped her tense stomach.

"Stop over-thinking it, Cate. All will be made clear very soon," he answered curtly, before taking her hand and leading her towards their wing of the castle. "Take her to her room," he ordered Alma who was waiting just inside the door for them, and she curtseyed. "Make sure she stays there," he added before teleporting away, and the iciness in his voice made Cate panic. She had to have done something wrong and was going to be punished, but she had no idea what she'd done to deserve his wrath.

"What did I do?" she pleaded with the witch as they walked slowly towards her room.

"It's not what you did or didn't do, it's who you are that's the problem. I can't answer your questions, but he will, and I'm not sure you're going to understand them," Alma answered, and Cate felt as if her whole body went cold, which was quite some feat being that they were in Hell. The high priestess then half guided, half pushed Cate forward, and she headed into her room in a daze.

I suppose you can't live forever and not have to mix things up every once in a while, Cate eventually thought, and she did everything she could to try and calm herself down. She was still confused, and tried to go over everything that'd happened again.

Their sire had insisted upon them both that she was destined to be with Devin and how he'd chosen them as his heirs. He'd told her himself how they were destined to have a family and carry on their strong line from the first conceived successors of Hell. It pained her to realise how that fate now belonged to Serena, and it worried her that she might now be heading to her room for a life of celibacy until someone else came along that Satan deemed worthy. Or perhaps he was done with her completely, and she'd be discarded, forgotten, unwanted and unloved.

Cate's stomached churned at the thought, and she thought she might be sick. If that were the case, she just hoped he'd be merciful and give her a quick death. But then again, it was the Devil she was dealing with, and he wasn't famed for his compassion. In fact it was quite the opposite.

CHAPTER EIGHT

Alma didn't say another word. She simply locked the door and left Cate alone with her thoughts. The Dark Princess slumped down onto the bed, and realised her current overriding emotion had changed from one of shock to anger. Annoyance rose up in her over the lack of information she'd been given following her master's destructive news, and she screamed into her pillow. She then lay back on her black sheets, staring up at the ceiling thoughtfully while she tried to figure out what was going to happen next, but genuinely had no clue. There was no guessing what was coming next, and a cold chill swept down her spine again as the deafening silence echoed the thundering in her ears.

She wasn't left alone too long, however, and a quiet knock at the door startled her. The lock turned and the large wooden door opened, allowing a man to enter, before it locked behind him again. He was spectacular looking, and Cate watched him in fascination. Her visitor was tall and slim, like Devin, but with more defined muscles that rippled in his arms and chest under his t-shirt. His chiselled features, piercing deep blue eyes and dark-blond hair framed him wonderfully, and Cate perked up straight away.

"Can I help you?" she asked, and he let out a gruff laugh that made her blush.

"I'm sure you can, Hecate," he said, startling her with the use of her pseudonym. She knew that voice though, and it took her a moment to place it.

"Is that really you?" she asked, and was getting more confused. As if he'd willed it, she then began to see through the changes in him. Satan did indeed have the same features she knew so well, but he was now much, much younger. Her Infernal Master had discarded the rough looking beard in favour of a fresh-faced look, and had slimmed himself down as well as having altered his age. Satan now resembled the twenty year olds Cate and Devin had associated with back on Earth, and his dark prowess and bad-boy demeanour only added to his sexiness.

"Yes, I've decided to change my look. What do you think?" he asked her with a cocky grin. He'd known every thought that'd gone through her head since walking through that door, and she guessed he wanted to hear her say the words out loud.

"Well, you're gorgeous, of course. But what's all this for?" she asked, and was still naïvely confused by his alterations. Cate slid down to the edge of the bed, where she stood to greet him, but Satan didn't answer. He stepped closer and took her in his arms, and she wondered for a minute if they were about to travel back to Earth, but when they didn't move she hesitantly glanced up to search his face for answers. He softened his features and allowed that strange back and forth of emotions and electricity to travel between them again, flooding her with a wonderfully sensual wave of adoration and desire.

"This is called *expression*, Hecate. It allows me to share a part of myself with someone that I don't normally allow others to experience, or even let show at all. You're the first being in over a thousand years that I've felt close enough to do it with," he told her, being honest at last.

Her head swam. The overflow from him was making her dizzy, and the strength of his words both scared and intrigued her.

"What's going on, father?" she asked hesitantly, looking up into his eyes, and Satan groaned.

"Don't call me that anymore, Cate," he whispered in return. For the first time since she'd known him, he sounded desperate, and she caught him looking down into her face and staring at her lips.

"Why?" she managed to ask, while mesmerised and taken aback by the strange vulnerability he was showing her.

"Because from now on, I want you and I to be lovers, equals," he replied, and then let out a deep, raspy laugh. Cate was still woozy from his *expression*, and now that he'd finally revealed his reasons, it made her gasp with shock. She was taken aback, and had no idea what to say in response. Yes, she'd felt the connection change between them recently, but it wasn't real. It couldn't have been, otherwise why had he sent her away? Why would he command her to be with Devin if he wanted her for his own? None of it added up.

Satan sensed her hesitation and she felt his hold on her tighten slightly, as though he was unwilling to let her go.

"We can't," she told him quietly, fearing his reaction. "I'm in love with Devin. I thought you saw me as your child, someone you nurtured and helped blossom into adulthood? Perhaps you don't understand your feelings towards me?" she asked, and knew straight away that he wasn't happy with her response. He hadn't really been anything more than a mentor to her, but she'd never consider him a potential lover either. Hell, he wasn't even a real person, but it all still felt so wrong.

The *expression* stopped immediately, but he remained where he was, holding her tightly, and their faces were just inches apart. Satan's eyes turned black as he regarded her for a few seconds, and Cate actually wondered if he might lash out at her. Instead, he kissed her. His deep and powerful show of forceful persuasion surprised her into submission, and he held his would-be lover even tighter.

Cate felt him luring her in. She knew there was even a part of herself that wanted him back, but she couldn't let it take over. She didn't know if what she was feeling was real, or just another order for her to follow from her dark master, and that realisation made her angry. After pulling back, he stared down at her, and then threw her down onto the bed with just a tiny push.

"No one says no to me, Cate. Not even you. I may have afforded you certain liberties in the past, but not anymore, not with this issue," he told her. His eyes seemed to grow even darker and his demeanour more ominous as he stood over her. Cate pushed herself backwards on her elbows, but knew there was nowhere to go, and certainly nowhere she could run. One thought kept running through her mind, a conversation she'd overheard one day between two level one demons, and she hated it. *It doesn't matter what we want. He comes first, and his needs overrule any of ours. What Satan wants, Satan gets. He can and will do as he pleases.*

He climbed onto the soft down and crawled over to Cate, and kissed her again. She swooned and couldn't help but kiss him back, succumbing to him involuntarily, but she was torn between the various rights and wrongs swirling around inside her head. She wanted him to open the *expression* link again to help her understand his desire, but he didn't. He kept himself deliberately closed off for some reason, despite her silent pleas. She realised then that perhaps she'd hurt him with her arguments, refusals and hesitations—both spoken and silent.

Cate truly did not want to disappoint her master, but she somehow knew that she didn't want to be with him the way he wanted—at least not without having some time to think it over first. He'd made her life so incredibly fulfilled since he'd come to her in the church that night, but all they'd had since was a relationship more like a student and her teacher than potential lovers.

She didn't know when his feelings towards her had changed, and found herself wondering if maybe it was that night at the penthouse when she'd caught him watching her, or was it before that?

Regardless of her frenzied thoughts, he continued his pursuit, and kissed her again. Cate's head swam while her lips tingled from his kiss, and her body screamed out for him to continue. It didn't matter that her heart and body were feuding internally, she knew she didn't want it to happen, and her heart soon won the battle.

He knew, of course, and reacted almost instantly to her thoughts. He kneeled over her, and stared down with black eyes. Rage and pain were clear on his otherwise gorgeous face, and Satan hesitated just for a moment as if not sure how to go about dealing with her.

"Please," Cate quickly begged, hoping to divert his attention away from the punishment she was sure he was deliberating over.

"So, it's a no?" Satan eventually asked, and there was no emotion in his tone, while his face remained completely unreadable. The younger look of his was a little alien to Cate, and she had no idea how to read him. It felt as though he was a stranger to her again. But that had to be the point, she wondered. He wanted her to see him differently, and had obviously chosen a look he thought she'd like, one that might help sway her decision in his favour. Evidently he wasn't impressed that it'd backfired.

"It's a no," she mumbled from beneath him, and couldn't meet his dark gaze. Satan climbed backwards and without another word stood up from the bed, reaching out for Cate's hand. She was confused, but took his offered hand and let him help her stand.

She looked up into his cold eyes pleadingly, unsure of what to say, but all words were lost to her. It felt as though she'd lost the two most important men in her life on the same day, and the thought of being left alone and miserable made her shudder. She wanted to beg him for forgiveness, and perhaps even give him the yes he desired, but knew it wouldn't be sincere, and that he'd know it. The way she felt now, she'd never be happy at his side. Could she force herself to lie to him, or to herself? The answer had to be no.

Before she could even try and fight the tense air between them, the familiar dizziness washed over her that told Cate they were teleporting away. She hoped they were going back up to Earth and back to Devin, but no. When the pair came to a stop, her heart almost skipped a beat, and she began trembling despite the heat.

They were in a deep, fiery pit. Dark red flames licked her body, burning her skin and singeing her hair. There was no way out, and the walls all around her were just inches away from her either side of her body, threatening to scorch her skin if she touched them.

Her master stood a few inches away, seemingly unaffected by the flames, while she was already blistering from just the proximity. Satan smiled maliciously down at her and kissed the backs of her hands.

"I might respect your answer, but it doesn't mean I have to accept it. I'll think give you some time to think about what you really want," was all he said before he disappeared, leaving her all alone in that terrible place with nothing but her thoughts and the flames for company.

***

Cate couldn't bear it all alone in the sweltering, fiery prison. She had no concept of how many days or weeks she spent there, but she knew her master was punishing her severely for her foolish resistance of his advances. She guessed she'd only be released when he was done seething over her refusal, and knew it might be a while. It wasn't in his nature to forgive and forget.

The walls and floor burned constantly with flames and running lava, and there was nowhere for her to rest or sit, so she was stuck standing in the constant blaze. The flames caused her just as much pain as any burn would, but because of the power given to Cate by the same man who'd imprisoned her, she would heal instantly, and it'd begin all over again. She figured she might find the irony funny if it weren't so painful.

Tears dried instantly on her cheeks the moment they were shed, and she prayed for death to come and take her, but it refused her. It was too much. Cate knew she was too weak to take any more and she cried out, calling for her almighty master and begging him to return for her, but he didn't listen.

After what felt like forever, she knew she was broken. Cate let out a bloodcurdling scream and fell to her knees. The once so tough Dark Princess no longer even had the strength to stand up, and while she cried out when the hot rock burned her legs to the bone, she simply hung her head in agonising defeat and let them tear away more and more of her burning flesh. She tried to summon the witches, warlocks, and every demon she could think of, but none of them came to her aid. They knew far better than to defy their Dark Prince's orders.

When he eventually returned, she could fight him no longer. She looked up into Satan's cold, black eyes as he stared down at her, and silently begged him to take her away from this awful place.

"I'm sorry, please," she moaned. "Please…"

He put a hand on her shoulder and obliged her pathetic plea. Satan returned Cate to her bedroom, where she was left alone, for now. She was filthy. Her clothes were so badly burned that she stripped and tossed them straight in the bin rather than try to salvage them. She then took a long shower and pulled on a heavy black dress that shrouded her entirely, and the dark look matched her gloomy mood. After a few minutes of uncontrollable tears, she tried the door, but wasn't surprised when she found it locked. Cate didn't know when her master would come to her, or how things would go when he did, but she had to assume he still hadn't changed his mind regarding his plans for them.

She fell onto the bed, exhausted, and slept for what felt like days, and thought maybe it even was. When Cate stirred, Satan was sat on the bed beside her, watching her intently. She could sense his intense gaze on her, but not the *expression* she still so desperately hoped for. She wanted to know how he was feeling towards her, and what he wanted now that she'd seen out her punishment. Cate was also anxious to know how best to approach her master and make him understand her reasons for saying no and to explain what she wanted, but didn't know where to begin.

She wasn't even so sure what she did want any more. "Thank you for bringing me home," she eventually whispered. The fresh young face peering down at her was unreadable. He was still gorgeous, despite his awful behaviour, and was equally as lethal, as she still couldn't read him.

"Did you have time to reflect down in your pit, my love?" he asked, and a sly grin curled at the corners of his mouth as he spoke. His evil pleasure showed on his face as he took in her painful memories of that terrible place, and she hated him for enjoying her misery.

"Yes, I think we both know I had more than enough time to think things over," Cate replied dryly. Satan shrugged and let out a small laugh, and then carried on.

"So, is it a yes now?" he said, leaning in to get closer to her. He seemed so insistent on having her full submission, and she thought it odd he was so desperate for her to willingly accept his barbaric methods at wooing her.

Cate realised then, in a moment of clarity, that free will was all that was stopping him from simply taking her by force. He needed her to say yes, otherwise she would never truly be his to possess. Her revelation stopped his advance, and he pulled back quickly. Satan's eyes darkened and bore into hers, and he laughed, although nothing was funny about the way Cate felt under his sinister scrutiny.

"Got me," he whispered and grabbed her hand.

"No, please," she cried out as her master pulled her away from her room. Cate was teleported away against her will again and materialised on her knees before her sire in a cold, dark abyss. She was crying and begging her master, pleading with him not to hurt her anymore, but Satan was cold and distant again as he towered over her. He looked through her as though she was of no care to him at all, and her pleas made no dent in his icy exterior.

A masked demon dressed all in black then approached and looked to his master for confirmation. A swift nod was all he needed, and then Cate was dragged across the jagged rock floor by an invisible force. When she reached the demon's side, she was bound by her wrists with thick rope and pulled up off the floor to hang there by them. Her shoulders throbbed and her wrists ached already, and Cate bowed her head in defeat. Her will broke with every moment that passed, and she knew she couldn't bear another sentence of lengthy torture. Satan approached and lifted her gaze to his by gripping her chin and turning her head up so she looked him in the eye.

"Let's see how you feel after another year of torment, darling," he told her. "We have all the time in the world to play these games, and you have no idea what other treats I have up my sleeve. You're right, Cate. I do get what I want, and whether it's wrong or right doesn't matter to me. In fact, the more I have to chase, the better the prize will be when it's mine."

Cate didn't get the chance to respond. With a smile, he teleported away, and she just sobbed as he disappeared, leaving her to her misery. She cried out uncontrollably when the first lash of a whip slashed open her clothes and drew a streak of blood from the skin on her back. Cate begged the demon to stop, but knew that he wouldn't listen. He couldn't defy his master's orders any more than she could, and knew he'd suffer a similar torture if he dared try.

Hours, days, and eventually months, passed by in a dark and painful blur. The demon whipped her unrelentingly day and night, but time mattered little during her isolation. She couldn't sleep, and her healing powers hindered her from numbing to the pain of each whip. Cate once again prayed for death to come for her, but of course, it never did. She felt utterly broken and powerless, and knew without a doubt that there was no fight left in her at all.

Her feelings for Devin had completely diminished over the time since she'd been taken away from him, and she was exceptionally aware of how alone she felt. Tears splashed down her cheeks, and would come and go as the torment continued, but would soon dry up again, as she knew all too well.

"Please, stop this!" she cried out over and over, begging for her master's mercy again. The sudden slash of her ropes then sent

Cate falling into a broken heap on the floor, and she watched as the binds magically disappeared moments later. She curled into a ball and looked around the dark pit, but didn't see Satan anywhere. Just as she began to wonder why the torture had stopped, she was then teleported away.

Cate closed her eyes as she was pulled between time and space involuntarily. She hoped she'd look up and find herself at home when she arrived wherever her master was sending her, but unfortunately, he didn't intend to release her from her torment quite yet. She instead found herself in an enclosed cell, surrounded by torture implements and weapons, just like the one Dylan had been in such a long time before.

"Let's really put your powers to the test, Prrrrincessss," said an ugly warlock behind her, his tongue rolling the sound of her title in disgust. Cate's instincts kicked in, and she leapt to her feet and tried to run away, pulling on the cage's door handle, but there was nowhere for her to run. She was trapped. The sniggering behind her made her turn, and the disgusting man delighted in informing Cate there was no hope for escape.

"Do your worst," she told him, and knew her fight was over. She was finally defeated. "I'm pretty much dead inside anyway," she added, and he shoved her into the metal frame. Without another word, the warlock then grabbed her right hand, proceeding to break each finger with a loud crack.

After many more days of torture at the hands of the vile man, Cate knew there was no use fighting Satan's feeling towards her anymore. Free will meant nothing if she had to endure countless beatings and torture in order to keep hold of it. She hoped he could hear her words, or even just her thoughts, and she whimpered as loud as she could between the beatings her hideous tormentor administered.

"Yes. It's a yes," she cried out with the last of her strength, and Cate then lost consciousness. She gave up, and it was the last thought she had before everything went black.

CHAPTER NINE

When she finally awoke, Cate was lying naked in a deep bath somewhere in the depths of the dark castle. She'd been immersed in some sort of thick, gooey, black liquid that had no smell, but felt strangely nice against her sore skin. She could feel it healing her body, drawing out the death that'd tried to creep in during her torturous imprisonment. Her evil master sat by the side of the bath, watching her come around with interest, and a sly smile.

"You fought hard, my love," he said, seeming pleased with her in a way she couldn't even begin to understand. Cate looked away. She couldn't bear to look at him, much less share in his pleasure following her submission. "Tell me again," he demanded, and grabbed her chin, turning her back round to face him. Satan drew her attention without a care for her pain, and her empty gaze met his. Cate then swallowed hard, struggling to fight the tears she felt hovering only barely beneath the surface of her stubborn expression.

"Yes," she said quietly, looking him in the eye. She was fighting back the sobs that threatened to expose her broken soul, and hated him regardless of having given into his desire for her. He smiled and touched her cheek lightly; seemingly uncaring that she was so damaged thanks to his aggressive methods of persuasion.

"Good. You need to stay here for a while to heal first, but then we'll be together," he told her with a smile, and then disappeared without another word. The realisation then dawned on her what she'd agreed to give him, and tears flowed uncontrollably within seconds.

Alma and a couple of young witches tended to her, keeping her under their watchful gazes, but none of them seemed able to soothe her broken soul. They encouraged Cate to rest, but she had no other choice—her body was too much of a mess to fight the sleep. Her mind was even worse. The memories of her torture haunted her dreams, but she was too exhausted and couldn't pull herself out of them. Her father would often appear in her mind, but as a Halloween style mask—silly and bright red with horns and a pitchfork. But, he would then grow larger and turn darker before sucking her in and devouring her. Other times, the image would take the form of the last warlock, and deliver her beatings or break her bones. When Cate would finally wake up, she'd be dripping with sweat and sob uncontrollably, before falling back into an exhausted sleep again.

When she was finally healed, Cate was taken to Satan's private chambers. The witches who'd cared for her teleported in alongside the Dark Princess, and not a single one dared say a word to either encourage her to remain strong or give her their sympathy. She guessed they'd been warned against it, and knew their master would know the moment any of them were disloyal to their almighty ruler. Ever since she'd said yes, Cate felt Satan's presence inside her even stronger than before, although she hadn't seen him since the black goo bath. Her thoughts were not her own, and she knew she couldn't hide anything from him. He crept in everywhere, haunting her day and night, and Cate actually thought she might go crazy.

She barely even registered the soft hands that guided and moved her body. The witches undressed her and then led Cate over to the gigantic bed, urging her to lay in wait for her master. She looked up at Alma before she left, and her face was warm, but tense. Even Satan's high priestess seemed too scared to say a word, and she and the other two witches exited silently before locking the doors behind them.

Cate lay still on the bed, shivering despite the heat. She closed her eyes, clearing her mind as much as she could. She knew she had to give herself to him, that there was no going back now, but she was truly terrified. It was one thing being the Devil's progeny with a future and fate decided for her by her almighty master, but it was another thing becoming his lover and the sole focus of his dark attention. His affection could be intense and overwhelming, and the thought of having more than just the usual fleeting fondness scared the hell out of her.

She felt his presence before she saw or heard Satan come into the room a few minutes later, and opened her eyes, taking in her dark master as he loomed over her. He undressed slowly, removing his black shirt and jeans, while taking his time to look her up and down before he climbed his way towards her on the bed. His body was fantastic, just the right amount of strong, toned muscles she might enjoy looking at if these were different circumstances, and his deep blue eyes bore into hers with such intensity she quickly lost herself in them. His cock was huge and hard as steel, ready for her, and he finally allowed the *expression* link to open between them. In that moment, he gave her a rush of emotion, lust, power, and finally—love. It overwhelmed her, but it was also exactly what she needed in order to go on.

Satan climbed on top of Cate, and slid between her trembling thighs. The tip of his length rested lightly on her navel as he kissed her, and her only conscious thought was how it was a good thing she didn't need to breathe. The kisses he planted on her lips were so intense and deep he would've cut off her air supply within minutes.

She gave in to him completely, and slid her arms around his back to grip his shoulders tightly, allowing him to kiss her deeper and more intensely with his authoritative tongue. He relished in her, flicking his tongue expertly between her lips, down onto her neck, and then to her breasts. Cate tried to fight the pleasure welling within her at his touch, but her body was defying her, and she writhed beneath him as he took her nipples between his teeth one at a time and bit down gently, sending painful pleasure signals throughout her core.

His hands then opened Cate's thighs wider and lifted her hips to meet his eager mouth. Satan groaned as he tasted her, delving two fingers inside her open cleft. She gushed as he rubbed her g-spot while sucking her throbbing nerve-endings expertly, and she came for him within minutes as he relentlessly pursued her.

Cate then called out incoherently as he climbed up and thrust his stiff hard-on inside her, and a second orgasm rippled through her almost instantly when he began thrusting deeper inside. As the last climax faded, she couldn't help the small sob that escaped her lips, but he ignored it. Her infernal ruler reached down and grabbed his prize, pulling Cate up onto his lap so he could kiss her while moving her up and down fast and hard onto his greedy length.

"See, you should've just said yes a long time ago, Hecate," he said while thrusting up inside her. "Can you feel how right this is? Can you see now how perfect I am for this body?" he asked as he ran his down her spine.

She knew he was right, but still couldn't fight the sense that it was still so wrong. Her body welcomed him, and wanted him inside, yet her mind still resisted. It didn't matter what he said, she wasn't ready to let down her walls and let him in quite yet. Satan eyed her ominously, and could tell she was still torn, but still pushed her on to orgasm after orgasm until he was finally ready for his own climax. He grabbed Cate tight and pulled her close, staring into her bright green eyes, and into her soul. "I hope you're ready for this," he whispered, and then the walls of the room started to shake violently. The bed beneath them vibrated and rose up from the floor a few inches, and Cate's body shuddered with her final release as he plunged deep inside her and came. He then lifted her face and kissed her, staying firmly rooted inside her while the walls seemed as though they might collapse around them thanks to the strange shockwave of power that'd emanated from him in that final crescendo of pleasure.

The moment over, they rested together in peaceful silence for a while, neither one asleep, but there were no words to express what'd just happened between them. The floodgates were well and truly open though, and she felt his *expression* coming thick and fast through their strange but still so strong connection. In her head, Cate was still unclear about what she wanted. As much as their lovemaking had been wonderful, she was still angry, and incredibly frightened. She agreed now that they *could* be together the way he wanted, but didn't know where to begin to try and talk to him about how she truly felt. She was still so defeated from the torture, and humiliated by his conquest, so she stayed quiet while her mind ran riot processing all the strange ups and downs she was trying desperately to get her head around.

It felt strange. Her adoration for him was still ever present, but now it seemed to be growing, changing. He'd come to her one night so long ago and told her he was family, and yet somehow all of that had changed. The man she'd readily accepted as a father had changed, and what he'd wanted from her had altered dramatically. The almighty being laid next to her had decided he wanted something other than an heir, and he'd evidently been willing to do whatever it took to make Cate change her mind.

She wanted to hate him, but couldn't. Affection for Satan as a lover crept into her once so steadfast resolve, and she knew he'd almost succeeded in seducing her mind as well as her body. She'd resisted him for so long and had done everything she could to push him away. However, he'd still wanted her, and had made love to her so powerfully and incredibly once he'd claimed his prize. She knew she might never be the same again. It didn't make her happy to realise no man might ever compare to the ancient being who now shared her bed, but for some reason she wasn't saddened by it either.

Taking in his chambers, she saw the mess and debris that littered the vast space following their intense lovemaking session. A snap of his fingers would sort that out no problem, she had no doubt about it, and Cate just wished she could be repaired just as easily.

Satan watched her, listening in on her thoughts as she worked things out in her head. This time around, he decided to stay silent while she figured everything out, even though her unease angered him. He'd hoped she'd come around by now, but knew Cate would get there in her own time; he would just have to force himself to be patient. The Prince of Darkness decided to let his actions speak louder than his words, and he pulled Cate close so that he could kiss and make love to her again. She obliged him, and it was a delight to read her thoughts and discover how much she was enjoying his touch, regardless of how much he'd had to break her to make her his finally so willing concubine.

***

The pair rested together for a while, and Satan was the one to eventually break the silence. He had been holding Cate in his tight embrace under the satin sheets of his huge bed for a long while, and he'd let his *expression* flow to her the entire time. Keeping her close while she wordlessly arranged her scattered thoughts was a necessary step in helping Cate recover, and he too had been considering how different everything would be from then on.

"I've been thinking. We need to figure out what you're going to scream when I make you come, Cate," he said, releasing her before leaning up onto one elbow with a bold grin. Cate smiled and nodded.

"What do you have in mind, master?" she asked, and smiled. After the hours spent in his tactile care, she now felt stronger and more comfortable in his arms than she thought she would've been. Cate guessed she'd forgotten how good it felt to be held so preciously, and soaked up every ounce of strength and emotion he seemed to want to share with her.

"Master's far too prim and proper, darling," he replied playfully. "After what we just did, there is absolutely no need for formalities any more, and you most certainly won't ever be regarded as my heir ever again," he added and then laughed, thinking on it for a moment. "I know…you, and only you, can call me Lucifer," he told her, and Cate smiled.

"Wow, really? No one has called you that in centuries," she asked, remembering the history lessons the witches had given her when she first came to Hell with him. He had reportedly been so angry when the angels had cast him out of Heaven, that when Hell started filling up and his minions would call him by the name the Council had chosen for him, Satan didn't like it. He wanted to be above everyone—respected and feared. It was how he became more powerful. As time passed by, and with every soul that was sent his way, he grew stronger, but even more so if they remained terrified of him. Eventually no one dared say his real name in Hell, and even on Earth for fear of his wrath. All his demons, witches, and warlocks addressed him formally on pain of torturous death. He had readily adopted the names of Satan or the Devil to heighten his prowess and control over the realm, and continued to strike fear into the hearts of any who dared speak of him with his ancient title.

"Well then, Lucifer it is," Cate replied with a smile. "I suppose that's okay with me," she added playfully, but she was overjoyed. It made her feel special to know she was the only one who was allowed to address him so informally, and had to admit, it was a worthy gift for her compliance. She liked it, and enjoyed knowing she'd earned the right to his heightened favour after everything they'd been through together.

***

The new couple hid themselves away for months, making love and mending the connection Lucifer had destroyed in order to break her will, as well as simply enjoying their new love affair. Cate came to realise that he cared for her so much that her resistance had hurt him deeply. He opened up tremendously during their time in isolation together, and she wished he'd just been honest with her all along.

"I've never opened up to anyone before, Cate," he explained. "And when I finally did, you told me no. You told me it didn't feel right, that you thought it was wrong, when everything inside me was screaming that we were meant to be. I kinda went crazy, and I knew that if I couldn't have you, I didn't want anyone to," he told her one night as they lay in a hot bath together. Lucifer was behind her in the deep suds, and Cate turned her head back to meet his gaze, utterly shocked by his admission. "I wanted you so badly, and nearly let myself force you. I just wanted to make you see how wrong you were about us. But, I knew you'd have to come around in your own time, otherwise we could never be together in the way I truly wanted. Even after you nearly killed yourself trying to defy me, I could still sense your hesitation, but I decided to be patient and let you figure it out in your own way."

Cate smiled, but couldn't help the sadness from creeping in when she thought about the terrifying way he'd swayed her resolve.

"And although I did come around eventually, I still can't believe you did all those things to me," she told him honestly, and her face fell. It still hurt, and she couldn't hide it, but a part of him didn't want her to conceal her emotions. They were his burden to bear too, and she knew he would—forever. Despite Lucifer having gotten his own way in the end, it'd pained him having had to hurt his true love so severely to get what he wanted from her.

"I'll spend eternity making up for it, my love," he promised, kissing her softly. "Without the drastic measures though, I might have never gotten you to see sense. I hope one day you'll understand that."

Cate had to admit he was right. Given the chance, she would've pushed him away and continued saying no forever, even if it'd meant losing Devin, and probably everything she'd built over the years with their father. Although it pained her to admit, he had been right to push her. She would never tell him that, though. Saying yes had already taken everything from her, and an added admission of defeat would be one too many burdens for her to bear.

CHAPTER TEN

Eventually, the time came that the witches and demons around them needed Lucifer to tend to his business. They both knew that things would be a bit strange for everyone at first, especially Devin, and Cate wasn't looking forward to seeing him again after all their time apart. Lucifer seemed understanding, but insisted she remain strong, and went off to convene the Dark High Council. She was alone for the first time since she'd said yes to him, and wasn't sure what to do with herself.

She teleported back to her bedroom and checked that her door was unlocked, just in case, before getting showered and dressed. Cate then stood looking at her naked form in the bedroom mirror for a few minutes. She took in her perfectly healed body, but could somehow sense every scar and scorch mark as though it were still there. Despite her awful memories, she chose to think of them as some kind of invisible shield—armour to protect herself from ever being hurt or broken like that again. Lucifer would lead and she would follow without question from then on, there was no doubting that, but she'd never let her guard down again. Cate was determined never to see the inside of those terrible pits or torture chambers if she could help it, but she would never forget, or get complacent with him ever again.

She also had to mentally prepare herself to face his council, and part of her knew she was stalling. Cate dressed all in black, her preferred choice of colour nowadays, and pulled a black metal ring from her jewellery case. It had a bright green stone in the centre, and it matched the hue of her eyes exactly. The girl who'd been given the ring by her master was a very different person to the woman who stood reflected back at her in the mirror. Nothing would ever be the same, regardless of whether she wanted it to be or not, and Cate finally accepted her fate. There really was no going back. No matter what, Lucifer was her future, not Devin.

Cate thought about the man she'd once loved with every fibre of her being. It'd been over three years since Lucifer had taken her away from him at the penthouse, and she didn't know if he'd been told what was going on, or if he would even care anymore. Lucifer's new heiress, Serena, wouldn't come of age for another fifteen years, and Cate hated that he didn't have a new lover to take his mind off her betrayal. Devin could've spent every day pining for her for all she knew. She had a lot of making up to do, Cate was sure.

She walked out the large doors and down the corridor headed to the main meeting room of the castle. Lucifer's council room was a huge suite where all her master's top minions and advisors normally met to discuss important issues with him in privacy. Cate had never been there unannounced before, and had certainly never been present when their ruler had convened his Dark High Council. Those meetings were usually strictly off-limits to anyone outside the council, but now the important issue they were due to discuss was her, and Lucifer had insisted she attend. An ancient demon named Lilith was waiting at the doors that led to the main council room, and she intercepted her as she reached the chamber. Lilith's face was stern and as unfeeling as ever, but she reached for Cate's hand before they entered in what she would assume was a gentle way, if it were anyone else. The powerful demon drew her gaze, and smiled uncharacteristically.

"Are you okay?" she asked, taking Cate aback with her moment of apparent care. They'd never been close, and Cate didn't trust her. Lilith was aggressively loyal to Lucifer, even against her, and she loved him more than any other being under his rule. The ancient demon did his bidding without question and always strived to gratify her dark master in whatever way he asked of her. Lilith had earned his respect throughout the years, and her coveted place as second in command of his underworld army. Nothing she said or did was about anyone but her master, or herself.

"Yes, I'm fine thank you, Lilith," Cate replied, smiling over at the dark haired demon. She was a short and slim framed woman, but Cate knew that beneath the human looking exterior, she was both incredibly strong and viciously cunning. Lilith was the leader of a council that convened to test and trial potential new demons as they tried to move up the levels that made up the hierarchy of demons below the royal family. She'd seen Lilith in action as she tested the souls who wanted to become new demons. Torturing them into submission or delivering dark punishments seemed like a hobby of hers, and there were many who tried and failed beneath her tutelage. Without batting an eye, Cate had watched her issue terrible orders for the wannabe demons to carry out in order for them to even be considered for the honour. Only the exceptionally evil would eventually carry on to complete their initiations and challenges under her watchful eye.

"Good," Lilith replied, looking back at her with a fake smile. "Because if you're happy, then he's happy, and you know how important that is to all of us." She reached out for the door handle. "I suggest you don't defy him again," she added, and opened the large door, ushering the seething Dark Princess inside.

The council members all looked up as the pair of them entered, and Lucifer ushered for Cate to sit by his left side at the huge table. Lilith went to his other side, and bowed graciously to her master as she took her seat.

"Some of you know already, and some of you do not. I've only discussed this with those absolutely necessary before tonight," Lucifer addressed them all, looking up and down the long table as he spoke. "Hecate is no longer going to live with Devin on Earth. He is now betrothed to Serena and is waiting patiently for her to come of age while he continues to run Black Rose Industries under my command. When such time comes, he will go to her, just like Cate did with him and become her teacher and lover."

He paused for a moment to ensure he had their undivided attention. "Cate is now my *inamorata*, my lover," he added, looking over at her with a satisfied smile. Lucifer then slid his hand over her thigh, sending wonderful tingles throughout her entire body, and she felt her cheeks burn. "From thus forth, she is no longer to be addressed as or regarded as my heiress. Anyone that does not treat her as my future Queen will be dealt with accordingly."

The room was so silent even Cate could hear the cogs turning behind the primeval demons' intense stares, but Lucifer seemed oblivious to their shocked expressions. "Those who are caught not following this order will be punished however I see fit. Perhaps, for example, I might dump said traitor in one of my many dark pits for all eternity with their eyes gauged from their sockets and their disrespectful tongues liberated from their mouths." He took a deep breath, relishing in the vivid imagery of the punishment. "Do I make myself perfectly clear?" Lucifer asked sternly, the rhetorical question more of an order to his small crowd of minions.

He then looked around the table to all the highest and most regarded members of his chain of command, and they each nodded in agreement. He took the time to look each and every one of them in the eye, reading their thoughts as they stared over at Cate or down at their hands, and none but Lilith dared to fully meet his gaze. She smiled at her Dark Prince and silently agreed to follow his plans without question, much to his pleasure, as usual. "Even you, Asmodeus?" Lucifer then asked a few moments later. He peered down the table at a demon sat third on his right with his face half covered by a dark cloak. "Your thoughts give you away, old friend".

"No, sire, not at all. I, I, I..." Asmodeus stuttered while trying desperately to be heard by his master, and Lucifer was glad to know he'd taken his threat seriously. "I just pondered that perhaps it is not the right match for the pair of you to have a proper marriage, and by that I mean having any children together, nothing at all to question the relationship itself. Your majesty's, please forgive my foolishness." The demon bowed his head and hoped that Lucifer was happy with his explanation. He stared at Asmodeus darkly for a moment before leaving the demon alone and addressing the group once more.

"And what about the angels in Heaven who are still as I once was?" Lucifer asked the question rhetorically again. "The many spirits who then went on to give birth to thousands more celestial beings. And let's not forget Adam and Eve, who then parented the entire goddamn human race," he added, and Cate could sense that Lucifer was getting angry, but he regained his composure again quickly. "Cate and I are going to be married. After that we have all eternity to try and make a family together," he informed them, and it was clear that was the end of the matter. Lucifer pulled her closer is if to prove his words were true, but all she could think about was what he'd said about them being married. While terrifying, it was also a wondrous thought to become a Queen at last. Not to inherit the throne if and when he decided, but to be crowned and beheld as ruler of Hell by his side. That, she certainly could do.

Cate was gladly excused from the council meeting soon after Lucifer's speech, and she went for a walk around the castle to clear her head. She was already so much clearer on everything that he now wanted from her, and had slowly come around to the idea of willingly giving him all that he desired. She supposed the whole marriage thing wasn't such a big deal. They'd already made the ultimate promise to love each other faithfully, and were committed to being together forever after all. Becoming his eternal bride would definitely put Cate at ease even further. She'd know then for sure that he would not simply change his mind again like he'd done with hers and Devin's relationship. A proper union and the higher status that came with his hand would hopefully give her more power, control and a say in her own life in the long run as well, and she welcomed the upcoming change in Hell's leadership.

Cate wanted more than anything to be loved, respected and happy. She also wanted to be trusted to make her own decisions and not to have to follow Lucifer's orders all the time, but have her own valid opinions as well. Becoming Queen of Hell was right. Cate could feel it. She was also excited about the prospect of children. It'd never occurred to her before that they could ever try and have a family together.

That evening as Cate undressed for bed, Lucifer teleported directly into her bedroom, and immediately went down on one knee before her.

"Darling. I know I let my intentions slip prematurely earlier, but I meant every word," he said as he took her hand and pulled a huge, black diamond encrusted ring from his pocket. "Will you be my wife?" Lucifer then asked, and Cate smiled, allowing him to slide the ring onto her finger.

"Yes," was all she could manage to respond, but it was the only word he needed to hear.

***

Up on Earth, Devin worked at his desk late into the evening, again. He'd had nothing else to occupy him other than Black Rose Industries during the last few years while he was waiting for Serena to come of age, but the monotony of the world bored him. He'd thrown himself into running the company as efficiently and successfully as possible since Cate had gone back home with their master, and had done it well.

He thought back to that night. The witch, Sara had taken him aside and informed him of Satan's new plans for his lover. She didn't even bother to sugar-coat the fact that Devin and Cate were no longer destined to be together.

"Cate has gone, and you must not try to find her. You're to wait here for Serena to grow older, and then you will go to her. You'll be for her what Cate was once for you—a friend, lover, and bridge between the world she knows now and the dark world she must embrace when the time comes," Sara had told him hastily. "Cate is a friend to you now and nothing more. There will be more changes soon, but they are your father's orders to command, not mine. In the meantime, you are forbidden from returning to Hell until he is ready to see you, Devin. I've been ordered to inform you to carry on your life here until further notice. Jonah will stay, and he'll take you to New York for Serena when the time is right."

She had then teleported away without a word of sympathy or understanding for the horrendous loss he'd just suffered, and Devin hadn't seen the witch since. It'd felt as though someone had ripped out his heart that night, and he'd felt the anger pour out of him as he wept openly for his lost love. They'd been so perfect together, so in sync and he couldn't imagine his life without her by his side. Jonah had sensed his rage at their ruler's betrayal, and had tried to calm his friend in the fear of him being punished by Satan for speaking ill of him.

"Our whole bloody union was *his* plan all along, and now suddenly he's just changed his mind?" Devin had bellowed in his fury, feeling both enraged and offended.

"He's not just your father, don't ever forget that. He's your master and King first, Devin," Jonah had told him following his outburst. "He can, and will, do as he chooses, and you'd do well never to forget that."

Now, it was three years later, and Devin no longer felt the

strong love-bond he'd once had with Cate. He could sense her power within him like an awareness rather than a formidable desire. It'd become nothing more than a small flame somewhere deep within him that linked them, but no deeper love, and no sexual need—not anymore.

He was completely indifferent to the women around him, both demonic and human again as well. Having been ordered to wait for Serena had bought about that familiar abstinence he'd had instilled in him before meeting Cate all those years ago, and he both understood and resented it. Devin felt as though he'd been forgotten about up on Earth. His master didn't visit anymore, and there'd been no further orders from him for far too many years.

Eventually, and out of the blue, he felt the familiar beacon as it called to him, and he was summoned back to Hell. He travelled there immediately and went straight into the castle, where he knelt before his master as he sat on his black throne. Devin immediately saw the age difference in him to the last time he had seen him up in the penthouse. He had to be twenty years younger looking than the familiar guise he'd always worn before, and it was a surprise to see him with a different look.

"Welcome back," Satan said, with an edge of warmth to his tone that began to ease Devin's anger towards him in an instant. He then beckoned for him to come forward, hugging him tightly when he did so.

"Thank you, father. It's good to be home. How might I serve you?" Devin replied, being careful to remain respectful, but still he hoped he might hear some news of his old flame.

"You need do nothing but listen, for I have some incredibly happy news," Satan told him, and smiled when Cate came in and joined the two of them. Devin's immediate reaction was to question the coldness behind her eyes, as if she were only half the soul she'd once been. There was a strange detachment there he couldn't understand, and when she smiled, those beautiful green eyes no longer lit up like they once had. "Cate is no longer my progeny, she's going to be my bride," Satan told him, and Devin couldn't hide the gasp that escaped him as his mouth dropped open in shock.

"And I suppose I was the last to know because it took you

such a long time to win her round?" he mumbled, and Cate shrunk back at his dismissive tone. "Or perhaps she wanted this all along?" Devin added, and shook his head at Cate in distaste. Hatred trickled out of every pore, and she was dumfounded by his assumption that she'd somehow instigated this entire plan to elevate herself into a position of power rather than share it with him. "Maybe next time you break my heart, you'll be a little more gentle, Hecate. Perhaps for pity's sake, you'll go as far to pretend for a moment that you actually care about anyone other than yourself."

She guessed he wanted to think the worst of her, and decided to let him. It was much safer for Devin if he hated her rather than blame Lucifer for how things had changed so drastically between them. Despite his awful words, she didn't want him to end up with the same punishment she'd endured, and knew her fiancé was capable of far worse if he were provoked enough.

"Perhaps…" she mumbled in reply, before walking away so he couldn't see the tears falling from her sad eyes.

CHAPTER ELEVEN

The world around them shuddered and shook violently as Lucifer climaxed inside his lover, and she wondered if the castle might fall down around them if they weren't careful. Cate trembled as the last of her many orgasms coursed through her body, sending wonderful messages throughout her entire core. By the time everything came to a halt, she was limp and exhausted in Lucifer's arms, yet exultant and relaxed. He lay her down and covered her with the black satin sheet, then clicked his fingers—repairing the damaged bed and surrounding furniture immediately. Cate lay back and wondered to herself if the whole of Hell shook when he came. If so, the beings around them surely knew when they were making love. Even if it were only the castle that knew, she'd still find it embarrassing. Lucifer laughed as he lay down beside her, reading Cate's thoughts again.

"No, I'm pretty sure it's just whatever room we're in at the time, darling," he answered her. "It only happens strongly down here, but on Earth it's more like a deep vibration. A bit like a blast of power that comes from me and anything in the immediate vicinity gets a beating, or an orgasm in your case," he added with a wink.

She smiled, but nodded. "Oh yes."

He then simply held her closer and savoured the feeling of having the woman he loved so much wrapped tightly in his arms, and Cate soon drifted off to sleep in his warm embrace.

***

Lucifer left her alone to sleep after watching her sleep for few minutes, which was his normal routine. He never need to sleep, so would often just wait for her to drift off before getting dressed and going off to his chambers, or to his convene his council and use the time to see to any issues that might require his attention. He was always needed. Eternally busy, but he couldn't deny his top priority these days was to make plenty of time to be with his future Queen.

He thought back to when she was just a baby. The existence of a child bearing his blood had altered history, and he'd known right away that she was special to him. It was inevitable that Cate would change his entire existence dramatically. It was as though from the moment she was born he'd known things would never be the same for him again, but had accepted it regardless. At first he'd thought it was just an extra special bond he shared with her as his first successfully conceived heir. After such a long time trying she was his most coveted prize, but in time Lucifer's growing feelings had taken his affection in a wholly different direction.

That night in the church was the first time he'd been with Cate in the flesh her entire life, which had been a necessity thanks to the white witches' involvement. To this day, he still couldn't understand how they'd discovered her and gotten so close, and knew he might never find out. His witches had played their parts along the way, though. They'd kept her safe and made sure her mother had enough money and security to keep a roof over their heads and food in Cate's belly. He'd even ensured that Ella hadn't ever married nor had any serious relationships after giving birth to her unholy child. It wasn't because he'd wanted her for himself, in fact he felt nothing at all for her. Like all the others, Ella had been a means to an end, an incubator and carer for the precious cargo he'd hoped to create with each full moon.

He'd kept possible stepfathers away simply so that Cate wouldn't be influenced or affected by having a male father figure in her life. Lucifer had wanted her weak and clueless when it came to men. Pliable to his every desire, and the epitome of the phrase, 'having Daddy issues.' Even back then, jealousy had stirred in him at the thought of another man loving her as his own. It was a wonder to him how he'd been so oblivious to his attraction to her for so long.

Now though, Lucifer faced a different future than the one he'd planned for Cate all those years before. He'd focussed his efforts in nurturing her mentally and ensuring she learned everything there was to know about him and her new home as soon as she'd come with him to Hell. Lucifer had even been forgiving that Cate had so many questions and hesitations rolling around in her mind when the time came for her to go and watch over Devin.

She'd continually forgotten back then that he knew everything, but part of him liked it how she wasn't always on her guard with her thoughts and feelings in his presence. Cate regularly let her mind wander, and Lucifer had enjoyed watching as her thoughts and memories played out in her mind. He'd found himself enthralled by the flow of her feelings, ups and downs through her unmasked responses to the new, strange world around her. Lucifer had especially enjoyed the way Cate had felt about him back when she'd first come of age. She had been so excited to discover what she truly was, and so eager to please her new master that she was acquiescent to his every request. The perfect underling to mentor and groom.

Since the successful inception of a second child, the plan had always been to bring Devin home once he came of age. His true identity would be revealed just as he'd done with Cate—by summoning the teen to a Satanic church and informing him of his true heritage, before asking his son to come home with him. He'd made the decision to send Cate to Earth early to meet Devin simply because he couldn't stop himself desiring her. It'd always been his plan that they'd be together. They were to become a superior couple that Lucifer believed would deliver his realm many more powerful heirs over the years. Their offspring would grow and become an eternal family, and by mixing his blood with human, he'd hoped his powerful bloodline might finally be allowed to rule up on Earth, as well as in Hell. He'd imagined them all going back and forth and taking over, piece by piece. Lucifer had even envisioned a world in which the saints were cast out into the cold and their churches burned to the ground, while the Satanic churches rose from their ashes. Any oppressors would then be punished and submitted to an eternity of torture at the hands of his demonic minions. It was a dark and ominous future that he'd wanted so very badly, bad enough to push away his personal desires to try and procure it.

And so, for his own peace of mind and the preservation of his dreams for the future, he'd sent her away. Lucifer had known Cate wasn't ready, but he knew he had to push her. He was sure he would've taken her for himself back then, and for that she was definitely not ready. That still so timid young woman and her fragile mind would've never been able to handle him. Lucifer couldn't be sure Cate could handle it all now, but there was no going back. He'd already waited as long as he could bear, and couldn't change things even if he wanted to.

His plan had worked for a while, though. With her gone, Lucifer finally had time to focus fully on his realm, where he felt her presence deep within him, as normal, but didn't hear her thoughts or feel the intensity of her prowess like he did when she was in Hell with him. It'd calmed him having her at arm's length.

It all changed again when Cate and Devin made love that first time, though. Lucifer had felt it, almost as if he were there—as if he were the one experiencing her first time through his son's eyes. He was somehow in Devin's thoughts, watching through his mind's eye. Lucifer had been working incessantly and had tried to rest his frenzied mind that night, but had found himself dreaming. It'd seemed so real. He was there, watching Cate make love to him, and he felt every thrust as though he were the one doing it to her.

When Lucifer had come back to himself, his right-hand demon, Lilith had come to him worried. She'd told him that he'd been missing for several hours and none of them could sense or find him in Hell or on Earth. He knew then that he must've gone into Devin's body for real, and not as a dream. It wasn't via possession, but more like a morphing of their consciousness. Lucifer didn't believe Devin even realised it'd happened, and had decided to keep it to himself at first. He later explained the strange phenomenon to his high priestess, Alma, who urged him never to do it again. She was worried he could get stuck in someone else's consciousness next time if he didn't know how to control the power properly. She'd also promised to find out as much as she could about the combining of two beings' minds though, appeasing Lucifer's curiosity on the matter for the time being.

After that night, he'd tried to occupy himself with either torturing the poor souls in his realm, or concocting new means of endless pain and suffering with his demonic council. He shut his two progeny's out from his mind and left them at the edge of his thoughts. That was until the witches informed him that the full moon approached and that Devin had come of age on Earth.

Once Lucifer opened his mind to them again, he became fully aware of their bond and adoration for one another. Devin was completely besotted with Cate, and she too loved him with every fibre of her being. His son was finally ready to come home, and despite him feeling a touch of jealousy for their bond, Lucifer decided it was time to go and retrieve the two lovers.

He went up to Earth right away, and the rush of emotion they sent his way were hard to ignore. When he'd got the signal from Jonah that Devin was at the church, Lucifer teleported towards the beacon and arrived there instantly, but didn't go right to them. He watched from the shadows as the pair sat down in the circle of warlocks. He was truly proud of Cate in that moment—she really was his ultimate treasure. He didn't know how she did it, but she drew his attention instantly, however Cate was not his intended focus that night.

Lucifer had instead walked right over and introduced himself to Devin. He read his thoughts before ushering him over to a dark corner so that they could talk, and knew the boy was nervous. His mind was racing, but it was also open and ready to accept his new fate. They spoke for a few minutes, and Lucifer outlined his real heritage while giving him the same speech as he'd given Cate on her same night of revelations.

"Now, any questions?" Satan had then asked with a grin. Devin had been utterly dumbfounded. His mind had raced and his thoughts were all over the place, but he'd seemed to handle it well, and had shaken his head. "Good. So, how do you feel about coming home with us to Hell?" he'd then asked him, and Devin had nodded, much to Lucifer's delight.

"Yes," he'd added, seeming unable to say much more.

"That's all I need." Lucifer had then led Devin back over to the group. He could tell Cate was worried about how things had gone, and she even wondered if Devin might reject her now. What a fool she was to believe anyone who loved her could ever forget her so easily.

Lucifer hadn't been able to stop himself from gathering her up in his arms, and he told her how proud he was. He knew she needed him to reassure her that Devin was okay, but he'd also felt envious. However then, there was something else, something unexpected in their embrace. Lucifer had sensed how Cate was somehow enjoying his closeness a little more than she should've been as well. He'd been able to hear her heart pounding harder while in his tight grip, and her body responded to him in a way he hadn't expected.

He had been overcome with his emotion for her in that moment, and knew then that he wanted her to feel his love. For the first time in far too long, Lucifer had allowed his *expression* to open for her. He'd let her into that tiny part of himself that felt passion and affection, and she'd soaked it up. Her thoughts had become dizzy with his offering, but Cate had relished his warmth, and lapped it up gratefully.

Lucifer had needed to force himself to release her, except by her hand. He'd then taken Devin's in his other hand and, after a quick explanation about the atmosphere down in Hell, they'd finally left for home.

As time had then gone on, Lucifer had continued to push his desire for Cate aside. Allowing the couple time to enjoy their new-found vigour and accentuate their power had been a necessary torment. He'd instructed the witches to teach them while he busied himself elsewhere again. No amount of women satisfied him, though. No number of deviant, sadomasochistic debaucheries with his usual lovers had made even a dent in his insatiable need or his unquenchable thirst for the forbidden fruit. He'd craved Cate. Lucifer had known it to his core, but had endeavoured to push those feelings away for as long as it took to hopefully quash them. She hadn't helped him though, especially when brazenly showing off her naked, just-fucked body without a care when he'd visited them to take her back to the white witch's cell.

He was more to blame than she, and knew full well that they were both still naked when he'd made his entrance, but Lucifer hadn't stopped himself. Curiosity had gotten the better of him. Cate had been so beautiful. Still rosy-cheeked and glistening with sweat from their passionate lovemaking session, the view had done nothing but feed his strange addiction to the tormenting pleasure of her. The cravings that the sight of her naked body had stirred in

Lucifer had overcome him, and he knew then and there that they could no longer be overlooked. Following that night, he'd wrestled with himself and his desires, and had soon decided to send them both back to Earth.

Once they'd gone, he hadn't cared for the quiet. Lucifer had summoned witch after witch, demon after demon, and ordered them to work harder and longer to help fill his time. It'd been no use though, and one Halloween when he went to Earth for three days during a full blood-moon, some good news had struck him dumb with inspiration. His suspicions had been right, and Lucifer received confirmation of a pregnancy with one of the human females he'd visited a few months before. Another female progeny of his was indeed growing inside the human woman, and would be born just a few months later.

The idea that Devin could be with the younger heiress was entirely feasible. He and Cate still weren't married, and if he tore them apart in time, Satan could then have her all to himself. That seed of doubt had then grown incredibly, no matter how much he had tried to push it away. The orgy he'd then instigated the following evening was all for her—Cate. The women that came along were nothing more than a distraction and a ploy to tempt her gaze and attention away from Devin. All he'd needed was a second and he'd know whether she felt that tiny seed of doubt, too. He'd hoped there was that small wonder of, *what else?* And indeed, he'd gotten it. Leaving again had been hard on him, but the moon demanded it, and he was as ever its unwilling slave.

Lucifer had always hated not having the freedom to come and go on Earth as he pleased. For thousands of years he couldn't go at all, until his dark witches finally found the loophole with the lunar phases. For some divine reason when the moon was full, he could go to Earth and roam freely until it started to wane again. Every year on All Hallow's Eve he also had from midnight to midnight should he wish to visit. When he'd tried to teleport up years before, Lucifer hadn't considered such things, and had evidently gone at the wrong time in the lunar phase. Within minutes, the fallen angel had started having violent headaches and begun losing his powers. He would then have nosebleeds and a consuming weakness of his usually intensely strong muscles, before eventually passing out. Luckily, he'd always ensured that at least one of his demonic council members went with him. Their job was to see to it that Lucifer was brought straight back to Hell once those reactions started, or else he wasn't sure might happen if he'd stayed. The longest he'd been able to stand it on Earth was a mere two hours per visit during those trials. He'd then given up for a long time, despite his desire to roam freely from Hell, and when the witches had worked out the lunar loophole out for him, he'd welcomed the news. He'd tested the theory during the next full moon, and had remained there for a full two days without any reaction at all. Lucifer had caused nothing short of chaos and mayhem during his first visits, with his demonic comrades Leviathan and Beelzebub at his side, as they corrupted and tainted the then sparsely populated world.

He thought how the times had changed, and how he'd changed. It was so strange to him to no longer be only thinking about only himself, but suddenly another. He'd always planned to care for his heirs like his family—as his children—but knew the moment he'd laid eyes on Cate that they weren't connected in that way. Their shared power seemed more of a mutually binding correlation, and a joining that once done could never be undone.

He thought back to when he'd returned to Earth to check on Serena after her birth, and how everything was perfect. The business was running smoothly, the infant was happy and healthy, and he could sense Cate's seed of doubt about her relationship with Devin still rooted within her thoughts, despite their happiness. His plan to lure her away had worked better than he'd imagined, regardless of her then refusing his advances.

Lucifer knew he'd acted coldly toward Cate in those first days back in Hell. He'd wanted her so badly he couldn't bear to punish her for denying him, and yet knew he'd have to break her will if he was going to make her see sense and change her mind. It was also the only way he knew how to handle the rejection. He'd not been able to bear Cate's thoughts and hesitations as they ran through his telepathic gift, or in those instances, his curse.

Lucifer had changed his appearance that day to try and help her cope with the changes he wanted her to make, and as a way to distract her from what he was asking of her, but it hadn't worked. She'd stomped all over his heart that night without even realising it, and instead of combating her refusal by focussing on winning over her hesitant thoughts, he had chosen to shut them out and punish her instead. Lucifer had never dealt with not getting his own way very well. In a moment of rage, he'd thrown her into the fiery pit where she might contemplate her decision some more, and left her there despite having hated every second of it.

Satan had then needed to double his efforts to remain busy while she was there in there. Through their strong bond he could feel the flames burning into her as though it were his own body being tortured, and Cate's pleading thoughts she sent him while held captive in the flames had been agonising. He knew then that he loved her. He had committed his body and soul to her completely, despite knowing he would have to wait for her fidelity in return. Lucifer had also commanded for her to stop loving Devin. He'd focussed on it with all his might, and after a while he could feel her heart shutting off to him. Despite all the concepts humans had that love could not be messed with, he had managed it. Opening Cate's heart to Devin had been simple, but closing it again had not been so easy. The torture had helped. The Prince of Darkness also knew that no matter how much he wanted her, he didn't want to order her to love him the way he had with Devin. He'd wanted it for real, forever.

Up on Earth, Devin had felt it too and stopped searching for her, stopped pining. Lucifer could sense that his son didn't understand why their master had kept Cate away so long or why he had banned him from coming to Hell, but he hadn't needed to know the details, and Lucifer knew he wouldn't approve of his methods to sway her resolve. He'd known nothing of what his ex-lover was going through down there at Lucifer's hands, and their master had intended to keep it that way.

When Cate had finally left the pit, Lucifer was sure she'd gotten the message, loud and clear. Her thoughts were open and honest, and she was afraid he would hurt her, but could also feel their connection growing. Lucifer had then made the mistake of letting her know the free will element of the deal, and straight away he'd known that she wouldn't give herself to him. Her thoughts gave her away, and he knew she'd exploit that pivotal rule in order to try and get more time to make her decision. His broken girl had been stronger than even he'd given her credit for.

Although it'd pained him to allow her further suffering, he did what he'd had to in order to break her will even more, and used a different approach. He'd known for sure though that once Cate had been broken and tortured enough, she would yield. Everybody cracked eventually.

It'd taken her longer than Lucifer had hoped, but eventually he got the *yes* from her he so desperately needed. He'd been strangely proud that she'd fought so hard, and had sensed her submission before the words had even left Cate's lips. A snap of his fingers and he'd taken her away from that terrible dungeon, and despite his eagerness to claim her, Lucifer had then delivered her straight to the witches' dungeon. They'd then tended to her wounds and bathed her in that special concoction of herbs and potions that would heal her quickly, and she'd needed it.

Cate had no idea just how close she'd come to a pure death. She was half human after all, and although she was an immortal being, she could still technically die if her body was hurt badly enough. They were all susceptible to one form of death or another. She would've then ended up in purgatory for however long it took to process her soul and then, he presumed, come back to Hell. By that time she would be just another worthless new arrival for them to torture, with no more powers or high standing than any other human essence. There would've been no place for Cate at his side if he'd allowed that to happen.

She'd been so defeated when Lucifer had come to her in the tub, a shell of her former self, and yet ever her so beautiful self. Even the night when they'd first made love, he could sense her fear and foreboding of him. By the time they were done though, she'd been putty in his hands, and her heart had opened to him like he'd always hoped it would.

And so here they were now. She was finally his, and would forever be, Lucifer would make damn sure of it.

CHAPTER TWELVE

"You are cordially invited to the wedding of His Infernal Majesty, Satan, and his bride, Hecate, on All Hallow's Eve. The ceremony will begin promptly at sunset," Devin read the invitation aloud to Serena, who grinned across at her lover as she listened. She clapped her hands excitedly while bouncing in her seat, and he had to warn himself against making fun of her daftness. While young, his new lover knew her mind, and Devin knew she would tell him off in a heartbeat if he let himself develop the bad habits of a humourless old man. Instead, he simply smiled back at her, and let her beauty fill his senses. Love had returned to him at last thanks to Serena's presence in his otherwise still lonely world, and Devin was glad to know that Cate and their sire were finally tying the knot. Moving on hadn't been easy, but as soon as he was with Serena their connection had flourished, and he'd forgotten all about the sense of abandonment that'd once consumed him so entirely. They'd now been together for just a few months, but she'd already embraced their dark world with ease, just as he had. Devin knew it was because someone they'd loved and trusted had shown them both how, and he pitied Cate for having been the first of their kind. It was no wonder their master had fallen for her. After all, he'd been her one and only semblance of the family she'd craved back then, and it seemed their ties had sprung to life during that relationship without either of them being aware of it. That was how Devin always thought about it, anyway. Theirs seemed a love forged out of both right and wrong, and yet they'd made it work. The past decade had seen a new world for all of them, and a new ruler. Satan was another being entirely for having her, and all their dark dominion agreed she'd become a welcome addition beside him on the throne. It was about time they finally made it official.

Devin hadn't risked any part of Serena's transformation, and had been with her every step of the way. He'd even offered to train and teach her all about her dark powers and abilities exclusively, and their father had agreed. The bright and bubbly young woman had taken everything in her stride, and was definitely the more relaxed member of their dark dynasty.

Cate seemed to love having Serena around to help ease the burden she obviously still felt when it came to having left Devin alone. He'd had hardly any explanation of what'd happened since she left, but they were friends again now, and the three of them had grown closer during the last few months since Serena had joined them in Hell. Devin had struggled with the betrayal and deceit at first, but had come around soon enough and accepted Satan's decision to be with Cate. He'd also had to accept, in the end, that there wasn't really any other choice in the matter.

Many years had passed since then, and Devin had accepted his new fate and was now with his true love at last. He was truly happy with Serena, and hadn't ever looked back since the day he'd finally been allowed to meet her. Devin was actually looking forward to celebrating Lucifer and Cate's big day. They'd become an enviable couple, and one that all of Hell revered, so he was glad he'd let her go rather than fight. His only regret was blaming her for his misery, but he'd had to hate someone, and even Cate seemed content to let his anger be directed at her rather than at their sire.

***

Cate had been bombarded with making wedding decisions and details for months, and part of her just wanted it to happen already so she could relax a little. The other part of her knew it had to be absolutely perfect, and so she gave it everything she had to ensure that every meticulous detail was planned out. Everything was black and red, of course. They had red roses and black dresses, but it was the fine detail that she obsessed over. Even if no one else noticed them, Cate sure would, and she knew that Lucifer appreciated them as well. They both needed it to be perfect—the event of the century.

When the day finally came around, Cate and the witches went

up to Earth early to get ready, while Lucifer remained in Hell with his demonic groomsmen—Devin, Beelzebub and Leviathan. The church was dressed beautifully in black decor and a dark red aisle for her to walk down, and it looked amazing. The finishing touches were already complete, and all that was left for Cate to do was to personally make sure their venue was secure, but she wasn't worried. Demons and warlocks guarded every entrance, while the witches strengthened the barriers restricting any light beings from crossing over the threshold, and she knew they wouldn't get close thanks to the immense dark power emanating from within their sacred ground.

"You ready?" Serena asked Cate as she applied her makeup, giving her soft features a delicate touch that emphasised her beautiful green eyes and red lips effortlessly.

"Absolutely," she replied, grinning back at her.

"You'll be the Dark Queen of Hell after today, Cate. Imagine the life you'll lead, and children you might have together—so wonderfully powerful," Serena added with a sigh. A dreamlike haze clouded her eyes, and Cate knew she must have been daydreaming about the future of Cate's potential dark brood.

"I hope so," she said, thinking of the possibility. The lovers had already discussed Lucifer's desire to sire more children, and she had to hope it might work for them. She was nowhere near ready to try, however, and simply held that optimism dear to her heart with faith it might someday come true.

***

The sun began to set over the church, and the red light streamed in through the stained glass windows as Cate walked down the aisle. She was dressed in her gorgeously flowing long black gown, and felt like the most beautiful woman in the world. It had a stunning fitted bodice and long skirt, and both had blood-red roses sewn on that went all the way from the bustier top down to the long tail behind her. The dress, like her marriage, was one of a kind, and she'd chosen only the most skilled seamstress she could find to make the custom piece for her special day.

Her bridesmaids—Serena, Sara and Alma—were dressed in black gowns as well. Their ones had stunning and sexy plunging necklines and open backs, with skirts that went all the way to the floor around their feet. The material also seemed to shimmer in the dark church, and the four women looked stunning against the black backdrop of the church. They followed her down the aisle as Cate walked the short stretch towards her groom, and each had their black rose bouquets in their hands and broad smiles on their reddened lips.

She peered down to the head aisle, and could only see him. Lucifer was elegantly dressed, in all black except for the red rose protruding from his lapel. Devin stood beside him and wore a matching suit to his father's, watching with a huge smile as the bride and her entourage walked towards them.

Lucifer opened his *expression* to Cate as she approached, and she beamed back at him. She welcomed his offerings of warm emotion and love as they poured into her, and could sense that he was eager to seal their union at last, just like she was.

The Satanic minister welcomed them, their family and friends to the church. He then bowed to Satan as he ushered the bride and groom to join him atop the steps before the altar. Cate was sure she saw him trembling as he led them, but he seemed to hold his nerves well despite the ominous occasion. The congregation then sat down and stared up at the almighty couple in absolute silence as they turned to one another.

"Please begin," the minister said to Cate, bowing to her again in respect. They'd decided to read their own vows to each other rather than to follow the minister's lead, and had written the oaths themselves. Cate took a deep breath and gazed up at her handsome groom as she recited her practised verse, and she had to fight back the tears pricking at her eyes. They'd come so far, and she couldn't deny how right it felt to be standing there with him at long last.

"From the darkness we came, and into the darkness I'll follow you. We are like two flames, but from one force, one endless black light. I'll never keep secrets, but share them willingly, and with love, trust and strength in our bond. I will love you now and for all eternity, and I promise to honour you every step of the way. I'll follow you forever."

She felt as if her heart might burst out of her chest, but Lucifer held her hand in his and let his *expression* tell her how much he'd adored her short verse. The promises were there, as well as the acknowledgements of their past, and she knew he accepted her solemn vows.

Then, it was his turn. The dark minister gestured for to Lucifer to recite his vows as well, and he did so without once breaking away from Cate's loving gaze, grinning broadly at her.

"My darling. I promise to smite all who might ever try to harm you. My love will not enslave or control you, but grasp you tight, and keep you safe for all eternity. I will never love another. You, and only you, possess my heart, body and soul. They are yours. I promise you now that I will take care of you forever. Just say yes."

Cate watched Lucifer with a wide smile, relishing in his wonderful words, and she felt true happiness filling her from within. He felt it too, and she could tell he was reading his bride and taking in the wonderful thoughts and feelings she openly shared. The minister then beamed at the two of them and finished the verbal part of the ceremony.

"Remember, your love should always be more powerful than your pain, and you should strive to make one another's dreams a reality. May the moon bring you strength, and may you live the rest of your days in true love and happiness as one," he said, and then concluded the ceremony by binding their wrists in black ribbon and pronouncing them as husband and wife.

"So mote it be," the pair called together, and Lucifer looked right into his beautiful wife's green eyes before he grabbed her and kissed Cate deeply.

"So mote it be!" The crowd roared, adding their shouts of praise to Satan and his new Queen. They all then stood and clapped for them as the happy couple walked back down the aisle together, their hands still entwined and their smiles wide.

The party that followed their wedding lasted for days. The witches and demons were free to celebrate and enjoy the dark delights thanks to their master's wonderful mood, and they happily took the opportunity to let loose. The London penthouse was transformed into a huge banquet hall where the upper level demons accompanied the royal family to celebrate their union. They toasted the happy couple and chatted loudly as the lower level witches served them fine wine and the King's favourite aged whisky.

"Here's to the happy couple," exclaimed Beelzebub as he approached, and he gave a small bow to the King and Queen as he did. He was wearing a black and grey suit, which looked wonderful with the shoulder-length black hair that fell around his ears. His deep brown eyes stood out handsomely above his pronounced cheekbones and strong chin, and Cate could see many of the witches looking over at him far too eagerly, hoping for some attention from the powerful and ancient demon. "Now that you've finally claimed your true love, do you think you'll stop being such a miserable bastard?" he then asked Lucifer playfully, with a huge grin across his face. He spoke to his ruler in such a familiar way that still shocked Cate, but he was never punished for it. Rather than be enraged, Lucifer knew his friend's humour far too well, and he laughed loudly along with him as Beelzebub roared at his own joke. The old friends clinked their glasses, and the demon patted his King on the shoulder to show his affection. Beelzebub never was one for hugs and kisses.

"You know I'll never stop, my adoring public would never allow it. And besides, who doesn't love a grumpy old bastard?" Lucifer answered with a wink, and he smiled as Leviathan walked over and joined them. He too raised a glass to Cate, who smiled and clinked her champagne glass with his as he bowed to her. He wore a dark suit and shirt like Beelzebub, and his was a grey colour with black pinstripes. Leviathan had the same cheeky, playful look as the other two, but his blond hair and blue eyes made his appearance seem brighter than his comrades, despite Cate knowing just how powerfully dark and dangerous he truly was.

"Do you need me to remove this cretin, your majesty?" he asked, indicating that he meant Beelzebub with a cheeky poke in his ribs. "Wow, you really can polish a turd," he added, joking and laughing with the pair of them for a moment longer as they exchanged their jibes. They stayed to chat for a few more minutes, and then bowed to Lucifer and bid them farewell before heading back off into the crowd in search of women and wine.

Lucifer and Cate stayed for a few more hours, but quickly decided it was time to leave. They needed some much deserved time alone. The newlyweds sneaked away without a word, and went into the huge master bedroom of the penthouse, complete with its four-poster bed and black silk sheets. Lucifer clicked the lock shut once they were alone inside and pushed Cate back against the heavy wood beam at the foot of the gigantic bed. His hand then reached up and gripped her neck to lift her chin to meet his eager mouth, and he held her tightly but didn't hurt her. In fact, the Dark King vowed to himself that he would never hurt her again. She gasped, desperate and eager for his touch, his love.

"Help me get this dress off will you?" she asked with an impatient grin on her face. Lucifer turned her quickly so that his bride faced away from him, and his lips gently traced the line from her shoulder to her neck as his hands moved swiftly over the ribbon that tied the corset style bodice of her black gown closed at the back.

The dress fell to her feet and Lucifer ran his hands down her naked back, stopping only to slip a finger inside the hem of her black lace panties and slide them down, too. Cate turned to face her husband and pulled the clip out that'd been holding her dark hair up in a high ponytail, letting the thick curls fall down to her bare shoulders. She then stepped out of her abandoned clothes, kicking off her black stiletto heels as she went, and stood before him without a shred of clothing on.

Lucifer stared down at her, his eyes hooded as he took in her beautiful body. He smiled and licked his lips. Cate reached up and ran her hand down the thick stubble on his cheek, and was glad he'd grown the short beard again. That, along with his short dark-blond hair that he had styled in a quiff at the front, was her favourite look for him. He'd completed the rock star look with a small black diamond earring, and looked positively striking.

"You're gonna need to take this off," she said, running her hands down the lapels of his suit jacket.

"You do it," he ordered her with a cocky grin before he pulled Cate closer and kissed her again, allowing his hands to explore her naked body as he did. She leaned back, smiling up at her lover as she pulled the knot of his tie down and threw it aside before moving on. Lucifer's jacket and waistcoat were then quickly discarded, followed by the shirt, and then Cate ran her hands over his thickly muscled torso, biting her lip teasingly.

"I want you, now," she told him, walking backwards to the bed and climbing up onto it. Lucifer couldn't bear to keep his Queen waiting, so unbuttoned his trousers and kicked them to the floor along with the rest of his outfit. He climbed up on top of Cate and slid himself inside of her straight away, lifting her hips up to meet his as he thrust hard and deep inside.

Cate's body had already been so ready for him and so tense with her desire that it wasn't long until she came for him. His touch sent her body into overdrive as usual, but so much more intensely now that they were finally husband and wife. She got the sense he was claiming her, letting a feral need instinctually mark her with his body, and she let him have every inch of her body and mind. He stared down into her eyes and stroked his hands through her long curls as he continued in his pursuit of more sweet cries of pleasure, and she gave him them. Lucifer held her gaze as they moved together, and they were so in sync with one another's bodies that it wasn't long before they shared their climax. The bed beneath them vibrated as Lucifer reached his wonderful release, and he poured himself into her while roaring with pleasure.

"Choose anywhere in the world you want to go," he asked later when they were lazing on the bed together, revelling in the afterglow of their epic first lovemaking session as husband and wife.

Lucifer knew they still had a few more days he could remain on Earth thanks to their chosen wedding day, and wanted to make the most of it. Theirs was a rare Halloween, which was exactly why they'd chosen it. It was an All Hallow's Eve followed immediately by a three-day full moon, and it marked the longest duration Lucifer had ever been on Earth before. He intended to use every moment to ensure Cate felt the most special woman alive.

"Paris," she answered, and smiled back at her husband. He nodded and climbed off the bed, offering her his hand to help her up before handing her a fresh set of clothes from the nearby drawers.

The pair of them dressed and then teleported away, and they

arrived in the beautiful city of Paris within seconds. They dined in the decadent cafes along the river Seine and climbed to the top of the Eiffel tower that afternoon. The loved-up pair spent hours taking in the fantastic sights as they went, walking hand-in-hand, and unable to release their tight grip of one another. She knew none of the humans who saw them would ever suspect who they were, and found she enjoyed the anonymity.

After spending the day enjoying their first stop, Lucifer asked her the same question again, and Cate answered by asking him to take her somewhere hot and all their own. He knew exactly where to take her, and teleported his bride to a private island off the coast of Hawaii, where she lounged with him in the hot sun and sucked his hard cock for hours. When he came into her mouth with such intense bursts, she fell backwards onto the hot sand, and laughed when he helped her up then returned the attention by focussing on giving her pleasure with his adept mouth. Lucifer made her climax ten times before eventually releasing Cate's sensitive clit from his strong and commanding grasp, and she was perfectly spent by the time he'd finished with her.

They lay back on the padded lounger and she nestled into him, resting her chin on her lover's chest. She knew Lucifer wouldn't allow any sleeping on this mini honeymoon, and she kick-started her dwindling energy again. Cate climbed onto his lap and slid his ready hardness inside her wet chasm one more time before they carried on with their whistle-stop world tour.

When they were ready again, she decided on the ancient city of Rome in Italy as their next destination. They both knew the churches and holy areas would be out of bounds in the picturesque city, but they happily wandered around the ruins of the old city and dined in exclusive restaurants, before partaking in a tour of some of the ancient crypts and catacombs. All the other tourists around them seemed both disturbed and intrigued by the creepy underworld of the city, but Cate devoured the historic sights. It was just the kind of gothic history she loved discovering, and they both revelled in the fear pouring out of the humans around them.

"This is so you," Cate whispered to Lucifer as they wandered the skeletal corridors and took in the dark vaults, still hand-in-hand, and he smiled down at her.

"I might've had a hand in it some time ago," he told her with a sly wink.

Before finally heading back to Hell, the newlyweds headed for their final stop on their honeymoon. They teleported to the forests of Greenland so Cate could watch the Northern Lights fill the sky for her first time. They stood atop the snow-covered mountains and watched in awe as the coloured waves hovered overhead. Cate had never seen anything so spectacular in her life, and couldn't speak as she let the breath-taking view wash over her. It was fantastic, and she was happier than she'd ever been. The last few days had been the most wonderful of her existence, and in all honesty, she didn't want them to end.

Lucifer held her closer than ever, and spoke quietly in her ear as they embraced beneath the shimmering colours. "I cannot read your thoughts any more, my Queen," he told her, and wasn't disappointed to have lost that bit of power over her. He welcomed the comfortable silence, and had noticed her mind slowly closing to him during their honeymoon. He didn't know how or why, but he gave into whatever higher power was driving them towards a different dynamic. "You have to tell me how you feel from now on," he added, leaning down to kiss her.

"I think I can do one better than that," she replied, and wordlessly sent him her love and emotion to him via their *expression* connection. Since she'd become the Dark Queen of Hell, Cate had slowly realised that her power had intensified, and understood why. She was becoming his equal, or at least it seemed that way.

Her power had reached the point where she thought she might be able to share that part of herself with him back through the strange link, where before it'd only ever been one-way. She'd been right. Her adoration poured out of her towards him, and they enjoyed each other wordlessly and thoughtlessly through their back and forth *expression*. Lucifer was lost for words. He simply revelled in her offerings of emotion and love without a sound.

Cate was glad he'd reacted so well. She felt more powerful than ever, as though he'd given her some extra omnipotence along with his hand in marriage, and she giggled at his surprised stare. It was good to know that her thoughts were her own again, as well as that her powers seemed to be increasing. While she had nothing to hide, she did enjoy the idea of being able to keep some things between them to herself from now on.

When the newlyweds returned to Hell later that night, they were greeted by shouts of hail and praise. Lucifer and Cate enjoyed the welcome, and he carried her over the threshold of the castle, before wasting no time in taking her to their now shared chambers.

She undressed slowly for him, enjoying every moment and teasing Lucifer with every seductive move. When he could handle it no longer, he grabbed her, ripping off her lacy underwear and taking her swollen clit in his mouth while she groaned loudly in response to his touch. Lucifer sucked and nibbled his wife into submission, and took great pleasure in feeling the throb of an orgasm pulsing through the exposed nerve as she climaxed beneath him.

He then moved his kisses up further over her torso to her tender breasts, and she yelped slightly as he bit down on one nipple, but lifted her chest up to invite him to push her further. Lucifer was driven wild by her insatiable need for him and quickly moved to the other nipple. He clamped down hard and sucked the tender peak deep into his mouth while curling his fingers around her still throbbing nub. Cate came again for him, lost in the moment, and she gave into the painful pleasure that swept over her.

When Lucifer thrust himself inside her, she felt him deeper than ever before. She couldn't resist his commanding influence and let go, relinquishing her power and giving herself to him entirely. Her need for him was strong as his now, and her dark powers increased as time passed by. They spent weeks in bed together, and basked in each other's wants and desires, climaxing together over and over.

CHAPTER THIRTEEN

A few months after the wedding, Alma knocked quietly on the King and Queen's chamber door, and Lucifer silently commanded for her to enter, having read the witch's mind. He already knew she was there to give Cate some bad news, but let her be the one to do the talking. They hadn't left their bed in days, and lay resting together after another lengthy few days of lovemaking, but she forced herself out of her slumber when she saw Alma's serious expression.

"Your majesties," she said, greeting them with a low bow. "I'm afraid I come bearing sad news, my Queen," Alma addressed Cate directly with a solemn expression.

"What is it?" she asked, sensing her trusted adviser's worry.

"Your human mother is old and is going to die very soon. I've just been informed of her condition, and it's very likely she'll be taken in the next few days," she added and bowed again, giving Cate a few moments to let the sad news sink in.

"Thank you, Alma," she replied, feeling wretched, and immediately guilty. She leaned up and looked to Lucifer for his guidance. "Do you think I could go and see her to say goodbye?" she asked him, requesting his permission to leave Hell. He nodded, and then gave the command to Alma.

"Take my wife to Earth and stay with her while she visits her mother," he said. "And, make sure she comes home safely, is that understood?" he asked, and the frightened witch nodded profusely. She then left without a word, rushing off to prepare for their visit.

Cate was worried about Ella's condition, but also felt terrible that she hadn't been to visit her in such a long time. Her guilt showed on her face as she wordlessly got herself dressed and ready to go, and tears were close to falling already.

"I know I cannot truly understand how you are feeling, my

love," Lucifer told her, looking over at his wife with a frown. "I do not value human life because I've never had any strong connection with a human. But, I can sense your sadness and I want you to have the opportunity to say goodbye. I think it'll give you closure," he told her. Cate knew it was hard for him to try to relate with her human feelings, and appreciated the effort. Lucifer really didn't have a clue, so it actually made her smile—relieving her guilt somewhat. "I can't come with you, the moon isn't right..." he began, and tailed off when she sent him her silent understanding via their *expression*.

"I know." She leaned down to kiss him. "And anyway, I want to do this alone. I need to say goodbye properly," she added, and he nodded in agreement.

A few minutes later, Alma returned and re-entered their dark chamber after a tiny knock on the huge wooden doors.

"Everything's ready, your majesty," she told Cate, who nodded and took the witch's hand in hers. She was glad Alma seemed ready to lead the way as her mind was too fraught to concentrate on teleporting, and she bid farewell to her husband before blowing him a kiss.

"See you soon," he told her, snatching her goodbye kiss from the air with a smile, and he then watched as they teleported away.

***

When she arrived on Earth, Cate immediately aged herself so people wouldn't ask questions when she arrived at the hospital asking to see her mother. She introduced herself to the nurse and was led to the small room where Ella was resting. Inside, there were no monitors or bleeping machinery hooked up to the frail old woman. There was just a small bed and an armchair for visitors. Cate knew this was the place they took the patients who had no hope of recovery, and that the end really wasn't very far away.

She was totally unprepared for the way she felt upon seeing her, and her tears fell as soon as Ella's green eyes lit up at seeing her long-lost daughter again. Cate could hardly recognise her mother, and hated that she'd abandoned her. So very many years had passed since she'd last seen her, but Ella knew Cate's face instantly, and regardless of the distance between them, perked up as soon as she went over to the bedside. She seemed so happy to see her daughter one last time, and smiled at her as she sat down in the armchair.

"Cate," she said, and her quiet voice faltered. "I thought I might never get to see you again. Where have you been?" she asked, and a small tear ran down her sallow cheek as she greeted her.

"I'm sorry, Mum. I've been living far away for a long time. I can't give you all the details, but please know I am truly blessed and very happy," Cate replied. She knew there was no point in revealing her life's twists and turns to her mother, and that she wouldn't understand even if she tried. All that mattered was that she was here now.

Ella looked over at her and took Cate in. She really did seem happy and healthy, and she was so pleased to see her only child at last that she couldn't be upset. She took Cate's hand and nodded in understanding, and didn't care if she wasn't prepared to be forthcoming about her life. After a long hug and a few more tears from each of the women, they chatted for hours. It was only when Ella was too tired to keep on going that they relaxed and the frail old woman drifted off into a deep sleep.

Cate decided to get some rest in the armchair beside her instead of leaving her mother's side, and was glad she had. She woke with a start when Ella reached for her hand in the middle of the night, her eyes wide, almost fearful. Her breathing was shallow, and they both somehow knew the end was close. Cate held onto her until her mother passed, and even caught a glimpse of an angel as it came to take her to Heaven. Despite her encompassed dark side, Cate knew that Heaven was where Ella belonged, and smiled as she bid farewell to her soul.

***

Cate and Alma stayed for a few more days while everything was put in order and Ella was cremated. The Dark Queen was in a despairing haze, but Alma helped with everything. She pretended to be a distant cousin of the family and facilitated with the preparations, along with overseeing the reading of Ella's will.

Cate decided to scatter her mother's ashes on the rocky beach where Ella would take her when she was a young child, and she sprinkled them over the rocks near the tide's edge with tears streaming from her eyes. She then watched the waves as they carried the ashes away to the ocean, and hoped her mother might at last be free. Cate then used her power to alter her age again as she looked out at the sea, and knew it was time to say goodbye to everything she'd once been. She was about ready to go back to Hell, but waited to watch the slow tide thoughtfully for a few more minutes as a light rain began to fall from the sky, masking her tears.

Up on a wooden bench overlooking the promenade sat Alma, and she'd been sure to sit around the corner so as not to be watching her Queen directly, but was close enough to be called upon when she was ready to go home. Alma never saw the white witch coming, nor had she sensed the lightness as the woman appeared silently from behind her. A blast of light power combined with a strong spell from over Alma's shoulder sent her flying off the bench to the ground. It'd knocked the dark witch immediately unconscious, and with a sly, satisfied grin, the white witch then continued down the path towards the beach.

Wandering along the water's edge, Cate suddenly felt eyes on her and turned around. She faced the witch as she approached, and recognised her immediately. The woman standing a few feet away was once her friend. Well, Cate had thought she was, but had eventually realised it'd all been a rouse to keep her under surveillance. The witch standing before her was in fact the high priestess of Dylan's coven from all those years before that'd tried to keep Cate away the night Lucifer came for her.

"Hello again, Angelica," Cate said as the witch neared her. "It's been a long time."

"Yes, Cate. It has," replied the witch. "How are you?" she asked, and she sniggered. They both knew she didn't care, and was only asking to stall her.

"What do you want from me, witch?" Cate spat, not answering her insincere question. She was growing impatient and thoroughly pissed off that Angelica had dared intrude while she was saying her last goodbyes to her mother.

"*I*, don't want anything," Angelica said, pointing to herself with feigned disinterest. "But your presence is requested by my master," she added, with a nonchalant wave of her hand. Angelica had always been somewhat theatrical. She loved any and all attention, but Cate didn't care for her games any more.

"Oh really, and just who might that be?" she asked, wondering if some angel may be trying to use her as bait to lure Lucifer to Earth. She wondered if perhaps the witches were after a fight in retaliation for her husband's treatment of Dylan a few years before, or if it could simply be about Angelica's bruised ego after her coven had failed the night Cate had been summoned to the church.

The Dark Queen waited impatiently for the witch to answer, to declare her master's name and their intentions, but she didn't reply. Angelica simply wandered nearer and when she was close enough to reach out and touch Cate's arm, she did so. She could feel her attempting to teleport her away, but her power wasn't strong enough. The powerful Queen had to laugh. She sent out a blast of dark power that caused Angelica to wince, and she pulled her hand back with a hiss. Cate could tell she was no match for her, and held her ground.

"Sorry," replied Angelica with a smirk, clearly pretending for a moment to be remorseful. She rubbed her hand as though it were still sore from Cate's blast of power, though, and the Dark Queen smiled. "Perhaps I should've said *our* master," she told her, and a sly smile curled at her mouth again. With that, another nine white witches appeared and encircled Cate. Once inside the white circle she quickly realised that she was unable to move or teleport away to safety. She tried summoning Alma, but when she realised she couldn't sense her witch through the impenetrable circle, Cate immediately gave up trying. Even she could tell that resistance was pointless, and instead she stood tall and held Angelica's gaze, waiting for the witch to make her next move. "Check-mate," Angelica told her with a snigger.

The coven then joined hands and stepped closer, tightening their circle around her. Cate noticed Dylan wasn't with them, but wasn't sure if that was a good sign or not. She was positive that her old friend was no longer her ally after what she'd let Lucifer's demons do to her in that terrible dungeon, and Cate held out no hope of finding a friend within the white coven.

The witches started chanting, and Cate could feel her head begin to spin. Their spell was taking control of her body, and a strange summoning took over her. She was then wrenched away from Earth, and couldn't control her course. She tried not to panic and tried to focus her mind and power on readying herself for whatever fight might be waiting for her at their destination. The main worry she had though was that she was moving up and not down, however she guessed the good guys might not be as into torture as her husband's legion of evil minions.

CHAPTER FOURTEEN

Cate lost consciousness somewhere during the ascent, and later awoke in a bright sunlit room. She was laid on a huge bed covered in white silk sheets, and she was dressed in a cream satin summer dress. Her hands had been placed over the heart—like the dead—and she knew she must look ridiculous. When she stood, Cate felt strangely woozy, and regained her composure after a few seconds, but was shocked to discover she was completely powerless. The witches must've somehow taken away her powers, and she made herself a silent vow to personally see to it that Angelica was beaten and tortured to death very soon.

"You have *got* to be kidding me," she mumbled when she looked over at her reflection in the mirror. She looked preposterous dressed all in white. After taking stock of her surroundings, she moved over to the door and gave the handle a try. It was locked, of course, so Cate decided to go over to the window and see if she could figure out where she was. A beautiful, white sandy beach stretched out before her, followed by an endless clear blue ocean and a cloudless sky. It was gorgeous, but she was starting to feel a chill down her spine that she couldn't ignore.

This place did not feel like Earth, and it was most definitely not Hell. There was no way she could be in Heaven, so she figured it must be some kind of dream, or alternate plain that the white witches had taken her to. Cate hoped she was right about torture being a no-no with the good guys, but wondered if she might be killed with kindness or something equally as pathetic.

"Welcome," a man's voice said quietly from behind her, and Cate turned to see where the sound had come from. She found that a tall, dark-haired man had silently entered the room, and already shut the door behind him. Either that or he'd teleported inside. He wore white khaki trousers with a white shirt, and was gorgeous, but not that Cate let herself notice. She had only one lover, and he seemed very far away right now.

"I suppose you're Angelica's master?" Cate asked, and the man nodded.

"I am everyone's master, Hecate," he said, eyeing her casually. "Even yours." She faked a small smile, and shook her head. He seemed harmless enough, but she didn't believe he could have any power over her. White beings weren't their overseers. As Cate went to respond though, he cut her off. "I am one of Lucifer's old friends, and his brother of sorts. So, in a manner of speaking, that makes me your brother-in-law. Does that sound about right?" he asked, then grinned and waited a moment for his words to sink in. Cate's face dropped.

"Holy shit," she mumbled, knowing she must be in the presence of one of the very powerful angels that'd cast Lucifer out of Heaven, and he laughed.

"Less of that please, darling. That's no way to talk to the Master of the High Council of Angels," he said, eyeing her with a smile. The title sounded about right, and she guessed perhaps he might not be quite as harmless as she'd initially thought. "My name's Uriel, and I am an archangel. Now then, that's us officially introduced," he added, while she still stared over at him in shock and surprise.

Uriel moved towards Cate slowly, taking slow but long strides across the room, and she knew she couldn't escape him. If she was right, this plain was probably just a square-mile or so of beach that he'd created as a place to hide her from Lucifer, and also to keep her just where he wanted her.

My very own prison, Cate thought as he neared.

"Exactly," Uriel replied, answering her thoughts just like Lucifer had used to do, and Cate jumped in surprise. It'd been a while since she'd had to be careful of her innermost musings and it shocked her having them answered again. "Make yourself at home, you're going to be here some time," he then added, inching closer until her back was up against the large window.

Cate could feel his power resonating through both her and every inch of the prison around her. He radiated light, and she could feel her inner darkness trying to fight it, but it was no use. His witches' spell had blocked her dark power, and trapped it somewhere deep within her. Energy couldn't die or be stolen, it could only be transferred, and she doubted any of his underlings would've wanted what was bubbling inside of her blackened heart. They'd found a way to suppress her power, and she wasn't happy about it. Cate felt an almost human-like weakness before him and wanted to curse him. Nothing about this situation gave her cause for hope, and she just hoped her kidnapper would get to the point sooner rather than later.

Uriel took a moment to take Cate in, staring at her lips and then into her eyes. He read her every thought, feeling and memory while he stood just inches away, and was entranced. Cate couldn't fight him, and she didn't even have the chance to try. His invasive examination was over so quickly it made her head spin.

"You and Sataniel are incredibly happy together," he said, and it seemed like a bemused statement rather than anything else. She knew he must have been processing the information she'd just wordlessly given him, and hated how he could know entire life story so effortlessly. "But why? After everything he put you through, how could you bear to be his wife?" he asked her, and was clearly genuinely confused by her love for Lucifer, and by her forgiveness for his terrible and selfish treatment of her. "Don't answer now, darling," he then told Cate before she could answer with a snarky comment. "We can discuss him in due time," he added dismissively.

Uriel placed the palm of his hand on Cate's cheek and rubbed her top lip gently with his thumb. She wanted to tell him to back off, but he advanced no more. The archangel just held her there for a few minutes before letting his hand drop, and he turned away. "Get dressed," he finally said, and surprisingly it sounded like more of a request than an order. "I want to make you dinner," Uriel added as he opened the door and went out into the rest of the house, leaving her bedroom door open and unlocked, for now.

She went to the closet and found nothing but a variety of white clothing. After rolling her eyes and giving the contents a loud "*tut*," she decided on a pair of shorts and a baggy shirt, and pulled them on. Cate caught a glimpse of herself in the mirror again and sniggered. She couldn't remember the last time she'd worn white. It didn't look right on her, but with no other options left she just had to go with it. It was wear them or else head out to dinner naked, and she wasn't prepared to play that game with her husband's greatest adversary.

She walked out into a long hallway, and wandered down to a room near the end where she could hear classical music playing. Uriel was there, humming along to the aria and tossing a salad while some steaks cooked on the hob. Cate was taken aback. *Who knew?* she thought as she watched him. He caught her eyeing him and smiled, beckoning her to sit at the table before he poured them each a large glass of red wine and went back to check on his sizzling meat.

"I don't see why we can't enjoy all things in moderation," Uriel told her with a wink. "After all, my council and I created these delights, so why can't I enjoy them?"

"I suppose you're right," she replied with a shrug before she took a sip of wine. *Damn, this is good,* she thought and took another, longer swig. A stern "tsk," from him told her that blasphemous thoughts weren't appreciated just as much as her actually saying them aloud, however she didn't care. Those weren't her rules, and regardless of where she was being held, she wasn't about to convert and serve Uriel or his council.

Cate watched him for a while, felling nothing of not more confused. This God-like angel was making her dinner and labelling her as some kind of extended family. But, she knew that Lucifer was his greatest enemy; his angelic brother-of-sorts who was cast out of Heaven for all eternity and forced into darkness and a torturous, wholly sinful existence at this very angel's hands. She couldn't understand why he'd brought her here. Or why he was taking care of her, cooking for her and now humming to music as if they were old friends enjoying a meal together. Surely his ultimate goal was to use her, or maybe even kill her to make Lucifer pay? Perhaps he was about to force her to make her husband come out and fight? What did he want, why had he bought her here? Cate's head was spinning again.

"Enough with the questions," Uriel snapped sternly, and he turned from the stove to face Cate, while his face darkened angrily. He composed himself immediately though, and set down a plate of tender steak before her. "You'll ruin this wonderful meal I've planned for us," he added calmly as he sat down opposite her and passed Cate the salad bowl. The petulant side of her wanted to push him, but her instincts told her it wouldn't be wise. Instead, she did as she'd been told, and got stuck in.

She ate everything Uriel had made for her. The steak was delicious, while the wine matched it perfectly and flowed easily as they ate together. The conversation was slow at first, but soon the two of them were chatting about everything and nothing, and they talked well into the night. Cate was confused at how easily she could relax around Uriel, and his warm nature drew her in as they chatted openly. The change in dynamic helped her overcome her grief for her mother, and Cate felt more relaxed than she thought she could be around such an intimidating archangel.

He kept the conversation light, asking her opinion on the current state of things on Earth while chatting animatedly about his hopes and dreams for the future of the human race rather than bring up her husband again. "Imagine if you will, my idea of a perfect world. No more war, no famines, and no governments vying for power and wealth. All we need do is create a higher race of beings that would take control. They would then rule over the humans and help to absolve them of their sins. Free will can be a nightmare, but if they are led, the humans will evolve and thrive," he told her thoughtfully.

Cate tried to fathom this potential future, but none of it made sense. After all, his God had reportedly created man to be free, so why would Uriel and the council seek to change that, to control them? That would go against everything the light power dictated, commanded, and expected from their followers. "That's the next problem. How would I go about it without disturbing the balance? The council has not agreed to my plan yet, but they'll see sense soon," he told her with a slight grin curling the corners of his mouth.

Cate knew that the angel sat before her was not to be trifled with. After all, he'd managed to cast out Lucifer, and then Leviathan and Beelzebub from Heaven for defying him, and after the millennia since she was certain his power had to have increased tenfold. She wondered if perhaps the other opposing members of the high council would simply be next on his hit list, and didn't envy them having to deal with his all-powerful expectations. Uriel smiled across at Cate with a twinkle in his eye that made her pretty sure she'd just hit the nail on the proverbial head.

He then moved on, quickly changing topic, and asked her how things were in Hell.

"Over-crowded," she joked, grinning at him over the delicious soufflé pudding Uriel had just set down before her.

"Unrepentant sinners are not welcome in Heaven, Cate. That will never change," he said seriously. The mood changed then and his expression grew sombre. She didn't like the tense silence, but also hoped that the real questions might be answered at last.

"Where are we now then, surely not Heaven?" Cate asked him in the hopes he'd decided to be open with her.

"On an astral plain between Earth and Heaven," Uriel told her, confirming her suspicions. "The angels all live on plains like this so that we can watch over the humans we're charged with protecting. This one though, is all ours," he told her and then paused for a moment. He let Cate take his explanation in, but he was simply confirming her earlier suspicions rather than telling her anything she didn't already know. "My turn," Uriel added before she could respond. He seemed to want the opportunity to ask his own questions in return for him opening up to her. "Do you really love Lucifer, truly?" he asked, watching her as he did.

"Yes," she answered without hesitation. "I gave myself willingly to him, and became his wife—so I should hope so," she then added with a shy smile.

"And do you intend to give him unholy, abominable children?" he pressed on, seemingly disgusted at the possibility.

"Someday, if we can," Cate answered, forcing herself to stay calm.

Uriel sat back, seemingly surprised by Cate's answers and thoughts on the subject, but he pressed on. He leaned forward and stared into her eyes with his bright blue, intense gaze.

"I don't get it. Why would you feel that way about him when he left you in that pit all that time, only then to be whipped and tortured by his dark servants? He ignored your pleas for mercy and forgiveness regardless of his affection for you. How is that behaviour worthy of your love in return?" he asked, seeming determined to know how she could possibly love him. "He broke you, Cate. He then manipulated you into his bed where he possessed you. That's not love, it's supremacy and control."

Cate was red-hot with anger at his rash assumptions. If he

were anyone else, she'd lash out and slap him for daring to question her so intensively while refusing to understand her loyalty. He didn't know the two of them, despite his power to read her thoughts. Cate knew full well that it'd been thousands of years since Uriel had even seen or spoken with Lucifer, so he had no idea who he now was or why he did the things he did. She knew him—truly knew him. Not every little detail, she was no fool, but she'd seen into his primeval soul, and gone far deeper than anyone else had ever been before. Cate also knew that the majority of his anger and pain came from the one rejection that'd happened a very long time before she was even in the picture. The rejection from his own dear 'brothers' had made him that way, along with his banishment and years of lonesome exile at their hands.

Uriel read her thoughts, and stood from the table without another word. Cate sat in furious silence watching him, then polished off her wine and stood up from the large table, aiming to storm off.

"Time for bed," he said, without looking at her as he began clearing the plates.

"It seems so," she answered, and turned on her heel. Cate stomped back up the corridor to her room, slammed the door closed and stripped off her disgusting white clothes. She couldn't stand them against her body, and let out an enraged groan when she wandered over to the white covered bed. Climbing in, Cate knew she might've pushed it too far, but didn't care. After all, if Uriel was going to read her thoughts all the time, he had to be prepared to hear some things he might not want to.

Despite her anger, she quickly fell into a dreamless sleep, not noticing the figure that watched her from the now open doorway almost the entire night.

CHAPTER FIFTEEN

The next morning as Cate roused, Uriel greeted her with a breakfast tray filled with bacon and eggs, served with buttered toast and fresh mango juice. Despite the events from the previous night, Cate thanked him. She didn't even shy away from the playful smile she received from her captor when she quickly covered her naked body and sat up in the bed.

She ate the entire plateful, and was oddly famished despite their big meal from the night before. Once she was finished with her breakfast and had gotten dressed, Uriel took Cate outside to enjoy the view. It was beautiful out there, and seemed warm and peaceful. She enjoyed the scenic tranquillity; despite her knowing it was all just an illusion. The sun felt nice on her skin, too. Cate had almost forgotten how enjoyable it was to bathe in the sunshine. The heat of Hell was more like an intense pressure, and although she was perfectly happy there, she had to admit it felt good to feel the sun's rays warm her pale skin again.

Uriel watched her every move, constantly reading her thoughts and feelings as she took it all in. She couldn't keep him out, but wished he would just talk to her instead. Surely he would know if she was lying, but at least they would have the opportunity to pass the time easier through conversation and interaction. He still wasn't giving anything away as far as his intentions were, and Cate wondered about those things openly in her mind, knowing he would hear her. She just hoped he might finally decide to answer her questions soon.

"What do you want from life, Cate?" Uriel asked her later that day over another delicious home-cooked dinner.

"To be happy," she told him honestly, surprising the angel somewhat. "I know it might not seem like much, but I think it's very hard to find real happiness," Cate added thoughtfully.

"It is a nice concept, but the problem with happiness," Uriel replied, taking a bite. "Is that it's dependent on your interpretation. What makes you happy, Cate? Love, power, purpose? Or even just a sense of belonging? But think what makes a serial killer happy, or a molester of children, or a rapist of innocent women. Everyone has been made to be different. They were created that way and those variances can mean a huge difference when the pursuit of happiness gets in the way."

"How do you know rape or murder doesn't make me happy?" Cate asked with a wry grin on her lips.

"You really do forget whom you're talking to sometimes," he replied. Uriel smiled warmly and reached towards her, touching her hand softly before lifting it gently into his own. Cate's whole body tingled in response to his touch, much like it did in Lucifer's strong hands, but this was a purer feeling—lighter.

"You can sense my light?" Uriel asked, seemingly surprised. Cate nodded, however she wasn't sure what that really meant.

"Yes, I think so. Why, is that not normal?"

"Not for a long time," he said, but added nothing else. The powerful angel simply let Cate's hand drop gently back on to the table between them.

***

He watched her sleep again that night, wondering the whole time how he might persuade Cate to join him in the light. Uriel had originally sent Angelica to take her from Earth with the intention of using her to lure Satan away from his dark domain.

The plan had been that when Lucifer left the safety of Hell, Uriel and the other angels would finally finish their feud with him once and for all. He hadn't decided which way to go yet, but it'd be either by a pure death or by persuading Lucifer to join them back in the light.

A lot of time had passed since they'd last seen one another, and they'd both changed immensely, but their feuding had created a seemingly unending void between the two worlds. It was a hollowness that would take an awful lot to bridge, and one of them would surely have to concede in order for that to ever happen.

Lucifer would have to yield or die, there was nothing else for it.

Thinking back over the past, Uriel knew he was right to become suspicious of his fallen brother's intentions when Lucifer had finally sired an heiress of his own, and he'd known he had to keep watch over the girl. He'd chosen to send a small coven of witches down to Earth so they could find out what Lucifer's plans for her eventually were, and also to try and keep Cate from going to Hell with him at all if they could. When they'd eventually failed, she'd completely gone from Uriel's reach. He couldn't know what she was doing down there in the darkness, what sinister lessons she was learning, and how she was being influenced by her evil master. Of course, he'd feared the worst.

The council had immediately assumed that she would bring about evil and death wherever she went when she travelled to Earth. They'd presumed she might bring about the apocalypse, or at the very least turn saints into sinners with every step she took— her influence over susceptible humans uncontrollable.

But no, she'd done nothing to force his hand, or even register on his radar when she came to Earth those first few times. Much to his and the High Council of Angel's surprise, she was discovered to just be living a seemingly normal life—as normal as the Dark Princess of Hell could have, of course.

Years later when Lucifer's second heir came along, Uriel was sure they would use him for the same evil deeds too, but again, no. A few sins were committed thanks to the siblings' influence over the humans that came into contact with them when they were later back on Earth, but nothing the council hadn't been able to handle.

Then the third child was sired, and still nothing. No war between their worlds and no attempts to contact their Council. No evil massacres, rituals or sacrifices in Lucifer's name that would add to his dark power. Uriel simply couldn't fathom his intentions back then, and he hadn't liked it one bit. That was why he decided he must kidnap one of Satan's heirs. He would then force them to give up their knowledge of their master, and use them as bait to lure Lucifer out of hiding.

When Cate had reportedly to have left Earth and returned to Hell without Devin, they'd had no idea that she was going through such torture and manipulation at the hands of her immoral master. When Uriel had heard the news that the pair of them had married a few years later, it was clear to him that she was the one he had to try and kidnap. Uriel's servants had watched the hospice, and he'd always intended to give the order to take Cate as soon as she was by Ella's side again, but something had stopped him. When he'd descended and stood looking through the window to Ella's room, he'd felt enough compassion to let her see it through. He'd watched for a few minutes at Cate holding her mother's hand in that hospital bed, and had been intrigued by her warmth and love for her human parent.

He'd been utterly captivated by the beautiful Dark Queen, and surprised by the tears she shed for the elderly woman's passing. The pain in her heart she showed so openly as her mother had died confounded him. He'd seen her true nature in that moment, and decided then that he would give her some time to grieve before she was to be captured.

Before returning to Heaven, Uriel had ordered for Angelica to wait. He didn't want to take her away before Cate could say a proper farewell to her mother, and he then watched from above with fascination as she'd gone through the motions and finally scattered the ashes into the ocean.

Uriel was sure Lucifer would never stand back while his wife was in captivity, and was convinced that he would endeavour to find his way to her soon. However, he had no way of knowing when it might happen. One of the biggest problems that they'd always encountered though, was that none of the angels could sense either Lucifer or his progeny while they were on Earth or in Hell. Their darkness concealed them from their reach, so he'd always needed to use other ways in which to find them. Tracking them down often took a lot of planning and forethought—and time.

The strange thing now, though, was that Uriel felt a connection with Cate that he hadn't counted on. It confused him. How could he ever plan for the possibility that after all these years he might finally sense something for another being other than the love he'd always felt for all mankind? He loved each and every human, angel, and being him and the council had created. Uriel loved Lucifer and his other fallen brothers still. He loved Cate too, but he realised now that it was in a different and strangely more potent way. He wanted to know her, to be near her and to touch her. He wanted to kiss her, and make love to her. She'd somehow infiltrated his usually so hard shell, and she didn't even seem aware of the power she had to compel him and everyone else around her.

Uriel knew that there was probably a part of him that wanted her simply because Cate was Lucifer's wife, but he was sure it was more than just his ancient rivalry that made him feel the way he did. He wanted to protect her, to make her smile, and to be the one to make her happy.

Anticipation flowed through him at the very possibility of a kiss, an intimate touch, or even the chance he might get to make love to her. He could feel himself growing hard at the thought of her at his mercy, and imagined Cate lying naked before him, begging him to take her.

By morning, Uriel had sorted through his thoughts, and knew that his objective had changed. Cate was the prize now—and he was determined to win.

***

Cate awoke the next morning to the same sensation of light power flowing through her that she'd felt after dinner the night before. However, it wasn't through Uriel's touch this time, but through his *expression*, just as Lucifer would often do. In honesty, it made her feel slightly nauseous. His wave was an overload of powerful emotion and light suddenly coursing through her entire body, and it caused strange, yet not unwelcome surges to collide somewhere deep within her.

She was used to the dark, dangerous, and intense emotions she received from her husband, but this lightness was new, and far scarier to her than the darkness had ever been. Cate looked over to the doorway and took in the Adonis before her. Uriel looked astounding. He was half dressed in white chinos and nothing on top to cover up his thickly muscled torso. He was beautifully tanned and perfectly toned, and gave her a cheeky, knowing smile as she stared across at him.

"Like what you see, Queen Hecate?" he asked, turning off the *expression* as he pulled a cream t-shirt over his head. Cate was left feeling disappointed, but shook it off immediately, and felt guilty that she even let herself look that long. She was a married woman after all. "I won't tell if you don't," Uriel told her with a chuckle. "Breakfast's ready," he then added, and sauntered off to the kitchen without another word.

Cate was hot and bothered all of a sudden. The energy between them had just changed dramatically, and she didn't know how to process the feelings that he'd passed to her while he'd opened that intense link. She got up and pulled on a cream dress from the closet, having given up her resistance to all light clothing now, and she then padded down the now familiar hallway to the kitchen.

She found Uriel sat at the large wooden dining table with a steaming cup of milky coffee. He watched Cate for a moment as she entered the kitchen, before grabbing the pot and pouring her a freshly brewed cup of the black nectar. He then offered the still confused Dark Queen a seat beside him.

"So, you can do *expression* too?" Cate asked, but then laughed to herself. "Of course you can." Uriel just smiled and nodded.

"All my angels can do it if their bonds with those in their charge are strong," he told her. Cate hadn't really thought about it being an angel thing before, but of course Lucifer was once like Uriel, so it made sense. "You can do it back to him now because of your marriage, but only with him," he informed her.

That made sense as well, although in all honesty she'd never tried with anyone else before.

"Does that mean our bond is strong then?" she asked, having realised what he'd just said. Cate knew she was pushing him a little, but sensed he was finally in a more open mood this morning.

"Clever girl. I suppose you could say that," Uriel answered, but Cate could tell he'd held back. She was ready to give up when he offered her a little more clarification after a few thoughtful moments. "The reason I opened my link to you this morning is because I believe there's a strong bond developing between you and I. And well, I want to nurture that bond and see where it takes us."

"As friends, or as your sister-in-law?" she asked. Cate hoped to discover whether all the desirous emotions she'd felt coming through the *expression* earlier were a quest for family ties, or if it was about something else.

"Neither," was all he replied, looking into her eyes intensely.

His deep blue irises burned into hers, and he held her gaze for a long time before he got up to fetch more coffee from the kitchen counter.

Cate knew immediately what Uriel had meant. She was scared and still more than just a little bit confused, but couldn't help the rush of adrenaline, and flutter of excitement thanks to his leading comments. By the time he returned with the coffee pot, the air was thick with tension between them. Cate could tell he was enjoying her response to his words, and he watched her curiously as she mulled everything over in her mind. "Don't feel guilty," he told her after a few moments.

Uriel took her hand in his and she felt the strange buzz pass through her again as their skin touched—his light somehow pouring into her through the contact. The strong and intense *expression* he then opened up to her was Cate's undoing, and she tried to pull back but he already had her at the tipping point. She was way over that line within seconds thanks to his intense eyes on hers, and before she could even focus her thoughts, Uriel planted a deep kiss on her lips.

His gentleness kept her wanting, needing more, and Cate leaned into his touch. She allowed his tongue to delve inside her ready mouth while hers flicked back, and quickly succumbed to his desire for her. Uriel then traced soft kisses down to her neck while she ran her hands through his dark brown hair and pulled him closer. He placed a hand on her neck to pull her closer, which excited her while intensifying the contact, and Uriel whispered in her ear.

"All I need to hear is one little word and I'm all yours," he said.

Her eyes flicked open immediately and she was bought well and truly back to the room with a thud. There she was all over again. Cate could've kicked herself for letting herself fall for it. She was just another piece in another game, and was angry as hell for being used so profoundly.

CHAPTER SIXTEEN

"How could I be so weak?" she cried, and she pulled away from his hold. Cate pushed back in her chair and stormed off out of the kitchen, heading straight to the front door of the house without another word. She then ran down the beach, kicking up the sand as she went, and then stopped just after she reached the line where the gentle lapping waves met the white beach.

Cate stood there for a few moments with her arms wrapped around her body, hugging it tightly. She stared out at the horizon as she let the water swell around her feet and the sun warm her body, and all the while she wept quietly to herself. Uriel watched from further up the beach, giving her a few minutes to calm down before he went and joined her at the water's edge. He'd been surprised by her reaction, but read Cate and quickly understood. The very mention of his required confirmation had brought back awful memories of her submission to Lucifer—memories that she'd pushed aside for so long.

He stepped close behind Cate and then slipped his arms around her stomach and held her close. Surprisingly, she spun around and held him back, letting her head fall on to his shoulder. Uriel could feel her emotions flood through him as he read her, but he kept quiet while she wept in his arms for as long as she needed.

***

A few days later, following another lovely home cooked meal, Cate sat quietly in the small beach house's living room. She was relaxing on the sofa and enjoying the calm quiet, but her mind was wandering, so she pushed all thought away in preference of the pleasant silence. Uriel came in a few minutes later with a cup of tea, another so seemingly normal gesture which still made her laugh, but she appreciated the effort he was going to and thanked him. They then sat quietly together for a while, and he left Cate to her thoughts as usual, but never seemed to want to physically leave her alone for too long if he could help it.

Uriel moved across and climbed behind her on the large sofa, where he embraced her as she leaned back into him, offering her a warm and loving circle of peace and safety. As much as Cate knew she shouldn't, she let him hold her. She hated to admit it, but she enjoyed being wrapped in his arms. Despite the guilt she had to constantly push away over her yearning for him, she didn't stop him from stroking her hands delicately before sliding his fingers through hers.

They'd grown closer over the last few days, and had talked for hours while lying on the sunny beach or devouring more of his deliciously cooked meals together. They were slowly becoming friends, and she'd soon found herself growing more relaxed in his company, regardless of the ever-present reminder that she was still his captive.

Uriel had dialled his affections back a notch though, and had agreed to allow Cate some more time to make sense of this strange scenario the two of them had found themselves in before pursuing her again. He hadn't changed his mind however, and still knew with absolute certainty just how much he still wanted her for himself. With his sights set on her rather than his plan for vengeance, he'd also heightened all security to their astral plain and commanded that more witches secure the portals, just in case. He no longer wanted unexpected visitors. Despite his original plan, Uriel now knew for sure that Cate was the only thing he wanted—the time of reckoning with Lucifer would have to wait.

"I love you, Cate," Uriel told her after just a few weeks at the beach house and her eyes widened in disbelief. She was shocked, and thought for sure that there was no way he could love her. They barely knew each other yet, and she was still the wife of his nemesis. Surely he just wanted to possess her for some crazy rivalry? "No, it's not that at all," he answered her thoughts again. This whole mind-reading thing was starting to really bother her now, and she pursed her lips with frustration.

A few moments passed in silence, but eventually Uriel

decided to let down his walls. "I do know you, Cate. I've seen your life from your memories and thoughts, as well as what you've told me about yourself since we came here. I listened to everything. I remember every detail. I don't love the situation we're in, where you came from, or how it is we came to be here together right now. But, I do love you. I love your laugh, your smile, and your warmth. I love the way you still blush at the memory of our kiss, and most of all, I love the way all you want from life is to be happy. Not power, not money, but happiness. I know you believe that you belong in the darkness, but I don't think so. I think you belong here in the light, with me." He'd finally given Cate the answers she so desperately craved, and her eyes widened in surprise at his heartfelt words.

She looked up into his intense stare and immediately felt the walls of her resistance come crumbling down. He hadn't resorted to breaking her will in order to make her say yes, she'd got there all on her own thanks to his patience and kind words. Cate then felt her heart fill with the light from Uriel's tender touch as he reached a hand up to touch her cheek. Their bond was suddenly stronger than it'd ever been before, and her resolve crumbled even further. The kiss that followed was powerful and intense. Both of them wanted more, and Cate knew—right or wrong—she couldn't keep away from him any longer.

"Will you make love to me?" Uriel asked her when he finally pulled his lips away from hers.

It was so wrong to want him so badly, and yet she'd been slowly seduced, and knew there was no turning back now that he'd won her heart. He overwhelmed her ready and willing soul, and she let him, no matter how much her love for Lucifer tried to tell her otherwise.

"Yes," Cate replied, and giggled as he pulled her up into his arms and carried her to the bedroom.

The kissing couple burst through the door with a crash. Cate was still in his strong arms, and had her legs wrapped tightly around his waist while their mouths explored one another's passionately. He shut the door and lay her down on the bed, leaning on top of his lover, and despite their eagerness, both of them remained fully clothed. Uriel took his time to kiss her deeply and enjoy their intense closeness rather than hurry. He didn't want to rush this, and vowed to take things as slowly as she needed him to. As much as he hated it, her guilt still welled up inside of her, and he knew he had to be patient while she worked through it.

She felt so much warmth and powerful emotion coming from her angelic lover that all she could do was lie back and bask in his energy. She lapped it up and was soon desperate for more. Cate kissed him and ran her hands through his dark hair, pulling him closer, tightening their embrace.

Their bodies screamed for each other, and it wasn't too long before she felt the strap of her dress being pulled down her arms. As her breasts were exposed, Uriel leaned down to kiss each of them, taking time to caress each nipple in turn with his gentle mouth. Cate groaned, relishing his touch, and as she arched her back he pulled her dress all the way down and flung it on the floor. His kisses then fluttered all over her stomach and down to her hips, before he pulled her knickers down and threw them aside—leaving her completely naked before him.

She opened her legs, watching with a grin as he licked his lips and nestled himself between her thighs. Uriel sucked her throbbing clit into his mouth and fluttered around it using his tongue while Cate arched up on the bed again, unable to control her intense reactions to his touch. Her body was so sensitive, tingling wonderfully, and threatening an orgasm already.

"Don't hold back," he then told her in a gruff tone. Uriel slipped two fingers inside her hot, wet opening and continuing in his pursuit of her release, and having him inside her sent Cate slamming straight into an immense climax. She cried out, calling his name and writhing on the bed as she flushed white heat throughout her entire being, and all thought was lost in that incredible moment of pure ecstasy.

When her body began to come down from the incredible high, Uriel started pressing his lips against her skin her again, this time over her thighs and down to his lover's feet. He sucked on her toes for a moment and laughed at her ticklishness, before finally letting her go. The sexy angel stood and pulled his t-shirt over his head, and then tossed it on the ground alongside the discarded dress and underwear. He was showing off that gloriously muscular body again, and it drove Cate wild in anticipation of what was coming next.

Leaving his trousers on, for now, he climbed back on top of her, pressing his body into hers as he leaned down to kiss her deeply again. She wanted him, and could feel his hard cock pushing against her core through the thin material of his chinos. His body's response told her he wanted her too, but he still didn't make his next move. Uriel took her mouth in his, and he delighted in Cate's touch and taste as he let his hand wander down her body to her breasts. He cupped each in turn and tugged on her nipples, firmly but gently, arousing her further.

She let her own hands wander down his torso as they kissed, the tips of her fingers stroking each perfect muscle before eventually reaching the belt of his trousers. She couldn't wait any longer, and slipped her finger under the band at the waist and pulled the hem down, taking Uriel's hard cock in her hands. He groaned and arched himself back up, taking his weight on his knees as she began stroking up and down on his rock hard length, gently pulling back and forth, but never taking her mouth off his. Uriel then kicked off the last of his clothing and pulled Cate around.

Before she knew it, she was up on his lap, and their chests were pressed together as he cradled her. She leaned into him, kissing him passionately, still pulling up and down on the hardness beneath her with her hands. "I want you to be in control, Cate," he told her, and she obeyed, climbing up and positioning herself above his erection before gently coaxing his tip inside her eager cleft. "I'm yours, take me however you want me," he groaned as she pushed him inside a little further. Cate's deep muscles tightened over him instantly, making her eager for more, and she flooded in readiness for the intrusion. She let herself ride down a few more inches before pulling up again, and then took all of him inside her at last. She was ready, and the thickness of him pulled every wonderful muscle within to its limit as she enveloped him greedily. She rose up, but her body was eager to have him back again, so she quickly pushed herself back down onto him. Soon she was going faster and pushing harder, welcoming him deeper with each delicious thrust, and she cried out in her pleasure.

Cate couldn't fight the orgasm that soon claimed her as she continued to cradle him inside of her. It lasted for so long she wondered for a moment if she could even carry on, but the wave eventually relinquished its hold of her and she started to move again.

Sensing her fatigue, he moved her round so he was on top. He moved slowly while the aftershocks continued to reverberate intensely within her for a few moments, and then faster and harder as she opened up for him more. Cate could think of nothing but her angelic lover and welcomed the wonderfully intense connection they now shared. Having him inside of her was a welcome distraction from the guilty emotions that still threatened to creep in, and she let go of everything while Uriel pursued his high.

The powerful orgasms that Lucifer had while they made love did little to prepare her for the intense bursts that came forth as Uriel climaxed inside of her a while later, and she exploded along with him. She'd thought she knew what she was in for, but was she wrong. She had to cling onto him for dear life while the world around them burned with a bright white light, and their makeshift home crumbled to absolute ruins around them. The walls then magically rebuilt themselves following the earthquake-like burst that Uriel gave off, and Cate was left feeling woozy and full of light from his release.

***

The days passed quickly, and the pair barely left the bedroom. They only took breaks to make a quick bite of food, but more often than not they just ended up making love somewhere else on their private island instead.

After months together, Uriel finally had to leave Cate alone to attend to some business in Heaven, and she decided to lie on the beach and soak up the sunshine. Her mind wandered though, and she started to contemplate just how different things might be for her now. She knew she could never go back home after everything she'd shared with Uriel, and the love she'd so willingly given him. And yet, there was still such a strong part of her that missed her dark family, especially Lucifer. She knew that if he were to welcome her back with open arms she would go to him without hesitation.

"This crazy love triangle is gonna be the death of me," she moaned to herself, and climbed up from the sun lounger to take a short walk along the water's edge. It was odd. She somehow felt like there was light power emanating from inside of her, and could hardly sense the darkness she'd readily accepted so long before. It was as though Uriel had given her the chance to break away from the binds her master had placed on her, and the freedom to finally choose for herself. Free will, she supposed, but perhaps in its truest form at last.

She laid back down on the lounger and fell asleep in the warm sunshine, but woke shortly afterwards thanks to Uriel's *expression* that was pouring into her from across the beach. He was so open with her, sending Cate his love, respect and desire through the bond, and she had to smile.

Cate's desire for him only made Uriel want her even more, and he happily gave every inch of himself to her, even though he knew that she was cleverly trying to hide away her earlier thoughts of Lucifer. He'd take whatever he could get from his captivating prisoner, and hoped he might find a way turn her head fully in time.

Later, as they relaxed on the sofa together before a warm fire in the living room, Uriel decided to ask one more thing from his lover, and tested the waters in regards to a possible future together.

"Would you ever consider giving me a child?" he asked, and Cate stared up at him open-mouthed. She was unable to answer at first. A million reasons to say no were flooding through her head. It was far too much, too soon, and she still had a lot to figure out with this crazy love triangle she was in. She sat up and looked over at him—the gorgeous, god-like angel that'd somehow found his way into her heart. He had to know that he was still fighting an unspoken war within her heart between him and his fallen brother for her true love and affection, and having a child would only complicate matters more. Cate was still torn, despite her insistence that she was happy there with Uriel. She was sure she couldn't answer definitively which powerful man she chose over the other, and hoped he'd never ask.

"No," she finally answered, but he knew anyway, having read her before she even opened her mouth. "Not yet anyway. At some point we will have to leave this plain and go back to the real world. We need to figure out how the future will pan out for us, or if it even could. We haven't actually considered how Lucifer's going to react yet," she added, and her face dropped at the realisation. He would no doubt already be so incredibly angry with her for her betrayal with Uriel as it was, and Cate couldn't even begin to think of how awful it would be if she were to return having had Uriel's child.

The angel was furious at both her words and thoughts. He quickly stood from the sofa and lifted the wooden coffee table with one hand in his rage. Uriel threw it through the window and out onto the beach with no effort at all. The hole that it left behind was half the size of the wall itself, and then he walked over and stood staring out at the beach, his entire body shaking with anger. Within seconds, dark clouds filled the sky outside and lightening came crashing down on to the sand around them, shaking the house with the electric blasts.

Cate was terrified. She'd never seen Uriel angry before and given his omnipotent power, knew she had to appease the situation otherwise things could get a lot worse. Hesitantly rising from the sofa, she slowly walked up behind Uriel and placed her hands on his bare arms. His white-hot skin burned her palms, but she held on, and forced her feelings out to him via her thoughts.

Please, she silently begged him. *Please stop this. I chose you, but I cannot give you more, not yet, but maybe someday.*

After a few moments, the clouds started to retreat and he stopped shaking. Tuning to face Cate, Uriel grabbed her hands and kissed her palms, healing the burns on them instantly.

"I've just never been so impulsive before, Cate," he told her. "But with you, I want it all and I don't want to wait."

She smiled, and was both flattered and grateful for his honesty. He looked down into her green eyes as he held her close, and then tucked a loose dark curl behind her ear before planting a soft kiss on her still trembling lips. "When you were more concerned with how Lucifer would react than you were about my feelings on the matter, it just made me crazy," he explained further. "I suppose you're right though, I hadn't thought far ahead enough. The fact remains that we will have to face the outside world some time, so we'll just need to be ready for the retaliation when it comes."

He gave off nothing but love, understanding, and warmth now, and Cate was glad he'd calmed down. Seeing this powerful angel's tiny bit of wrath had made her sure she never wanted to see it, or anything stronger from him, ever again.

CHAPTER SEVENTEEN

"Would our child have to remain on Earth, like Jesus?" Cate pondered aloud a few days later as they relaxed together in a warm, soapy bath. Uriel had gone back to being his calm, wonderful self, and hadn't raised the subject again, but she hadn't been able to help contemplating how it would all work.

"Yes. The fact remains that you're still Lucifer's blood, and your offspring would bear his mark regardless of my, *contribution*, so to speak. Neither of you could ever be welcome in Heaven," he told her, and his explanation convinced Cate more that she wasn't ready to make such a commitment to him. She actually felt disappointed that she hadn't considered it earlier.

If she gave Uriel a child, they would both be stuck on Earth permanently. They definitely wouldn't be welcome in Hell with her family any longer. She would be an outcast, and so would her angelic child. They wouldn't have their father around to help them grow up either, and might even be persecuted by the humans who didn't understand or comprehend their existence. Add to that, the undeniable probability that they'd be hunted by the dark beings her husband commanded at the same time. Cate couldn't think of a worse future for herself or her potential offspring.

As the dark thoughts washed over her, she then felt very defeated all of a sudden. Guilt and regret crept in more than ever since her time with Uriel had begun, and she wanted to cry.

He knew, of course, and tried in vain to distract her with his *expression*. Uriel held her closer as he sent his love and emotion to Cate through their link, but they both knew it wasn't enough. Uriel wanted nothing more than to make her happy, hoping to make her fall more in love with him, but there wasn't any more they could do while he still held her captive. She wanted more, but there was still this little niggle—a small doubt she simply couldn't shake.

Cate knew for certain she wouldn't be able to clear her conscience until she was free to leave their wonderful prison, take a breath, and decide for herself what she wanted for her future.

Uriel wasn't ready to give her the freedom to yet though, despite her moment of clarity on the subject. The world could just stop turning, and things could just stay as they were for now. He would deal with the real issues in time, just not yet.

***

Before long, Uriel had to start leaving more often to attend to his angelic business. After they'd been in their astral plain for a few months, he knew he'd taken liberties with his time away from his charges, and reluctantly gave Cate some alone time here and there while he saw to his responsibilities. She enjoyed the quiet, and usually spent the time sat basking in the warm sun. The only thing she hated about being alone was the dark thoughts that flooded her mind uncontrollably in his absence. It was as though her privacy brought with it a tidal wave of forbidden thought and emotion from deep within her, and Cate knew it was everything she'd forced aside when she was in Uriel's lucent presence. He'd promised to stay out of her head for the time being, but she'd also figured out how to guard her thoughts a little more wisely following his outburst. She'd started to use some of the diversionary tactics she'd used on Lucifer years before, focussing only on the important details while pushing her more risky thoughts aside to deal with later on. As far as she could tell it seemed to be working.

One afternoon, Cate decided to go for a swim in the crystal clear waters that surrounded their island. She kicked off her sandals and sarong, and then waded into the shallow pool near her usual spot on the white wooden lounger. The warm water was lovely, and she immediately swam out into the depths. For some reason, she then decided to keep going out as far as she could, and part of her wondered if she might magically return to the beach if she kept on going. She picked a faraway star and followed her line in the horizon, out of curiosity more than anything else, and didn't stop for a long time. When Cate looked back after taking lots of long strides through the waves, the island was far away in the distance. Turning back towards the horizon, there seemed to be an endless expanse of water still stretched out ahead of her, and she guessed her assumptions that she'd go full circle had been incorrect.

She pushed on through the waves regardless, but then not long later, Cate felt her foot push on a stone or some kind of rough floor deep beneath the water's surface. The ocean somehow started to get shallower as she continued on, even though her eyes told her that it still went on for miles. It was just an illusion though, and she soon started to climb the odd ridge. The water got shallower, until eventually just her ankles remained submerged.

"I'd stop right there if I were you," came a voice from behind her. Cate turned around to find Angelica's smug face moving towards her as she walked slowly on the water's surface towards her. "You'll drop off the edge, and more than likely fall to your death. My master wouldn't be very happy with me if I let that happen now, would he?" she asked, rhetorically, with an unimpressed wave of her hand.

"It'd be worth it knowing just how much trouble you'd be in for letting me fall, witch," Cate couldn't help but snap back. Angelica simply smirked, but didn't advance further, her eyes boring into Cate's as she contemplated her next move.

"If you'll please follow me," Angelica ushered Cate back in the direction of the island, but couldn't hide the tiny bit of fear that flashed across her eyes. She was obviously afraid that their captive might try to do something foolish.

Cate wondered why the witch was so scared of her master, but knew she would never answer her even if she asked the question aloud. She did as she'd been asked though, and silently glided back through the water as her guard wandered impatiently along beside her on the water's surface.

When they arrived back on the beach, Angelica turned to leave, but hesitated for a moment. "Quit fucking around, Cate," she then said, her voice low and her eyes wide. "He always gets his way, so you'd do better to just give in now and save yourself the torment," she said, her eyes sad. It seemed as though the usually so playful witch was remembering something she shouldn't be, and the fear in Angelica's eyes scared her.

Cate froze, completely taken aback, and she wasn't able to

respond right away. Angelica seemed to sense her foreboding, and teleported away before she could find her voice again.

"Holy shit," Cate then muttered to herself, it suddenly dawning on her just how deep in it she really might be.

Uriel didn't come back to their astral plain until the next day, and by then Cate had made sure to file the previous day's events with Angelica to the very back of her mind in case he decided to take a peek. She greeted him with a smile and a kiss, while making coffee and openly fantasising about making love with him. Cate found it was an effective distraction, and stopped him from interrogating her on what she'd done in his absence.

"Everything okay?" she asked, knowing he wouldn't give her any information on the goings on in Heaven, but she had to ask, hoping to find something to talk about with him. There really wasn't much left for them to discuss any more. She'd made her feelings clear about their future, and they both knew that her life there really was just a comfortable imprisonment. Nothing would change until she was free to choose her own path.

"Of course," Uriel replied, accepting the hot drink with a warm smile. Cate peered up at him and was still taken aback by his beautiful features. His hair was almost black, not unlike her own, but his incredible blue eyes still took her breath away. He wore a white shirt and jeans that framed his toned body wonderfully. It was a look she'd somehow gotten so used to now. Even her own white wardrobe was no longer quite so alien to her any more, and she would pick out her clothes for each day without even a grumble at the white fabrics. In many ways, she felt she'd lost herself to him. But, then again, Cate wasn't sure she truly missed the woman she'd been before arriving on the astral plain either. She wondered if there even was a real person beneath all the façades, or whether she was simply another version of what once had been moulded to Lucifer's preference. No part of her life had ever been her own choice. Not once that she could ever remember.

***

As time went by at a snail's pace, Uriel was called away many more times. When she was alone, Cate often ended up thinking about the day she'd swam to the edge of their fake world. The solace gave her many opportunities to let her mind wander, and she soon found herself thinking of the various escape possibilities. It wasn't much longer before she began regularly imagining herself swimming out to the edge again. She'd envision herself fighting with Angelica before throwing herself over the edge of the plain and falling to Earth—and to her freedom. Yes, she could die in the process, but at some point wasn't that a better alternative than remaining hostage, even if her captor wasn't bad company at all?

If she were truly honest, this place was boring her, and her feelings for Uriel had started to wane. She missed her old life, and began to contemplate actually carrying out those drastic measures if that was what it took to get back to her friends and family. More than four years had passed since she was bought to Uriel's island, and although her time there hadn't been terrible, Cate couldn't stop herself from feeling incredibly homesick.

She was also truly ashamed of herself and her actions, and was unafraid of the potentially fatal consequences that falling to Earth might pose. Cate wondered if perhaps she was just bored and welcomed a change to this mundane existence, despite the dramatic and potentially life threatening method. If and when she eventually found her way to Earth or Hell, she'd have a lot of explaining to do to her husband, and could definitely wait for that day to come around.

Weeks later, Cate awoke from another dreamless sleep to find a note beside the bed telling her that Uriel had gone up to Heaven for business, again. She stretched, and started to climb up out of the bed, but was forced back down onto the white pillow as a bright wave of light slammed hard into her bare chest. She collected herself, but quickly realised that she couldn't move. A mysterious force trapped her, and Cate couldn't see or fight against it.

A few seconds later, Dylan appeared in the doorway to her room. She stood there, watching Cate intensely, but didn't say a word to her. There was no warmth in her face as she scowled down at her, but there had to be a reason she'd come, and Cate hoped she was there to help rather than to hurt her. She looked up into Dylan's cold, hazel eyes as she approached, hoping for some answers, but the witch remained stoic. She didn't say a word until she reached Cate's side.

"Hello, old friend," Dylan said as she sat down on the edge of the bed, and there was no softness to her tone. She looked her same, beautiful old self, but Cate could see that she was wrestling with herself internally. Dylan seemed undecided on how she intended to deal with the woman who was once her best friend. The woman who had no doubt broken her heart the day she'd stood by and let her be tortured.

"Hi," was all Cate could think to respond, and her voice faltered as she took in the sight of her damaged friend. They hadn't seen each other in such a long time, and their last encounter had been truly awful. The memory of it made her want to reach out and hug her, but Cate could see the hurt and anger behind Dylan's eyes even now, and knew it wouldn't be welcome. She deeply regretted the treatment her friend had suffered at the hands of her husband's vengeful ire, but knew there was nothing she could do to take it back. What was done was done, and it was just another burden she would have to bear for all eternity.

There was an awkward silence as they took each other in. "What're you doing here?" Cate eventually asked her, and she kept the tone of her voice soft and warm towards her old friend. Dylan didn't respond, but her eyes seemed to flash brightly for a moment, as though she'd made up her mind about something at last, and she stood. The witch's mouth then started to move over strange, whispered words, and she recited a spell that Cate couldn't hear. Her arms were still pinned to her sides, and her body felt as though it was being pushed harder into the mattress as Dylan spoke the incantation.

"Are you ready to die?" she finally asked after a few moments, and her voice was calm and steady as she reached a hand around her back and pulled something from the back pocket of her blue jeans. She then raised a huge, golden dagger over Cate's chest and grinned, as though excited to finally have her revenge. Dylan held the blade high over her frozen body as she continued reciting the spell over and over again. Cate wanted to fight back, but she couldn't move. She was paralysed by both her own fear and by Dylan's powerful incantation, and could do nothing but watch.

"No!" she screamed, but the witch ignored her. Dylan leaned

over and began lowering the dagger, and Cate screwed her eyes shut. She waited for the pain to come, for the dagger to silence her final heartbeat, and then for her transition from life to death to begin. Oddly, she felt like she deserved it, and just hoped it'd be over quick.

The golden tip penetrated not only her body but her soul too as Dylan pushed the blade into her chest. She continued to whisper her spell repeatedly as she pushed the dagger deeper and deeper into Cate's body, but she didn't utter any kind of farewell to her old friend. Cate cried out and tried to speak, she even tried begging Dylan to stop. It was no use though, the dagger's sharp blade eventually went right through her heart, and she lost consciousness in seconds.

CHAPTER EIGHTEEN

"There's still no news of her, your majesty. They have the Dark Queen well hidden," Alma told Satan. She was shaking in fear as she said the regretful words again, and kept her eyes on her King's feet and her thoughts full of apology. Despite her very best efforts and exhaustive searching, she still couldn't find even a single trace of Cate. They were all confused by the lack of ransom or other such stipulations by the angels, but knew full well who was holding her captive.

Lucifer said nothing in response to her pointless update, and stood from the desk where he'd been sat when Alma had entered. She knew without him saying so that she was dismissed, and backed away slowly and made her way out of the door. The huge wooden desk then narrowly missed her small frame as it was sent flying past her in his rage, and went crashing through the wall to her right.

"You mean, *he* has her well hidden," Lucifer said, to himself rather than to his high priestess. The rage inside him seeped out of him and into the walls of his home, and he knew everyone in the castle could sense it. The mood in Hell was more than dire, it was disastrous. He didn't care enough to turn things back around though, and couldn't concentrate on anything long enough to try. His worry for his wife and the thoughts of what Uriel must be doing to her haunted the living nightmare he was in, and he was consumed by his hatred for everyone and everything.

Lucifer was alone and empty, but he craved no companionship at all. He'd even sent Devin and Serena to Earth to live in one of their secure mansions nestled in the Yorkshire countryside rather than in one of his city penthouses. There they would be safe and secluded, and out of his sight for a while. He simply couldn't bear to look at them. Their presence constantly made him think of Cate, and he actually found himself resenting the pair for not being the ones Uriel has chosen to kidnap.

It'd been years since she'd been taken, and he'd heard nothing from them ever since. Lucifer couldn't sense her at all, their connection now blocked, or perhaps broken somehow—he didn't know for sure. There'd been no demands, no declaration of war. There was simply…nothing.

Lucifer had ordered the kidnap of any white witch that his dark minions could find, but they hadn't come across a single one since she'd been taken. Alma had tried to convince Lucifer that the reason must be because the High Council of Angels would need all of their witches' power combined in order to keep Cate prisoner. She was far too powerful for just a few witches to have taken her captive, and so their disappearance from Earth had to mean she was okay. He hoped she was right, and that Cate was just being held somewhere out of his reach. All that mattered in the long run was that she was safe and, most importantly, alive.

Even contemplating an existence without her drove Lucifer to madness, rage, and thoughts of annihilation and all-out massacre. Should the worst ever happen to her, he knew that his need for vengeance would lead him to Heaven's doorstep, even if it meant sacrificing everything, including his own existence, in the process. He'd meant every word of his dark wedding vows, and would not stop until he found her again.

Lucifer's insatiable adoration for Cate never waned in all the time she'd gone, and he never even considered taking another lover. In fact, their forced period of separation told him more than he'd ever needed to know about his self and their relationship. If he'd ever had any doubts as to the extent of his love for her, he knew they were futile after this absence. Nothing mattered to him more than she, and he'd do whatever it took to have her home with him again.

***

Waves lapped quietly on the shore not too far away, while seagulls squawked, and the wind rustled through the trees. Cate started to rouse, wondering where Uriel was and why she felt so strange. For some reason, she was utterly exhausted. She tried to open her eyes, but they didn't want to work just yet, so she just lay there and listened for a few minutes to the familiar sounds of her island paradise.

"Oh good, you're awake," Dylan's voice bought her screeching back into full consciousness, and the memory of the witch's spell and her piercing dagger came rushing back to Cate's mind. Her eyes fluttered open and she tried to sit up, but was far too weak. Her mind was racing and her head was fuzzy, but her body was even worse. She felt terrible, worse than she'd ever felt before—even following Lucifer's strong persuasive tactics all those years earlier. Dylan laid her hands on Cate's shoulders, urging her to lie back down on the bed, and she begrudgingly did as she was silently told.

"Am I dead?" she asked.

"No," Dylan replied, with a cold edge to her voice that Cate knew she deserved. "I had to take you near to death in order to free you, though. It was the only way. I knew I'd need to take drastic measures to try and get you out of there, but it worked, so that's a bonus," she told her with a shrug. Dylan spoke as though she hadn't actually been sure her spell would've worked when she'd cast it, and had chosen to blindly stab her old friend through the heart with only the vague hope she'd be successful. Cate shuddered at the thought, but then forced herself to focus her eyes on Dylan's soft face at last. She didn't look any older than when she'd last seen her, but there was a pain behind her hazel eyes that was never there when she'd known her before. It seemed a combination of weariness and a defeated sadness that Dylan just couldn't quite hide.

"Why did you do it? Why bother saving me?" Cate asked her, looking up at her from the bed. "Why care after everything I put you through?"

"Well, for one, *you* didn't put me through anything per se. It was your dick head of a father—I mean husband—who ordered it. You were simply blinded by his affection for you. Oh, and by the way, I think you two being together is very wrong, you know?" she added, chastising her. The rant made her sound a little bit more like her old self, and Dylan giving Cate a speech about right and wrong was exactly like old times. She smiled to herself, but kept quiet so Dylan could finish getting things off her chest.

Cate knew she owed her much more than just the chance to vent a little, but it seemed like a good way to start. "I truly did love you once, Cate," Dylan continued solemnly. She stared down into her face intently, and her features softened as her emotions finally came to the surface. "I don't think you ever really realised just how much. I wanted to keep you safe, to take you where the dark witches couldn't find you, and do you know what *he* told me?" Dylan asked, raising her eyes to the sky, clearly implying Uriel. "He told me no. He said you were an abomination who could never be trusted. He said that a partnership of light and dark would bring about nothing but chaos and bedlam to the Council's perfect world," Dylan told her with a bitter edge to her voice she didn't even attempt to disguise. "But, when he decided he wanted you, all those things were somehow irrelevant. He had to have you, no matter the cost. He's left the Earth unguarded by white witches for years. Subsequently, the darkness has flowed freely, and the sins soon started pouring in. He didn't care when he chose fucking you over answering the prayers and pleas of his loyal servants, whose friends and families became easy pickings for the demon's who'd been left to roam here on Earth. Innocent people suddenly started selling their souls for fame and fortune, with no-one to stop them, to help them see the righteous path," she seethed, a forlorn expression on her face.

"Dylan, I…" Cate knew there was nothing she could say, so let her voice tail off. The witch didn't seem to even hear her anyway, and carried on with her rant.

"Uriel then called us to him, and said that he expected us all to accept you as his lover. Just like that. Because he said so. Talk about an unholy partnership!" Dylan added, she then took a deep breath and calmed herself for a few seconds while Cate lay still on the bed. She tried to take in everything that she'd just heard her friend fume about, but the overload was exhausting her even more. After a few minutes, she decided to change the subject. Her pounding headache was making it hard to take in much more of the serious talk, despite her being glad to help Dylan and her need to offload.

"Where are we now?" Cate asked, although she was quite sure she already knew.

"Earth," Dylan replied. "But don't worry, he can't find you

here. The spell I cast has hidden you from both him and all the other white witches under the Council's command. I've renounced them, so he cannot use me to find you either," she then added.

Cate gasped, but Dylan just shrugged her shoulders, looking downcast and defeated. "You don't go through everything I have and keep believing—keep trusting in just the good. I think I've honestly seen much more darkness than light in my time, and both sides are just as terrible as each other. I guess I realised that I'd rather be on whatever side you're on than blindly believing for the sake of it. I think it's safe to say I've never gotten over losing you."

Dylan then got up and busied herself with sorting out some bags of clothing she must've bought while Cate was out of it. She was grateful for her honesty, and sensed that Dylan had said all she wanted to for now, so she didn't bother asking for more information. It could wait until later.

They spent the rest of the day reconnecting, and Cate was glad to find that Dylan wasn't holding too much of a grudge with her. They reminisced and talked openly about what'd happened since the night of Cate's coming of age reunion with Lucifer, and why things had ended up the way they had. The pair then talked about many things, but didn't go into too greater detail about Dylan's torture. The scars still seemed too fresh for either of them to bear reopening those awful floodgates.

Instead, Dylan told Cate how she'd been misinformed by Angelica that Lucifer was keeping her in Hell by force, and that he was torturing her into submission. She said she couldn't bear the thought of him hurting her, so had acted—rashly yes, but she hadn't been able to help it. Cate adored her for trying so hard to keep her safe, and knew she'd never find another friend like Dylan in the entire world. Even after their time apart, and the fact that she had known their relationship was never going to be allowed to go any further, she'd always felt a deep void since losing her that night in the field. Cate knew she truly loved her in return, and always would. She was glad that Dylan still felt that way, and she finally opened up about what Lucifer had then gone on to do. Angelica had almost been right, just not at the right time.

"You're the first person I've told about it…"

"How can you love him?" Dylan asked her when she'd finished explaining what'd happened, and was clearly disgusted by Cate's disturbing admissions.

"Don't, Dylan. Please," Cate answered, unable to bear an interrogation from her. "He's my home, my absolute everything. Despite the bumps in the road, we're meant to be. After everything I've endured, I still know that for sure. I couldn't stand it if you didn't accept us."

"I do, and I'll accept whatever makes you happy, Cate. That's all I want for you," Dylan told her, smiling warmly at her, and the Dark Queen grabbed her best friend and hugged her tight.

***

Later that night, after scoffing Chinese food and watching television in the sanctity of their hotel room, the pair finally settled down to get some much needed rest. Dylan looked over and watched Cate as she began to lull and drift off to sleep, and she knew she'd done the right thing. Despite the bad blemishes in their history, she was happy to have her back in her life, even if it meant her having to pledge her allegiance the dark underworld in order to do so. She too drifted off after a few minutes, but her dreams were fretful and scattered despite her exhausted body. She had worries and fears for the future that seemed to be affecting her more than even she'd realised, and knew she needed a definite plan.

The next morning over pancakes and fresh fruit, courtesy of room service, Dylan was back to being her playful and fun self again, and wondered aloud about the current state of Cate's love-life.

"Maybe there's something about you that people cannot help but fall in love with? Everyone that knows you loves you in one way or another, have you ever noticed that?" she asked, popping a strawberry into her mouth. "Whether they want to fuck, marry, protect, or even just be your closest friend. Everyone is drawn to you in some way. Most of the time they cannot understand it themselves," she mused, looking to Cate for her input, but all she could do was blush and shake her head.

"Surely not?" she finally answered a few moments later, but

also had to wonder if Dylan might be right. What if it was all just part of some strange power she'd not yet mastered? Or some all-consuming evil influence that drew others to her? Was all of her tumultuous love life her fault because of a power she'd inherited, yet even Lucifer had no idea of? Serena didn't have this problem, so why her?

As Cate sat and wondered about all these terrible possibilities, and her thoughts eventually settled on her husband. In all honesty, she was scared to face him, and hated the reality that she'd have to tell him of all the things she'd let Uriel do to her up on that astral plain. Now that she was away from that place, and the powerful angel, she could think so much more clearly. Cate knew for sure that she never truly loved him, but had been coerced into submission by him and his powerful prowess. She hated the thought that she'd succumbed to such intimidation again, but in a different form of it this time.

Cate knew would have to be honest with Lucifer when she saw him again, there was nothing else she could do. She was truly disgusted with herself for giving in to Uriel's advances so readily, allowing herself to be possessed by him, and giving him the *yes* so quickly. There was even a part of her that didn't actually want to go home just yet. She wanted to hide away for a little while, to give herself time to think about how she might explain these things to her husband, and how she might go about begging him for his forgiveness for her forced betrayal. Despite her best intentions, Cate always seemed to end up hurting either herself or those she loved, and she hated it. *Perhaps that's just another one of my fucked-up powers too?* she contemplated, but couldn't bear to decide on an answer to her inner musings.

After a couple of days resting at the hotel, Cate felt much better. Although still not remotely at full strength, she was finally ready to get up and face the world. Things with Lucifer would be tough, but she knew she had to attack things head-on, no more stalling.

She and Dylan had agreed on a plan during their recuperation time, and had decided to wait a few days until she was stronger and then find a Satanic church. Once there, they intended to gain entry and travel together to Hell using the dark witches' help. Cate would then—when she was hopefully welcomed back arms wide open—speak for Dylan and ask Lucifer to allow her safe passage to Hell. She would also request that she be able to join his ranks as a dark witch. She owed Dylan far more than a place in Alma's coven, but it was a decent place to start.

There was only one other complication. For some reason, Cate hadn't regained any of her powers at all since they'd returned to Earth. She couldn't teleport, and she couldn't sense or summon the witches or demons. There was no beacon drawing her to her husband yet either, and it made her worry that Uriel had somehow kept her powers locked away at his command. Without them, she feared she might not be strong enough to return home, but knew she had to try.

Even Dylan thought it was strange, but the pair both put it down to either the spell she'd cast, or perhaps the on-going healing process Cate might be going through. It wasn't until they tried walking over the threshold to the church later that day that it all became clearer.

Dylan stepped over the invisible line that surrounded the dark church without any resistance, and that act alone made clear her lack of allegiance to the High Council of Angels. Cate took a deep breath and then lifted her right foot, trying to follow her friend over the threshold. There was a little push back at first. It was just a small amount of resistance she barely even registered as she pushed on through, but it was mere seconds more before a strange sensation then flowed through her. Suddenly, as though a brick wall had slammed into her chest, Cate was sent flying backwards, and she landed hard on the concrete floor behind her.

"What the?" she started to ask, but Dylan came running back over and pulled her away from the church in a panic. She hurried Cate along, and both of them ran as fast as they could without stopping until they were well clear of the hallowed ground.

CHAPTER NINETEEN

Huffing and puffing, the pair slumped in a shop doorway to catch their breaths. Cate was shocked, and so completely baffled she couldn't speak. She looked to Dylan for answers, finding only another perplexed face looking back at her.

"Why couldn't you cross into the churches inner circle, Cate?" the witch finally wondered aloud, and was clearly shocked and worried by the rejection of the Dark Queen from her own church as well.

"I don't bloody know. I was hoping you might have an idea!" Cate cried in response, her green eyes wide with worry. "Why did we run?"

"We don't know what we're dealing with here," Dylan told her. "What if the dark witches couldn't see you, perhaps my spell hid you from them, too? They might have only seen me wandering up like I belonged there, and would've kidnapped me and zapped me to your Dark King in less than a second. You would've been left there, stranded, and with no idea how to get home, while I would be tortured for all eternity!"

Cate nodded, understanding what Dylan was trying to get at. They both quickly agreed that they needed to stick together and figure this out. Eventually, they'd try again, but for now, it seemed as though Cate was stuck on Earth. She was, however, a little relieved that she could put off the family reunion for a little while longer.

Dylan insisted they planned to constantly move around, only ever staying in one place for a few nights at a time. They would have to be careful which magic Dylan performed, as it would leave a small trace of them that the witches, whether light or dark, could use to follow them if they picked up on it.

The pair travelled around for a while, staying in hotels for a few nights at a time, but they never settling longer in fear of being followed. After just a few months, Cate was exhausted. She still hadn't gotten her powers back, and the stress was taking its toll on her.

"I can't do this anymore, Dylan," she told her friend after they'd hungrily tucked into some cheeseburgers and chips. They were poor, dirty, and beyond exhausted, and Cate knew she had to do whatever it took to get back home.

"I'm going to try to get into the penthouse. Maybe Devin is there, or at least Belias?" she wondered, sipping on her sweet tea and enjoying the warmth from it as it spread throughout her body. "The moon is full tonight as well, so you never know," she added, tailing off thoughtfully.

"Maybe," Dylan replied, understanding immediately what Cate was hoping to find. "Okay, but let me come in with you," she added, stuffing her mouth with salty fries. Her lips were covered in mayonnaise where she'd devoured her dinner so hungrily, and Cate threw her a napkin from across the table.

"Absolutely not," she replied, shaking her head. "If I find anyone there, I'll come and get you before going home. I promise." She couldn't risk Dylan's capture, even though they'd both wondered if it might be one of the only ways to get their attention. If any of the dark beings caught Dylan, she would undoubtedly be taken to Hell. Lucifer would read her mind, and he'd find out the truth at last. Dylan might have to take a beating first, but had insisted it'd be worth it to help ensure they both got there in one piece. "Whoever it is might decide against chit-chat and kill you on sight, did you ever think of that?" Cate asked her friend, who shook her head. "I'd never be able to forgive myself, and would rather we live on the streets than me lose you, Dylan. You're my best friend and I would die before I let anyone hurt you ever again," she promised, and they both knew she meant every word.

They took the train that evening to the penthouse and gazed up at the gloomy building for a moment before Cate went inside, alone. Dylan agreed to wait in the tube station for her, but Cate knew that she would be clock-watching the entire time she was inside.

"You've got twenty minutes," Dylan told her, tapping her

black wristwatch with her index finger. "And then I'm coming in to get you, I don't care who's there."

"Okay," Cate replied with a warm smile. She pulled Dylan into a tight hug and then turned on her heel and headed off towards the huge building. A human man opened up the huge glass door for her on his way out, and Cate thanked him before heading inside. She was incredibly aware of the lack of resistance she felt as she entered the building, indicating that there was either no protective threshold or that she had managed to pass over the invisible line without being rejected this time.

The lobby was empty, which Cate wasn't sure was a good sign, but she wandered over to the lift and pressed the call button while her eyes darted around looking for any sign of life. Moments later, she was making her way skywards. She felt both impatient and scared of what might be there to greet her when she arrived at the top floor apartment she'd once lived in with Devin. Many great memories came back to her as she ascended, though. It felt like such a long time since she'd lived there, but it was also as if it were only yesterday that they'd be back and forth, holding parties and running Black Rose Industries with Devin while living their fake married lives together.

After a few minutes, Cate arrived at the dark hallway that led to the main door to the penthouse flat, and she flicked on the light switch. It was cold in there, and she noticed that no fresh flowers adorned the antique unit beside the doorway. She could hear nothing but silence, broken only by her own footsteps as she walked towards the huge, dark wooden doors. Cate pressed her index finger down onto the bell in anticipation, before waiting for a few seconds and then pressing it again, just in case.

No answer came, despite her hopes, and the realisation quickly dawned on her that the flat must currently be empty. No humans, witches, or demons were there to greet her, and most importantly—no Lucifer.

Cate burst into tears and fell to her feet, curling herself into a tight ball on the floor while she wept. She felt so desperate, so lost, and she sobbed even harder as the silence of the hallway enveloped her further. Uncontrollable tears fell down onto her knees as she hugged them, and her heart broke.

Strong arms wrapped around her a little while later after Dylan ran over to her from the elevator's open door. She didn't say anything; she simply held Cate tight and cradled her friend as she fell apart.

"It's as if God himself is trying to keep me out, as if he's trying to keep me away from him?" Cate cried between sobs, and knew her despair and desperation was clear in her tone.

"I thought you didn't believe in him?" Dylan asked, with a small laugh. She'd always believed in the higher powers of both good and evil that drove both sides, and had told Cate her theories many times, but her ideas were always met with a blank stare and a shrug. It was only now that Cate could fathom the idea of it all, and she had to wonder if that strange divine intervention was now forcing her into exile for some reason.

"Perhaps I'm coming around to the idea of a higher power," she eventually admitted, looking over at Dylan with a forced smile at last. She then nodded and the pair stood and got back in the lift, going down to the empty lobby before heading back out to the street.

On the train out of the city the next day, the pair decided it was time to stop searching for answers. They both needed a break, and it'd only be until they could figure out what was going on, or until the universe made its next move. Cate and Dylan both agreed that they'd have to find a quiet little town where they could settle in for a while and decide how they might plan their next move.

"The use of magic will have to stop completely," Cate said, and Dylan nodded in agreement.

"Absolutely. It's the only way we can be sure there's no way for any of the witches to track us," she replied. They both knew it'd be hard, but were tired of the running, so knew it was worth it.

They stopped off on their way out of London, deciding to consult an aura reader as their last attempt at figuring out what was going on with Cate and her powers. Dylan had searched for a spiritual reader using her own divining power, and they decided to give one last avenue a try before they then disappeared for good, or at least for as long as it took for Cate to get her powers back. When they reached Paddington station, Dylan worked her last bit of magic on a young guy behind the desk of a nearby car rental agency, convincing him to let her take a hire car away for free. She signed the forms using a fake name and signature, and then produced a couple of crumpled up receipts from her pocket that she magically manipulated him to believe were her identification and credit card.

The pair then sped off, and programmed the satellite navigation system to take them to the aura reader's address just outside the city. When they arrived at the small house, the two of them were welcomed into the reader's home by his wife, a kind lady who offered them tea and a plate of delicately decorated cupcakes. Dylan scoffed some down, while Cate just nervously took a few sips of tea as she sat back in the large, throw-lined sofa.

The house was cluttered. Bookshelves lined every wall of the living room with hardbacks detailing the use of gemstones and horoscopes, along with incense burners and scented candles. The woman was dressed in a floating, paisley printed dress and leather sandals, and she gave off a faint scent of lavender when she passed close to Cate. She assumed the woman must prefer a few drops of flower's essence on the her clothes rather than her wearing actual perfume, and she liked the smell—it reminded her of Ella.

When she was ushered into the back room, Cate didn't even need to speak. The grey-haired man waved his hand for her to sit with him at the crystal covered table, but then stared at her for a moment before he spoke. What he said immediately took her breath away.

"You are full of light, my dear. Many, many congratulations!" he told her excitedly. "I've never met anyone with such a strong light power inside of them. It's almost as if God himself filled you up with the most wonderful present and power to ward off evil," he cried, raising his hands to the sky with a triumphant joy she could not even begin to share. Cate found herself simply staring open-mouthed at the aura reader once he'd spoken the glaring truth, unable to say a word in response. She mentally kicked herself for not having realised it sooner, though.

"Of course!" Dylan shouted out from the other room, before jumping up and storming into the back. She quickly handed the man some cash and dragged Cate away. "How did we not figure this out before? You're full of light, Cate. Get it?" she almost screamed at her as they climbed back into their rental car and sped off.

"Yuk," Cate replied, but nodded. "Okay, so I'm full of light, no darkness. There's our answer. So now what?" she asked, not able to hide her petulant attitude.

"We wait, I expect," Dylan offered. "Eeeew, I suppose you're kind of, *infected* with light then," she added, laughing even harder when Cate slapped her hard on the shoulder in response.

The pair then headed off towards the motorway in search of somewhere to call home for as long as it took for Cate to be cured of her lightness, however long that might be.

CHAPTER TWENTY

Cate and Dylan decided to spend a maximum of three years in any one place, and for the next six years, they did just that. They'd get set up, find themselves somewhere to live and odd jobs, while assuming different identities each time—just to be safe. They managed far better than they'd first thought, and kept to themselves while staying under the radar. They also spent time searching for any ways in which they might try and contact Cate's infernal family, but missed out at every turn.

Meanwhile, the rekindled friends grew closer over the years. They confided everything in one another, and Cate knew she would have Dylan by her side forevermore. Their friendship had somehow survived their horrific ordeals as well as the tests of time, and she had every hope they would continue working through the hardships side-by-side.

After their third move, Cate really missed home. She'd had enough of being stranded on Earth, and was ready to face the music back in Hell. She still had no powers, and living a fully human life was hard without them. Dylan still wasn't using her magic for fear of the watchful eyes and the keen senses of her old coven, and she would complain daily about having to carry out their mundane chores. Neither of them aged, strangely, which meant that they would've had to keep on moving anyway, but as they settled into their third new home, Cate felt lost.

Choosing a new town had been simple, and Dylan assured her that the ley lines of England would help keep the pair hidden, so they'd followed the line westwards from the capital. The ancient power reportedly interfered with the witches' magic, both light and dark, and would help keep their senses scrambled should any come close enough in search of either Cate or the absconded witch.

Regardless of the hardships, Dylan was glad she had this time to be with Cate. They really were best friends again, and being by her side made her happier than she'd been in years. Helping and protecting the Dark Queen gave her a profound purpose, and she knew she'd much prefer a lifetime in her service than to ever go back under Uriel's command. They accepted each other, warts and all, and Dylan considered them to be a remarkable team. There was nothing sexual about their relationship this time either, and she was fine with that. As long as she was in Cate's life, she was happy.

Cate let her guilt overpower her desires, and didn't take any lovers at all during their exile. She remained abstinent, while Dylan frolicked with many a cute guy or hot girl she found along their travels—enough to make up for both of them. She was definitely enjoying her preparation to becoming a dark witch, and had really come into her own since allowing that side of herself to flourish. Dylan had always had a fun and carefree nature, and being back to her old self took her mind off the big issues she'd run from for so long. Being with Cate again brought back many memories from their days as friends, both good and bad. She often thought back to the years she'd spent being the doting best friend, all at the behest of her angelic master, but they were an amazing few years.

She'd gone willingly to the school, where plans had been made and their ages altered to match that of the devil's so-called evil heiress. Angelica was in charge, and her dominance over the rest of them was clear and unyielding. She commanded her coven with an iron fist, and Dylan had always struggled to get on with her. She'd decided to go against her orders the day she'd gone to the girls' toilets and met Cate though. Dylan had purposely gone there to lie in wait, and was in prime position for when she came in to hide from P.E class.

It wasn't long before she'd heard her silently enter and hide away in a cubicle, and within minutes, Dylan drawn Cate into a conversation about how much she hated long distance running, making her giggle and agree wholeheartedly. She'd known at that moment that they were going to be great friends, and hadn't regretted defying her high priestess.

They now knew almost everything about one another, but for some reason she still had secrets she hadn't confided in her yet.

Dylan hadn't told Cate about her true family. In their many long and intense conversations about the past, she'd kept quiet, and often wondered why she'd chosen to keep the truth to herself. It was common knowledge among their kind that witches could be either created or they could be born, to witch and warlock parents—like Dylan. Her mother had been the high priestess of all the white witches hundreds of years before, and she had married the chief white warlock. The powerful couple had four children, two of whom still served their angelic master's in their white covens, and one who'd died when Dylan had been four years old.

She was the youngest of the family, and the only daughter. Her eldest brother, Gabe, had joined their father's coven at only fifteen years old. He'd responded to his father's calls for help following a demonic attack one night, but had gotten home too late. Gabe had found their father curled up and alone in his bed after having been poisoned by the demon Asmodeus during a battle. He'd then died in Gabe's arms just minutes later, and the loss of their father had caused vengeful desires to well up inside her brother like he'd never felt before. Gabe had disappeared that same night, and for over a year neither Dylan nor the rest of her family knew what'd become of him. That was until his broken, dead body was left at their family's doorstep one crisp winter morning.

Her mother had then fallen into despair. It was a kind of depression none of her kind had ever seen before in such a strong white witch, and it overwhelmed her usually so strong prowess. Darkness had then crept into her every pore; changing and affecting her in ways she didn't even know herself until it was too late. Dylan had been told years later by her brother Mike, that one night when the full moon rose in the sky, their mother had felt the darkness summon her from deep within, and had gone straight to the Satanic church. She'd reportedly crossed the invisible threshold with no resistance, and was then taken to Hell. She was brought before Satan to be tried, where she'd begged the Dark Prince to take her life, but he was not so merciful as to grant her the much-desired peace.

Lucifer had reportedly looked down upon the broken spirited witch as she knelt before him, and read her thoughts with intrigue. He'd sensed the power and strength she possessed within, and had coveted it. He knew that if she could be fully turned, her power would be infallible—a dark force no white witch would ever be strong enough to thwart. Lucifer had seduced her that night, turning her anger, pain, and hate into a new and disturbing sense of love and loyalty to her evil master.

From that day on, she'd been his to command, and had then pledged her allegiance to him for all eternity. Her mother, Alma, was then promoted to high priestess of the royal dark coven, and Dylan hadn't seen her since, even when she herself had been tortured and beaten at the hands of Satan's legion of demonic soldiers. She had no idea what'd become of her, or if she'd ever see her again, but she hoped she might one day at least rekindle some kind of relationship with the mother who'd been drawn from the light in much the same way as Dylan had. She too had been seduced, but had turned away from her angelic master willingly, and knew she'd never return to him.

***

Cate and Dylan had been living in a small town called Avebury just a few miles from the infamous Stonehenge for a little over two years, when Cate finally felt things start to change for her. She had assumed the identity of Dana Williams, and Dylan was known there as her big sister, Nina.

Cate still looked every inch the twenty year old, fresh-faced young woman, despite her now being close to one hundred years old in official terms, and Dylan looked to be in her early twenties even though she was actually double Cate's age.

Just like when she was younger, Cate had taken a job working at the village pub over the last couple of years, and she enjoyed the laughs and jokes she'd often have with the patrons, no matter whether they were there to drink down their problems or to celebrate and have fun. Cate even found some of the men quite charming as they drooled over her and kept her tips generous, but she wasn't interested in any of them, of course. Her heart still yearned for Lucifer, even after all their time apart, and she knew now that she was ready to see him again. Regardless of how awkward or scary it might be at first, she was sure they'd find their way back to each other eventually. They were worth fighting for, and she had to hope he still felt the same way.

She tried many times in vain to summon her power into her. Cate meditated, prayed, and even used summoning spells to try and focus on her lost sense. She downright encouraged the humans around her to sin in the hopes that the dark doings would rid her of the light's power, but it was no use.

"Don't bother," Dylan snapped one morning when she'd found Cate sat at the kitchen table immersed in a Satanist's bible she'd purchased online, desperately looking for some kind of ritual or demon summoning spell she could try out.

"I can't just sit here waiting for my light to go so we can head home, Dylan. I need to try and push it along a bit," Cate replied, and was angered by her friend's uncharacteristically impatient attitude. They both knew that the future wasn't going to be an easy one, but she was sure that she could be happy in Hell again. She hoped she could go back to her rightful place as Queen, and would make sure Dylan would remain by her side for eternity.

Cate took a sip of her hot coffee and caught Dylan's curious eyes on her over the top of the black leather-bound book.

"You're horny aren't you?" she cried, and burst out laughing. She shook her head in mock disgust, and her ash-blonde hair fell loosely down her back as she did so. Cate loved the colour of it in the sunshine, and thought it was a shame Dylan kept it hidden in a ponytail most of the time. This morning's bed-head look even suited the witch's round face, and Cate had to smile back at her.

"You can't blame me, it's been *far* too long!" she informed her, blushing slightly. "And anyway, what's your problem today?" she asked, wondering why Dylan had snapped at her.

"I've got a guy *and* a girl asleep in my bed right now, and I need to kick them out. Why the hell did I invite them back here?" she asked rhetorically, and Cate just shook her head with a wry grin.

"Because you're a deviant dark witch who cannot keep her legs closed," she replied, earning herself both a laugh and a slap on the shoulder from her best friend.

Dylan shrugged and headed back to her room to get dressed for her shift at a local supermarket, a job which she despised, but it bought in some cash so that was all that mattered. Ever since they'd left London, the pair had found it much easier to find little jobs that wouldn't require too much in the way of references and identification in order to get a foot in the door, and they'd been all the healthier and happier for cash they brought in. It was worth the mundane life to have food in their bellies and a roof over their heads.

Cate thought of her old, privileged life she'd led when living on Earth the last time. She'd give anything to go back to that lavish lifestyle, but guessed those days were over. After attempting to make contact with Devin and Serena a few times without any luck, she'd all but given up. Her emails bounced back to her every time, giving Cate the usual, *undeliverable*, message back in response. She'd even called the lobby of the London penthouse not too long ago, but it was still empty. The doorman admitted that he hadn't seen anyone there in years. He told her that Mr Black's family back in Germany had inherited Black Rose industries after his death, which led Cate to believe things were being handled from afar once more. Unfortunately, the man said he had no contact information for any of them, and she knew the entire organisation was lying dormant until Lucifer was ready to let it flourish again.

***

Later that night, Cate got ready for her late shift at the pub. She climbed into her favourite black skinny jeans and a red t-shirt, adding a splash of colour in an attempt at being less gothic in her choice of outfit. She'd been trying to add more variety to her wardrobe recently, but more often than not would still end up in mostly blacks and the occasional reds. She then pulled her dark brown curls away from her pale face into a high ponytail and applied her usual light makeup, before sliding on her black leather biker boots and jacket, and heading out across the village. Thanks to Dylan's paranoia having rubbed off on her over the years, she'd also taken a moment to make sure the door was double locked behind her.

When she reached the pub, Cate ditched her jacket in the back room, and quickly went about taking over from the young barmaid who was finishing up from the day shift. She kept herself busy behind the bar for the first few hours, while waiting for the place to fill up and help her pass the time more easily. Cate chatted to a couple of men who were regulars at the Lion's Head while she poured them their beers and handed over peanuts and crisps, and thanked them for their kind and generous tip, but refused when they'd asked her to join them for a drink during her next break. It seemed like a game many of them liked to play, as if they kept on asking in the hopes that someday she might just say yes. She'd always made sure the regular patrons knew that while she was happy to be warm and friendly, she wasn't flirting with them. Many a time she'd even had to avoid getting set up on blind dates by the older women from the village, all of whom seemed dead-set on setting her up with someone they knew who would apparently be perfect for her.

There was only one man perfect for her, and she pined for him rather than let any new face crumble her vow to remain loyal to him. Despite all of Cate's carefully closed-off emotions though, she felt a connection with one of her new customers who came for a drink that night. She felt strangely attracted to him as soon as their eyes locked over the pint of lager she placed on the bar in front of him, and she actually did a double take. Cate was careful to maintain her usual cool and calm composure, but couldn't help enquire after him when he sat down opposite two young men who were small business owners from the village.

"Do you know who that is?" she asked another regular who was sat at the bar, an older woman called Lily who was on her fifth glass of white wine. She also happened to be one of the nosiest people she'd ever met, and knew everything when it came to the comings and goings in their small community.

"He's just moved here. Apparently he's going to be the new doctor, or so I have heard," Lily told her matter-of-factly. "Harry, I think his name is. Cute too, hey," she added with a wonky smile before focussing on her wine glass again.

"I suppose," Cate replied nonchalantly, and inadvertently looked over at his table. She caught him watching her as well, and quickly busied herself wiping down the bar area.

Harry looked across at his new friends over the wooden table. He'd only moved into Avebury a few days before, but had already made friends with both Jamie and Marc when he'd popped into the small supermarket Jamie owned in the village centre. They'd got on well, and had chatted for a while before he'd then agreed to go for a drink with them, and Harry was glad he'd said yes now. The barmaid was stunning, and he knew he had to know more about her.

"Who is she?" he asked, gesturing over to her with a nod.

"Ah yes, we see you have finally met Dana," replied Marc, smiling at him over his whisky and cola. He owned the village bakery and was what Harry would call, a little on the chubby side, but was a nice guy all the same.

"She's the ultimate, unattainable woman," added Jamie with a sigh. "She's lived here for a couple of years now, and I've never seen her even go out on a date with a guy, let alone anything else. You'd think she was a prude or something, but her sister's the biggest slut around, and Dana doesn't seem to care," he added, as though that was supposed to mean something to Harry. He shrugged and looked over at the bar again, taking in the beautiful woman as she chatted warmly with another customer, and he finished off his beer.

"Who wants another?" he asked with a grin, and the two guys nodded. Harry stood, grabbed the empty glasses and then made his way over towards the bar, his sights set on Cate.

"He's got no chance," Marc said quietly to Jamie, who laughed and nodded in answer. Both of them had tried to pick her up many times too, only to have their best chat up lines and warmest smiled shot down by the mysterious and much admired girl.

"Hi, um," Harry started to say when she looked over at him expectantly from the other side of the bar. He was desperately trying to think of something cool and impressive to say, but his mind went completely blank once he was under her beautiful gaze. Those intense green eyes of hers had him mumbling like an idiot, and he forced himself to speak some words. Any words…"Can I grab two beers and a whisky and cola please?" he then asked, and gave up on trying to be smooth. He peered over the wooden bar at Cate with a shy smile, and was mesmerised by the woman staring back at him. As he looked into her stunning face, he was lost in her allure. When she smiled back at him before taking away the empty glasses, he was spellbound.

Cate felt a pounding inside her chest that she didn't recognise, and it took her a minute to realise it was her heart beating extra fast. She'd already noticed how his light blue eyes lit up when he laughed, but when they were locked with hers, she saw how wise they also were—as if his soul was centuries old. She had to admire the set of his strong, square jaw, and even memorised the little dimple in the centre of his chin. When he smiled, she bet all the women swooned.

"Anything else I can do for you?" she asked as she placed the fresh drinks down in front of him, and she had to remind herself to breathe when he shot her an awkward smile. Dread finally reared its ugly head, and Cate suddenly felt nauseous. Regardless of their connection, she knew it was no use getting close to anyone, least of all hot doctors with cute dimples.

Harry shook his head, handing her a twenty-pound note.

"Just one for yourself as well, okay?" he offered. His warm smile was back on his gorgeous face, and Cate thanked him.

He knew he was hot, and had been quite the womaniser in his past, but he'd decided it was time to stop looking for one-night stands any more. Harry had known for a while that he was finally ready to find the right girl and settle down, but his studies had kept him so busy he hadn't had the chance to meet the right kind of woman for the job. That was until he'd met the unattainable barmaid. In just a few days he'd not only met some new friends, but also a woman unlike any he'd met before, and he'd been dumbstruck for the first time in his entire life.

Harry returned to his new friends with his head low and his ego dragging behind him, but laughed as the guys joked with him about his lack of skill in the pickup-line department.

"You did better than me, mate," Marc said as Harry sat back down at the table. "I was in here about three times before I could even get the right drinks. I'd get so flustered from trying to talk to her, I would forget what I supposed to order every time!" he cried. Harry laughed and shrugged, thinking perhaps he hadn't done so badly after all then.

CHAPTER TWENTY-ONE.

By the time Jamie and Marc had finished drinking, it was almost closing time at the Lion's Head. Harry bid farewell to his new friends and took the empty glasses over to the now quiet bar. He was glad to have met them, and even more pleased he'd agreed to meet them for that drink after all.

"One more for the road?" Cate asked him, and Harry nodded, smiling broadly at her as she quickly went about pouring him another pint of cold beer.

"Thanks, I'm Harry by the way," he told her, with his boyish grin firmly back on his face. His confidence was back thanks to the several pints of beer that he'd already consumed, and rather than get flustered, he let himself enjoy the beautiful barmaid's attention. He handed Cate some money and waved his hand when she offered him the change.

"Cheers," she said, eyeing him warily. She couldn't figure out why she felt drawn to him, but she felt safe in his presence, and more alive than she had in almost a decade. He confused her, but she didn't want to push him away like all the other men and women who'd dared try to get close over the years. She could tell he had a gentle soul, and she wanted to get to know him. Despite them having only just met, there was a connection there already. "So, Harry. I hear you're the new doctor?" she asked, making small talk, but she was genuinely interested in his plans.

"Soon to be, yes. I have a placement at the village practice for a year before my final exams," he told her with a smile. "It's nice to know you've been asking about me though," he added, and Cate rolled her eyes playfully, but grinned back at him.

"The name's Dana," she told him. "But I guess you already know that about me, too, don't you?" she asked him with a knowing look.

"Touché," he answered with a gruff laugh before taking a long swig of his beer.

They chatted for a while as she cleared up, and could both feel their immediate kinship to one another. They didn't talk about the things she thought normal people talked of in bars, but discussed philosophy, debated religion, and he wowed her with the scientific advances that were now part of his everyday life. Cate enjoyed the attention from him, but let Harry know straight away that she wasn't looking for a boyfriend. Regardless of their connection, she would never risk her cover, her heart, or his safety. He smiled, appearing to understand, or at least to accept her wishes, and seemed even more like the most perfect gentleman she'd ever known because of it.

"Can I walk you home?" he asked as she locked up, and seemed to genuinely want to make sure she got back safely. As they left the dark pub though, Dylan's face came into view from just a few metres up the road that led to their part of the village, and she did a double take at discovering Cate wasn't alone.

"Hey sis, who's your friend?" she called, concern clearly etched on her face. She could sense he was human though, and calmed down as she neared the pair of them.

"The name's Harry," he said, shaking her hand. "I was just offering to walk your sister home, but I see there's no need to worry now," Harry added with a smile, before heading off in the direction of his flat. His mind was racing with both excited and anxious thoughts of the barmaid that had already stolen his heart, and he had to literally force himself to walk away. No woman had ever made him feel that way, and he couldn't resist taking a peek back over his shoulder at her before she disappeared from view.

"He's cute," Dylan said, eyeing Cate curiously while the pair of women walked off in the direction of their flat.

"Kind of," replied Cate, but smirked over at her old friend as she did so.

"Be careful," Dylan warned, and Cate knew without her having to explain exactly what she'd meant by that. They were both at risk if she let anyone get too close, and she owed it to Dylan to make sure she never suffered because of her again. They linked arms and wandered home, chatting quietly as they went, and Dylan told her fake sister all about the man who'd shared her bed that evening.

***

Harry returned to the Lion's Head the next night during Cate's shift at the pub, and then the next. He soon became a regular and would often sit with Jamie and Marc, but eventually started heading straight over to the bar after just a few visits. He found he preferred to chat with Cate rather than hang out with the guys, and guessed they didn't mind. In fact, they seemed more impressed than offended.

They quickly got to know one another well, only as friends of course, but she honestly loved having someone else to hang around with other than just Dylan. Cate had kept everyone so far at arm's length she didn't really have any close friends of her own, and it was nice having someone new to spend her time with.

Harry was the first person she'd ever let break down some of her carefully built walls. He was both understanding and patient, despite her secretiveness towards her past, and their friendship grew incredibly stronger over the few months that followed. So much so, that a year later when Dylan raised the issue of them moving again, Cate told her no.

"I've had enough, Dylan. We've been stuck on Earth for years, and we don't know for how much longer. I couldn't bear losing everything I've made here as well," she told her best friend. They both knew she meant Harry, and Cate blushed at the admittance of just how much he meant to her.

Dylan already knew how close they were. Just because they weren't in a sexual relationship didn't mean they weren't obviously a close couple. Their connection to one another shone so clearly when they were together that everybody but the pair of them seemed to see how perfect they could be together. Most people often mistook them for boyfriend and girlfriend, mistaking how natural and easy their deep friendship was. Dylan was the only one who knew why Cate wouldn't admit her feelings for Harry, even to herself. She couldn't stand to put him in harm's way by taking things any further, regardless of the strong bond she had with him—too strong. He was in love with her, they all knew, but he'd to keep that unspoken truth firmly pushed to one side to make things easier on her. Cate knew it had to be hard on him, but made it clear he wasn't to push the boundaries.

"Okay, we'll stay," Dylan agreed, and seeing Cate's face light up thanks to her words was bittersweet. It seemed the tides were changing, and she desperately hoped Harry wouldn't bear the brunt of Lucifer's anger when those waves finally collided.

Cate and Harry continued spending almost all of their spare time together. He kept her company during her shifts, and she took him out for long walks to try and help clear his head of all the medical terminology he'd been studying relentlessly. They often went out for meals together in their favourite restaurants, all the while chatting and getting to know each other even more. Cate regaled him with her knowledge of languages and history, while Harry taught her about sports and educated her about the movies he was shocked to discover she'd never seen. Their shared love was music, and her face lit up when he reeled off a list of his top bands, many of which were her favourites, too.

Harry was open and honest about everything. He told her about his childhood and his family, as well as his hopes for the future, while Cate had to lie about everything she'd been through in her life. It was the first time she'd ever regretted not being able to share the part of herself that was so important, yet so scary. She was positive that revealing the truth would either make him concerned for her mental health, or too scared to remain friends with her. Either way, she and Dylan would then be forced out of Avebury and she would lose him forever.

When Harry finally asked her one night about the black diamond ring she still wore despite all her years away from her husband, and Cate couldn't even bring herself to look down at the dark stone that signified her union with Lucifer. Instead she rubbed it absentmindedly with her index finger. He'd already tried asking about her previous relationships before, and she always tried to skirt around it. This time though, she decided to tell him just a few details about her former lovers.

"Well my first boyfriend, Devin, was a wonderful man," she revealed. "I loved him very much, but one day I fell for someone else—Luke. When he came into the picture I just couldn't say no." She had to stifle her laugh at those words, thinking just how literal they were. "He and I were, and still are, each other's soulmates. He stole me away and turned my world upside down," she told him, and Harry's face dropped. What she'd told him wasn't too far from the fundamental truth, and although she hated hurting him, Cate needed to let him know just why she was so unavailable. She'd referred to Lucifer as Luke, his normal alias from his visits to Earth, and it felt strange talking of him again after such a long time.

The way she spoke about him spoke volumes to Harry, who knew she was still in love with him. This 'Luke' was the reason she and Harry weren't together. She was pining for a man who wasn't even around, and he hated him for somehow still commanding her heart. After a few moments of awkward silence, he finally asked her the one question that was burning away at his insides.

"So why aren't you together now?" he said, with a cold and bitter edge to his voice he couldn't hide, but he needed to know.

"Something, or should I say *someone*, always manages to come between two people in love," Cate told him. Her eyes were so sad, but he didn't stop her. She continued, telling Harry just a little bit about her last partner, despite how hard it was to talk of him and her most recent heartbreak. "I have no excuse for it. He seduced me and I fell for all of his lies. I learned my lesson there, and eventually realised just how manipulative and controlling he truly was, but by then I'd already lost everything," Cate told him, fighting back the tears.

She then confided a little more in Harry, knowing she could trust him. "Nina and I had to move away. We needed to run from him. That's why I'm so careful now," she added, but couldn't really say any more. She'd skimmed over the fine details as much as possible, being careful not to get Harry too intrigued in the crazy history behind her sad eyes. She couldn't bear to talk about it in any further detail anyway, or risk giving too much away about her love triangle of darkness and light.

It finally seemed to register then. Harry knew for sure just why she'd closed herself off to men. Cate had always known that he liked her, and deep down she also knew that she really liked him back, which was all the more reason she couldn't let herself fall again. When the time came that Lucifer would return for her,

Cate knew full well what fate would befall any human who might've dared touch her, let alone having loved her. Lucifer would want to take out his fury in one way or another, and would surely not go easy on Harry if he found out that the pair of them had been together during their separation. Cate cared too much about him to let him suffer because of her foolish actions, so was surer than ever just how much she had to keep their affection for each other locked away.

A few weeks later, Dylan and her current girlfriend, a young woman named Sophie, begged Cate and Harry to go with them to a music festival. Cate still loved listening to her favourite bands. It was a passion she'd almost forgotten while in Hell, but one that she and Dylan had rekindled since they'd been living their human-like lives on Earth again.

They travelled for a few hours by car to a huge field in the countryside that'd been transformed into a massive arena with three stages. After they arrived at the huge site and pitched their tents, they quickly got ready and donned their boots before heading off in the direction of the loud rock music.

Cate loved every minute of it, and quickly remembered just why she loved live music so much. She crashed around happily with the throbbing crowd and sang along with the bands as the various artists played. Harry joined her in the throng and grabbed Cate's hand protectively, standing close behind to ensure she didn't get washed away or hurt by the masses that surrounded the pair of them.

Their electricity was immense, and the feel of Harry's hand in hers gave Cate a long forgotten pang in her once empty heart. He leaned closer and sang the deep and heartfelt words to a delicate, acoustic song in her ear.

"I want you, I need you. Be mine," he sung, and the lyrics made her heart pound as he whispered them, while his breath sent shivers down her spine as it tickled her skin. "I'm crazy, I'm lost. Hold me, be mine."

She turned and looked up at him, suddenly forgetting about the dancing, and peered up into Harry's gorgeous blue eyes. She didn't pull back this time, and knew she couldn't push him away again. Cate quickly realised that she didn't even want to anymore.

She looked into his warm face and climbed up onto her tiptoes to inch closer, before hesitantly caressing his lips with hers. Harry kissed her back with every ounce of unspoken desire he'd kept at arm's length for so long, and he wrapped his arms around her waist while hers went up around his neck. They swayed together, enveloped tightly by the heavy crowd, and they caressed each other tenderly. Cate let him hold her closer to him, and by the time he let go, she was buzzing. She was so happy, and enjoyed the carefree adoration as they embraced one another and took that next step at long last. Rational thought was long gone, and she let her heart rule her head for the first time in her entire existence. What she had with Harry was unlike anything she'd known before, and yet it was somehow more terrifying.

Harry cherished every moment, and held her close for the rest of the afternoon. He didn't ever want to let her go, and hoped to God she would never leave him or push him away again. The rest of the first day at the festival went by in a blur, but all the while Cate and Harry were inseparable. They simply couldn't let go of each other, not that either of them tried. He knew she needed to take things slowly, but didn't mind at all, and lapped up her affection as she allowed him in at long last. They danced for hours, and didn't stop when the rain lashed down and clagged their boots in mud. She seemed happier than he'd ever seen her, and it was a thrill knowing he'd been the one to put that smile on her beautiful face. Harry knew he'd remember their day for the rest of his life.

Later that night as the music began to die down and the crowds of festivalgoers returned to their tents, someone gave Cate a tap on the shoulder. She'd been stood talking with Harry off to the side of the now quiet stage, waiting for Dylan and Sophie to come back from a run to the beer tent, and she jumped. She turned to look at who'd interrupted them with a scowl. It was one of the burly bouncers she'd seen watching the crowd earlier, but who now stared down at her with a seemingly forced smile.

"Hi, how would you two like a free VIP wristbands?" he asked her and Harry, lifting up two thick, red cotton bands, and she could make out the promised upgraded access that was embossed along it in black writing. The bands would allow them admission to the special, behind the scenes area where she knew many of the band members were now hanging out, and Harry nearly jumped out of his skin with excitement. However, Cate just smiled and shook her head. She'd been taught well by her magical best friend, and was suspicious of the man's motives.

"No, but thank you," she replied, taking Harry by his arm and starting to walk away.

"These usually only go to the band members and their entourages, you two are very lucky to have even been offered them," the man answered back teasingly, but she saw through his façade. He wasn't going to take no for an answer, and there had to be a reason for it. Cate tried to search the dissipating crowd for Dylan, but she was nowhere to be seen. She could tell Harry couldn't understand her hesitance, and so she took a look inside the VIP area behind the man, where she caught a pair of dark eyes watching her from a dimly lit tent. They called to her, summoning her closer. Curious, she finally conceded.

"Okay, go on then," she said, and they put on their bands and followed the burly man through the gate into the VIP area. They were quickly led over to where one of the rock bands they'd been watching on the stage just an hour or so before were sitting having a drink together. Harry was immediately star struck, and shook hands with them all before chatting animatedly to the lead guitarist about how much he loved their new album. Cate smiled and greeted them all as well, but quickly sat down next to the band's lead singer and the owner of that intense stare she'd locked eyes with minutes before. He was none other than her old friend, the demon Berith. He looked different to the last time she'd seen him, but knew right from the moment she'd found herself in his presence it was him. Cate didn't quite know how to act or what to say, but it was Berith who spoke first, saving her the worry.

"Well, then. Hasn't it been such a terribly long time, my Queen?" he asked her with a wry, knowing grin. He took care to keep his voice low in front of the humans he was now associating with, and she was glad he seemed intent on keeping their secret. His long dark hair fell to his shoulders messily, but he was clean-shaven now, and looked almost like a normal human, apart from his array of new tattoos and piercings. "There are an awful lot of different beings looking for you in this big wide world, and in those above and below. I can see now just why they haven't had any luck," he added, grinning broadly while looking Cate up and down, as though seeing something she couldn't. Berith's brow furrowed, and he seemed distant for a moment, but then shook off whatever memory had stirred in his ancient mind.

"What do you mean?" she asked, and had to wonder what it was he was looking at. "You can see me though, and you knew it was me, didn't you?"

"Yes, Hecate. I knew it was you," Berith answered, and his dark brown eyes bore into hers as he leaned in closer. Cate could tell he was finding it hard to explain how or why he could sense her, and wondered if he knew the answer himself. "I cannot see your true form, it has somehow been hidden. Those looking for the Dark Queen will not be able to find you as you are now; the spell concealing your nature is so strong they would pass you in the street. I see you today as just an ordinary human girl. The darkness that lies beneath that guise is well hidden by both magic and by light power that still courses through your veins. It's as though the combination of the two has blocked your powers and true presence from coming through, despite the passing of time," he told her with a clearly confused look on his face.

"Then, how did you know it was me?" she asked, glancing over to Harry and giving him a smile as he continued chatting away happily with two long haired, black clothed, band members.

"I never forget a pretty face, whether human or otherwise, and especially one as infamous as yours, your highness," Berith told her with a quiet laugh. "I was drawn to you instantly, and liked watching you have fun. You do know I am bound to report this back to my master when I can next have an audience with him?" he added, looking over to Harry and then back at Cate, and he gave her a knowing look. "All of this—including what I saw the pair of you doing in the crowd today." Cate's stomach dropped. She could kick herself. Of course the one day she'd let her guard down would be the day she'd get caught. Wasn't that just her luck?

"I've not cheated on Lucifer with him," Cate told the demon quietly and calmly. Her green eyes peered over at him, pleading with him to believe her. "There would be no need to anger my husband with unnecessary bad news, not when we can finally be reunited at last. How might I convince you to leave out the part of the story that involves the human, and keep my reunion with Lucifer a wholly joyous occasion?" she asked hopefully, and

Berith nodded solemnly. "I've tried to gain access to the churches, and even went to the old penthouse in London, but there was no one there. Please tell him I tried everything I could," Cate implored him further. "But, I couldn't get into the church, the light inside me blocked my darkness, and I couldn't cross over the threshold. The only reason I had to hide away is because the white witches would take me back up there if they caught me, and I couldn't. I...I just couldn't. Please old friend?"

Berith pushed a stay lock of dark hair behind Cate's ear with his hand, and she looked up into his almost black eyes, feeling slightly uncomfortable beneath his gaze. He smiled and then leaned closer, whispering into her ear.

"I understand completely. I tell you what, sell me your soul and my lips are sealed," he offered, then sat back and grinned, seemingly to enjoy watching Cate squirm as she mulled over his incomprehensible proposal.

CHAPTER TWENTY-TWO

"It is not mine to give, you know that," Cate told him, disturbed somewhat by Berith's lack of loyalty to her husband.

"True," he admitted, and then pondered on it for a moment. "Okay, well how about we just go with one good, hard, fuck?"

"You do realise you'd be tortured for all eternity by your Dark King?" she replied, smirking over at him now as she realised he was just messing with her.

"True," he replied again, and then thought about it for a moment. "A kiss?"

"Still dodgy ground, don't you think?" Cate replied with a shrug. She was so relieved he'd been kidding, and gave him a playful smack on the shoulder.

"Okay, well how about a kiss off your friend over there instead?" he asked, and Cate was surprised he wanted a kiss from Harry. She hadn't heard of him taking male lovers before. Then, she followed Berith's gaze to the opening of the VIP area, where Dylan stood glaring over at them with her hands on her hips, and she was clearly angry as hell.

***

"I'll keep your friend out of it," Berith told Cate the next morning as he hugged her goodbye. "Granted that nothing else happens between the pair of you, I will never tell. But you know he has ways of finding out the truth even in the dark corners of our minds," he added, and Cate knew she had to be careful, but nodded solemnly. She hoped the demon was adept at disguising his thoughts, and just hoped that Lucifer would be so distracted by their reunion that he wouldn't be interested in hunting Harry down. She would make sure to keep him well occupied.

Berith had gotten much more than just a kiss from the promiscuous Dylan and her open-minded girlfriend the night before, and seemed more than willing to help his Queen get back to her King's arms safely. She gave him a small, folded piece of paper with the address written inside for the flat she shared with Dylan, which Berith slipped in his pocket and then he gave her a nod. Cate knew it wouldn't be long until her husband knew that his wife was safe, and how she was ready to see him. The realisation that her exile might all be over at last left Cate feeling both scared and excited all at the same time.

"Deal," she promised the demon. "And, make sure you tell him I love him."

"I will," he smiled and climbed aboard the tour bus, waving goodbye to Dylan as they drove off.

Cate heaved a sigh of relief, but she couldn't be too happy to have found a way home at last. Her body yearned for the freedom she'd discovered the day before while wrapped in the arms of a man who wasn't her husband. She felt like crying.

"Wow, how amazing was that?" Harry asked loudly as he joined them. He'd been walking on air the entire night and was still buzzing thanks to his first VIP experience, and had no idea Berith's unwitting followers had been commanded to keep him occupied while they talked. She and Dylan laughed, but hooked their arms in his and led Harry back into the crowd so they could enjoy the final day of the music festival. They'd been able to keep the VIP passes so watched from just in front of the stage as a handful of bands finished off the wonderful weekend. Cate felt terrible for having led Harry on, but knew she had to push him away again. There was no doubt about it now. Lucifer would come for her soon, and she knew that Harry had to be far away from her when he did.

He could sense Cate's coolness straight away, and tried not to let it show that he was bothered by it. She barely looked at him as the music played, and didn't seem half the woman she'd been the day before. It was as though she was too lost in thought to even enjoy herself, and she didn't go anywhere near him, as though she was scared he might try and pick up where they'd left off the night before. Harry quickly realised she'd pulled away again, and thought perhaps the tiny amount intimacy from the previous day was all he was ever going to get from the beautiful woman he desired so very much. He wondered if maybe it was just time to let her go, and save himself the torment of loving this unattainable girl. Better to walk away than get his heart broken, but he feared the damage there had already been done. Dylan sensed their silent disconnection too, and gave Cate a supportive squeeze as they watched the finale.

"It's the only way," she whispered in her ear, and she wiped away a stray tear that rolled down Cate's cheek as the realisation finally hit her. They returned to the camping area in silence, dismantled the tents quickly, and then made their way home. Cate closed her eyes all the way back, and felt utterly exhausted. She slept a little, but also wanted the quiet time to think over everything life had thrown at her so far, wondering what she'd ever done to warrant all the heartache that seemed fated for her.

Dylan drove while chatting away to Sophie in the front seat, and Harry just sat in silence, watching the world whiz by out the car window beside him.

***

The next few weeks were agonising for Cate while she waited for the moon to become full. She wondered if Lucifer would even come for her when it did, but truly hoped he was planning on it. She was unsure whether she could even go home or not when he finally did come to take her back to Hell, but knew she had to try. Life on Earth hadn't been terrible, especially the past few years, but now she was ready to leave it all behind. She hadn't seen Harry since the music festival, and knew he'd stayed away on purpose. He didn't answer her calls, avoided her when she tried to intercept him at the supermarket, and in the end, Cate decided to write him a letter. He needed to know that she was planning to move away again soon, and that he shouldn't try to look for her.

Dear Harry,

I'm truly sorry for my behaviour. I never meant to lead you on and I will regret hurting you for the rest of my miserable existence. You deserve the chance to find someone who can love you and put that love above all others. I tried to tell you as much as I could about my past, but you just wouldn't have understood if I told you everything. I cannot be with you, and I cannot keep you safe or make you happy.

Nina and I are moving away again soon, and please do not try to find me. It's better if you just forget about me completely. Live your life to the fullest Harry, and I hope you find your soulmate.

Goodbye.

It pained her to push him away so forcefully, but it was for his own good. For his safety, she'd do it.

On the night of the next full moon, Cate waited at home in the hope that her husband would come to her. But for some reason though, Lucifer didn't appear during that full moon, nor the next, and she began to fear that he'd rejected her. She tried to call to him, and to summon Berith to her side, but it was no use. Her powers were still blocked, and she had no way of knowing if or when Lucifer would decide to find her. Cate felt so lost and alone, and couldn't settle her body or mind. Dylan tried to help, offering her support and comfort while never leaving her side, but nothing eased her, and she felt miserable again, just like she had in the hall outside the penthouse.

Cate reached out to Harry, foolishly she knew, but she couldn't help herself. She was so damned desperate to see a friendly face, but he still refused to return her messages. Cate hadn't received any response from the brutal letter she'd sent, or the texts and voicemails she left for him since. She'd ruined the best thing she'd ever had, and it broke her heart in two knowing he was done with her. Dylan kept on telling Cate that it was for the best, but she felt miserable knowing she really had lost him so completely.

***

When the next full moon shone in the night's sky, Cate was sick of waiting in the flat, so agreed to do a shift working at the pub. She kept busy, clearing the tables, and re-stocking the fridges, all the while dispensing with the small talk. She was so morose that hadn't felt the shift in pressures, or the darkness that'd begun creeping in around the small village. The patrons were even gambling more readily in the bar's fruit machines as the night drew darker; giving into their greed while others drank more than usual in their gluttony. Cate continued to busy herself with cleaning and tidying the bar area, instead of noticing the men and women who were flirting more openly in the corners of the room, so ready to commit sin as though being influenced somehow.

"Whisky on the rocks please," a voice said from just inside the doorway, and her heart immediately fluttered wildly at the oh-so familiar sound. She knew it was Lucifer before even seeing him, and turned slowly to face her husband as he wandered into the pub just like any other Friday night drinker.

He looked fantastic, dressed in black jeans and a grey t-shirt teamed with heavy military style boots and the same cargo jacket he'd been wearing the first night she'd met him. It was strange how much she remembered from that night so long ago, and how different their lives together had become since then. His blue eyes were dark and brooding, and he didn't take them off Cate's for even a second as he took her in, despite her being aware he was undoubtedly reading every mind in the room.

She could hardly breathe. Her mouth opened and closed as though she wanted to say something, but she was unable to find the words to even start their long and hard journey back to each other. Lucifer smiled across at her, taking Cate's breath away again, and she dropped the glass she'd been holding, but didn't even register the smash as it hit the ground and shattered at the her feet.

"You're here," she said in a whisper, finding her voice at last.

"I'm here," he confirmed, walking through the crowd with a smile before coming around behind the bar so that he could stop within inches of his trembling wife. She still had no powers, but could feel the electricity passing between them as though it were lightning, and Cate knew then that neither of them had lost their love for one another despite their years of having been forced apart. "Your housemate didn't want to give up your location, my love. She wanted to bring me to you herself, but I made her an offer she simply couldn't refuse," Lucifer told her after a couple of silent seconds. His words sent her into immediate panic, and she began worrying for Dylan's safety.

She peered up into his warm face pleadingly. "Don't worry," he told her, and a gruff laugh escaped his lips. "Berith told me everything. She's been rewarded for keeping you safe." He took her face in his hands, staring deeply into Cate's green eyes. "She's joined the dark coven. Dylan's perfectly fine."

She let out a sigh of relief, her head going fuzzy as she accepted his explanation. Her body screamed out for her lover and she stared back up at him, willing him to take her home. But, they didn't go. His defeated sigh a few seconds later gave away Lucifer's frustration, and she could tell he'd just tried to teleport her away, but couldn't. He looked down at Cate, seeming just as desperate to reignite their flame, and he gave away his only weakness—her.

She reached up and touched her King's cheek tenderly with her hand, and revelled in his touch and embrace after such a long and lonely time.

"I'm so sorry, for everything," she said, staring up at him, and Lucifer smiled warmly back down at her. He kissed her palm and then put it back against his cheek.

"I know," was all he could reply, and then leaned down to kiss her lips tenderly at last.

"Well, if we can't go home. Perhaps we can go somewhere more private?" she asked him, and giggled excitedly as Lucifer gathered her up in his arms and carried her from the pub. None of the patrons seemed to have even noticed the dark entity that'd been among them, or the fact that Cate had then disappeared off into the night with him. She didn't care, and assumed that he must've been working some kind of mind control power on all of them, ensuring they had privacy during their wonderful reunion, and was glad for it.

They walked quickly, hand-in-hand in silence, revelling in each other's company at last as they headed across the village towards the flat. In her hurry, Cate then fumbled with the keys for a moment before her impatient husband grabbed them from her, flung the door open, and pulled her inside. Lucifer wasted no more time, and he pinned Cate to the wall with his strong body. He kissed her deeply as he ran his hands through her long, dark hair. One arm came down and grabbed her left thigh, pulling her body up into his strong arms and towards him as they kissed.

Cate relished in his strength as he devoured her. She was so weak before him, but gave every part of herself to her lover, willing him to possess her entirely. He pulled her other leg up and around his waist, and pushed her harder into the wall. The world turned upside down for Cate and she gasped for breath in his arms. Her body screamed for his, and she thrust her hips forwards, wrapping her thighs tighter around Lucifer and gripping him eagerly. He then carried her to her room in his arms and dropped down on the bed, allowing her to straddle him as they continued to kiss lasciviously.

She leaned back, gasping for air and giving him access to her neck, and he kissed it eagerly, popping open her black shirt as he kissed lower and lower down Cate's chest. Her top was quickly discarded, and Lucifer moved on to unclip her bra, and sent that flying across the room also. He cupped her tender breasts, tweaking her nipples with his fingertips as Cate gasped and then lunged forward into another deep kiss.

He fell back onto the duvet, and she followed, straddling him as he lay beneath her. She arched her body over his, and began pulling his shirt up over his head, before then tossing it to the floor beside the bed. She took the time to kiss each of Lucifer's nipples, suckling gently on his sensitive peaks as he groaned. Her kisses then moved further down to his toned stomach muscles, licking and kissing every ripple that she could get to. Her hands moved to his belt, undoing the metal clasp and pulling the leather strap free, before opening Lucifer's fly and gripping the hems of his jeans and boxers with her small hands. She looked up to her lover with a grin, and then pulled down, slipping off his clothes and releasing his ready erection in the process. It'd been so long, and she was ravenous for him, ready for the pleasure, and even the pain, if that was what it took to show her husband what he meant to her.

Cate began sucking his tip gently, taking more and more of him in her mouth with each pull, but it wasn't long until Lucifer reached down to stop her. After stroking her face gently, he demanded that she remove her skirt and knickers. She stood at the bedside and obliged her King, of course, and felt sexy as hell giving him a striptease.

He sat up, watching her eagerly before ushering her to straddle him again. Cate climbed onto Lucifer's lap, but he didn't enter her right away. Instead he kissed his wife with insatiable passion one more time, before leaning back and letting his powerful guise slip a little.

"Don't ever leave me again," he told her. His tone was more of a command than a request, and Cate stopped her barrage of kisses. She stared deep into Lucifer's eyes, and sensed the pain and hurt in them.

"Never," she told him honestly, before kissing his lips softly.

Lucifer grabbed Cate and lifted her up by the thighs. The opening of her wet, ready cleft was just millimetres from his hard cock, and she let out a groan of anticipation. He held her there for a few moments longer, refusing to give her what she desperately craved—what she needed. Not yet. He delighted in drawing out her pleasure, keeping her from him, while he made himself even clearer in his commandment.

"Never," he demanded again, his eyes swirling with black flecks and expression ominous. "You are mine, Hecate. Forever." Cate stared lovingly into Lucifer's gaze, holding it, and she made sure she didn't hesitate for even a second.

"Forever," she promised him, kissing the tip of his nose as Lucifer dropped her onto his hard length. She cried out as the stretching feeling of him inside created both the pleasure and pain she'd anticipated, but refused to stop. She might be weak and feeble—as good as human—but it wasn't going to stop her giving her lover everything she'd just promised, and more.

He lifted Cate, up and down, faster and harder, with his powerful arms. She had no control, even though she was the one on top, and lost all conscious thought as he pummelled her from below. Lucifer lifted her effortlessly and sent her crashing down hard onto his hard-on, again and again. Her muscles throbbed and tensed inside, enveloping her master greedily, and he grinned as he watched her come undone. She climaxed hard and intensely, but he pushed her on even faster, unrelentingly, until he reached his own glorious end. The walls shook around them and Cate cried out as another intense orgasm seemed to ripple throughout not only her entire body, but also her very soul. Lucifer emptied into her and held her close. He watched her as they came down from their joint high, not willing to let go of his true love ever again.

They stayed in bed together, making love well into the next

day. Cate's fragile body struggled to keep up with Lucifer's powerful sexual prowess, but she couldn't stop even if for some reason she'd wanted to. They both had a lot of catching up to do, and she was pretty sure Lucifer wanted to fill her with as much darkness as he could in order to try and take her home with him before the moon waned. If she still couldn't travel home then, he'd have no other choice than to leave her there until the next full moon, and both of them hated the sheer thought of it.

"I can't bear the prospect of being alone in Hell without you again, not even for a day. Let alone another month," Lucifer told her, and Cate nodded.

"Now that I've found you again, I won't be able to survive without you, Lucifer. I need you to take me home," she mumbled, snuggling against him beneath the sheets. It felt good to be in his arms again, and she knew she couldn't leave them again.

A loud knock at the door to the flat that afternoon disturbed their satiated peace following another epic bout of lovemaking. Although Cate had said to ignore it, Lucifer couldn't help his mischievous self. He had to go and see who it was, and hoped it might be a disgruntled neighbour coming to complain about all the sexual noises that he could mess with. He pulled on his jeans and slicked back his tousled hair before heading to the door, while Cate hastily tried to get herself dressed.

Harry stood in the doorway to the flat, having hoped that Cate would be the one behind the door as it was quickly pulled open. He was shocked to see the half-naked man standing before him, but immediately presumed he must be there with her sister. Lucifer stared at him expectantly, both scaring and intimidating Harry without having uttered a single word.

"Urm, is Dana here?" he eventually asked. Trying to hide the look of disgust that crossed his face when Lucifer smirked over at him.

"She's a bit, *busy*," he replied, eyeing Harry curiously. "But, please come on in." He opened the door wider, ushering their guest inside. He wanted to read him, to figure out his connection with Cate, but needed to make contact in order to properly read the human boy's thoughts and memories.

Harry hesitated in the doorway for a second, but Lucifer

smiled insistently, doing his best to come across as warm and friendly. It didn't seem to be working. Harry frowned, but eventually went inside and headed through to the living room, where he took a seat and stared down at his hands awkwardly.

"Beer?" Lucifer asked him, standing over him still only half dressed.

"It's two o'clock in the afternoon?" Harry answered, but quickly changed his mind when he saw that Lucifer didn't care what the time was. "Actually, yeah please," he quickly corrected his attitude and smiled up at his host uncomfortably.

Cate came running in from the bedroom, looking from Lucifer to Harry and back in silent anticipation. She didn't quite know how to tackle this, and decided to say nothing, yet. She raised her hand to Harry in an embarrassed half wave, and then followed Lucifer into the kitchen, where she watched as he grabbed a couple of beers from the fridge. Cate took a tall bottle from the fridge's door, poured herself a large glass of Chardonnay, and took a big gulp. Lucifer eyed her; curious as to why she was so nervous.

"Friend of yours, darling?" he asked her quietly, with an accusatory tone clear in his voice.

"Yes, and just that," she replied, placing a hand on Lucifer's chest, and she stared him in the eye solemnly. He gave nothing away as he peered back down at her; he simply grabbed the beers and left the kitchen without another word, while Cate trailed behind him in her tracksuit bottoms and t-shirt. They re-joined Harry in the living room again, and she tried to seem relaxed as she made the introductions.

"Harry, this is Luke," she told him, and Harry understood immediately. He nodded and took a long swig of the cold beer. Funnily enough, he was now glad to have said yes to a proper drink after all.

"Her husband," Lucifer added. He watched the pair of them keenly, but hated not being able to read either of them enough to know for sure if there was something he was missing. His senses were off thanks to the intense reunion with Cate, and he was struggling to tap into Harry's mind from afar. Lucifer put his hand out to him, wanting the physical contact so that he could properly search the boy's memories.

Cate had to stop herself from intercepting the connection. It was the last thing she wanted, but knew that it would look much worse if she intervened. She had to let it happen, and would face whatever consequences came her way once it was done. She was tired of running, and remained still as Harry reached up and shook her husband's outstretched hand in his. They only kept contact for a couple of seconds, but it was enough. Lucifer knew everything.

CHAPTER TWENTY-THREE

The three of them made small talk for a little while, but when the time came for Harry to go, he was relieved. He didn't like Luke at all, and thought he wasn't at all the way she'd described him. He seemed the possessive, controlling type, and was a pretty scary guy, if he were completely honest. Harry was glad he'd had the chance to make his excuses and leave, and knew for sure that this really was their last goodbye. Cate saw him out, and hugged him tightly. Their awkward final exchange left him feeling depressed and anxious though, rather than getting the closure he had desperately hoped for, but he left without another word or even a backwards glance. She'd made her choice weeks ago, and he'd given up fighting for her.

Cate made her way back to the living room where Lucifer sat, calmly finishing off his beer and fiddling with the paper label. She cautiously stood near the doorway but didn't say a word, waiting for his reaction to Harry's visit. She watched him closely, sensing his rage, but wasn't sure how to act or what to say. A second later, the now empty beer bottle came hurtling across the room, and it smashed just inches from Cate's head.

She squeezed her eyes shut as the shards scattered nearby, and by the time she'd opened them again, Lucifer was standing right in front of her, inches from her face. He pinned her to the wall with his strong body, but there was nothing exciting about his hold this time. His hand gripped her by the throat, holding on tightly, and he pulled her face closer to his as his blackened eyes bore into hers.

"You kissed him!" he growled, and Cate could feel him shaking with anger, the powerful rage threatening to burst out of him if she said the wrong thing in response.

"It was only that one day. I was just so alone, Lucifer. So desperate. It was nothing but a big mistake," she cried, and her voice sounded hoarse thanks to his tight grip he had around her throat.

"He's in love with you, Cate. Do you love him back?" he shouted, thumping the back of her head hard into the plaster, and she winced but didn't cry out. His other fist came around a moment later, and in his rage he smashed a hole the size of a bowling ball through the wall behind her.

"No, you know that. You must've read his mind!" Cate eventually cried out, desperate to make him understand. "It was one moment of weakness, and it didn't happen again. I was never with him, ever." The tears streamed down her face as she pleaded, begging him to believe her words and trust that they were true. He might not have been able to read her own thoughts any more, but surely Harry's version of events was clear enough?

Lucifer stared at her, seemingly absorbing her words and working over her explanation in his head. He was so still, unblinking and unflinching, as he processed it all in his mind. Cate had to try and bring him back to her again, to calm him and to loosen his hand that still was wrapped tight around her neck. "Please, Lucifer," Cate begged, her voice quiet again. "You're hurting me." His grip on her released at once, and he backed away a few steps.

He'd read Dylan's thoughts before going to the pub to meet his wife, and was aware of the friendship Cate had with Harry, but he hadn't realised just how strong the pair's bond was. Harry was completely in love with her. He was consumed by it, but she'd never realised just how strong his feelings were. She was telling the truth though, and Lucifer knew that she'd pushed Harry away at his every advance, except for that one day. The image of the pair of them together echoed painfully in his mind though. It was one of the down sides to seeing into another person's head he knew all too well, and he had to force the shared thought away.

He knew from those memories he'd just plucked from Harry's mind that they really were only friends, and yet Lucifer couldn't help but still feel angry at their connection. Perhaps it was sheer jealousy that they were so close, he wasn't sure. He honestly didn't know how to even begin processing all the things that'd happened to Cate in the years since she'd been taken from him at the beach, but he knew for sure they needed to get her home again during this full moon. The thought of leaving her there with her 'friend' angered him further, and a flash of rage came bubbling to the surface uncontrollably.

"If I ever see that boy again, he will wish for death. He'll beg me for mercy, and you know he will not get it. Is that understood?" She nodded, the sobs escaping from her uncontrollably as she peered up at her master. His eyes soon turned back to their usual deep blue, and he smiled down at her as though nothing had happened. "Good. Now, let's go back to bed."

Lucifer took Cate's hand and led her back through to her small bedroom. She followed, but was still shaken and needed some time to calm down. Cate had to sort herself out before she could even think about forgetting that whole thing had just happened and carry on as they were.

"Give me a minute, okay?" she asked, excusing herself for a few much needed minutes alone in the bathroom. She stared at her reflection in the mirror, refusing to let herself cry, despite the more than willing emotions that threatened to burst out of her. She splashed her face with cool water and then dried it with a nearby towel, heaving a huge sigh into the cotton.

Cate thought back to her wonderful days with Lucifer before Uriel had come between them. She thought of their fantastic wedding and romantic honeymoon, as well as their happy reunion just the night before, and smiled to herself again. Lucifer was her true love, and she decided then and there that she'd never dwell on her memories of Harry ever again.

Thanks to the flood of happiness that filled her soul again, it wasn't long until she felt ready to face her husband again, and she wandered back into the bedroom. Cate looked over at Lucifer as he lay on the bed reading one of her magazines. He was his usual calm self once again, while she was still a little bruised by his actions, both on the outside and on the inside.

He knew she was hurting, despite her best efforts to hide it, and took her in his arms as she joined him on the bed, embracing Cate tightly.

"I love you so much, my Queen. It feels like a century since I last held you in my arms. I want to murder anyone that so much as even looks at you," he told her honestly, needing Cate to understand his anger towards her relationship with Harry.

"I know. But I'm yours, my King. Always and forever," Cate assured him with a smile. "I love you."

"I love you, too."

Rather than urge her back into bed, Lucifer then ran Cate a bath to soothe her weak and aching body. She slipped into the hot, soapy water, and groaned happily, making him laugh. He joined her, sitting opposite Cate and massaging her feet as she soaked for a few minutes with her eyes closed. He took her in, watching his wife as she relaxed. She was so beautiful, vulnerable, and human-like without her powers, but mesmerising. Her dark curls spread out around her in the water, clinging to her pale skin and she still looked so young, almost innocent and pure.

Cate reminded him of the night she'd first come to meet him in the dark church. Her features were still soft and delicate despite all the years she'd lived and the hardships she'd faced. Lucifer's mind was racing with questions, but he couldn't bear to ask her yet what Uriel had wanted of her up on that astral plain. However, he knew by the still strong light he could sense inside of her that the whole truth might be more than he could ever handle knowing, and thought perhaps he'd never ask. He wanted to forget the last chapter of their lives completely, to wipe out the last seventeen years that'd been terrible for them both, but he knew there was no way. For now, he would settle for having her back in his arms, and back in Hell where she belonged.

There was only one way he thought for sure that he could rid Cate's body of all of the lightness and fill it entirely with his dark power once again. Lucifer sat forward, startling her awake, but then she opened her eyes and smiled over at him as he peered down at her with a broad grin.

"How do you feel about giving me a child, Cate?" he asked, and she stared up at him, her eyes opening wider. The dread-inspiring words brought her crashing back to Earth from her restful state, and she swallowed the lump that'd formed in her throat. Cate sat up and leaned forward so she could look into his eyes. She wanted to feel his *expression*, to understand his motives, but her lack of power seemed to be stopping their wordless connection. He had to tell her more. She needed to know more.

"Why?" she asked him, eager to know before she could even fathom being able to answer him.

"I'm ready to be a proper father, my love. You're the only woman for me, and I want you to give me full-blooded heir. Our child would make our reunion complete, and I'm positive it'd make us whole again," he said, looking over at her with an open and earnest expression on his gorgeous face. "Also, I have no doubt that having a good dose of my darkness along with my child inside you would ensure you could travel home safely. And once we're there, you'll be able to work on getting your powers back, once and for all," he added.

"And we'd all stay there together?" she had to ask.

"Forever," Lucifer answered, and it was all Cate needed to know before she made her decision. She stared over at him, open-mouthed and completely taken aback by his honesty, but was so incredibly happy he'd opened up to her about his feelings.

She knew now that his desire for a child hadn't been because of any need to have power or control over her. It was only about his love and how he wanted to strengthen their bond. She thought back to their conversations about children from a long time ago, and remembered how scary the idea of having a family was to her back then. Now though, things had changed. She had changed, and while she wanted nothing more than to go home and be loved and happy by Lucifer's side, Cate knew that she was finally ready to give her love to a child of her own as well. She knew she needed to earn her husband's trust and respect back, but also that she wanted to rid herself of the goddamn light Uriel had forced inside of her. Cate was ready to regain her dark powers again, and agreed that this had to be the best way to do it.

"Yes," she told Lucifer after settling her thoughts, looking back at him with a huge smile. "Of course, it's a yes."

Lucifer sprang towards her in the hot water, sloshing it over the sides of the bath and onto the floor accidentally as he pulled Cate into his arms, but neither cared for the mess. He then laid her back in the warm water, kissing her eagerly, and didn't care about anything other than her and their future. Sliding inside Cate's welcoming body was effortless in the warm water, and it felt so right, so natural.

She gasped as he thrust hard into her ready and willing opening, and whispered her affirmation over and over again in his ear between her deep kisses. He plunged into her eager cleft over and over again, and she was lost in his heat, his hungriness, and his desire for her.

The room span around them as they came together, and Cate cried his name as Lucifer lifted her out of the suds and emptied into her with a powerful thrust that caused her entire body to tremble beneath him. Their bodies seemed in perfect sync again, and the world around them struggled to catch up. She'd never been happier.

"I only have a few more hours left," Lucifer told Cate a while later when they stood drying themselves off, and he climbed under the sheets of her bed. It was almost midnight, and Cate knew he'd have to be gone by sunrise. She looked over at the all-powerful man beside her, taking in his darkly handsome face, and she adored the light bit of stubble that'd grown on his cheeks over just the past day. His tousled hair had lost its stylish quiff now thanks to the hours they'd spent in bed already, and also the water that still dampened and darkened the usually dark-blond locks. It now fell messily across his forehead, framing the oceans in his eyes perfectly in the glow of the bedside lamp.

Lucifer looked worried, and Cate knew that he was desperately hoping that she'd be able to go with him. He propped himself up onto his elbow, lying on his side so that he could look down at his beautiful wife, and she gazed up at him with a smile. She turned onto her side to mirror him, leaning in so she could snuggle into his warm, safe body. "I can help make sure you're full of darkness, if you'll let me?" he then whispered, and Cate leaned back, looking up into his face with a frown.

"How?" she asked. He didn't say anything at first, but then used his fingertip to slit open and inch of skin on his neck, which he offered to her.

"Drink of me, Hecate. Take what I willingly offer." Cate was gobsmacked, but knew it was common practice for demons to blood-share, and guessed it was worth a shot. They'd never done it before, at Lucifer's insistence it wasn't needed to strengthen their bond like others needed, so she wasn't sure what to expect. Cate leaned toward his open vein and lapped at the blood while screwing her eyes shut to avoid having to watch the crimson flow. She tried to imagine it was tea, rather than blood, but still couldn't fight her gag reflex as she gulped. It stayed down, and she was glad. Surely it had to work, and she just hoped that his blood along with his dark seed was strong enough to bring life into existence within her. Lucifer was patient, and he didn't push her to drink more than a mouthful at a time, but simply reminded her why they were doing it to help spur her on.

When she could drink no more, he lifted his leg over hers and wrapped his free arm around her back, enveloping Cate tightly with his strong body while he leaned down and kissed her deeply. When he released her mouth, she snuggled against him, feeling sleepy, and he watched as she rested her chin on his chest and closed her eyes, as though drifting off to sleep.

Lucifer could sense that she was weak, but that her tired body was struggling to stay awake in his hold. He intended to let her rest for a little while, happy to keep her safely cocooned within his protective grip as she did so, but then his wife jerked slightly. She forced herself awake again, and looked up at him with a smile.

"How will we know if it's worked?" she asked, automatically placing her hand over her belly as she stared up at him thoughtfully. Her green eyes seemed to shine bright even in the dim light, and they hypnotised him as he looked down into the face of the woman he loved so very much.

"I'll sense it," he answered her. "Well, I think so anyway. I did with all three of you, but it was weeks after I'd been on Earth, not right away," he added, referring to her, Devin and Serena. It was odd hearing him talk of her that way. It'd been such a forbidden connection that they hadn't acknowledged in so long, and felt strange to be reminded of her true heritage.

"So, we have to wait?" she asked him.

"No darling, we keep on trying," Lucifer replied, and grinned as he climbed on top of her. He stopped to briefly check that she was ready, aware that her frail body was still struggling to keep up with him despite wanting to keep going, and he shot her his most seductive smile.

"Yes," she said, gazing up at him as Lucifer pulled up her hips and slid himself inside her wet chasm again, and again, until they both reached another glorious climax.

"Okay, let's do this one more time," Lucifer said, gripping

Cate's hands tightly as she stood before him by the bed. She raised an eyebrow playfully and he laughed. He didn't need to read her mind to know she was having dirty thoughts, and shook his head in mock astonishment. "Not that," he whispered in reply, with a wicked smile on his lips.

He had only a few minutes left until the waning moon would begin to affect him, and knew it was time to try and take her home again. Lucifer called to every ounce of his dark force to empower him, and focussed his mind on his dark realm.

He held Cate closer, closed his eyes, and attempted the teleportation again. A second later, he could feel them pulling away from Earth, down towards Hell, and he dedicated all his strength on taking his wife home at long last. It worked, and as they shifted between the worlds, a tiny spark of new power came into his almighty consciousness. It was like a small flame, and Lucifer knew right away that it was the essence of a life that was just beginning.

The pair of them teleported straight into their castle chambers this time, and Cate caught her breath quicker than she'd thought she would without her powers. She then looked up into her husband's eyes with a satisfied smile, and was so happy to be home at last.

He smiled down at her and pulled her into his arms, kissing her passionately. It was just seconds before he was telling her the wonderful news, and Cate broke down in happy tears that their plan had worked. She was going to be a mother, and while she was terrified, she was also ecstatic.

CHAPTER TWENTY-FOUR

The entire underworld welcomed Cate back home with joy and relief. She was at Lucifer's side as he convened his dark council, and even his closest and most loyal demons cheered loudly. They congratulated her on having found her way home at long last, and even Lilith seemed relieved to see her. The ancient demon smiled warmly over at Cate when she took her seat beside her husband at the top of the huge wooden table, and while it was a surprise, she couldn't resist grinning back at her.

The celebrations that followed her return lasted for many days, thanks to the King's good mood that simply could not be overlooked. They partied hard, and celebrated without a care. As Cate reconnected with her friends and family, it was quickly revealed to her how not a single hellish being had been able to sense her existence at all during the long absence, and they were all glad to have her back where she belonged.

"He's been so lost without you," Serena told her when they were stood to one side together later that night, watching the party from the side-lines. The upper level demons and witches all continued to party around them in the great hall of the dark castle, and the energy was electric. "He went to Earth many times to try and find you, but he kept coming back empty handed. There wasn't even a hint of you, and I swear he came back a little more defeated every time. We didn't even know that you'd escaped until a couple of years ago when Alma managed to make contact with one of that angel's white witches, Angelica I think her name was. She told her that you'd gotten away from that bastard a long time ago, and took great pleasure in finding out that you still hadn't returned home. It took every ounce of strength Alma had not to kill the bitch for daring to mock her," she added. "Where were you? Why didn't you come home? She asked, and paled as she pieced the story together. Serena smiled awkwardly over at Cate, who'd gone quiet thanks to her unwittingly harsh words. "I'm sorry, is it too hard to talk about it?" she then asked, her cheeks flushing almost as red as her hair in the dark hall when she realised how upset Cate was.

"Yeah it is. I just hadn't even thought about it from the other way around. I didn't realise how little you all actually knew about what'd happened to me. Dylan has given Lucifer all the details now, but I suppose I'll have to tell my side before too long as well."

Cate shook her head when Serena started to respond, somehow knowing she was about to ask for more information. She knew she had more questions, but wasn't even close to being ready to answer them yet. "That stuff's definitely off limits for now. It's far too soon for me to talk about it. Part of me never even wants him to know," she admitted, looking over at Lucifer with a pained look as he chatted happily with Devin a few metres away.

Both men instinctively looked over at her, sensing her eyes on them. While Devin smiled, Lucifer frowned. He managed a supportive half-smile and Cate knew that he must've either overheard their conversation or he'd read Serena's thoughts while the pair of them had chatted. They came back over, and Devin kissed her cheek before hugging her again.

"Hey, are you okay?" he asked, and his genuine concern made her smile again. She was glad they'd mended things a long time ago, and it was nice knowing he hadn't lost his affection for her after all. Of course, now it was because of both his loyalty and protective urges towards her as his Queen, rather than any of his old emotions.

"Yes. I'm fine, Devin. I honestly couldn't be any better," she answered with a wide grin, looking at each of them while a contented pang shot through her still healing heart. It was great to be home. She instinctively brushed her hand over her stomach, and caught Serena's mouth as it dropped open beside her, the realisation hitting the Princess like a sudden bolt of intuitive insight. Thankfully, she didn't say anything. Serena knew the King and Queen would want to tell everyone their happy news themselves when they were ready. She just beamed over at them and bounced on her feet excitedly. Lucifer grinned down at Serena and afforded her a wink as a silent thank you.

"What I'm about to tell you is strictly between us for now, okay?" Satan asked, looking at both Devin and Serena with a serious expression, and they both nodded in understanding. "Cate's expecting our first child," he told them, reading their happy thoughts as they both smiled up at their master. Serena reached over and took Cate's hand, and gave it a gentle squeeze before pulling her into a tight hug.

"Congratulations," she told them both, and she leaned up to give Lucifer a soft kiss on his cheek. He hugged and kissed her back, and then patted Devin on the shoulder, pausing for a moment to gaze upon his family with a smile.

Before any of them could say another word, Leviathan ran over to the royal brood, grinning mischievously at Cate. He bowed to Lucifer who smiled back at his friend, and then ushered for the demon to join them.

"Hail to the Queen," Leviathan bellowed as he stepped forward, grabbing Cate and lifting her up off her feet for a few moments as he twirled her in his arms. Devin and Serena laughed at the demon's playfulness, and left the three of them to talk. They headed back over to speak with their coven, but bowed to the King respectfully before they left his side.

"Get off me, you bloody fool," Cate chastised the demon jokingly. She wriggled and climbed down from his tight embrace, slapping him hard on the shoulder. After stepping back, she giggled as he feigned pain at her feeble hit, and then felt strong hands grab her waist from behind. Cate then felt Lucifer's stubbly chin rest against her shoulder as he peered over at the demon and wrapped his arms tighter around her, his hands resting over her stomach protectively.

"Hands off, Levi. She's all mine," he ordered him, but was still being playful with his friend. He knew Leviathan didn't have any ill-conceived ideas towards his Queen. He wouldn't dare.

"My sincerest apologies sire," he proclaimed, bowing down overzealously at their feet, and making them both laugh even more. He rose after a second and they continued chatting for a while, each of them enjoying the relaxed atmosphere and long overdue calmness that'd descended over the entire castle.

***

Being back home at long last affected Cate much better than she'd ever thought possible. She hadn't realised just how human she'd become again during her forced time away. The Dark Queen had to adjust to everything all over again, especially the lack of everyday comforts.

"I'd do just about anything for a cup of tea right now," she mumbled grumpily to Serena after just a few days back in Hell. She already missed the ability to eat and drink, and was sure that it must be her cravings setting in. Milky tea with a handful of biscuits to dunk in it was all she could think about for some reason. Her sister simply laughed and rolled her eyes, but soon doubled her efforts to keep her busy. Cate knew it was all a ploy to take her mind off both the things she missed from Earth and the more unsavoury reminders of her recent past, but was willing to take any distraction she could get.

They sat together in the royal quarters, working hard, and Cate tried again to summon her dark power. She wanted to bring it back as quickly as possible, but something was still getting in the way. The Dark Queen huffed, annoyed once again at her failure and still weak body, but she tried again despite the setbacks.

By the next night, Dylan had been fully initiated into the dark coven and was allowed to visit Cate and Lucifer's private living area. Alma presented her to the King and Queen, promising Lucifer that she'd completed her transition and had encompassed her dark powers fully. He stood and approached the kneeling witch, looking down at her with a stern expression on his face as he read her mind again.

Seeing the pair of them like that, Cate was reminded of the last time Dylan had been in Hell, and just how awful those days had been for her. This time though, it was going to be completely different. The past was long gone and their amazing new life was just beginning, and she'd help make sure of that. Lucifer nodded to Alma, who visibly let out the breath that she had been holding in anticipation.

"Rise," he commanded Dylan, who immediately did as she was bid. She didn't dare meet Lucifer's gaze, looking over at Cate instead with a longing, almost shy smile. "You may now greet your Queen," he added, walking back over to where she still sat, and Dylan followed closely behind him.

Cate stood and walked to meet them, lifting up onto her tiptoes to kiss her husband when he reached her.

"Thank you," she whispered into his ear as he gripped her waist. She kissed him again before he released her, and was glad he'd trusted her enough to leave the two of them alone. Alma followed the King's lead and left the living area too, perhaps adhering to a silent order from him, Cate couldn't be sure.

Dylan's face lit up when they were finally alone, and she almost ran the last few paces to get to her friend. She quickly gathered Cate up in her arms, hugging her tightly.

"We finally did it," she said as they pulled back from their hug, beaming happily at her. Cate grinned back at Dylan, revelling in her friend's happiness. She was so glad they'd made it to Hell together safely, just like they'd always hoped they would, and was pleased to see she hadn't been harmed.

"We sure did, are you okay?" Cate asked her, looking across at her and checking her over as she asked.

"I'm better than okay," Dylan replied, putting her at ease immediately. "I finally have everything I ever wanted, Cate. And, it seems you do, too," she added, looking down at her stomach with a sly grin. Her cheeks flushed red and she gasped, shocked at how Dylan could already know her secret.

"Can you sense it?" she asked, genuinely surprised. Her old friend nodded. Dylan knew her better than almost anyone, so it made sense that she was the first one to notice the changes in her.

"It's more like a feeling, and you smell different somehow. I only realised it for sure once I was close to you," she explained. "How fucking amazing is all of this?" Dylan then shrieked, jumping up and down excitedly, and Cate was pleased to see she hadn't lost any of her usual vulgarity during her transition to dark witch.

Cate pulled her back into a tight hug, and held her close for a few minutes. When she pulled away, she ushered for her to sit at the nearby table beside her.

They caught each other up on the events from the last few days, and Dylan told her all about how Lucifer had come to the flat that night and found her there rather than Cate. "I opened the door and totally freaked out. I didn't know what to do, so I just fell to my knees before him. I opened my mind before he could even react to my being there instead of you. Somehow, it worked, and luckily he spent a few minutes reading my thoughts rather than just opting for interrogation," Dylan told her. "I let him have all of it, and didn't hold anything back. All my thoughts and memories, especially my knowledge of the astral plain and the spell I'd cast up there in order to get you out. He knew I wanted to join his coven, and he must've read my mind to know where you were. He clicked his fingers and teleported me straight to Hell, without having actually said a single word to me."

"Whoa, well I'm just glad it worked out that way. I know it can't have been easy for you seeing him again without me there. I guess Alma was commanded to be at the dark gates to greet you?" Cate asked, and Dylan nodded, but immediately looked away from her intense gaze.

"Yes, she met me. It was awkward at first though, because there's something I haven't told you—something else that draws me to Hell as well as my connection with you. It goes deeper than just our friendship," she told her, looking worried.

"What is it, you can tell me anything, Dylan," Cate promised, and her mind was racing as to what her friend might be about to reveal. She'd never known Dylan to keep a secret from her since releasing her from Uriel's captivity, and was eager to hear the truth.

"Alma's my mother," she finally admitted, her eyes still down. "I don't even know why I never told you about it. I just never found the right moment to bring it up, and I guess I didn't really want to re-live it all. She kind of abandoned me when I was just a little kid, so I guess I was always too torn up and angry all these years to deal with it. But, we've mended so much between us in just the last few days together, and I finally feel like I have the answers I needed. I'm now truly ready to serve you and the King completely, and I'll keep no more secrets from you from now on. I promise, and I understand if you can never forgive me for not telling you the truth sooner."

Cate reached over and grabbed Dylan's chin, pulling her gaze back up to meet hers. She stared at her friend for a moment, and was taken aback by her worried words. Cate smiled across at her, silently letting her know she could never be angry with her, and Dylan couldn't stay sad. Her usual playful smile crept back in after a few seconds.

"It's okay, Dylan," Cate told her quietly, but earnestly. "I'm so very happy to be here at last, and it's all thanks to your hard work. You deserve to be happy, but it's a reward only you can find for yourself," she told her with a smile. "It seems that we've both been able to come home and be with our family at last, and that's all that matters." Dylan grinned broadly, seemingly unable to help herself.

Cate was right; she was home at last.

The pair talked in private for a while longer, and they loved being given some time alone to process the events from the past few days. Lucifer graciously left them to it, and Cate felt more relaxed and happier than ever. It was a wonderful realisation to know that both her family and her best friend would be by her side for eternity. Together at last—and always.

CHAPTER TWENTY-FIVE

It wasn't long before being back in Hell made Cate feel so much more like her old self again. Thanks to her stubborn sessions with Serena, she quickly began getting stronger and her senses keener again, and her powers soon made their way back under her control again at last. It did help, of course, that Lucifer's darkness coursed through her body again thanks to their rekindled relationship, his continued blood-sharing, and his child that now grew inside of her. Those key elements all added to her recovery tenfold as the pregnancy progressed, and she felt better than she had in years.

After just a few weeks, Cate was able to teleport herself around the castle at will, and the superior strength she'd once had returned to her body, allowing her to keep up with Lucifer again as they made love for hours. She desired him with every inch of her being, and often downright demanded that he satisfy her powerful cravings for him. Cate was insatiable, and her powerful husband was the one and only outlet for that passion. Lucifer was the one drug she needed, or wanted in order to get her high, and luckily, he was always keen to oblige.

"Pregnancy becomes you," he told Cate one night with a sultry smile. They were lazing on their huge bed, lying on the black satin sheets while surrounded by black roses that'd been manifested as a treat for them from Alma.

He trailed kisses down Cate's already slightly swollen belly, her ready core in his sights. She groaned loudly as he sucked her sensitive nerve endings into his mouth, and flicked his tongue over them expertly before sliding his fingers inside her gushing cleft, while he continued to devour her delicate, tender nub. Cate came within minutes, but hadn't had nearly enough of him. She gripped Lucifer with her strong legs and pulled him closer for a kiss, sliding him inside of her within seconds of her previous comedown. He followed her lead, revelling in her increased strength and incredible sex-drive. It was hours before she'd had enough, and snuggled down to rest in her husband's arms.

As the next few days passed by, Lucifer and Cate quickly realised that the pregnancy could not be hidden any longer. All the witches seemed to sense it as soon as she was within a few feet of them, and many would give her a knowing smile. They said nothing, and Cate guessed they'd been made well aware that they weren't to speak a word until Lucifer had made a formal announcement, which he finally gave during their late-night gathering to celebrate the spring equinox. The news was met with cheers and praise, as expected, and the Dark King and Queen didn't stop smiling the entire time.

Following Dylan's initiation, Alma had been free to watch over Cate with increased effort, and the Dark Queen could feel the witch's presence around her almost all the time, as if she couldn't stay away. Alma still hadn't forgiven herself for failing to stop her from getting captured up on Earth, and begged her Queen to punish her however she saw fit. It was as though she wanted to be tortured for her shortcomings, rather than carry her shame so heavily on her shoulders, but Cate wouldn't hear of it. She was a fair and merciful Queen, despite her dark core, and couldn't blame Alma for the unfortunate events that'd happened up on that beach all those years before. The witch had tried her best, as always, and she wouldn't punish Alma for Uriel's disturbing doings. None of them could've ever anticipated his plans. In fact, Cate was glad Alma had simply been knocked out and then left for dead while Angelica and the other white witches completed their mission to kidnap her. She almost certainly couldn't have taken on a whole coven of white witches alone, and Cate couldn't bear to even contemplate the possible outcomes if she'd tried to fight them off single-handed. She refused to fret on it, and urged the high priestess to do the same.

Dylan had seemingly gone through her trials and initiation with relative ease, although Cate could still sense her fear and trepidation of the King when she was near him. The scars were still fresh, and although neither of them raised the subject, it was always the elephant in the room whenever she attended to them. It was nice to see that she and Alma had grown closer still, and one night, while they were relaxing together before a roaring fire in the royal living area, Dylan finally told Cate the story of how her mother had come to be at Lucifer's side. Cate listened to Alma's story intently, but there were parts of the story she hated hearing. She wasn't comfortable knowing that their high priestess and her husband had once been lovers, but she chose to let it go. There were more than just a few women in his past, and she couldn't bring herself to dwell on either of their pasts, especially when it came to their lovers.

Cate just enjoyed their rekindled love and happiness, while trusting that Lucifer only had eyes for her. It was good learning the truth about Dylan's past, and she opened up with her in return about her fears and guilt. Dylan was a calm and assuring friend as always, and both women enjoyed the closeness they could still share, even if it had to be in private. Lucifer's understanding of their close bond was an element of their new life she simply couldn't live without, and it felt good to have a true friend around.

Her King had also gone one step further, and appointed Dylan her official protector, thanks to her unflinching loyalty and love for the Dark Queen. She was more than worthy of the role, and seeing Dylan flourish under the dark reign empowered Cate even more.

Cate strengthened more as the days passed, which in turn pleased Lucifer immensely. He was still incredibly angry at the way their marriage had been forcibly split in two, but couldn't blame his wife for Uriel's doing, nor for hiding away following her escape.

Lucifer summoned Dylan to explain the situation the other council members in greater detail one night during one of their regular meetings, having informed them he refused to put Cate through the ordeal of reliving the painful past in front of the council. After Lilith's seemingly relentless questioning, the witch was released, and they all had to agree that the Queen and her witch had done the right thing. They all knew that if Uriel had found her on Earth again following her escape, there would be no chance of her evasion a second time.

"We need a plan, just in case," Lilith advised him when Dylan had gone. "If this ever happens again, we go up there baying for blood. Do you agree, your majesty?"

"I do," he replied. "All we need to do is find the perfect pawn, and I think I know just the one." He knew Uriel would be ruthless in his seduction a second time, and he would force her to say yes to his every desire. That would never be allowed to happen again, and they all agreed the Queen should remain in Hell for the foreseeable future.

Later that night, Cate rested in her husband's arms as they lay on the large sofa together. He tried to force them away, but couldn't fight Dylan's memories of her time with Cate invading his thoughts. Envisioning the sad, tender moment the pair had shared together at the empty penthouse, as well as Cate's first few days back on Earth, brought him nothing but pain. Reliving Dylan's memory was like a movie playing in his mind of the desperation Cate had faced, and he loathed seeing her so lost and afraid.

"What are you thinking about?" she asked him, looking up into his deep blue eyes. Cate could tell that Lucifer was pensive. She'd been lying in his arms quietly as he cradled her from behind, but he hadn't spoken in a while.

"You're not ready to talk about it yet, my love," he told her, gazing down into her bright green eyes adoringly as he spoke, and his meaning was clear. He was desperate to uncover the truths about what had actually gone on in that astral plain.

"You can still ask. I understand there are many things that have been left unsaid. If I'm not ready to answer, I'll say so," she promised, turning onto her side in his embrace so that they could see each other more easily.

"Dylan's memories, they've told me almost everything I need to know," he told her, and he twirled one of her ringlets between his fingers absentmindedly.

"Almost," she muttered quietly, but urged him to carry on.

"The spell I can understand, and see what it made you untraceable, but I just cannot seem to get passed the fact that you were full of so much light? Why did he keep you so long, Hecate? What were you doing?" he asked, and his eyes speckled with black flecks as he contemplated her answer.

"I don't even know where to start, Lucifer," she answered

honestly. "You won't like my explanation no matter what, and I'm so ashamed I don't think I could bear to even say it out loud. He wanted vengeance at first, but then his goal changed. He wanted…"

"You," he answered. And Cate nodded.

"Yes. Please can you ever forgive my foolishness?" she asked, curling into a ball in his arms, afraid of his reply.

"Only if you can forgive mine, too," he told her, hugging Cate tightly.

***

"I can hear something strange," Lucifer told Cate as they lazed together in their huge bed. She was lying on her back under the black sheets, while he lay next to her with his head snuggled into her chest. His legs were wrapped around hers protectively, and she loved how close he always kept her now that they were back together. His strong hand ran up and down her stomach, and the baby continuously kicked the palm of his hand, making him laugh.

"Like what?" she asked, and was delighted to share every moment of her first pregnancy with her husband. She knew he'd never been able to enjoy such moments in the past while his heirs had grown within their other mothers' wombs. She often wondered why and how it'd finally worked after his many years spent trying, but he always refused to talk about the details with her, and she had to respect his need for privacy. Cate hoped someday she'd get the truth, but for now it was just another mystery only he had the answer to, and it didn't bother her enough to pursue it.

"It's like a strong thumping sound," Lucifer told her, and climbed down to lay an ear against his wife's swollen belly. He listened hard. She was now around halfway through her pregnancy, and had begun getting the frequent strong kicks and prods on her bladder that let her know the little one was bouncing around in there quite happily. Lucifer often talked to the bump, saying he could sense the energy that grew from deep within her, referring to it as a dark flame that developed and grew stronger and more powerful every day.

"Do you think it's the baby's heartbeat?" Cate asked, eager to figure it out. She propped herself up on her elbows and looked down at him, drinking in the sight of his gorgeous face and rugged beard she loved so very much with a contented smile.

"Perhaps, but if it is—that means there are two of them," Lucifer answered, grinning as he pulled Cate up out of the bed. Her eyes grew wide with surprise, and he laughed. "Come on, let's go and ask the witches," he added. They dressed quickly and Lucifer teleported them to the witches' chambers immediately, which were littered with dark spell books and bottled potions. It always occurred to Cate how they were highly organised and incredibly clean—no big cauldrons or spider webs like she'd once imagined thanks to children's stories and movies she'd pored over as a child. They had every potion imaginable, and never seemed short of an answer for whatever Lucifer tasked them with, and this request was no exception.

Alma tried her best but couldn't see into Cate's thick womb lining using her magic, and informed them it was completely normal for the offspring to be too powerful for the magic to penetrate the protective layers. When two mighty beings mated, the pregnancies were often unusual, so she wasn't at all surprised that it'd happened to the Dark King and Queen. If they went to Earth, she hoped the electronic hospital equipment might be able to see, but that was still absolutely out of the question for either of them. The risks were far too high.

"Next suggestion?" Lucifer demanded, and Alma set about searching their ancient books for a spell she might try instead. After reading through the old texts and having a feel of Cate's belly for a while, she believed there to be two foetuses as well. The knowledgeable witch took a few more minutes to press on Cate's stomach, gently prodding and poking her while they chatted. All of them were incredibly excited at the prospect of there being two babies on the way, and Cate was surprised she wasn't afraid.

"Wow, imagine that," Dylan whispered as she joined them, leaning down to lay her hands on Cate's stomach. The strong kicks she received in response to her touch made both her and her closest friend laugh. "Cheeky," she told the bump playfully. They then agreed to try some other methods, as long as they didn't cause any harm to the Queen or her offspring. Sara and Dylan put together an alternative version of a chant they'd found in an old almanac, while Alma concocted a potion for Lucifer to rub on Cate's belly.

The idea was that the combination of potion and a spell would hopefully allow him a glimpse of what lay beneath Cate's protective layers—almost like a second sight.

It wasn't long before the witches all began reciting the altered incantation, and Lucifer rubbed the gooey potion over Cate's belly. Only he was powerful enough to try and have a look without causing harm to her or the baby, or perhaps babies. Lucifer closed his eyes, keeping his hands firmly on his wife to keep him grounded, and he concentrated on the witches' powerful words.

The Dark King soon felt his consciousness shift, somehow going out of himself and into his wife. It was like an awareness, moving down through the layers of her skin and muscle, and then into her protective womb. She made sure to lie completely still, wordlessly sending Lucifer the go ahead via Dylan, who watched her like a hawk knowing her thoughts were being read. Cate also let him know via their *expression* that she wasn't being affected by his actions in any way and to continue.

Lucifer quickly became aware of her strong body trying to push the intruding presence away, but he pressed on. He wasn't there to harm them, and the resistance eventually halted. It wasn't long until he saw a tiny pink-skinned baby. The arms and legs were scrawny, and he could see its veins through the thin skin, but the foetus was moving around with strong movements. Their child was opening its tiny mouth and sucking its thumb as he watched in awe for a moment, and Lucifer could tell right away that the baby was a little girl. He then urged his consciousness to shift around some more, trying to see the whole space that was available to him. He nearly withdrew after a few minutes, but then there it was—a second baby, just as he'd thought. The other one was a boy, and he was moving around just as strongly as the girl, but was a little larger than his twin. The boy baby was sucking his little thumb eagerly while moving gracefully in the amniotic fluids. He was content and healthy, just like his sister.

Lucifer watched each of them for a moment longer and then retreated gently. With careful gestures, he allowed his mind to push through the layers and come back to himself, and back to Cate. When he eventually opened his eyes, Lucifer grinned at his wife.

"Twins!" he exclaimed. He was clearly in shock at the

incredible news, and had a mixture of surprise and excitement he couldn't seem to hide on his usually so stoic face.

"Whoa," she replied, laughing at him. Both Alma and Dylan insisted on Cate being checked over before they left, but were happy that the spell had been a success, and quickly congratulated their rulers on their fantastic news.

***

The pregnancy continued without any complications. Both Cate and the babies seemed powerful, strong and healthy, and when the day came that her water's broke, Lucifer was by her side the entire time. He banned anyone other than Dylan and Alma to attend to his Queen during childbirth, deciding not to allow anyone else to interfere with her or their babies during Cate's moment of vulnerability.

The labour progressed quickly, and Lucifer held her hand while Cate's now strong body took over the birthing process wonderfully. She was tough, and yet still showed the same frailty as any human woman would during the birthing process. Her pain consumed her, but she pressed on in readiness to deliver their precious bundles, and he was in awe.

"I'm ready now," she called out, looking up at Lucifer from the bed as soon as she felt the urge to push, which was only an hour or so after the contractions had started. Dylan and Alma stood at the ready, watching and helping her as much as possible while her body took over. Cate's inner muscles clenched strongly as the next contraction took over and she screamed, sending their first twin, the boy, into Alma's ready hands. He cried out with strong lungs right away, and Lucifer took him into his arms immediately. He wrapped the child in a warm towel, and cleaned him up while Alma cut the cord.

Lucifer then leaned down to show their son to Cate, who smiled and touched his tiny head gently, and kissed him. She let the happiest tears of her life fall down onto her red cheeks, but it wasn't long until she was ready to push again, and she readied herself one more time. Their little girl was born just minutes after their son, and she too cried loudly at first, just like her brother had done. She settled quickly though, already seeming relaxed, and snuggled into her own soft towel before Dylan put her into her mother's awaiting arms.

Cate was delighted, and looked up into Lucifer's eyes as they held their two newborns. He seemed absolutely besotted with his son, but soon placed him in Cate's empty arm so she could hold them both close. The doting father then took their baby girl into his embrace so his wife could greet her son properly at last, and she couldn't take her eyes off his gorgeous face.

The babies soon both fell asleep, seemingly peaceful in their parent's arms, and each then groaned when Alma and Dylan took them away again. They needed to get the twins cleaned and dressed thanks to the mess of blood, but they worked quickly, before handing them back to the blissful couple.

While they were sorting out the babies, Cate could feel her muscles tensing from deep within. Her body seemed to be strengthening with so much force that it felt as though a strong pulse reverberated through every inch of her, but luckily it only lasted for a few minutes. She quickly felt her pains subsiding with each powerful wave, and by less than an hour after the birth she'd completely healed. Cate was back to her old self in no time at all, and was glad her dark power had grown so strong during the last few months.

"What shall we call them?" Cate asked Lucifer when they were relaxing together a little while later. She'd just climbed out of a roaring hot shower, and had to admit she felt amazing. The witches had left them alone at last, having been satisfied that both she and the babies were fine. Even the usually playful Dylan had insisted on doing numerous checks with them first, and while she'd loved having her be part of the birth, she was glad when they'd left. Cate wanted to have some time alone to enjoy their little family in peace. It felt strange to suddenly be a parent, but she adored the sense of all-consuming pride she had for them, and discovered how instantaneous her need to protect them was.

Cate also marvelled at her body's reaction to her hungry offspring. Her belly was flat and her soreness gone, but her breasts swelled with her milk, and she fed the twins with natural ease. All the while, Lucifer couldn't take his eyes off the three of them.

"What do you think of Blake?" Lucifer answered, looking down at their son. He seemed so sure, it was as if he'd known what he wanted to call his new son all along, and she smiled. She supposed that this was the first time he'd actually had any control over their names, and remembered how he'd wanted her to be named Hecate—a name she'd readily assumed regardless of it not officially being her full name. "And, how about Luna?" he asked, kissing his daughter's tiny forehead as she slept peacefully while suckling away at Cate's breast.

She nodded in agreement, and kissed her husband when he looked up at her with a shy smile at last.

"They're both absolutely perfect names, yes to each of them," she told him, and was glad to give him this. He was so naturally warm with them, and she'd never seen his hardened façade slip so far as it had in that moment. Lucifer actually seemed vulnerable, and Cate was pleasantly surprised by his tenderness, but truly loved both the names he'd chosen for their beautiful dark babies. It was decided, and she whispered their names to them as Blake and Luna finished their feeds and drifted off into a blissful sleep.

CHAPTER TWENTY-SIX

By four years old, the twins were bright, powerful little dark spirits. They'd brought so much happiness and love to both Lucifer and Cate in their short lifetimes, more than the almighty couple could have ever hoped for, and life was finally good. Their unusual family was complete, and they all thrived thanks to the twins' powerful energy and strength that'd somehow connected all the dots along the way.

Despite Lucifer's initial worries for his heirs' safety, Devin and Serena were living up on Earth again. They'd wanted to continue adding to their successful following, and Lucifer had agreed, however he'd insisted they return home regularly. The pair had agreed, and brought with them gifts for their young niece and nephew each time. They regaled the twins with fun stories and strange tales from up on the mysterious realm, and the children both loved hearing all about Earth.

The twins always asked Cate to tell them stories of her old home when she tucked them in at night, and she couldn't resist. She animatedly retold her children the story-lines of old movies and books that she'd read when she was younger, and they lapped them up with huge smiles she found infectious. Cate basked in their excited shrieks and eager pleads for more of the fantastical stories, so would indulge them happily. She often told them about her childhood, and of their grandmother, Ella. Despite how sad it made the Queen to remind herself of her guilt, and of the awful memories that thinking of Ella's passing would summon within her, she spoke warmly of their lost grandmother.

"Don't you have a Daddy then, Mummy?" Luna had asked her one night, with such an innocent tone to her question that Cate couldn't lie. She had to laugh at her intuitiveness, though, and knew Luna was a clever little Princess already.

"No, baby girl, I don't have one," she'd replied with an awkward smile, and shook her head before she kissed her goodnight.

As well as teaching the twins to play games and read, Cate had also ensured they encouraged the children to learn about their powers from a young age. Blake and Luna had powerful beings around them at all times, even when they were asleep, and each was there to keep them safe, as well as to teach them all about their powers and dark lineage. With the help of both their parents and the witches and demons, they'd already learned how to teleport and had also developed a strong mental link with one other, allowing them to share their thoughts via a strange psychic bond. Cate had even felt their messages creep into her dreams and thoughts at times too, proving how powerful they already were.

She thought about their differences, and how each had developed over the years, and her heart swelled with pride when she thought how far they'd both come. Luna was a gentle little soul. She was kind and warm hearted, and she loved making her mother smile. She had soft green eyes and dark brown hair that already curled into huge lockets around her tiny shoulders, just like her mother, and Cate found staring into her face odd—as if she were staring at herself from when she was the same age. Blake had the same hair and eye colour too, but unlike his twin he was neither soft, nor gentle. He was incredibly strong though, and even at such a young age, and they could sense his power swelling and extending inside of him. He was decisive and stubborn, a trait he had to have gotten from his father, or so Cate would always joke. But he too could be kind, and would show his sensitive side on rare occasions, usually only when he was alone with his mother.

Blake would also revel in Cate's affections, and yearned for more from her, eager to hear her laugh or keep her attention on him as long as possible. She loved them both so dearly she couldn't bear not to lavish them with hugs, kisses, smiles, and encouragement along every step of the way and she guessed they needed the steadiness her tenderness offered them. Her human side seemed intent on teaching them the important lessons in morality and kindness that Lucifer unfortunately still seemed to have no concept of, and the balance between their two sides was working wonderfully.

***

Cate winced and cried out as her head began pounding again with agonising throbs of a sharp, shooting pain. The royal living area of the dark castle began spinning around her and she swayed, unable to stay on her feet. She even had to grab the nearby wall to steady herself properly. The headaches had started a couple of months before, and had been happening more and more ever since. Neither Lucifer nor any of the powerful dark witches within their premier coven could figure out what might be causing the affliction, but they all worried what the pain might mean. The strange episodes would come and go once every few weeks at first, but were happening much more frequently, and when they did, she'd be overwhelmed by blinding agony for a few minutes while each bout lasted.

This time though, something felt different. Cate's nose felt hot and throbbed as the pain raged inside her head. She raised her hand up to her mouth, having reached up to wipe clean a trickle from just above her lip. She thought it odd to have a runny nose, but when she pulled her hand down, Cate paled nauseously at the sight of her own blood. She quickly reached for a tissue from the table before her and sat down on the nearby sofa, and Dylan ran to her side. She grabbed a towel, soaking up some of the blood with a worried expression while Cate shooed her away.

"I'm fine," she promised weakly, and Dylan shook her head.

"Liar," she replied, but said no more, concentrating instead on ensuring Cate recovered from her moment of illness.

Alma looked over at the Dark Queen and her protector from across the room. As soon as she'd noticed the nosebleed, a shiver had run down her usually steadfast spine. Lucifer had summoned her to discuss Cate's health with him again, but he now had a sneaking suspicion he wasn't going to like her theory. He had tasked her with creating a spell or a potion that might stop these strange attacks, but without knowing the cause of her illness, Alma hadn't had any luck in providing the Queen with a solution. They were both worried, especially Lucifer who looked forlornly over at his wife, but there really was nothing either of them could do. Together they watched as Dylan tossed the blood soaked towels into the fire before her, and grabbed another.

"My lord," Alma said, beckoning him closer to speak with him more privately. "I think I've seen something like this happen before," she told him, and it was a bittersweet realisation as it hit her at last.

"When?" Lucifer asked her tersely, urgently wanting to find out more from his high priestess and her speculations on Cate's condition.

"Many years ago, when you travelled to Earth without the moon to protect you," Alma replied, looking dejected. Lucifer hoped she was wrong, but knew in his heart that his loyal servant might've finally found the key in solving Cate's malaise.

"What does this mean?" he asked, and knew the answer, but still hoped he may be wrong in his depressive assumptions.

"I believe the Queen needs to return to Earth, master. I fear she may get a lot worse if we ignore these symptoms," Alma told him, already thinking of what healing potions she could adapt. She wondered how she might use them to cure Cate in time, but for now she worried that time might not be on their side.

"I will not let her go up there without me," he bellowed angrily, looking down at the short witch with black eyes, showing the rage bubbling beneath the surface. "She's stayed in Hell before without this happening?" Lucifer added, questioning the worried and frenzied thoughts she was having.

"Yes master, but maybe she was stronger before, or her human side wasn't revolting against the invading darkness? She was going to Earth regularly back then as well, whether in practising her teleportation or when we went to meet Devin. She's never stayed here for more than a couple of years at a time, and since everything with the angel, the pair of you have remained here permanently for her safety." Neither one of them needed reminding about that absence, but Lucifer added up Cate's time in Hell, and knew Alma was right—she'd never been there so long before. "That was five years ago now, my King. I truly believe that her human side is protesting—or maybe dying—I don't know for sure. But I cannot know until I am able to investigate further and test out some ideas for potions. If I'm right, this could be the end of her completely if her body is too weak to stave off the death I fear has already begun creeping in." Alma stared at Lucifer's feet while she gave him her predictions, and she shook with fear before him. Even after the last few years with the wonderful twins in his life to soften him, Lucifer was still an almighty dark force that no human or demonic being would ever want to mess with. The same went for delivering bad news.

He didn't respond, but stared through Alma absentmindedly, deep in thought.

"Daddy," Blake called to him from across the room, breaking the King's reverie. "Mummy fell asleep," he informed his father, pointing over to where Cate had fallen from the sofa onto the hard floor, unconscious. Alma ran to the Queen. She lifted her up in her tiny, yet deceptively powerful arms, and placed her back up on to the nearby couch. Dylan went running back in, Luna's tiny, pale hand in her own as she led her back into the main living area.

"Get them out of here," Lucifer commanded her, patting Blake on the head. Dylan followed his order and led the children out into the hall, heading for their bedrooms to play a game, despite her fears for Cate's health and her desire to be by her friend's side.

"The Queen will have to go to Earth, master," Alma told him again, and this time Lucifer knew there was no other choice.

"Hide her from him, Alma. Do you understand me? Make sure she stays within the confines of the church at all times, and as soon as she's healed, or you figure out a cure, you bring her back to me," Lucifer commanded with a stern expression. His eyes began swirling with black specks again at the very thought of losing her all over again, and it took everything he had not to explode with rage. "Is that understood?" he asked again, and Alma nodded and bowed to her master.

She summoned Dylan back to them, and when she re-appeared, instructed her to gather some things and come with them to Earth. The witch nodded in agreement and left, tears already welling in her hazel eyes.

Lucifer took a moment to be with his wife. He leaned down and kissed Cate's soft lips, but he felt utterly useless. He then headed off to sit with the twins for a while, needing their company to help him to calm his frenzied mind.

CHAPTER TWENTY-SEVEN

Alma arrived at London's Satanic church, carrying the still unconscious Queen, and Dylan was right behind them. Thanks to the lower level witches who'd received the silent commandment from their master, a room had already been made up for her in the back of the vast, dark church, and Alma took her there without delay. There would be no stopping to explain the Queen's predicament to them, and the others stepped aside as they passed.

Cate was immediately slid under the covers to rest, while Dylan unpacked the belongings she'd brought from home for her, but she didn't even seem aware that they'd left Hell at all. Alma then sat beside the bed and watched as her mistress slept for two solid days. She never moved from the Queen's side, nor did she let herself drift off to sleep even once. After what felt like forever to the two witches, Cate slowly began to rouse. She was drowsy, but lucid as she opened her eyes at last. When she came to, she was shocked to find herself on Earth, and looked over questioningly at the witches beside the bed.

"How do you feel?" Dylan asked Cate, and was unable to hide the worry from her usually so relaxed face.

"Like crap, but better already. Did you manage to heal me?" she asked. She tried to sit up, but quickly slumped back down on the bed weakly, and Dylan urged her to rest. "I'm guessing it's a no, otherwise why would we be up here?" Cate answered her own question, seeing Dylan's disappointed look. The witch updated her on the unfortunate build up to her necessary sanctuary, and then climbed up on to the bed with her best friend. She held Cate tightly as she began to cry, and didn't begrudge her a moment of weakness in the slightest. "How long do I have to leave it before I can go back?" Cate asked Alma when the powerful high priestess came over to join the pair of them.

She sat up, and felt calmer and stronger now already. She then gratefully accepted the cup of sweet tea that the witch offered her, and dunked in one of the accompanying chocolate biscuits with a smile. One thing was for sure, she'd really missed the food on Earth, and she hungrily dunked in another. Cate then laughed at Dylan when she did the same with her own cup of tea and pile of biscuits, breaking the sombre mood.

"You need to stay here until you're at your full strength, your majesty. I believe your sickness to be your human side's rejection of the long stay in Hell. When you're well again, we'll try taking you home a little bit at a time—just at first. Perhaps then we can bring you here each full moon to stave off any more illness, at least until I can make a potion for you," Alma informed her, smiling over at Cate with motherly affection. "For now though, you need to rest. You must stay within the church's boundaries at all times. It's for your safety, and this is what the King wants for you." Cate nodded, and trusted Alma's words were true. She knew Lucifer had to have given them the order to send her to Earth. There was no other way she'd be there without him otherwise. She also understood, that as long as she stayed within the church's protective circle, she'd be safe. To step over the threshold and out into the open could render her powerless to stop the white witches from finding her again, and that absolutely could not happen. Now that Dylan's spell was no longer keeping her hidden, tracing her was a very real possibility, and Cate shuddered at the prospect of Uriel succeeding in having her taken away again.

After few more days spent resting, Cate had to admit she already felt much better. She'd had no more headaches or any of the other symptoms since her return to Earth, and felt more energetic than ever. Regardless of the improvements, Alma ensured she continued to rest. The motherly witch had played the part of the caring nurse well, but had also been quite pushy whenever she thought Cate might be taking things on again too quickly. Dylan stayed by her side, both by Alma's order and by her insistence of being close to her Queen at all times, and Cate was comforted at having her best friend close by.

"I hadn't been feeling right for a while, but I never told anyone," Cate finally admitted to her as they relaxed in front of the television one night. They were just tucking into a gorgeous meal of spaghetti and meatballs cooked for them by the other lower level witches who lived at the church, Suzanne and Bea, and she groaned in satisfaction of their amazing cooking skills. The pair had been slowly making their way through all the newest movies and television shows that they'd missed out on during their time in Hell, and had actually been enjoying themselves, regardless of the circumstances that'd led them here.

"We could all see that you weren't right, Cate," Dylan replied, sipping on a glass of juice as she stared over at her friend. The Dark Queen had gone noticeably paler and skinnier over the last few months, and had been much more tired and lethargic than she'd been at all since returning to Hell with Lucifer years before. Despite her insistence that she was okay, Dylan had known something wasn't quite right. "I actually thought you might be pregnant again or something," she added with a shrug, smiling over at Cate's shocked face as her incredulous assumptions took her by surprise.

"I wouldn't mind if that was the case," she replied after a few thoughtful seconds, blushing at the idea. She and Lucifer hadn't discussed the possibility of having more children yet, but she was sure that she'd want more when the time finally came for them to decide. "How long until the full moon?" Cate then asked with a sigh. She'd found that thinking of them made her miss Lucifer and the twins terribly, but wouldn't let it upset her. Yes, she'd enjoyed the relaxation time with Dylan, and having the human food at her disposal again, but nothing compared to having her family with her.

"A week," Dylan informed her with a sly grin, her hazel eyes twinkling playfully. "Wow, you must be feeling better if you're already planning your next fuck," she teased, and had to duck an airborne meatball that Cate then sent flying over at her. The now stronger Queen threw it with such speed that the gooey meatball hit the wall behind and splattered into a huge, brown, sloppy mark that stayed stuck there, rather than bounce off the wall and onto the floor, and the squishing sound made them both giggle. "I must be right," Dylan then added. She then laughed loudly and threw a sticky string of tomato sauce covered pasta in Cate's direction, having eaten all of her meatballs already. Cate simply caught the strand in her mouth and sucked it into her pursed lips, giggling again as Dylan shook her head in mock disgust.

"You always take it to a dirty place, I think maybe it's you who needs a good sorting out?" Cate replied with a wide grin, even though Dylan had been spot on—she was incredibly horny.

"Don't remind me," Dylan replied, feigning a pained, forlorn look. "It's been *so* long," she added with a forcefully sad expression on her pretty oval face.

"What, like a week? You're such a filthy fiend," Cate cried with a wicked grin. She discarded her plate on the low coffee table and then slumped back into the cushions of the comfortable sofa she was sprawled on, laughing so hard she snorted. Dylan laughed too, and she just shrugged in response, her lack of a witty reply telling Cate she was absolutely right.

Alma came in and cleared up the empty plates and cups, but not before telling the pair of them off for making a mess with the flying meatball. Dylan climbed up from her armchair and cleaned the splattered mess off the wall, bowing to her mother apologetically before she then left the two of them alone again.

Cate had found herself watching the two of them with intrigue during their short moment together. She'd always loved watching the pair of them interact since they'd been reunited at last a few years before. Dylan was still such a strong and playful character, and she'd seemed to settle into the darker way of life with complete ease. Alma, however, was of a much quieter nature. She'd always seemed focussed on her duties so entirely that it was almost hard to imagine the mother and daughter as anything other than a high priestess and one of the witches in her coven. Cate had often caught them talking quietly together, though. Alma's usually so serious features would grow softer as she spoke to her daughter privately, and Cate hoped they were connecting bit by bit over the years. She remembered how she'd watched with a smile one day as Alma had held Dylan's hand protectively while they'd worked a powerful spell together. Their bond, combined power, and strong connection, had seemed to increase the magic's potency somehow, and even Cate could sense that their bond was slowly creating a formidable duo.

She hoped that the twins would be that way with her and Lucifer when they were older, but that nothing would come between them like with Dylan and Alma. She had every hope that their powers would combine and strengthen each other's as they grew, rather than them vying for more power or rebelling against their parents as they got older, and was sure they'd soon become quite the powerful pair. So far their natures seemed to be in perfect balance, and she looked forward to a future in which that steadiness would undoubtedly lead them onwards, together.

***

Lucifer came to Earth as soon as the next full moon allowed him to teleport to his wife's side safely. He appeared in the doorway to Cate's bedroom, and watched as she napped peacefully for a few moments, sensing that she was already doing much better. Dylan lay beside her on the king-size bed, asleep too, but she quickly awoke from her nap, having sensed her master's presence. She stood and bowed to her King before she hastily left the pair of them alone, and he was pleased she'd never lost that healthy bit of fear in his presence. Lucifer read the witch's mind, and knew that his beautiful wife was not only well, but also more than ready for him to come to her.

He smiled and shut the door behind him, and wandered over to the bed, stripping off before climbing under the covers with her. Cate didn't even stir as he leaned up on his elbow beside her and watched her sleep for a few moments longer. With a salacious smile, he then slipped his head under the warm covers and climbed between her legs. She slept on even as he lifted her nightdress and nestled himself above her hot, wet cleft, opening her legs further so he could access her delectable core.

Cate soon started dreaming of her husband, of his mouth against places that'd gone untouched too long, and devouring her with his strong mouth. In her dream, he flicked his tongue over her swollen nub and his fingers delved deep inside of her to stroke on the sensitive spot inside with expert precision, making her moan in delight. She climaxed within minutes, her body shuddering as the strong release pulsated throughout her entire body. Cate flushed with heat and jumped awake, and lifted the covers to look down at her body in sleepy bemusement. Lucifer's smiling face greeted her from between her trembling thighs and she laughed, releasing the confused tension she'd felt when she first awoke.

"Well, hello to you, too," she whispered down at her husband, before allowing her head to fall back onto the pillow. Lucifer groaned in response, laughing gruffly as she twitched beneath his touch. He was still stroking her sensitive insides wonderfully, and he began lapping at her clit again. Cate writhed and gripped the covers in her hands, arching her back as Lucifer pursued another climax from her, and she soon fell headfirst into a glorious wave of pleasure.

He then gripped her hips forcefully with his free hand as he tongued her effortlessly, pulling her closer to his eager mouth and heightening her climax. She cried out his name as she trembled and revelled in the aftershocks of his deep, pleasurable gift. She was so sensitive that Lucifer's hot breath made her shudder, but he didn't pull away. Cate lay back and panted as he trailed soft kisses up her belly to her breasts, sliding beneath her nightdress so she couldn't wriggle away. He commanded her pleasure, revelling in it himself as he devoured every inch of skin he could reach, and she didn't even try to fight.

Lucifer had worried so much for his wife during the last couple of weeks spent apart, and was delighted to sense how strong and well she now was. He'd take this over her frailty, even if it meant they might have to spend more time apart until an answer could be found for her illness. He knew Alma would come through for him, and that they'd soon have a solution for the adverse effects Hell had seemingly been having on Cate's human half. In the meantime, he'd gladly settle for nights like this.

She arched her back and then pulled the cotton dress up and over her head in one quick move, exposing her dishevelled husband who was still leaning over her now naked body. He caressed her breasts one at a time with his powerful kisses, soliciting more delighted groans. Lucifer looked up at her and smiled, his deep blue eyes playful and excited in the dim light of her small room. His dark-blond hair was tousled thanks to his antics under the heavy covers, but he somehow looked even more gorgeous to her. She took in his warm and happy smile, and reached down to cup his coarsely stubble-covered cheeks. Cate then pulled him up so she could kiss her beloved husband's soft lips at long last. It'd been far too long since she'd kissed his mouth, those lips, that face, and she let him know just how much she'd missed them.

The enamoured couple chose not leave Cate's small bedroom for the duration of the full moon's time over London. They decided to enjoy one another for as long as they could, rather than worry about what would have to happen once the moon waned. Lucifer laid beside his wife, basking in her attention and lapping up the beautiful afterglow she now radiated with following her numerous climaxes. He pulled Cate into his arms and hugged her tightly.
"I don't want to leave you," he whispered into her ear, allowing her to sense his tiny moment of weakness. She was still the only being he ever showed that small side of himself to, and while she loved that he could open up to her, she felt sad not to be going back home alongside him. His words were a reminder that their time together was only short, but at least it was only for a little while.
"I don't want you to go either," she told him, snuggling into his neck and wrapping her legs around his muscly thighs as she breathed in his musky scent. They lay there together for a while longer, but eventually she felt him pull away, and he climbed up from the bed to get dressed. He peered down at her sadly before leaning down to give her a kiss goodbye, but she simply wasn't ready to watch him leave. As Lucifer then began to teleport home, Cate sprang up from the bed and grabbed his hand, travelling down with him to their home regardless of his orders for her to stay behind. When they arrived, he pulled off his cargo jacket and wrapped it around her naked body before staring down at her angrily.
"Cate," he groaned, but she raised her mouth to his, stopping him from finishing his chastisement by placing a deep and powerful kiss on his lips.
"I'll follow you forever," she then whispered as she pulled away, smiling up at her lover and melting his resolve.
"It's not safe yet, you need to be well," he said, stroking her pale cheek with his hand as he stared into Cate's deep green eyes.
"Okay, but can I just see them. Only for a moment and then I'll go back, I promise?" she asked, and Lucifer knew she was talking about the twins. He nodded and immediately teleported the

pair of them to the children's bedchambers, where they found their dark offspring playing a game of hide and seek with the demon Berith. All three beings smiled widely at the Queen as she entered, and Berith immediately teleported away to give them some privacy. Cate hugged the children tightly and beamed down at the pair of them, taking in their happy faces. "I can't stay, my darlings," she told them, feeling her smile falter slightly as she spoke. "But Daddy's here, and I'll come back as soon as I can. Be good for him, okay?" she asked them, and both Blake and Luna nodded in agreement.

"Get better soon, Mummy," Blake said as Cate stood, seeming to understand so much despite his young age. She smiled down at him and nodded, seeing the worry in his tiny, green eyes.

"I will, baby boy. I will," she told him before she padded back over to Lucifer and kissed him goodbye. Cate then teleported back to her bedroom in the church, feeling weak after her first sneaky few minutes back in Hell. She fell into bed exhaustedly as soon as she arrived, but before she could drift off to sleep, Dylan burst into her room. She was shouting and bellowing at her friend in annoyance and worry.

"How could you be so bloody reckless?" Dylan demanded, but Cate just curled up under the covers. She began falling into a deep sleep, mumbling her insincere apologies as she drifted off. Her heart was still back in the underworld, entombed forever in the two children she and Lucifer had created together, and regardless of her illness, it'd been worth the trip so she could see them.

CHAPTER TWENTY-EIGHT

After her first visit, Cate tried teleporting again every few days. Soon she was managing to go back to Hell for a few minutes here and there, splitting herself between the two worlds for a few more weeks, before building up to longer periods of time each visit. It wasn't perfect, but it was working, and at least that way Cate got to spend some time with the twins. She hadn't been away from them at all before her illness had struck, and she missed them terribly.

Each time the moon was full again, Lucifer came to Earth to be with her. They delighted in each other's company for as long as they could, shaking the church walls around them whenever the Dark King climaxed inside his lover, but the couple of days passed by in a fast blur each time. It was over far too quickly and always left them both feeling unsatisfied, having been used to being together every day again after her return to Hell.

After a few months, they decided to let the children come up to visit Cate at the church during one full moon. They weren't entirely sure, but they presumed the twins, like their father, couldn't stay up on Earth once the moon waned. Lucifer believed that because of his full darkness and Cate's half dark heritage, the twins were surely on the heavier side of the scale. He suspected the moon would bind them just as it did him, but they didn't even want to risk trying the theory out on the pair of them yet.

Cate loved spending time with Blake and Luna for longer than just the few hours she'd built her tolerance up to in Hell before the headaches crept in, and after that first successful visit, the twins were allowed to go and visit Cate during most of the full moon's that followed. Lucifer kept them close, holding their hands as they teleported up to the church excitedly, and they didn't leave their parents' sight the entire time. Both children enjoyed the change of scenery, despite the restrictions, and they'd happily watch the world go by from behind the safety of the church's big windows.

One night though, Blake's curious nature got the better of him and he decided he wanted to see more. He waited until his father was busy elsewhere and then sneaked out of the church's side entrance. Within seconds, he'd crossed over the sacred line and was out in the open world.

Lucifer caught his son after just a few steps, and grabbed him tightly. He pulled Blake back into the safety of their hallowed ground, scolding him immediately for his careless behaviour, and his vicious temper flared at his son's foolishness. Blake ran back inside in tears and curled up next to Luna in front of the fire in the main living area at the back of the church, nursing his bruised ago. Cate knew she should be angry, but couldn't bear to scold her precious boy any more than his father already had for his moment of curiosity. After all, they'd raised the twins to be powerful little dark beings who knew their own minds, and she couldn't bring herself to disparage him for having followed his curious heart.

It wasn't long before Blake became intrigued by the outside world again, though. During each of their visits to Earth after that day, he managed to sneak away undiscovered. The Black Prince had even managed to hide his thoughts from his father, cleverly figuring out how to close that part of himself off to Lucifer's mind reading capabilities, and no one even knew he was doing it. All he did at first was cross the threshold and stand in the real world for a few seconds before ducking back inside, but he soon began exploring farther each time. He'd listened intently to the stories of the terrible white witches, and had paid attention when he'd been told it wasn't safe outside of the church's protection. But, he still didn't understand why his oh-so-powerful father was so scared. As far as Blake could see, there was nothing to be afraid of. Devin and Serena seemed to be able to live on Earth safely, so he figured why couldn't he just explore a little?

One night, Blake and Luna were playing quietly in their room while Cate was resting in her chambers. Lucifer had gone to Hell with Alma for a short while to check out a potion she'd finally managed to concoct in the hopes of curing Cate's symptoms, and Blake had an idea. Dylan was watching over the twins, and agreed to grab them some hot chocolate if they promised to go straight to sleep after they'd finished. The pair grinned innocently and each fluttered their eyelashes, making her smile down at them, her resolve quickly disappearing.

"Okay, I will be back in one minute. Stay right here," she told them, before ducking out into the kitchen to grab some hot drinks.

"Luna, come with me," Blake quickly whispered once Dylan had gone, taking her hand and pulling her out of the church. She obliged, but trembled in fear when they crossed the quiet road and headed towards a play park he'd found around the corner from the church. Luna tried to say no, but her curiosity got the better of her, and she soon stopped trying to pull her brother back towards the safety of the church.

"It's okay, I've played here lots of times. I know it's safe," he promised, and despite her fear, Luna joined him in the fenced play area. They swung on the swings together, slid down the slides, and span giddily on the merry-go-round—laughing loudly and enjoying their thrills as they spent the next few stolen minutes acting like real five year olds.

Neither of them noticed the group of women that began encircling the fenced park, moving silently and gracefully through the still night air. They drew closer, chanting quietly and tightening their circle around them as the children played on obliviously for another few minutes. Eventually, Blake looked up and noticed their presence, but it was too late. He grabbed his sister close to him, sensing her panic, but there was nothing either of them could do. He held Luna as she cried, trying to be brave, but he knew he'd done something so incredibly wrong in taking her there. A heavy sensation welled in Blake's stomach, and for the first time in his life, he felt truly afraid.

***

Cate awoke with a start, and knew immediately that something was wrong. Luna had sent her a mental flash, some kind of telepathic cry for help thanks to her strong power, and it scared her to have seen the white witches through her daughter's eyes even for that split-second. She looked for Lucifer, but he was gone from their bedroom, and she remembered that he'd headed home to talk with Alma about the potion.

There was nothing else for it, and she jumped out of bed, pulled on her black boots and ran for the church's exit, feeling her daughter's mental beacon emitting from just across from the back entrance to the church. Cate ran outside and crossed the protective threshold without a second thought. She rounded the corner and she saw them immediately—a white coven. They were being led by Angelica, and encircled her two precious children, trapping them within their circle.

The twins were trying to get through their wall of witches, but they couldn't penetrate the powerful white circle. Both Blake and Luna pushed at the women, kicking and hitting them, but the witches didn't flinch. They also didn't grab at them, or try to bind them in any way. Cate was confused as she watched them for a moment, but kept on towards the group as she tried to figure out how to defeat them, or find a way to break their circle long enough to free her children.

She was so busy focussing on them that she realised too late how the real reason the white witches weren't reacting to the twins' retaliation was because they weren't there for them. They were using the children as bait to lure Cate out of hiding.

A second coven then appeared, and teleported around the Dark Queen, strategically encircling her. She didn't even have time to react to their presence, and felt a burst of light power course through her body, weakening her instantly. Cate clutched at her aching chest, and cried out as the witches blocked her path, while each of them smirked at her delightedly. None of them spoke, but she soon felt the familiar feeling of them teleporting her skywards and knew why they'd come.

She tried to resist, but knew from previous experience that she couldn't fight them, so quickly gave up. Cate couldn't see clearly in the blurry white haze that flashed past her as they travelled up and away from Earth, and she quickly realised she couldn't move at all. She gave up trying, allowing herself to be teleported away without any further resistance—it was pointless and she knew it. Cate couldn't stop her thoughts turning to Lucifer, and her heart ached as his face flashed across her mind. She pushed the thoughts of him away, and focussed on Luna and Blake instead. She hoped the witches had left them behind, but also suspected they might've preferred that their bait accompany them.

Please don't hurt them, she thought, sending out a silent plea to the master she knew must've orchestrated her abduction. Cate was also pretty sure she knew where her destination was and who would be waiting there for her once she arrived there, and her stomach dropped at the sheer thought of what she knew he wanted from her.

CHAPTER TWENTY-NINE

Cate landed with a thud in the oh-so-familiar living room of the bright beach house, and it was both reassuring and disturbing to discover that it was no different than it'd been all the years before. The smell of the ocean and the bright sunshine that streamed into the windows bought back many memories, and not all of them were awful ones if she was completely honest. Things were very different for her now than they'd been when she was last here though, and she'd changed very much in that time—in both herself and her priorities.

She scanned around and saw that to her left sat her two clearly terrified children. They'd been left on the soft white sofa in the centre of the room in front of the large fire that was, for now, unlit. They weren't visibly restrained, but neither of them seemed to be able to speak or move, and Cate could see the struggle behind Blake's sad eyes. He was clearly trying desperately to fight whatever spell or commandment was holding them in place, but with no luck. Cate tried to go to them, desperately wanting to wrap the pair in her arms and tell them everything was going to be okay, but she quickly realised that she too was stuck, unable to move or speak despite her best efforts. She stood still as stone over her equally motionless offspring in wait for their captor—a strange and eerie sight against the backdrop of the bright beach house.

Cate began to think of the possible escape options, and anything she might use to bargain with Uriel for the twins' release. Her mind was completely blank though, and she couldn't help but feel lost and powerless. Dylan had freed her before, and she was far away down on Earth with no hope of gaining access to his astral plain. She wondered if Dylan even knew that the three of them had been taken. Cate didn't know if or how Lucifer might try to get to them and attempt a rescue, but she very much doubted that Uriel would let his guard down a second time, and the presence of the two covens had already proven that.

A cool, steady breath fluttered along Cate's collarbone from behind her, and she felt his presence before Uriel even spoke or came into view. She was so angry, and wanted to lash out and hurt him, but was still unable to move or react thanks to his powerful commandment holding her still. With an inward curse, she let her hatred pour out of her via her thoughts, but her captor didn't seem to care at all.

"Welcome back. I've missed you," he whispered, and he inhaled her scent. "The way I see it, my love, you have two choices," Uriel said quietly into her left ear, gesturing with his hand towards the two babes who looked innocently on at them from their forced resting places on the sofa. Cate could see the tears that were running down Luna's cheeks, and knew that she had to be incredibly frightened. Being imprisoned inside her own body was obviously scaring her profoundly and she silently pleaded with Uriel to free her poor children, but he ignored her. "You can say yes, or you can say no," he continued calmly. Uriel then stepped around to face Cate, and he looked her straight in the eye. His eyes burned brightly as he took in her memories and thoughts for a few moments, and she didn't even try and fight the mental intrusion. "And, I have two choices too," he said as he inched closer.

He pressed his torso into her statuesque frame, and moved his mouth so close to Cate's that he was almost kissing her. "Leverage, or blackmail," Uriel added with a vile grin, and then watched her squirm beneath his spell. She wanted to tear his eyes out, but at the same time she knew fighting him was pointless. It no longer mattered what she did or didn't want, she was helpless and they both knew it. With that thought, she was released from the spell that'd been keeping her trapped in her immoveable body. Cate stumbled back slightly, but he caught her with a strong hand against her lower back. Uriel captured her in his tight grasp again, and held Cate's body firmly against his.

He didn't have to say anything more. It was abundantly clear to her what he was willing to do, and whose lives he was willing to sacrifice in order to blackmail her. Cate trembled against his hold, feeling defeated.

"I thought you were meant to be the good guy?" she asked him, her pained voice just a whisper, but he heard her clearly enough. He didn't answer, but pushed her back so she stumbled. Uriel then used her moment of confusion to his advantage, and pinned her to the wall. His strong body held hers tightly in place as his hands reached up her waist, over her breasts, and then to her face. He cupped her cheeks, running his fingers over her lips and then up through her dark, curly hair. In another life she might've enjoyed the passion in his eyes or the care he touched her with, but not now—and never again.

When he planted a soft, delicate kiss on her lips, Cate put her hands on Uriel's chest and tried to push him away, but she couldn't stop him. Her strength was no match for his. The angel's mouth expertly caressed hers, and he soon felt her relax ever so slightly into his powerful kiss. Cate was giving in to him at last, despite her mind still running through her possible escape options, and he smiled against her mouth. They both knew she really had no choice anyway, so the sooner she submitted, the better.

When he finally released his hold of her soft, red lips, Uriel pulled back and searched Cate's face, taking in the beautiful Dark Queen. He'd missed her so very much since she'd been ripped from his grasp all those years before.

She looked up at him, taking in the gorgeous angel that stared back at her. His deep blue eyes still mesmerised her as she stared back into them. What a paradox he was, and Cate considered it odd that beneath his light power and angelic cause, Uriel might perhaps be one of the most evil beings she'd ever known. She was terrified for her children, and of what he was willing to do, and that fear dominated her every thought as she awaited his response. Cate was unable to hide her emotions from the powerful being whose touch was already sending light coursing through her, and so stopped trying to fight.

"Do you still not realise by now, darling that the whole *good versus evil* thing is all about interpretation? I told you about a similar concept once before, do you remember?" he asked, and Cate nodded, feeling woozy thanks to her pounding heart and the frenzied emotions that'd taken over her body. His touch also gave her that tell-tale tingle again, even after all the time they'd spent apart. Despite her indifference to him now that she was no longer under his once so seductive spell, her body reacted to him, and it annoyed her that he was still able to affect her so strongly. "Man believes us to be the good guys, so even when we do something bad it's simply seen as God's will," he went on, his sly grin still firmly in place.

Cate didn't care what he thought or how he justified his evil deeds. She could tell he was incredibly pleased with himself for getting her back here at long last, and truly despised him. Uriel didn't care, and carried on with his rationalisation. "But, man believes Lucifer to be evil, no matter what. Regardless of what he does, or any of you dark bastards do in his name, it is, and always will be, considered an evil deed," Uriel explained running his hand down her cheek again.

"The road to Hell is paved with good intentions," Cate muttered, with a low laugh despite there being nothing funny about the angel's words. He nodded, pleased that she was already getting his point. "So no matter what we do, we'll always be the bad guys?" she asked, her green eyes looking up sadly into his as he continued to pin her to the wall.

"That's right, but don't forget that being bad is not the same as being hated. It was my will that he be cast out from both Heaven and Earth, but not by fear, and certainly not because of hate—it was for love. We love him still, and yet the council and I cast him down into that dark pit regardless. It was done that way so that he'd thrive, become powerful, and become his own master. We needed to appoint someone as the ruler of the underworld, so had to choose one of our angels to fall, and he was the obvious choice. Lucifer was the most stubborn and headstrong of all the high council," he informed her, making Cate jump with shock at his side of the story of how her husband had been cast out from Heaven.

"So you wanted him to question your orders? Encouraged him to disagree? You probably told him to speak out, didn't you?" she snapped back angrily, and the smile that curled in the corners of Uriel's lips told her that she was right.

"In order to encourage someone to reach their full potential, you do not deliver to them the object of their desires. You open up a world of possibilities to them and encourage them to find that power or possession for themselves. They need to earn it.

Sometimes the ones we love meet our expectations adequately, other times they fail miserably, and every once in a full moon they might just surpass our ambitions for them entirely. They accomplish far more than you ever thought them capable of, and you then find yourself envying them for all that they then possess," he said. Uriel eyed Cate with a dark expression before he leaned down and kissed her again, pressing her even tighter into the wall.

"So am I just a possession of his that you want for yourself then?" Cate asked him quietly once he pulled back again. "Hardly the pillow talk I was always so used to with you, Uriel," she added, aiming for a playful distraction from their intense conversation. It worked, and Uriel smiled down at her, the tension in his own body subsiding slightly.

"I wasn't just talking about him. I was talking about you, too." Cate was utterly taken aback by his openness, but urged herself to calm down, knowing that she needed to keep the conversation light and her wits about her. She was still desperately aware that the twins remained trapped in their seats and how she still needed to negotiate their release with their captor. Cate searched his face, but the angel gave nothing away, and she hated that she had no way of knowing what his next move would be.

"I wonder," Cate pondered aloud after a few quiet moments passed. "Is there a way I can persuade you to release the children from their binds and send them home? We can then use the time alone to talk about all of these issues in more detail," she tried, and hoped he might at least give her the peace of mind of knowing that her babies were home and safe with Lucifer in Hell—even if she couldn't go with them. Cate didn't want to dwell on thoughts of her husband, especially under Uriel's gaze, but knew the number-one priority right now was the safety of her children. She would find her own way back to their father as soon as she could.

"Do you give me your word you'll stay with me?" Uriel asked, stepping back and looking her square in the eye. "Do not answer lightly, as I will hold you to your word, Cate." He took her shoulders in his strong hands. "Do you promise to stay here with me until I release you?" he asked again, looking down at her with a stern and unrelenting expression on his face.

"Do you give me your word that they'll be delivered home safely, Uriel?" she asked, her own tone strong and demanding, and her counter-offer firmly on the table. Giving into him was the only way, but she was determined to do it on her terms.

"Blake will be delivered to his father instantly, I promise," he responded, a sinister grin creeping in around the corners of his mouth.

"And what of Luna?" Cate asked.

"She's the blackmail," he answered. The response made her gasp, but she also knew she had no other choice but to accept.

"Let me say goodbye first?" Cate asked him, and Uriel nodded in agreement.

He stepped away, releasing her from his command, and he watched as she walked tentatively over to the sofa. She knelt down in front of Blake and waited as the spell holding him silent and still was quickly removed. Uriel watched them from beside the sofa with intrigue as she embraced her child tightly, and a satisfied look crossed his face as he took in the sight of her. Cate was so different now that she was a mother, but her actions only served to make him want her more. Her selflessness had brought her right to him, and now he intended to utilise that same instinct to get exactly what he wanted from her.

Both Cate and her son sobbed together as they cuddled, and Blake's muffled apologies could be heard clearly from within her tight grasp.

"It's okay. You didn't mean for any of this to happen, so you be strong, baby boy," she told him, leaning down to whisper in his ear. "Be strong for Daddy and Luna, Blake. I love you," she insisted, kissing his forehead and fighting back her own tears. He nodded in promise.

A moment later, Blake was gone. He'd been magically teleported away right from within her arms thanks to the powerful angel, and the emptiness made her heart ache. Cate's sobs shuddered through her uncontrollably, and Uriel just stood and continued to watch her, his curiosity aroused. He was bemused somewhat at her reaction, but was also pleased that she was such a maternal woman. He then decided to give her a few minutes to calm down in privacy, taking himself off to the kitchen to make them both a glass of wine, just like old times.

Despite the bright sunshine, the clock on the mantel struck six o'clock in the morning on what would've been the end of a dark, cold night on Earth. Panic quickly rose in Cate's chest, realising what that meant. The night would be over very soon and the sun would then rise down on Earth, beginning the waning process of the moon, and indicating the end of her husband and children's safe time away from Hell.

She quickly stopped her sobbing and looked down at Luna. Tears still lay on her daughter's cheekbones from where they'd fallen earlier, and were almost dry after her long imprisonment in her own body. It broke her heart to see the fear in Luna's gaze, but before she could soothe her, the reaction began. Despite the spell's incredible power holding her still, Luna let out a muffled cry. Her nose then started bleeding and she closed her eyes. Cate jumped to her feet and charged quickly down the hall to find Uriel. He was still in the kitchen, pulling the cork from a deep red bottle of wine in his hands.

"You have to send her home now!" she cried, begging him. "The moon's waning and she's already started showing symptoms. Please Uriel," she bellowed and fell to his feet. Cate grabbed his light trousers with her hands and bowed her head before him, almost as though she were praying. He smiled, enjoying watching her fall to her knees for him.

"I will save your daughter's life today, Cate," Uriel told her. "But, you must say yes to me first."

She looked up at him, tears streaming down her face, but knew that there was no other choice. She nodded and rose to her feet, taking Uriel's hand in hers as she then led him back to the living room.

"Lift the spell, please. I need to see if she's okay," Cate pleaded when they were stood staring down at Luna. Uriel didn't say anything, but nodded, and Cate knelt before the child as she slumped down onto her side, moaning and crying out as she went. She leaned forward to grab her, wanting to lift Luna off of the sofa and into her arms, but Uriel reached down and stopped her from going any further. He grabbed Cate's arm and pulled her back to her feet, turned her around and pushed her forward, flattening her cheek against the wall opposite the sofa. He then pressed himself into her back, pushing her stomach and chest hard against the wall.

Cate didn't resist. She let him take control of her, and knew she was going to have to promise to be his to command now, and that she'd have to do whatever he demanded of her. Every part of her body that he pressed into the wall ached terribly, but she didn't cry out or push him away. Her strength would be no match for his, even if she had wanted to fight back.

All Cate could think about was Luna. She knew there was no other choice for her, and she had to do whatever it took to save her daughter's life.

"You reek of him, even more so than before," Uriel moaned in her ear. "Are the rumours true? Do you drink from him like some vampire from the horror stories?" She knew he was teasing her, riling her up to get a bite, and her thoughts gave her away before she could even try to fight them, so she spoke up regardless.

"I was borne of his blood, and took it again so he could share his strength, his power, and more. Mock me if you must, but at least it worked in getting rid of the light you'd infected me with," she spat.

"Lapping at his vein like the good little puppet you are," he mocked her further, but Cate refused to answer back with the vicious retort on the tip of her tongue. Time was of the essence, as was Luna's life, and she didn't have time to waste standing there arguing with Uriel about the gory methods she and Lucifer had used to set her free of him the last time. She'd do it all again to get back to his side, but this time Uriel wasn't taking the time to woo her, leaving her full of light like before. Nothing about his actions this time reminded her of his once so romantic ways, and she promised herself—perhaps foolishly—that she wouldn't give up her mind so easily a second time around. "I don't need your permission to fuck you, Cate," Uriel told her, whispering impatiently in her ear. "You gave me that before. But you will say yes to giving me a child this time, or else you will watch your daughter die today." With one quick move of his ankle inside hers, he pushed Cate's legs open while still pressing her harder against the wall. He pushed his erection into the back of her thigh, running his hands down to her waist as his entire body ached for her. She gasped, finding herself both angered and aroused at his forceful desire for her. She knew she had to give into him, and forced the words to leave her mouth even though she hated saying them.

"I am yours, Uriel. And yes, I will give you a child," she told him, and her entire body felt weak and defeated after the submission. She would give him her body to use as he pleased, but she wouldn't give him her heart, or her soul. Cate had to keep something of her own if she were to survive a future beyond this realm, and he could have her body, but nothing else. "Now please, send my daughter home to her father," she begged.

"Good girl," he replied, and she could tell without looking that he was smiling. Less than a second later the commandment keeping her child in the astral plain was lifted and Luna was gone. Cate wanted to scream.

"How can I know for sure they're safe?" she asked, in a hushed and scared voice. She remained pressed firmly into the hard wall by Uriel's immovable frame, yet she had to know for sure.

"Because I said so," he told her angrily, turning her around to face him in one quick move. He kissed her deeply, lifted her up into his arms and wrapped her legs around his waist. She gave into his silent order and held on, allowing her new master to carry her down the hall and into the white bedroom, his mouth not leaving hers for even a second.

Cate's black clothes were ripped from her body by an unseen, powerful force, as Uriel's eagerness to dominate her overruled his usual carefulness. Once she was naked, he lay her down on the bed before him and undressed himself with a click of his fingers, watching her. "Don't fight me, Cate," he told her, and she halted in her attempt to cover her body from his prying eyes. It was fruitless, and they both knew it.

"I wouldn't dream of it," she answered sarcastically. Uriel then climbed onto the bed and leaned over her, nestling himself between her legs with a satisfied smile, and he stared down into her stunning eyes. She wasn't ready, but he refused to wait, and gave her just one more kiss before plunging himself inside with one deep, heavy thrust.

She cried out, grabbing his shoulders tightly as the tender membranes inside took a few seconds to stretch for him, and she dug her nails in hard. He didn't stop, and pushed deeper with each thrust of his thick, hard length. With her body betraying her, Cate closed her eyes and tried desperately to concentrate on Uriel and her oath to him, rather than anything else. She knew she needed to focus on anything other than Lucifer and the children, but was also terrified by the very real possibility of giving him a child.

Despite her rollercoaster of emotions, Cate's physical impulses took over, and she climaxed quickly. The wonderful and still familiar feel of him inside her, along with the twinges of both anger and guilt she felt deep in her gut, quickly led to an outburst of both physical and emotional release at the same time. She didn't hold back, and lifted her hips up towards him, thrusting herself to meet his strong advances as he penetrated her deeper. Uriel groaned loudly as she tensed around him and then flipped Cate over to lie on her belly, and he grabbed her hair roughly as he plunged back inside her soaked core. He then closed her legs beneath to and wrap tighter around him inside her hot, wet cleft as he delved harder and faster in pursuit of his own climax.

She soon began to writhe beneath him and called out as she came for him again, panting exhaustedly as the aftershocks coursed throughout her body. He'd never been rough with her before, but this time she guessed he was punishing as well as pleasuring her, and Cate couldn't deny it was a thrill. Uriel then pulled her hips up towards him, and he shuddered and gripped her hips tightly as he allowed his own climax to burst out from him like a wave of intense pleasure.

Their beach house practically crumbled around them as he came. The small earthquake that erupted from his body sent a shockwave that tore through the hard stone walls and rippled across the sand on the beach that surrounded the house. The powerful burst carried on out into the ocean, sending waves crashing back through the deep waters in an incredible display of Uriel's almighty power.

Less than a second later, the damage to the beach house was repaired thanks to another of his silent, powerful commands. Despite her frantic panting and still shuddering body, Cate didn't hesitate to obey her new master when he leaned down and whispered in her ear that he was ready to start again. She climbed on top of him as he lay back on the bed and eyed her eagerly. Cate leaned back on her heels, welcoming his hardness deep inside her again as she rode up and down on his thick length, and all the while forcing herself to fight back the tears still prickling at her eyes.

CHAPTER THIRTY

Uriel lay beside Cate, cradling her tightly as she wept. She'd turned her body away from him, but he continued to hold on regardless. He knew she was still angry, and didn't want him to see her while she was so vulnerable, but he couldn't walk away. She belonged to him again, and despite being aware that he was the reason for her tears, Uriel refused to leave her side. He'd pursued her relentlessly for three days non-stop, and she was now utterly exhausted and incredibly sensitive. Her desperation and worry seemed to be bubbling up inside her uncontrollably, and even though she'd tried to fight it, the emotion was currently overwhelming her.

Cate had given herself to him entirely, and had even allowed herself to enjoy the rolling orgasms that came with the territory. But after days of nothing but sex, she needed to rest, and her body was crying out for sleep. She had a deep void inside of her that she knew was that of her tremendous loss, both of her children and her husband. She didn't know when or if she would see them again, and the sobs that came pouring out of her was her grief for them forcing its way out of her at last, refusing to be stifled any longer.

Uriel climbed up from the bed, snapping his fingers once again to repair the damage to the walls and furniture around them. He went to the bathroom where he ran Cate a hot, deep bath, complete with bubbles and candles. He approached the bed and stroked her damp cheek, making her jump. She looked up and took his hand, following him into the warm bathroom without a word. Cate then climbed into the red-hot water graciously and closed her heavy eyes as she relaxed in the soothing suds, trying desperately to calm down.

Uriel decided to leave her alone for the first time since she'd said yes to him again. He had to trust that she wasn't going to try anything foolish or try and escape. Doing so would only force his hand to deliver her another lesson in what he was capable of, and he had the sneaking suspicion she might not survive another punishment. She just needed some quiet time, and he couldn't deny that it brought him no pleasure to see that she was hurting. Cate looked exhausted, and pale. Her pain was coming though via her thoughts and emotions she was so openly sending to him, seemingly unable to hide or mask her feelings at all, and he could tell it was consuming her.

He went to the kitchen, fixing her something to eat as he mulled over the events of the past few months in the build-up to getting her back. There was still an incredible amount of love he felt for Cate, despite all their time apart, and her escape the last time they'd been there on his astral plain together. He knew that Dylan had been the instigator of her release rather than Cate herself, though. Although he knew that she'd welcomed being set free, Uriel still hoped she might find a way to love him again despite her resistance.

The anticipation had almost driven him mad waiting for her to come back, and he thought back to the night he'd eventually received word that she was up on Earth again. Angelica had sensed a shift in the balance of light and dark, and had come to him immediately. She was a formidable witch, her instincts only ever having been surpassed by her predecessor Alma, and Uriel had ordered her to look into it immediately.

She'd soon discovered that not only was Cate on Earth, but that she'd given Lucifer two children, one of whom was a curious child, and that he could be used as bait to lure her out of hiding. All they had to do was be patient and he would bring Cate to them, which was exactly what'd happened.

Uriel knew that he had all the power. Although he wouldn't have willingly hurt the twins, he'd known he would have to push the boundaries of his own will to its limits in order to force hers to bend and eventually break the way he needed it to. When Cate had knelt before him in the kitchen, he'd known then that she had finally submitted to him entirely.

It'd felt so good having her ready, waiting, and willing to give him everything he desired. Being proven right was fun, and he'd enjoyed seeing her on her knees, begging. Uriel was well aware that his darker urges had stirred up in him then, and they'd spurred him on towards his only goal that night, but he'd had to have her, he'd had to win.

Uriel made Cate a cup of sweet, milky tea and a couple of slices of buttered toast, taking it to her where she still lay in the centre of the misty bathroom. She smiled up at him from her resting place in the large metal tub, and gratefully sipped the tea.

It tasted good, and her stomach rumbled for the rest. Instinctually, she leaned sideways and held the toast over the side of the bath so she could eat it without getting any crumbs in the deep water, and had to remind herself that she needn't care about making a mess.

The angel looked down at her thoughtfully as he perched on the edge of the sink. His dark hair fell into his eyes as he smiled playfully, feeling ready her again, but he fought his urges. She needed a bit longer to rest first. He watched as she finished off the toast and set the plate down before lying back against the incline of the tub with a satisfied smile, and then slipped off his white linen trousers and climbed in behind her. He urged her to lie back and rest against his chest rather than on the hard metal basin, and was pleased when she did as she was bid.

Cate leaned forward and pushed open the hot tap, quickly topping up the water to re-heat the warm cocoon around them, before lying back in his strong arms. Her mind was blank, and Uriel couldn't be sure if she'd forced all her feelings aside, or was just becoming more and number to them. Either way, he knew that she couldn't bear for him to question her on it, so he resisted. Holding his lover close for a few quiet moments, he hoped she'd find comfort in his arms, rather than just sadness and fear.

"I love you," Uriel told her after a while, knowing that Cate didn't feel the same way about him, but he didn't care.

CHAPTER THIRTY-ONE

Within a few weeks, the beach house was in absolute ruins. Uriel decided to give up on the repairs, and instead he'd simply left them a huge, white bed in the middle of the sandy beach for them to lie together on and do as they pleased. No one else was allowed on his astral plain, so there wasn't anyone around to see their antics anyway. The beach house simply couldn't withstand the shockwaves he continually gave off due to their relentless lovemaking, and he couldn't be bothered with trying.

Despite the time that'd passed, Cate still wasn't pregnant even after his continual efforts. Uriel was disheartened, but carried on, enjoying being with his lover far too much to worry about the details regarding their child's inevitable conception.

She'd grown emotionally numb over the last few weeks, her mind usually blank or despondent, but her body responded willingly to her new master's orders, and her strong muscles gave him everything he craved. When she allowed herself a moment to think, Cate would quickly realise that she preferred it when her mind was blank or they were making-love. Both denial and the distraction kept her occupied, and helped stop the terrible thoughts and feelings from trying to creep back in for just a little while longer.

A few days later, she stood on the beachfront, looking out at the crystal clear waters that stretched out before her—a seemingly endless ocean although she knew it was all just an illusion. She'd been there for four weeks, and soon found herself wondering absentmindedly if the moon was full again below them, and whether Lucifer was down there on Earth trying to find a way to them. Cate couldn't help but hope he might be on his way to take her home, but she also knew that it was impossible. She felt lost, and couldn't know for sure where he was or what he was doing.

Her connection to both him and the children was completely severed again, thanks to Uriel's strong power over her once again.

Thickly muscled arms then came around from behind her and held Cate tight, and her arms were pinned to her sides as he stroked down her bare forearms to her hands.

"Feeling thoughtful, my love?" Uriel asked her, serving a reminder to his captive lover that he knew exactly what she'd been thinking about. Cate didn't reply, but pushed the thoughts of Lucifer away at once, and shook her head. He laughed gruffly and leaned over her, kissing her neck softly before trailing gentle kisses down to Cate's collarbone. Uriel tugged at the thin straps of her white summer dress, each of which then fell down her arms to her waist, exposing her breasts. He cupped them gently with his hands, trailing kisses up and down her neck and shoulder while she continued to stare blankly off to the horizon.

"Get your fucking hands off my wife," a voice then boomed behind them, disturbing their isolation.

Cate jumped. The voice had startled her, and she was scared but also desperately yearned to see the face of the man who'd spoken those words so assuredly from behind them. She wondered for a moment if she was dreaming, hallucinating, or even if it was Uriel playing tricks on her to test her loyalty. Cate knew one thing for sure though, she'd felt the angel's strong body tense from behind her, telling her she hadn't imagined it. Uriel quickly pulled the straps of her thin dress back up her arms to her shoulders, covering her naked body again, yet he kept his arms tightly around her as the pair of them turned to face the intruder together.

Standing just a few feet away was the Dark King, his eyes jet-black with his power, while anger and hatred billowed out of him towards his angelic foe. He glared over at the pair of them, and there was darkness in him that scared Cate when he looked at her in disgust for a second before focussing his attention on Uriel again. Lucifer looked older somehow and he too seemed numb and broken. His usually playful prowess was long gone as he took in the sight of Uriel holding onto her so protectively.

Lucifer was wearing a black shirt and jeans, both of which were splattered with red blood, and in his arms he held the body of a beaten and bloody, blonde haired woman.

"Angelica," Uriel whispered gruffly, looking to and from the lifeless witch and the monster that carried her in his arms.

"Yes," his brother-of-sorts replied with a sneer. "She tried to fight at first, but she was no match for me, of course. I promised the stupid witch I wouldn't kill her if she took me through the portal to your astral plain," Lucifer said as he dropped Angelica's clearly dead body to the ground. "I lied," he then added with a smirk.

Uriel's grip tightened on Cate's shoulders, hurting her as he pulled her closer. She was the only leverage he had, and he was determined not to let her go.

"Cate's mine now," he told Satan.

"And what makes you think you can simply have her? My blood runs through her veins, my power gives her the life-force you yourself are so drawn to, and yet you believe you can own her?" Lucifer smirked, and had the gall to laugh at the angel's audacity. "I alone possess her, do you understand? Hecate is mine, and always will be. She'll infect you with my darkness before I allow you to taint her with your light again. She and our children will do my bidding for centuries to come, and you can do nothing to stop us."

"You're wrong," Uriel demanded. "Cate belongs to me now."

"And, what do you hope to achieve in keeping her?" Lucifer asked him pointedly. His voice was clear and his stance powerful now in the face of his long-time adversary, but Cate was gobsmacked by his selfish words. Part of her hoped they weren't true, that he was simply taunting Uriel, but she had the sneaking suspicion they might stem from a real place within him. Perhaps the second betrayal was one too many, and she began wondering what the future might hold for them once all of this was over.

"I yearn for the same as you, I suppose," Uriel replied thoughtfully. "Love, family. You have your heirs, and she will now give me mine. Cate has already said yes, she has given herself to me," he added matter-of-factly.

If hearing Lucifer basically call her his trophy hadn't wound her up enough, listening to Uriel speak of her like an object that way quickly made her downright furious. Intense rage built up quickly inside of her, and the powerful emotions that she'd tried to push away for the past few weeks suddenly burst out of her uncontrollably. She wrenched herself away from Uriel's hold, ignoring the intense pain that flared up on her skin from the grip his hands had once had on her shoulders. Cate moved sideways and stood between the two of them, and then took a step backwards. She wanted to edge away from both of them, and stared angrily at the pair of almighty beings that fought so obsessively for her affections.

"I'm not some fucking baby maker you know!" she cried. "Nor am I a possession for either of you to own or use at your bloody convenience." Both Lucifer and Uriel looked taken aback by her strong words, their gazes each flicking over to her anxiously before returning to one another. "I don't think either of you even know how to truly love another person, or what that word means," she added, looking down forlornly. "Perhaps monsters are real after all," she added, a whisper to herself more than to either of them, and she had to grip her gut as a pang of angst swept over her. She felt broken. Utterly and so profoundly lost it was soul-destroying.

Lucifer looked over at her for a second, saddened by her powerful words, but he quickly returned his gaze to his adversary. He focussed his anger and pain on Uriel, rather than his wife, despite her hurtful speech. He started edging over towards Cate, but the angel took note of his movement and took a step in her direction too.

The hate in Lucifer's eyes flared again, and he stepped forward this time. He slammed his fist into the angel's left cheekbone with a punch that would render any human dead without question, but not him. Uriel retaliated instantly, his powerful counter attack sending a shockwave through the ground beneath Cate's feet, stirring the air all around the pair of powerful beings. Before she could beg for them to stop, a wave of power rushed her, and she was sent flying backwards through the air. She was thrown far away from the beach thanks to the strong blast that'd hit her, and crashed into the deep water with a huge splash.

Cate broke the surface and looked towards the now far off beach, seeing the two powerful enemies brawling on the sand. Their matching strengths were giving off such blasts of power that the water's current seemed to have changed course because of it. The waves were being forced away from the beach by the shockwaves created on it by the feuding men. Pure power surged through the water, pushing Cate farther out with the tide. She tried to swim towards them, to push back through the now powerful force of the current, but it was no use. It was only a few seconds before she found her footing, just like before, and the water quickly began to shallow beneath her as she was pushed back thanks to the strong waves.

She was just about able to look above the waves at the beach, but quickly realised that she must also be very near to the edge of the astral plain. Cate began to panic that she might fall over the side and away from the protection of the realm that was, until very recently, her prison. It was now the only thing keeping her from falling the thousands of feet to the Earth below, and potentially to her death if Angelica's previous words of warning were to be believed.

When only her ankles remained covered by the water, Cate stood and stared out, trying to catch a glimpse of the fray ahead. Uriel and Lucifer were so far away. She could only just about make out a blur of quick movements along with loud cracking noises, which she assumed must be their powerful blows as they rained them down on one another. Dark black clouds began moving in overhead, and Cate could hear the sound of deep, ominous thunder that rumbled through them. A second later, a large fork of lightning shimmered across the sky all around her, landing on the beach. Cate watched as the bed she'd once shared with Uriel exploded thanks to the blast from the power, and shrieked.

She stood there for a while longer, contemplating her options, but a huge wave then sprung up in front of her, pushing her backwards. The edge of the astral plane felt as sharp as a knife's edge under her bare feet, and she immediately lost her balance. Cate toppled backwards, and was soon plummeting downwards, away from the plain. The wind whistled loudly around her and enveloped her as she fell towards Earth, picking up speed uncontrollably. She looked up, trying to see back to the plain as she descended, but she could see nothing except the swirling black clouds that sparked with incredible cracks of lightning and boomed loudly with thunder from above her.

Cate fell faster, unable to control her descent, and after a few seconds she closed her eyes. She tried bracing for the impending impact as much as possible, and curled around herself. Thoughts of Blake and Luna's smiling, happy faces came to her, with the sad acceptance that her death may come soon. She hit water, and was grateful for the slightly softer landing, but still fell fast through the depths, despite the tide that pushed back against her powerful plummet. Within seconds, the deep, dark water swirled around her and blackened the view all around as she sank further down to the ocean floor. She nearly blacked out, but urged herself to stay lucid in the hope she might find a way to resurface. The lack of oxygen caused her chest to tighten and the shocks of pain that coursed through her entire body made Cate jerk and writhe in agony as she yearned for a breath of air.

You don't need it, she thought, knowing it was that way in Hell. She couldn't help but wonder, or rather hope, that maybe she didn't really needed oxygen while she was on Earth, too. Cate finally managed to calm herself down, mentally relaxing her tense body and slowing the painful pangs that plagued her chest as she began to slow down at last. Jagged rocks soon came up to greet her as she descended, and Cate winced as she slammed into them. The searing pain as another rock crashed against her head caused her to lose consciousness at once, and her lifeless body floated away at the behest of the current.

CHAPTER THIRTY-TWO

Cate stirred and forced herself awake, ignoring the dull aches that still throbbed throughout her entire body, threatening to pull her back into the sleepy abyss. Part of her welcomed it. The emptiness would help her block it all out and let her heal a little while longer. However, she needed answers, and pushed herself to rouse. It felt as if she was breaking the surface of the dark water that had not long before swirled all around her, and she took a deep, loud breath as she sat up in the strange bed where she'd been lying.

Cate looked around her, taking in the unfamiliar surroundings. She was in a small metal room, almost like the ones she had seen before on ships and cruise-liners. After taking a deep breath she thought back, trying to piece together the events that'd brought her here. An overwhelming barrage of memories hit her, and she lay back down in the bed, sobbing loudly as everything came rushing back. A few minutes later, the large door opened slowly, and a young man entered. Cate figured he couldn't be any older than twenty years old, and he tried not to look at her directly as she wept, seemingly embarrassed to have walked in on her crying. The tall, skinny young man stood beside her bed for a moment, and he awkwardly set a tray of food on the table to her left. He then made to leave silently before she stopped him, clearing her throat and wiping her eyes with her hands as she stared up into his dark brown eyes from the bed.

"Thank you," she mumbled, and he smiled kindly down at her. "Where am I?" Cate then asked, feeling completely lost, on many different levels.

"We're on an oil rig not far off the coast of Norway," he told her, his accent thick, but his English was still very good. He sat down on a solitary chair that was near her bedside and handed her a bottle of cool mineral water from the tray, which she took with a smile.

"Thanks," she said again, and introduced herself. "My name's Cate."

"Torstein," he told her shyly.

Cate was grateful for the nourishing drink, and once she'd taken a long gulp she looked across at the tray he'd bought in. She could see that he had kindly prepared her a delicious smelling bowl of soup and some buttered bread, along with a pot of yogurt and a chocolate biscuit. She smiled over at Torstein, thanking him again before propping herself up a little bit more on the pillows so that she could eat and drink a little easier. Cate winced as she moved her still tired and bruised body, but she pushed herself on nonetheless, knowing she would heal properly in no time. "You washed up near our rig. Just appeared out of nowhere," Torstein told her bemusedly. "We weren't even sure if you were alive at first, but we fished you out of the water anyway and bought you here to the infirmary." He waved a hand around as if to motion that was where the two of them were now.

"Thank you, I don't think I would've survived otherwise," her voice faltered, and she stared intently at her water bottle.

"It was a wonder we even saw you through the rain and wind of the storm, the waves were so high it was almost as though they carried you up here on purpose," he continued, still looking at her with a confused look. Cate just nodded, understanding his bewilderment, but she couldn't even begin to explain her strange predicament or how it was she came to be in the ocean near his rig.

"Oh yes, the terrible storm. How long did it last?" she asked, wondering how many hours her two feuding lovers had continued their battle.

"It's still raging outside," Torstein told her, his eyes wide with excitement and fear. "It's some kind of freak weather phenomenon, no one can explain it. The whole world is experiencing the terrible weather, it's all over the news," he told her animatedly, seemingly excited to give her the strange update.

"How long has it been going on now, then?" Cate then asked him, her eyes growing wider as she propped herself up higher on her elbows. She was still unsure how long she must've been unconscious, but knew that this was bad news, and could only mean that the pair of them were still fighting up there.

"It's been eight days since it all began," he told her, and Cate flopped back down on the bed, exhaling loudly.

"Eight days?" she asked, wondering aloud. "Whoa, this is bad."

The young rigger didn't seem to know how to respond to her, so he said no more. He just stood and lifted the tray from the bedside onto her lap.

"Eat this before it gets cold, Cate. It will make you strong," he said with a grin, and his feeble attempt at a stern order made her smile. She nodded and saluted him playfully with one hand.

"Yes sir," she joked, and Torstein laughed. He then nodded triumphantly and walked over to the metal doorway, looking back over at her before he left.

"I'll be back to check on you later," he promised, heading out and leaving Cate alone in the ward room with her food and her thoughts.

Another week passed by before the terrible storm finally started to pass. It was a week in which Cate rested and recuperated with the help of Torstein and the other riggers, and she finally felt more like her old self again. She didn't know what the ending of the storm finally meant, whether it was because Lucifer and Uriel had both stopped fighting at last, or if it meant that one of them had finally been defeated. Either way, Cate was worried and still full of so many mixed emotions she didn't even know where to begin to process it all. She was glad to be alive and back to her normal strength again, especially after what she'd thought might be a fatal fall from that astral plain.

Cate tried to teleport back to Hell a few times, but every time was unsuccessful, much to her dismay. She couldn't even teleport elsewhere on Earth, and could only imagine it was because of Uriel's light being inside her once again. Cate hoped she would hear news of the fight and its outcome when she finally reached home, but was still unsure how to get there without being able to teleport. She knew she had no choice other than to wait and hope for the best.

When the ocean around the rig was calm again and the sun shone brightly in the sky overhead, Cate looked up at the blue expanse above. She felt full of hope and wonder, and knew then that it was the right time to go in search of answers, and hopefully a way home. She packed a small backpack with a couple of changes of clothes given to her by the generous riggers and some food packs, before saying a huge thank you to Torstein and all the others that'd helped her over the past couple of weeks. Those mere humans that she'd somehow begun to take for granted in her long life had taken great care of her and had never asked for anything in return. Cate was absolutely positive they'd saved her life the day they'd fished her out of the stormy waves, and vowed never to forget their kindness.

She boarded a small boat and headed for the shore, having to sleep rough in the ferry terminal for a night before she managed to talk her way onto an overnight boat headed for England. She'd met a middle-aged lorry driver who offered her a seat in his cab in return for her company for the evening, and she made it clear she wasn't about to give him more than a kind smile and some polite conversation. Cate made sure that the man drank his weight in vodka, smiling and chatting warmly with the rotund man who lapped up the attention from her with a twinkle in his eye as she poured him shot after shot of the potent drink. When he eventually passed out drunk in his seat, she sneaked away and headed for the quiet lounge to find a comfy spot in which to sleep for a little while.

When Cate arrived in Hull the next morning, she disembarked and made her way over to the nearby bus stop. She couldn't deny it was a sorry sight, and she was shocked to find the port still in such a tragic mess following the storm's damage. Cate headed into the local town and was gobsmacked to discover more destruction and ruin that'd affected almost everything in sight. The streets and homes there were either covered in branches and debris, or had been boarded up and left behind while the occupants made their desperate attempts to flee the coastal areas in fear of tidal waves or flooding. The sight sickened her, but she knew it wasn't her doing. The devastation was the work of her two formidable lovers, and she hated them both in equal measure for what they'd done.

As the evening grew darker, she still had nowhere to stay and had very little money, so Cate wandered around in search of inspiration. She eventually found a small bed and breakfast, and talked her way inside, promising to help the old couple that owned it if they gave her shelter for a few nights. They agreed, seemingly happy for the helping hand, and Cate spent the next two days there, working hard through the day helping them recover from the storm, and all the while she was well fed and taken good care of by the elderly owners, Bob and May. When she finally said her goodbyes, May thrust some money in Cate's hand.

"Take it. Go and find your family," she told her, and Cate was taken aback by the kindness showed to her by yet another stranger. She took the money, grateful that she could now afford her train fare to London, and hugged the kind woman goodbye. Her plan was to go to the Satanic church in the capital, where she hoped to find some witches who could use their magic to send her back to the twins. She could figure out things with Lucifer later.

Cate was still disheartened that she hadn't felt any of her usual power since she'd woken up on the rig, and not even a glimmer of the usually strong beacon she'd normally felt with Lucifer. Her powers were completely gone, just like before, and she hated it. She knew it wasn't quite right, but kept on going in the hope that she would find some good news once she got to the church.

That evening, Cate left the tube station and crossed the busy street. She then headed down a dark alleyway, where she stepped over the invisible threshold to the dark church without any resistance. Inside she found the two lower level witches, Suzanne and Bea, whom she'd met during her time living in the church not too long before. The two of them were alone in the large central room, and were huddled around one of the warm, glowing lanterns that'd usually lined the walls, each of them looking dishevelled and dirty.

"Your majesty," Suzanne cried as Cate approached, her brown eyes wide with shock, and she smiled broadly at the Dark Queen. "You're alive!" She climbed up from her spot on the floor, pulling her dirty brown hair out of her eyes and into a scruffy ponytail in an attempt to tidy herself up.

"Well, yes, of course I am," Cate answered, and she couldn't help her impatient tone. "Has there been any word from my husband?" she asked them expectantly.

"No, your majesty, nothing," Bea told her, looking sullen.

"We've had no word from anyone since the King went to retrieve you. Alma and Dylan are with your children back home, so don't worry, but he hasn't been seen or heard of ever since the full moon."

"I cannot feel his power, can you?" Suzanne interjected, looking worried. Cate wondered if the pair of them had been holding out in the hope she would bring them good news, just she had for them, and she realised that none of them were any clearer thanks to having found each other again.

"No, I can't sense him either," Cate told them honestly. "The storm, it was Lucifer and Uriel. They had a terrible fight. I got away, but I was badly injured," she explained.

"He can't be, you know...*dead*, can he?" Bea asked, looking as though she might cry.

"I sure as hell hope not," Cate replied with a gulp. "Can you take me back home?" she asked hopefully, having had enough of their depressive conversation, but the two witches shook their heads forlornly.

"We have no powers, mistress," Suzanne told her. "We've been stuck here since the storm started."

***

Cate stayed with the witches in the cold church that night, not really sure what else to do with herself now that she knew for sure that she was stranded on Earth. The dark church, it seemed, offered no real protection without their powers or the invisible threshold to keep the white witches out, but there was no other place they could go. She and the witches needed to stay put, and Cate was positive that Lucifer's first instinct would be to go there, just like she had done. As she lay awake in the early hours of the next morning, cold and scared, Cate knew she might need to find herself somewhere safer to hide out until they had more news. Weeks had already passed without a sign of him, and she was unsure just how long it might take for them to hear from her husband.

She drifted back off to an uneasy and anxious sleep, and woke up starving a couple of hours later. Cate leaned over and rummaged in her backpack, finally finding her last bit of food, a cereal bar, which she wolfed down in seconds. She then lay back on the hard bench, wondering to herself where Lucifer might be, but within a couple of minutes, her stomach began to churn painfully. She climbed up out of her makeshift bed and ran down the hall to the toilet, only just making it in time before she was violently sick.

"Oh hell no," she whispered to herself when it was finally over. She wiped her mouth clean and took a deep, calming breath and stared in the mirror, the realisation suddenly dawning on her. Cate placed a hand over her tender stomach and thought back over the last few days, realising that she'd been feeling woozy ever since she left the oil rig, and had just been too busy and focussed to take notice of the signs.

She knew the signs were there, and wondered if the unthinkable could really be happening. It absolutely could be. She'd said yes after all.

Tears streamed from her eyes without warning, and she put her hand over her mouth so the witches wouldn't hear her sobbing. Cate cursed Uriel, wherever he was, but also cursed herself.

CHAPTER THIRTY-THREE.

"I'm going to see if I can find anyone else that might be able to help us," Cate informed the witches later that same morning. "If we gather as many of us together as possible, I hope that maybe we can combine our darkness to bring back our powers. I'll check in with you regularly, so stay here in case anyone else comes to find sanctuary at the church, okay?" she added, staying strong despite her fears and frenzied thoughts. The witches both nodded in agreement, despite them worrying for the Queen's safety, and each of them hugged Cate goodbye. She had to hide the anxiety in her own face as she left the familiar safety of the church, but she simply had to be away from all of them, especially any dark beings who might realise what was going on with her, or who could sense her suspicions regarding her *condition*.

Cate knew exactly where she needed go, and whom she had to seek out. There was only one being on the entire earthly realm that she could truly trust—Harry. She took the underground and boarded a train heading southwest, fretting the entire way over what she'd say when she finally found him. Cate arrived in Avebury later that same day, and then headed straight for the Lion's Head pub. She hoped to see some familiar faces there from her old days as its barmaid, days that seemed so long ago now that so much had happened, but it was still a comfort seeing the village again. The same old regulars were there, and she waved over at Jamie and Marc who'd stared at her as she entered with the same bemused faces and drunken grins. Cate then spoke with the young girl who was working behind the bar for a couple of minutes, but she wasn't of any help, not seeming to know anyone named Harry that lived in the village at all. Her face fell. She turned to leave just as her old boss, Joe, poked his head around the doorway that led through to the rest of the house.

"Blimey, Dana. Look at you!" he shouted to her, running through the entrance before grabbing Cate and pulling her into a tight hug. "My God, you don't look any different. How long has it been? Six years?" he quizzed her, smiling and ushering her to join him through the back.

"Seven," she corrected him, grinning warmly at her old employer and friend. He'd always been a kind man, and a fair boss. She'd enjoyed working with Joe and, most importantly of all, Cate knew she could trust him. In the living room above the bar, the pair caught up over coffee and cakes, and Cate thanked him but refused when he later offered her a stiffer drink.

"I'm trying to find Harry, does he still live around here?" she asked him hopefully.

"Yeah, but he got married about two years ago and moved to Marlborough I think," Joe told her, and Cate's stomach dropped. She knew she had no right to be jealous that Harry had moved on after she'd left, but she honestly felt a little disheartened. "I think he moved back into his old place a few months ago when it all went wrong though," Joe added with a sorry look as he took a swig of his beer. Cate knew she shouldn't be glad to hear of Harry's failed marriage, but she couldn't help but be a little relieved at the revelation that he was back in the village, and that he was single.

"Thanks Joe, it's been great catching up, but I'd better get going," she said, rising from her chair to leave, eager to see her old flame.

"It's late," Joe replied, and after looking over at the small clock on his living room wall, Cate realised it was almost midnight. "Have you got somewhere to stay?" he asked, and she shook her head. "Hey, why don't you just stay here tonight? You can have my room and I'll take the couch. It'll just be one night until you can get yourself sorted," he offered, and Cate had to smile, glad she wasn't about to spend the night sleeping rough. She nodded, grateful for the offer of a warm bed after the previous night's restless sleep in the cold, unguarded church.

"Thank you, Joe. You always were a good man," she said, smiling over at him. He stood and grabbed her backpack, slinging it over his shoulder as he then led her out to the hallway and down to his bedroom.

"I'll get some fresh sheets, and help yourself to the hot water,"

Joe added, seeming to know she'd appreciate the hospitality, and she grinned gratefully.

It wasn't long before Cate emerged from a lovely hot shower and then climbed under the freshly changed bed linen Joe had made up for her. Safe and comfortable once again, she drifted off to sleep almost instantly, dreaming of Blake and Luna as they played in the dark castle, smiling and cheering as she watched them with a huge smile.

***

The next morning, after getting dressed and calling herself a taxi, Cate thanked Joe for his hospitality. She refused breakfast just in case, and then went off in search of her old friend. After a few minutes, they pulled up to the familiar row of Victorian houses, many of which had been split into apartments that lined the wide road. The cab came to a stop outside Harry's ground floor flat, and Cate could see the clear number thirteen inscribed on the doorway—an omen that'd always made her laugh. She paid the driver and hurried up the path. Anticipation was welling up inside her as she stood on the doorstep for a moment, hesitating for a minute before she eventually rang the bell.

It was a Saturday morning, and it was only early, so Cate wondered for a moment if he might still be in bed. She almost took a step back, thinking it might be better if she went back later, when she heard a sound on the opposite side of the door. The latched lifted, and a key turned, and Cate waited impatiently for the door to finally open. When he answered, Harry looked neat and comfortable in his black tracksuit trousers and a t-shirt emblazoned with a superhero slogan. He looked good. The pair stared at each other for a moment, and she smiled up at him, feeling happier than she had in weeks.

Harry hadn't changed a bit. He was older looking of course, and even had a few grey flecks that speckled his brown hair to show for the years that'd passed since their last encounter. His blue eyes widened in disbelief as he took in the sight of Cate standing there staring up at him expectantly from his doorstep, and he stood motionless for a second. It seemed as if he needed a moment to process the sight of his long-lost friend—the unattainable object of his affections he'd tried to forget. Harry then burst into a huge grin, and he scooped her up off her feet and into his arms. Cate gave in to his welcome embrace, needing the safe and warm protectiveness more than she'd even realised, and held him back tightly.

"What are you doing here?" he asked excitedly, finally putting her back down on her feet, but he kept her close. "It's been ages, too bloody long," he added, scalding her mockingly with one eyebrow raised.

"I know. I'm so sorry, Harry," Cate told him. "Can you ever forgive me?" she added, and then started sobbing uncontrollably into his strong arms. He pulled her close again, shushing her, but Cate couldn't hold back the tears. She didn't want to, feeling incredibly vulnerable yet completely safe in his presence.

"I couldn't find you," he told her, his voice almost a whisper against her dark curls as he leaned his head down and breathed her in. After a few seconds, Harry leaned back to look upon her face, searching for a sign of why she was crying. "I tried to track you down, to track Luke down, but I found nothing. It was as if you two didn't even exist," he told her, and his face fell. "Did he hurt you?" Harry asked, a solemn look crossing his gentle face, and Cate shook her head.

"No, but I really need a friend right now. Are you willing to forgive me for running off on you?" she asked as she looked up into Harry's gorgeous eyes, searching them for forgiveness, and she found it, of course.

"I could never be mad at you, Dana. You know that," Harry told her, wiping the tears from her cheeks with his thumbs. He then beckoned her inside and she gratefully accepted the invitation, following him into his small flat. It still looked exactly the same as it had all those years before when they'd much of their time there together as friends, and he took Cate's bag and placed it by the sofa. "Do you want a cup of tea?" Harry asked, and a gentle, knowing smile crossed her lips as he did so.

"Always, you know that," she answered, grinning over at him, and the pair then wandered into the small kitchen to chat some more. Harry boiled the kettle and grabbed two large mugs from the cupboard, looking thoughtful.

"So, are you gonna tell me where you've been all this time?" he asked, placing teabags in the mugs and then adding the boiling water and a dash of milk. Harry then reached up into another cupboard for the tin of biscuits he knew she'd want as an accompaniment to her hot, milky brew, and set it down without having to ask. Cate wanted to laugh at how well he still knew her, but resisted, choosing to enjoy the familiarity rather than tease him about it.

"Somewhere far away, but it's kinda hard for me to explain, Harry," she answered, reverting straight back to her old diversionary tactics to stop him from asking questions. She then caught the disappointed look on his face and stopped herself from telling him more lies, and felt a sudden urge to tell him everything. A longing for full honesty came over her and she wondered, why not? Harry was her only friend and was absolutely the only person she knew she could truly trust with her secrets. If she didn't tell him the truth, it was a real probability that Harry wouldn't be willing to take care of her and the baby she was sure was growing inside of her like she needed him to.

Cate knew it was time to reveal all at last, regardless of her old, yet necessary closed-off nature. "Okay, I'm going to tell you everything," she told him, and Harry's face lit up, clearly pleased that she'd changed her mind. He'd always known there was more to her story than she'd revealed to him in the past, and he was eager to hear it at long last. "But you're gonna need to sit down for this," she added, looking over at the table in the corner of the room.

Harry started to laugh, sure that she must be joking, but quickly stopped himself when he saw the seriousness in Cate's eyes.

"Urm, okay," he said, leading her over to the small table with its two chairs that he'd squeezed into the corner of the kitchen. After depositing the mugs between them along with the biscuit tin, he took a seat. Cate sat in the chair opposite, staring into Harry's gorgeous eyes for a moment, taking in his handsome face. She basked in his gentle expression before she reached forward and grabbed a biscuit. After soaking it in her tea, she devoured the sweet treat whole and stared down at the hot mug she had cradled in her delicate hands.

"Well, firstly I guess you need to know that my name's not really Dana, it's Cate. And I'm not just the normal, human barmaid you once thought I was." She took a deep breath. "The girl you knew as Nina isn't my sister, she's my best friend. Luke *is* my husband, but we have what you might consider to be a rather strange relationship. We'll get to that in a minute," she said, still staring down at her hands. "Oh, and there's one other thing. I'm pretty sure I'm pregnant right now with someone else's baby," Cate added, feeling butterflies in her stomach as she finally admitted it to him, and to herself, for the first time.

"Whoa, I really am glad I'm sitting down now," Harry muttered, looking at her intently, but then stopped himself from commenting further. "Okay, go on," he added, urging Cate to continue after seeing the vulnerable expression on her face. She knew it was time. Now or never...

"I never had a father growing up, and when I was eighteen I found out why," she hesitated slightly at the next part, taking a long swig of her tea as she thought hard how to word it. "Don't freak out or call me a weirdo, okay?" she asked, looking up at him, and Harry nodded, unsure what she was getting at. "I wasn't the same as you. I was different, and I discovered that the reason why, was because my father's the Devil, Harry," she added finally, and his mouth dropped open. He stared at her incredulously, obviously trying not to freak out as he sat back in his chair and tried to work it out.

"No way, what?" he blurted out after a few awkward seconds of silence had passed between them. Harry was watching her intently as though hoping she might burst out laughing and reveal the strange punch line, but she didn't. Cate remained perfectly still, and watched him with a serious expression.

"It's true. I'm now over a hundred years old. That's why I don't look any older than last time I saw you," she went on and she saw the realisation hit him then. She wasn't joking.

"Yeah, I did wonder about that," he admitted, scratching his chin before swigging his tea. He then grabbed a biscuit and shoved it in his mouth.

"I lived in Hell for a while before meeting my first love, Devin, who I told you about before. Now, this is going to be strange—perhaps stranger than everything else I've already told you so far. But, please try and take it in, okay?" she asked, needing him to hear her out rather than judge her and her strange family before she could explain it all better.

"Okay, but are you sure you're not having me on?" Harry asked, checking one last time, and then shrugged when she raised an eyebrow at him impatiently. "Alright, no more questions. Carry on," he said, raising his hands and then pretending to seal his mouth shut and throw away the key. Cate sucked in a deep breath, letting it out slowly before continuing.

"Devin was like me. A Devil's heir. He wanted us to be together, but our master changed his mind. Devin's now married to another like us, Serena, and they're in Hell at the moment," she told him, talking fast in order to get that part out as quickly as she could. Cate then looked at Harry, checking that he was following and he hadn't already had his mind blown, before she continued on to the next revelation. "Luke's the Devil, Harry. Also known as Lucifer, Satan, etcetera," Cate said, catching the shocked look as it passed over his face. She sat back in her chair, giving him a moment for it all to sink in while staring over at him from across the table as she desperately tried to gauge his reaction.

"What the actual fuck?" Harry cried, jumping up from his seat angrily before he began pacing the small room. "Didn't you tell me before that he stole you away from your first love? Seems more like he groomed you rather than wooed, if you ask me!" he bellowed, his face contorted with rage.

"You promised me you'd try to understand, Harry," Cate said calmly from her seat, watching him stride up and down. Harry stopped pacing, and stared back at her for a moment before sitting back down at the table. He stared across at her, his expression a mixture of sadness, anger, and confusion.

"I'm sorry Dana—I mean, Cate. This is just so crazy; I can't get my head around it. I don't even know where to begin to make sense of it all," he told her. "I'm trying, I promise."

"I know," she said, reminding herself just how young and uninformed he really was about the world. She knew she couldn't expect him to understand all of her craziness right away. "I guess I've had a lot longer to figure it all out, haven't I?"

Cate smiled. She then she reached across and took his hand in hers, and was glad that he didn't pull away from her touch. "I need you to know everything before I can let you ask me any more questions, does that make sense?" she asked and Harry nodded, staying quiet once more so Cate could continue. "Thank you. So, Lucifer and I eventually got together and we were married. I resisted him at first, but you know what, we do work and we're happy together. I know it might seem odd to you."

Harry shrugged, but said nothing in response, his ego still seemingly bruised from that day he'd met him at the flat all those years before. "I came back up to Earth to say my goodbyes to my mother a few years after our wedding. She died holding my hand, an old lady in her bed, and I scattered her ashes at the beach near where we'd lived when I was a young girl. But, while I was there, I was kidnapped," she said, her voice faltering here and there with the raw emotion she felt at reliving the story.

"By who?" Harry asked, unable to control his intrigue.

"A coven of white witches," Cate told him and he gazed over at her, seemingly transfixed by her strange story. "They took me to an astral plane near Heaven where an angel named Uriel held me hostage for five years." Harry continued to stare over at her, his mouth dropping open in shock.

"Why?" he then asked, incapable of stopping himself again, but she let him off.

"At first, it was to use me as bait to get Lucifer out of Hell. I think Uriel wanted a fight, but then he changed his mind. He wanted something else," Cate said, and her face dropped.

"You?" Harry guessed, and she nodded. "Sweet Jesus," he replied, and then covered his mouth quickly.

"No more of that, okay? We only blaspheme where I come from," Cate replied with a smirk, trying to lighten the mood a little. "But seriously, no more, okay?" she insisted, and Harry nodded, a smile creeping into his lips, too.

"So, is he the one you said manipulated and controlled you then?" Harry asked her quietly.

"More than you'll ever know," she replied forlornly, nodding and taking a final swig of her tea.

"So much for him being one of the good guys, hey?" he asked absentmindedly, finishing off his brew. Cate chuckled darkly to herself at his poignant comment, and nodded in agreement.

CHAPTER THIRTY-FOUR

Cate gave him a minute to absorb what she'd told him so far, and then continued with her sad story. She needed Harry to know every detail, and it felt good telling him the truth at long last.

"Well, Uriel wanted me to give him a child, but I refused, and I managed to get away. Nina, whose real name is Dylan, used to be a white witch. She was and still is my very best friend, and she helped me to escape using a powerful spell. Since then, she's stayed by my side and renounced the High Council of Angels as her masters. She turned dark for me, Harry, to save my life and to protect me," she said, letting him know that doing so had meant an awful lot to her. "We couldn't go home when we got away though, and I know this sounds gross but I was—how do I put it—full of light?" Cate said pulling a face.

"Eeeew!" Harry replied, laughing at her awkward expression.

"I know, right? Well, I had to wait until it was clear, so to speak, so we moved around and that's when I met you. I had no powers so couldn't get any messages to Lucifer that I was free, oh yeah I have powers most of the time, but not then, and not right now," she told him, laughing at how odd it sounded. He couldn't help but laugh with her, thinking just how strange his life had recently become, but he didn't care. He was glad to finally know her story.

"The day of the music festival, do you remember?" she asked him.

"Of course I do," Harry replied, his awkward smile making Cate think back to their wonderful kisses that day, and she blushed at the memory.

"Well," she continued, pushing herself on. "The singer that I was chatting with in the VIP area is actually a demon named Berith. He recognised my human form because we'd met years before when he was in another band. He took a message to Lucifer for me, telling him where I was, and that was why I pushed you away. I'm so sorry I hurt you, but I had to," Cate said, and she blushed at the memory of her couple of days spent in bed with Lucifer when he'd returned to her. "He would've killed you when he came to find me if he found out we'd done anything more. Lucifer was angry as hell about our kisses as it was, imagine what it would've been like if we'd done more?" she asked, and Harry nodded. He finally understood both the strange chemistry he'd sensed between them that day, and the way 'Luke' had been with him.

"He scared the shit out of me," he told her honestly, and was glad to finally be able to tell her how he'd felt about meeting her husband. "Now I know why. Whoa, no one would ever believe me if I told them I have met the Devil and shook his hand, or that I'd kissed his wife..." he added with a cheeky half-smile. "I remember thinking he couldn't have been the love of your life you'd told me about. He just seemed so wrong for you, so moody and controlling. But then I saw the way you two were together, so in sync and obviously in love. It was a no-brainer," Harry admitted, looking down at his hands, and he'd forgotten she was holding them.

"I'm sorry," Cate said again, giving his hand a squeeze before she continued. "Well, we had to go back to Hell the next day as he can only be up here during a full moon. One of the setbacks of being the master of all evil, is they don't want him on Earth too often," she told him. "So we tried filling me with his darkness, yuk I know, sorry again." She blushed. "We managed to get me home just in time for the waning moon, and it was all thanks to me having been pregnant," Cate added, and Harry gasped, looking up into her eyes again.

"You have a child with him?" he asked, genuinely taken aback by her remark.

"Yes, well two actually. It was twins," she told him, knowing that full honesty was her best approach, even if it meant hurting his feelings. "They're in Hell now, being cared for by Dylan and the other dark witches."

Cate's expression grew serious then, and she looked Harry square in the eye as she braved the final part of her dark tale. "I stayed in Hell for as long as I could after they were born, but as

I'm half human, I had to come back to Earth for a while. Being in Hell too long had started to make me sick. The children came to visit during some of the full moons, but one night the white witches cornered them outside the protective boundaries of the church. I had no choice but to go to them, I had to help."

"Was it a trap?" he asked, understanding more than she'd thought she was giving away.

"Yes, and the three of us were taken back up to that damned astral plain. Uriel used the children to force my will, to make me agree to conceive a child with him. They were more than just the bait, and he called them his leverage and blackmail," she told Harry, and a tear ran down Cate's cheek as she thought of Luna's limp body when she'd reacted to the moon's power over her. Harry leaned forward and wiped the tear away with his thumb, and the delicate touch soothed her instantly.

"And so, you think you're pregnant. I'm guessing he's the father?" Harry asked, breaking the silence, and Cate nodded. "Does anyone know?"

She shook her head. "No. Lucifer found his way to us on the plain. They started fighting and I was thrown down onto Earth. Luckily, I fell straight into the ocean and passed out. I washed up near an oilrig and was saved by the riggers there. They were fantastic and let me rest there until the storm was over."

"The storm!" Harry almost shouted, jumping back in his chair. "Whoa was that them fighting?" he asked and Cate nodded, burying her face in her hands. Harry quickly calmed himself down and sat silently again, watching her intently from across the table for a few seconds, before she lifted her head back up and looked back at him worriedly.

"I don't even know the outcome of the fight, or if either of them are still alive. I managed to find some dark witches at our church, but none of us have any of our powers. I can usually feel Lucifer's presence too, like a beacon, but now there's nothing. I realised just yesterday that I might be pregnant, so I knew I had to find a safe place where I could go to figure everything out away from either the light or dark influences. You were the first—no, the only person I could think of, Harry," Cate told him, staring into her empty mug, feeling suddenly exhausted from her emotional rehashing of her life's ups and downs.

Harry looked across at her, his soft gaze sweeping over her beautiful pale face as he stared into her sad eyes. He reached over and absent-mindedly tucked a stray dark curl behind her ear.

"I'm here, Cate. For whatever you need. And you can trust me, of course," Harry told her, his voice unwavering as he spoke his promise. "You know I love you. I've always loved you, and I won't hide it away any more, but please know that I will never expect anything from you in return. I would never try to manipulate or control you because of my love. I want you to know that, and remember it always, okay?" he said, cupping her cheek in his palm while gazing into her eyes adoringly.

She couldn't fight the smile his words brought her, and knew that it was exactly what she'd needed to hear. Cate nodded to him and leaned forward so she could hug Harry tightly, feeling safe again at last.

"My turn to make the tea," she said after a moment, refilling the kettle while he raided the biscuit tin again.

He grabbed a chocolate bourbon as he watched her potter around the small kitchen, still in shock after her story. Harry knew he wanted Cate in his life, regardless of the strange sequence of events that'd led her there, or how dangerous it was for him to continue down this path. He still couldn't help but wonder if it was really happening. How could the girl he thought he knew so well but something so mysterious and powerful, while at the same time so frail and scared? Either way, there was no turning back, not that he even wanted to.

***

"So," Harry said later as they chatted over a Chinese takeaway. "You're the Queen of Hell then?" he asked, a smirk on his face at the strange title. Cate chuckled and nodded, digging into another bite of crispy chilli beef as she wrapped her legs under her on the comfy sofa.

"Well, yes. But you can call me, your majesty," she then replied with a cheeky grin, and Harry laughed, shaking his head. He sat opposite her on a matching couch, and there was a small coffee table between them on which they had laid out the delicious meal.

"Not a chance. And I won't be serving you breakfast in bed or any other such nonsense you may be accustomed to down there," he replied, and they both laughed. The whole thing seemed ludicrous in his ordinary little town and normal human life.

She didn't have the heart to explain why they didn't eat, so kept quiet. Cate simply leaned forward and re-stocked her plate with spring rolls and chicken chow mein, looking across at Harry thoughtfully.

"You got married then?" she asked him, not sure how to broach the subject of his ex-wife. "Joe told me."

"Yeah," he said, looking back at her over his own second helping of food. "We were happy for a while. I guess she kind of filled a void I had inside of me after you left," Harry told her, and Cate felt herself blush. The butterflies in her stomach made another appearance, and he smiled at her reaction, but carried on, pretending not to have noticed. "It felt good at first, but then somehow, once the dust settled I just knew we weren't right together. We argued constantly towards the end. She desperately wanted to start a family and I wasn't ready, or maybe I knew we weren't going to last. Either way, she ended up running off with a colleague of hers, and I filed for divorce the next day. She got pregnant straight after that with his child, and I don't think he even stayed with her in the end either."

"Whore," Cate said, smiling mischievously as she chomped down on a prawn cracker piled high with noodles. Harry laughed, but she knew he was hurting from thinking back to his ex's betrayal. She was glad to be there with him, and wondered if maybe they could help each other through all their relationship woes.

"You know I'll have to go to work on Monday, so I won't be able to stay with you all the time?" he informed her as he finished up and put down his plate. "Will you be okay?"

"Hmmm, yeah. I guess I hadn't thought of all the details yet. Where are you working at the moment? Do you think there's anywhere there or close by that I could get a job, too?" she wondered, and Harry shrugged. He didn't know for sure, but was willing to pull some strings if he had to.

"I'm a qualified doctor now, maybe I can try and get you something at the practice? It'd be great if we could work together, and at least that way I can always be close to keep an eye on you, and you'll feel safer." He stood and began clearing the used plates. "How's your telephone manner?" Harry asked as he took the empty cartons into the kitchen and discarded them by the sink, returning to give Cate a protective squeeze before he sat down next to her on the sofa.

"Not great, got anything where I don't actually have to deal with people?" she replied with a smile, but she was honestly so happy to have a plan in place so quickly that anything would do.

Later that night, Cate drifted off to sleep in Harry's double bed, while he had kindly pulled out a blanket and snuggled down to sleep on the couch. She slept deeply, relaxed and happy for the first time in weeks. The pillow smelled of her long-lost friend, which comforted her, and she woke the next morning feeling full of hope. Harry insisted that they needed to get sorted, and he took her shopping that afternoon. He seemed eager to get rid of the unflattering clothing the riggers had given her, and encouraged Cate to buy herself a whole new wardrobe, including her usual choice of dark clothes. She opted for a few pairs of black skinny jeans, grey and black t-shirts along with biker boots and a leather jacket.

"Thank you, Harry," she said gratefully, hugging him as he handed over his bank card to the cashier. He grinned down at her, and hugged her back, taking the bags. Harry then pulled her towards a nearby café, his hand in hers as they walked. They ordered two lattes and shared a brownie, chatting quietly to one another as they devoured their treat. Harry still had many questions to ask about her strange life, and Cate was more than willing to answer him honestly. She was just glad that there were finally no barriers between the two of them.

An hour later, and after a second coffee, Harry finally felt like it was all much clearer in his head. Regardless of the strange events that'd bought them here, he loved the fact that he was sitting opposite her again, and he lapped up her attention as she opened up to him further.

"There's one more thing," he said when she stood to go and use the bathroom. Harry reached into his jacket pocket where he pulled out a small box wrapped in a paper bag. He handed it to her and Cate peeked inside, finding a pregnancy testing kit.

"Harry, I'm already pretty sure," she started to say, but stopped herself when she saw his stern look.

"I want to be absolutely, one-hundred per cent sure. At least then I'll know if I get to keep you here for a least the next nine months, or whether I have to stop kidding myself that you'll be able to stay," he told her, smiling up at her from his seat.

Cate blushed and nodded, heading over to the ladies' toilets. She peed on the test strip and sat nervously waiting for the result to show on the plastic window for a minute, but she didn't need to wait. The double line showed up almost instantly, confirming her suspicions once and for all—she was pregnant with Uriel's child.

CHAPTER THIRTY-FIVE

Cate's waters broke with a huge gush eight months later while she was stood washing the dishes at the kitchen sink. Harry was at work, and she'd only just left to go on her maternity leave from the medical practice the day before. Cate had worked there as an administrator since Harry had arranged it for her after her return to Avebury, and she'd held on as long as possible before finally slowing down and leaving the job behind.

She called Harry on his mobile phone, calmly telling him that things were starting and to get home as soon as he could. They'd already agreed that he would deliver the baby himself, but Cate knew there wasn't long. She still distrusted everyone but Harry, and even he agreed that no one else could be dependable with her and the baby while she was helpless. So, he lied. He told his colleagues he felt a migraine coming on and excused himself from work, all so that he could get away without telling anyone that Cate was in labour. He grabbed his things and set off towards home, readying himself to welcome her baby into the world.

They'd told all the people in their lives that the child was Harry's, and that it'd been conceived straight away when they'd rekindled their romance upon Cate's return to the village. Everybody that knew them both from before and after her reappearance had believed the story, and they played the besotted couple easily as there was so much natural chemistry between the two of them. Harry didn't have to pretend at all, and as he'd told her that first day, he never once hid his loving feelings for the dark girl who still kept her distance.

Cate didn't need to pretend or put on an act to show her love for Harry to those around them either, but she still fought those same feelings for him when it came to their private hours. Her true allegiance was to Lucifer, and she still believed he'd return one day. When that happened, he'd come to find her just like before. If they forgave each other, life could continue on as it had been. Even if they couldn't, they were still bound to one another and would have to come to an arrangement for the twins' sake. Either way, Cate looked forward to being able to return to Hell and be with her children again, but she didn't want to have the added fear for Harry's safety. Lucifer had told her already that if he ever laid eyes on him again he'd kill him, and she didn't doubt it for a second.

It wasn't that she didn't love Harry. In fact, she adored every moment they spent together and dreaded the day she'd have to leave. She was happy and content with Harry by her side, but she knew she could never let herself forget her place both in this world, and in the underworld. She thought of Blake and Luna all the time, and missed them terribly.

Cate used her thoughts of them as a constant reminder not to take her time on Earth for granted. Her little family would soon have another member, a secret member, and Cate vowed to herself that she would not put the baby or Harry in harm's way ever again. Lucifer could never know she'd even been back in touch with him.

They'd also discussed the return of her husband from another perspective, too. Both of them agreed that first and foremost, the baby must be hidden from him at all costs. Harry understood how much was a stake, and he was prepared to take the child and run from him—from them all—if it came to it. Cate hated the very thought of losing the pair of them, but knew that someday it might be their only choice. If it meant saving their lives, she would do it. She'd prepared a backpack already, and stashed it away for such a time. It was packed full of money and maps of the ley lines, along with ideas of small towns and places she and Dylan had lived in where he and her child could to live safely together. Harry vowed to Cate that he'd make sure the baby was safe, and most importantly, away from the reaches of both Lucifer and Uriel. Either influence could prove to be devastating, and both Cate and Harry had made a solemn promise to one another that they would protect it, no matter what the cost.

Cate clung to the kitchen chair as another contraction clenched her tender muscles, hunching over it as she concentrated on slowing her breathing. She knew she had to be careful to keep the noise down so the neighbours didn't call by to see if she was okay, but her strong body was already taking control and she had to bite her lip to stop from crying out. The few minutes she had between contractions allowed her to recover quickly from each painful episode, but the gap was shortening with every intense contraction.

Harry arrived home in hardly any time at all, and dropped his things in the hall quickly before running to find Cate in the kitchen.

"Are you doing okay?" he asked, cupping her face in his hands and taking Cate in for a moment. He gave her a once over, and she nodded, smiling back at him. Harry kissed her forehead and grabbed the antibacterial soap from its wrapper beside the kitchen sink. He then vigorously washed his hands, scrubbing them with a well-practiced technique thanks to his medical training. There were clean towels and blankets already out on the kitchen side and he dried his hands carefully.

He was trying to stay calm, but was glad that they'd prepared themselves well for the impending arrival. He might be a doctor, but he'd never delivered a baby before. He'd read up on it as much as he could in preparation, though. It'd helped, and Harry was sure he would be running around like a headless chicken if everything weren't already organised for him. "How far apart are they?" he asked, grabbing the rest of the linen.

"Two minutes, I think," Cate answered him between the contractions, before taking his hand and allowing Harry to lead her into the living room. He laid down a couple of the large blankets, covering one of the small couches as well as the floor in front of it, and she perched on the edge of the sofa, her legs open and trembling. Cate panted as another contraction took over her body and Harry took her hand in his, groaning as she gripped onto it tightly. As the pain relinquished once again, she let go and apologised.

"It's fine, don't worry. Can I check how dilated you are?" he asked, an embarrassed look on his handsome face, and Cate laughed and nodded. She pulled the hem of her nightdress up so he could check on the baby's progress, and didn't feel at all uncomfortable by his presence between her thighs.

"We should've planned your first time down there much better," she told him playfully, laughing as she heard a loud "*tut*" from beneath her bump.

"It's almost time," he told her as he reappeared, smiling up at Cate excitedly. She grinned back at him, relishing in his warm smile. She was tired, but ready, and slid down onto the blankets to rest on the floor.

The next contraction came hard and fast, and Cate quickly felt the familiar urge to push. She looked to Harry for guidance. "Go for it," he told her, kneeling between her legs as she gripped her thighs and breathed deeply. She bore down, and just a few minutes later gave birth to a healthy and beautiful little girl. Harry checked the baby over quickly before cutting the cord and wrapping her up in a soft towel. She was perfect, and hardly even cried. He smiled lovingly down at her, kissing her forehead quickly before placing her in Cate's ready arms.

***

Less than an hour later, Cate was completely healed. Harry was absolutely astonished by how fast her body had gotten over the trauma of childbirth, and he'd barely finished clearing up the bloody towels and blankets when she came sauntering happily into the kitchen, holding the cleaned and dressed baby to her breast.

"I'm starving. What shall we have for dinner…Chinese?" she asked Harry, startling him with her nonchalant attitude.

"Bloody hell, Cate," he said, his doctor's urges taking over uncontrollably. "You should be resting."

"I'm fine," she told him with a smile. He could be so over the top sometimes, but she also loved his caring nature. "I'm all healed up and I'm bloody starving. Come on Daddy, I need some grub," Cate ordered him, grinning cheekily as she leaned over to give him a kiss on the cheek. He blushed but kissed her back, and then leaned down to kiss the baby's head as she suckled gently on her mother's milk.

"I like you calling me that," he murmured, and she grinned. It was necessary for them to call him Daddy, but it'd also felt good, and right. He was going to be a wonderful father, Cate knew it. "What shall we name her?" Harry then asked as he pulled the menu for the Chinese takeaway out of the kitchen drawer. They hadn't really discussed names much in the build up to her arrival, and they hadn't been sure if the baby was a boy or girl. There was a part of her had even wondered if it might be twins again. They'd chosen not to go for any scans during the pregnancy as Cate wasn't sure if there would be some strange light or unusual goings on inside. She wouldn't be able to explain something like that away, so they opted instead for a natural approach. The pair had told their friends and colleagues that they'd decided to just wait and see. Cate lifted the now sleeping baby away from her chest and handed her to Harry, staring down at the already calm and peaceful babe.

"I really like the name Lottie, and I was thinking it'd suit her, too. What do you think?" she asked, looking to him for his opinion, and he smiled and nodded. Harry's blue eyes lit up as he stared down at the child he cradled so protectively. He didn't care that she wasn't his, he loved that baby with every inch of himself, and knew he always would.

"Lottie, it's perfect. Do you know what that name means?" he asked, gazing up into her beautiful green eyes.

"No, why do you, *Mr Baby name dictionary*?" she asked, joking with him.

"I do actually, and only because a friend of mine called her daughter Charlotte and she told me," he replied matter-of-factly. "It's actually pretty perfect by the way. It means, free," Harry told her with a loving smile.

***

In two corners of the world, two young men lay in their hospital beds. The first, Lucifer, was unconscious in a hospital room in Moscow, Russia. He was in a coma, having been so for nearly nine months already, and had no signs of any brain activity or response to the doctors' tests. He'd been admitted to the hospital the day after the freak storm had cleared at last, with no form of identification on him, and he'd been wearing nothing but bloody, ripped clothes.

All the attending doctors and nurses guessed that he must've been caught in a flash flood or avalanche during the storm, and so regardless of his lack of identification, he was taken straight to the intensive care unit. Lucifer had many deep, severe cuts and bruises to his entire body, along with badly broken bones in his legs, arms, and spine. It was a wonder he was alive at all, but apart from his unconscious state, he'd healed physically in record time. His broken bones had snapped back together, requiring hardly any casting or physiotherapy in order to mend. Lucifer had also needed no help in order to breathe, or for his organs to function normally on their own, so the only strange thing was that he just would not wake up. It was as though he were simply in a deep sleep. Marvelled by his record-breaking healing, the doctor in the ER had kept a bed free in the hope he'd wake up and regale them with his story, however they'd eventually had to concede. The bed was needed, and the strange patient had been moved to a small room on a quiet ward in the back of the hospital. Since then, the unknown man hadn't had a single visitor. They couldn't find a match for him on the missing persons' database either, but his nurse, Yelena, regularly checked back for updates.

Yelena took her responsibilities very seriously. She soon began talking to him and telling him stories in the hope he might be listening to her from somewhere in his deep, dark slumber. She was a lonely woman, and had immediately felt a strange kinship to the handsome man that was all alone in her care. She would buy flowers for his room and play him music, or sing to him as she cleaned him up and changed his sheets. Sometimes, she sat chatting away to him for hours, as though they were actually having a conversation, and she'd soon created an entire identity for him in her mind. Yelena would occasionally curl up next to Lucifer on the bed, rather than go home to sleep, and she'd nestle into him as she drifted off. She often slept on his chest, listening to his shallow breathing, and regularly pulled his arm over her as though he were holding her tight. Yelena found she couldn't help herself. She had a strange attraction to the unknown patient, and somehow found her darker urges came to the forefront of her mind more and more with every day that passed by.

In Rio de Janeiro, Brazil, a small local hospital housed the other man, Uriel. He was awake and physically well, but had suffered with complete amnesia. Thanks to him also having no form of identification on him, he'd been allowed to stay in the hospital until they could figure out who he was, when they'd send him safely on his way. He too had been brought into the hospital the day after the storm had ended, his body battered and broken. All the staff had been working overtime thanks to a tidal wave that'd destroyed part of the harbour, so they'd all just assumed the unknown man had been caught up in the destructive wave too—and regularly told him how lucky he was to be alive.

The doctors had helped him, tending to his wounds and setting his bones, which had also healed impressively fast. Despite having broken bones in both legs and his neck, he'd managed to walk again after just a few weeks of bed rest and physiotherapy. The local nurses had quickly referred to him as a *miracle from God,* and they'd soon discovered how more and more of his wounds had healed each time they unwrapped them to change the dressings. The brain specialist that came to visit him after a few months could find no visible damage to his nervous system or brain function on the numerous tests he carried out, and was unsure what might be the cause for the amnesia. They'd then tried hypnosis and even shock therapy to try and help him recover, but without any luck.

Both the staff and other patients in the care community he now resided in flocked around him constantly. They were drawn to him in a way none of them could really understand, and not a single one of them were in a rush to send the unknown man on his way. They enjoyed the way he made them feel far too much to say goodbye. He made them feel good, and became someone they flocked to for guidance and understanding. He didn't know who he was or from where he'd come, but he knew how to bring people serenity, and did so without knowing how or why he had an affinity for bringing peace. He guessed he was simply a natural.

CHAPTER THIRTY-SIX

Lottie was a happy baby, rarely ever crying, and from just a few weeks old she had a warm smile and happy nature to her that drew everyone's attention. She looked just like Cate, with dark hair that was already growing in ringlets around her ears, and she had deep green eyes the exact same shade as her mother's, too. Cate had come to suspect that perhaps there really wasn't any physical trait for the divine omnipotence that her children's father's possessed that could be passed on to them. Thinking aloud one night she asked Harry for his opinion, having showed him a photograph of her mother. She'd managed to find it online from the archived website for the legal firm Ella had worked at for all those years, a firm owned and run by Lucifer and his demons, she had later come to find out.

"I did wonder that, too," Harry replied, handing her a freshly brewed cup of tea. "Especially when you described how the twins look the same," he added.

She looked down thoughtfully at the sleeping baby in her basinet, who rested so calmly, and Cate loved that her relaxed nature had already begun showing in her. Lottie and Luna could've been the same baby. Their natures were so similar and their delicate features almost identical to one another's, and Cate couldn't help finding herself thinking more and more of the twins as Lottie grew. "I know you miss them," Harry said quietly, knowing that far-off look she would get when she thought of her older children. "I have absolutely no doubt they miss you like crazy, too. But Dylan will love them like her own, and they'll always feel your love through her," he told her. She knew he was trying to offer her a little bit of his intuitive insight and a slight respite from her guilt, and as she thought about it some more, his words did bring her comfort, as always.

"You're right. Dylan loves us all so very much, and I'm sure she reminds them every day just how much I love them," she replied, her face losing its sadness at last. Harry put his mug down on the coffee table and then pulled her into a tight hug. His warm embrace was a welcome and needed comfort, as usual, and she wrapped her arms around his back, breathing in his familiar scent with a contented smile. She really did adore him, and often wished they'd met in far different circumstances.

Before long, Cate accepted that it was high time she went to the church to check on the witches. She had to hope for news of Lucifer at the same time but, if she was honest, she'd been putting it off. She was terrified that there might, in fact, be news of his return, and if there was, it would mean she couldn't go home to Lottie and Harry.

It was something she needed to do, though. Cate owed it to them to show she still cared, and she hadn't been able to go back to London during the pregnancy because it would've given the secret away. Now that Lottie had arrived and could safely stay with Harry in Avebury, Cate knew she needed to start at least showing her face every now and then to the witches and demons that might still be sheltering there.

"I'm their Queen. I need to show them support. I cannot be selfish. They need me," she told her reflection in the mirror before heading to bed, trying to give herself the kick up the bum she so desperately needed. The rehearsed lines weren't convincing her at all, but she still repeated them over and over in the hope she'd leave her fears behind.

The next morning, she packed some clothes and toiletries in her trusty backpack, and then prepared herself to set off. She hesitated at the doorway on her way out of the flat, wanting nothing more than to just turn back and wait it out for just a little while longer, but Harry's stern look urged her onwards.

After one more hug and kiss from them both, she was finally on her way. Cate reached the city centre within a few hours and parked her hire car easily beside the seemingly derelict building that was the old Satanic church. Inside the main hall, she could see that the former aisle and seats had been transformed into makeshift beds for the many beings that were now taking shelter there. It seemed many of the others had come to the same conclusion as her after all, and had flocked there to find their dark kind. She looked around, counting no fewer than ten dirty and uncomfortable looking beds, and was glad she hadn't stayed. Cate searched for Suzanne or Bea, and eventually found them sat amongst some other lower level witches and a couple of demons that Cate assumed were their new roommates.

After greeting them with a wave, she made her way over to the group and the pair of them stood, their faces lighting up at the sight of her. The two witches quickly bowed to their Queen, as did the others around them once they realised who she was. Cate hadn't met the new refugees before, and without their powers or keen senses, she could forgive them for not knowing her human form, this time. Either way, all of them seemed relieved to see her.

"Do we have any more information on my husband yet ladies?" Cate asked, addressing them casually. They both shook their heads, grave looks on their scrawny faces, and their disappointment was clear.

"No, my Queen," said Suzanne. "We hoped you might bring some news?"

"No, I'm afraid to say I've found nothing either," Cate answered, touching each of the witches shoulders lightly with her hands to comfort them. "How have you managed?" she asked Bea.

"Not great. There's not much food, but we can keep a fire going, and as long as the doors are shut tight the heat stays in," she answered, indicating with her hand around the large room. Cate noticed that the once magnificent windows were now boarded up and air tight. She nodded and gave Bea and handful of pound notes from her bag, instructing her to buy supplies sensibly and to hold tight.

"I'll be back again soon. But for now I must keep searching for news of the King," she told them, and they bowed their heads, a quiet prayer to him on each of their lips.

Cate then said her goodbyes and went out towards the car. She hadn't stayed nearly as long as she ought to, but was grateful to be out of that dirty place and back in the fresh afternoon air again.

"My Queen," called a voice from the shadows just as she clicked the unlock button on the car key. Cate looked in the direction of the familiar sound, and had to go closer to see the person who'd called to her more clearly. Just as she thought, it'd been Berith. He'd never really been a fan of sunlight, more of a night-time creature, so Cate joined him in the shadows. She even hugged him tightly as she greeted the demon, and was glad he was safe.

"Long time, no see," Cate said with a smile "I guess you're stuck here too then?"

"Yep," he told her. "I've heard no word from the King since he left, yet the storm subsided around a year ago. I must admit I fear for his wellbeing," he told her, his usual humorous and fun nature hidden behind his forlorn features, and his worry was obvious. Cate knew that Berith was fiercely loyal to Lucifer, as loyal as Dylan was to her, and she also knew he was not one to be underestimated, despite him having helped her in the past.

"Me too," Cate admitted. "I'm trying to figure out where he could be. Surely we would feel something if he were on Earth, don't you agree?" she asked, trying to gauge his suspicions.

He nodded in agreement, his long, dirty hair falling from behind his ears into his face.

"I've actually been wondering about purgatory," Berith said, not finishing his sentence, but Cate knew what he meant.

"Perhaps," she agreed, looking into his brown eyes earnestly. "I would assume that if Lucifer and that bastard angel were there, we probably wouldn't be able to sense them until each eventually returns to their dominions. That would also explain the lack of powers on both sides."

"So, we wait then," he said, another statement rather than a question.

Cate nodded, and bid her old friend goodbye, feeling grateful that he hadn't questioned her further to find out where she was staying while they were all forcibly exiled to Earth.

Before she returned home though, she decided to hold out for a little while longer, and checked into a cheap hotel by the motorway. Cate wasn't sure why, but she was worried someone might've decided to follow her from the church, and her conversation with Berith was especially playing on her mind. She sent a text message to Harry, letting him know she was fine, but that she'd be home the following day. She'd decided to put some safety plans in place first and would explain it when she got home.

Later that evening after a quick dinner, she sat at the hotel bar enjoying a glass of wine as she browsed through some web pages on her laptop.

"You come here often?" a voice behind her asked, his tone playful. It was Berith. She guessed he must've followed her from London, and Cate knew to trust her hunches again in future.

"No," Cate answered curtly, and was genuinely angry that he'd been tailing her. "What are you doing here, Berith?" she demanded.

"It's just, it occurred to me after you'd left that I never asked where it is you've been going that keeps you so busy looking for our Dark King. I wondered if perhaps you were holed up wherever it was you were living before, with that boy, what was his name? Henry?" he questioned her, and she didn't correct him, being careful not to rise to his accusations.

"And why would I bother? You know Lucifer wouldn't take kindly to me consorting with humans unnecessarily, especially men. Not that I need to explain myself to you, Berith, but I've been travelling around England, doing odd jobs for cash and looking for any sign of my husband," she told him pragmatically. "I was also thinking about getting myself a permanent base somewhere in London. I'm sure Lucifer wouldn't begrudge me a better state of living than those poor people squatting in the church. Don't you?" she asked, her tone flat and unfriendly.

"I'm sorry, your majesty," Berith answered apologetically. "I didn't mean to infer that you were up to something. You were just not very forthcoming earlier, and it made me suspicious."

"Well, maybe when your master returns you can talk to him about your suspicions, but until that time comes I'm in command, and you do not want me on your bad side," Cate replied sternly, and Berith bowed his head in respect as she stood and turned to leave. "I suggest you carry on with your business as usual, Berith. I'll see you again when Lucifer returns, and if I even get a sniff of you following me again, you really will be sorry," she promised. Cate then went back to her room, furious but more determined than ever to put extra measures in place to ensure the safety of her secret little family. She then researched late into the night for any sign of her husband, or of Uriel. News of either would be something at least, but she still found nothing.

She also checked out some flats for rent near London before settling down to sleep, and emailed a few of the landlords to request long term rental options, before snapping the laptop closed and turning out the light. Cate decided she would rent a place where she could go during the full moons without Harry and Lottie anywhere nearby, assuming that when Lucifer returned to her he might be bound by the moon as usual. She decided that she would go each and every month and wait there until the moon waned again. It'd be awful leaving them so regularly, but hoped it would ensure that when the time eventually came that Lucifer came to her, she'd be there instead of at the flat. Although it pained her to even think of it, she knew it was the best scenario. It was the only way she could leave her new family behind, knowing they were safely hidden from his all-knowing radar.

The next day, Cate found the perfect little place. It was a one-bedroom flat near Brixton just outside of the capital city. She'd be close to the church, but to not too close to invite anyone from the dirty refuge to come to her doorstep unannounced. Cate signed a one-year lease agreement there and then, paying up front, and taking the keys from the overjoyed landlord before she got in the rented car and headed back home.

She arrived at Harry's small home later that night; having checked what must've been one hundred times that she was no longer being followed. She crept in quietly, finding Harry asleep with Lottie in the basinet beside him in the bedroom. Neither stirred as she sneaked in and gave the beautiful baby a kiss, her heart full of love for her precious bundle. Cate then stood there for a moment, watching Harry as he slept soundly in the bed. He'd been a wonderful man, friend, and father the past year, and she couldn't deny, she yearned to add lover to that list. Her heart beat for him, despite her efforts to quieten it, and she knew she loved him.

"Hey gorgeous," he whispered, startling Cate who was so deep in thought she hadn't even realised he was awake.

"Hey yourself," she whispered back, sitting down to perch on the edge of the bed. They'd always slept separately in the flat, Harry usually sleeping on a sofa bed in the living room while she had the bedroom along with Lottie. He'd slept in there to be next to the baby throughout the night while she'd been away, and Cate felt a little naughty being in the bedroom with him. She also couldn't help herself from feeling excited as she stared down at Harry, and her attraction to him seemed to come bursting out of her all at once. She quickly realised just how much she'd missed them both over the last couple of days, and that she was incredibly happy to be home.

Cate reached over to Harry, unable to stop herself. She gently caressed his face with her hand before stroking her palm slowly down onto his lightly haired chest. He smiled up at her, not knowing for sure what she wanted, but not stopping her in the hope he might finally get a taste of what he'd coveted for so long.

She leaned down, planting a soft kiss on his ready mouth, and they both moaned in readiness for more. He grabbed her shoulders and pulled Cate closer, instantly deepening the kiss, and she let him. The unadulterated closeness with the man she truly trusted to take care of her every need was sheer bliss, and she knew she couldn't fight it any longer.

Cate climbed on top of Harry, straddling him on the bed. She was still fully clothed on top of his duvet, while underneath she knew that he was naked. Harry always slept in the nude and the thought of him so pure and exposed beneath her turned her on even more.

They lay like that for a few minutes, kissing each other passionately and intensely for the first time in far too long. Harry let his hands run through her long hair, grabbing it gently and pulling her closer, not letting her mouth come away from his for even a second.

"I need you, Harry," she eventually told him, an almost silent whisper escaping her lips between his ravaging.

"I've always needed you, Cate," he told her back, looking up at her as she leaned over him in the darkness. "Take everything, for without you, I'm nothing…"

CHAPTER THIRTY-SEVEN

Cate grinned and sat up, leaning back on Harry's lap, and she could feel the tell-tale bulge of his need beneath her thigh. He watched her with a smile, intent on savouring every moment, and didn't take his eyes off her as she pulled her black shirt off and then slipped off her bra. He wanted to resist, to hold back and let her lead, but his hands instinctively reached up to caress her breasts. Cate heaved a sigh, savouring the feel of his hands on her at long last, and leaned back down for another deep kiss, while he let out a guttural groan. She giggled but didn't stop him as Harry gently cupped them, before he then carried on down to her jeans so he could unbutton them.

She then rolled onto her back beside him, pulling the black denim trousers down her slim legs, along with her knickers, which she then kicked off the end of the bed.

Harry took her in for a moment—the beautiful, dark goddess that lay bathed in the moonlight before him. He was so eager to touch her, to taste her, but he knew she was still in a delicate place and needed to be the one in complete control. It wasn't the time to pounce on his would-be lover, and he was more than willing to wait. Harry would please her in whatever way she commanded, and they both knew it. Cate smiled coyly over at him and climbed up onto one elbow to look him in the eye, while his gaze swept up and down her naked body.

"Well?" she whispered expectantly, "your turn," she added with a cheeky grin. Cate tugged at the edge of the duvet she was laying on top of, the only thing keeping her away from his naked flesh, and grinned. Harry quickly shuffled himself free of the linen and climbed on top of the bed covers to join her, and she took her turn to gaze upon his gorgeous body. His arousal was hard and ready, sticking out prominently against his slim body, and she wanted to touch and feel it more than anything.

"Will you make love to me, Harry?" Cate asked him, an almost shy tone to her voice as she spoke, and she looked up into his eyes in the darkness.

"Oh yes, I thought you'd never ask," he told her, never having wanted anything more.

"Then come over here will you?" she asked him playfully, and Harry conceded. He climbed on top of her and kissed her passionately again before trailing his kisses down her neck to her breasts and then stomach. She groaned loudly as her body responded to his delicate touch, and he shushed her, laughing to himself as his kisses continued further down towards his sweet prize. Harry's mouth soon surrounded her swollen bead, taking it between his lips. He began suckling on it gently, yet firmly, and revelled in Cate's squirms of delight. She thrust her hands into his hair, urging him to continue, which he did with vigour.

Her thighs began to tense, signalling her rapid closeness to the glorious orgasm she needed and wanted. Harry took her commands for more without comment, and continued his unrelenting deliverance of pleasure to Cate's aching core. His hands gripped her thighs tightly while his tongue flicked over her clit for a while longer, before he then delved it inside of her hot, wet cleft, making her gasp and moan again.

Cate came, her back arching on the bed, and she had to stifle a louder moan that threatened to escape her lips as she did so. She instead let out a quiet, satisfied groan and released her grip of his hair, revelling in the aftershocks of her first orgasm in far too long.

Harry wasted no time, continuing his kisses again as he climbed back up onto his knees and laid his mouth against her stomach and breasts as he glided back up towards her mouth. She kissed him feverishly when he reached her soft lips again, tasting herself on his tongue, but didn't care at all.

Cate stared up into Harry's eyes a few moments later, a broad smile on her lips as she reached down, running her hands over his slim stomach. When she reached his waist, she grasped his still rock-hard cock between her hands and stroked it. He gasped, delighting in her touch as she guided him towards her. Cate then lifted her hips up to meet his as he leaned down, and the tip of him finally entered her wet opening. She held his gaze as she welcomed him inside her at long last, and the world around them disappeared when he plunged inside. All that mattered to Cate was Harry, and her heart ached for him, and only him.

The pair kissed each other hurriedly as he thrust into her, neither holding back as her body opened up for him. She wrapped her legs around his waist and pulled him deeper inside of her, eager for him, yearning, and yet she was desperate to please him too. She had to know it felt right for him, and loved watching as his body told her everything she needed to know. He plunged deep, thrusting harder and faster in tune with her body's silent commands, while taking what he needed to reach his climax as well.

Cate called out his name as she unravelled beneath him, throwing all caution to the wind as she shuddered with the wonderful surges of pleasure that seemed to collide wonderfully with the raw emotion she felt gushing out of her from within. There was no guilt, no shame, and certainly no regret. Unlike with her previous lovers, she'd made love to him by her own choosing, and wished she could continue doing so for the rest of her seemingly endless life.

Cate slept in the bed with him after their wonderful lovemaking, and had woken Harry by wrapping her mouth around the tip of his long shaft. Lifting the covers, he'd grinned broadly down at her, and gladly urged her to continue. She drank him down, and then laid kisses over his torso and up to his chest, having taken her time to suck his nipples, biting down gently as she went. Harry gasped, but his sharp intake of breath had done nothing to stop her eager mouth. She then lay in Harry's arms, both of them feeling happy and relaxed as they enjoyed their embrace.

Cate turned to gaze up at him in the morning sunshine, and was pleased to find he was ready for her again. She climbed on top of him, wet, and more than ready herself, too, and slid him inside. Cate rode up and down on his lap, his long cock pressing on just the right spot inside of her. She came quickly, riding on and on despite her tenderness from the night before, and Harry sat up so he could kiss her. He cradled Cate in his arms and pressed himself even deeper into her while her muscles tensed around him. With a kiss, he brushed the hair away from her face with his hands so he could stare into her eyes as she started moving slowly on his lap again, and his own climax soon followed hers.

They lay back down, dozing happily in each other's arms until their daughter woke up, ready for her morning feed. When she eventually stirred, Harry scooped Lottie up from the Moses basket and placed her in her mother's arms. After giving them both a quick kiss, he then headed off to the kitchen, where he made them both some coffee and buttered toast.

Harry bought the tray of food in and placed it on her lap, taking Lottie from her so she could eat while he burped her and changed the baby's nappy. The three of them then relaxed in bed together for a while, Harry lying back against the pillows with a happy smile. He silently took in the wonderful sight of the two girls before him that he loved more than anything else in the world. He had a pure and contented feeling inside that he just couldn't hide, and he felt giddy when Cate looked at him, making him pretty sure he had to be the happiest man alive.

It felt to Harry as if there were a secret bond the two lovers now shared. It was like a final, utterly complete, and unadulterated connection to one another existed, and they could both finally enjoy it after being denied the freedom for so long. The intimacy they'd shared, the pleasure, and the love that'd finally flourished between them made him smile to himself as he remembered every moment, every touch. Harry wanted to shout it from the rooftops, to proclaim his love for her to anyone that would listen and beg her to be his, forever.

There was still that little niggle in the pit of his stomach though, and he knew that there always would be. There was an annoying little voice in the back of his mind that knew it couldn't last forever, but while he had Cate and Lottie there in his feeble little human life, he was determined to enjoy every minute of their time together.

Cate watched him as he lay there with a far-off look and a relaxed smile. Her feelings for him were stronger than ever, and utterly determined not to be pushed away again. She'd denied herself his love, simply because she didn't want to put Harry in harm's way, but knew it'd been pointless. Cate had convinced herself it was the right thing to do, but she realised that she'd already put him in the crosshairs for the demonic wrath that might be coming her way anyway. No matter how her future with Lucifer might pan out, he was already ruined, already fated to burn thanks to her. It was the one thing she truly regretted most in her long and immoral life, but, there was no going back, and she figured if they were both damned, they'd better make the most of what little time they had left.

"Are you okay?" he asked, catching her thoughtful look.

"I'm wonderful," she answered, making him smile.

"But," he persisted, a knowing look on his face as he placed Lottie back in her basinet.

"But, I can't help but think I'm going to be the death of you, Harry, and worse," she told him, a sad half-smile on her pale face. "Not only have I asked you to take care of me—the wife of the most dangerous, evil being in all creation. But, I've also asked you to help me cover up the existence of a child that is potentially a ticking time-bomb dependant on how her future might go for her," Cate said, reaching across to stroke his cheek with her hand, and she stared into his gorgeous blue eyes. Harry's smile didn't falter, he just gazed back at her, looking into Cate's eyes with his heart on his sleeve, and his soul hers for the taking.

"The beauty of free will," he told her, covering her hand with his own, and giving it a squeeze. "Is that it's my choice, and I choose you, Cate. I don't care what he does to me for loving you, I'd rather live my life knowing I'd been fortunate enough to love my soulmate for as long as possible, than ever running away in fear. I know I can never keep you here when he returns, but until that time comes, I'm going to love you for every minute of every day. I'd sell my soul if it meant you could stay with me," Harry told her. He leaned down and gave his lover a deep, desperate kiss, sealing his devoted promise to her before he pulled her into his arms. She reached up and ran her hands through his slightly wavy hair, pulling him into her embrace as she feverishly returned his kisses—stunned by his macabre pledge.

She'd known the second she chose to find him again that she'd asked him for an incredibly dangerous favour, and at first had offered him nothing but her company in return for his protection. And yet, he'd still said yes. Cate was astounded that Harry had been so ready to take care of her and Lottie, regardless of the high risk and potentially little reward for himself. He truly was a good man, and she couldn't help but fall even more in love with her secret lover with every passing moment.

The many years of suppressed desire, love and passion had come pouring out of Cate the night before, and she refused to shut it off, run or hide it away any more. She wanted Harry, and had always loved him, but was blinded and consumed by the terrible love triangle she'd found herself in, twice. The devastating affect it'd had on her had meant she hadn't been able to see that he was the one for her. Harry truly was her soulmate, and she wanted to be a part of his life for as long as she could as well.

Cate cocooned herself in Harry's arms and legs, relishing in his protective circle as they continued to kiss, neither one ready to break their connection. She finally felt free, as though she could take a step back from the situation at hand and stop being selfish. The bigger picture was most important, and she owed it to him to make the foreseeable future the best she could provide for him and Lottie. Cate vowed to herself that she would be strong and decisive from then onwards. She would dedicate herself to keeping them both safe, and no longer worry about herself or her fate.

She realised then, in a strange moment of clarity, that her own future actually did seem set out for her. It was suddenly apparent that whatever higher power appeared to be keeping her powers at bay might also be keeping her two omnipotent lovers lost in whatever abyss they'd found themselves. This higher power she'd never believed in had somehow steered her on the path to eventually having Lottie and Harry come into her life. There had to be a reason, and somehow, she believed it would all work itself out in the end. All she had to do was sit back and wait for the rest to play out. It seemed she'd found some faith for the first time in her entire life, and couldn't deny it felt good to have hope.

***

The morning before the next full moon, Cate held her beautiful Lottie close. She smelled her soft, dark hair, and kissed her forehead, watching as the baby slept peacefully in her arms.

"I'll be home in two days," she told Harry, who nodded and kissed her after she'd handed over the precious bundle. They'd talked a great deal about her plans to go and stay in the flat during the moon's full phases, and he'd agreed that it was a good idea. The plan made perfect sense to Harry, but he still hated the idea—the reality—that one day Lucifer would come and find her. Just like before, he would take her away again, and just like before, there would be nothing he could do to stop them.

It made him sick with worry knowing that at some point the full moon would claim Cate once and for all, and that when it did, she might never return home to him and Lottie. He didn't show her his fears though, urging her out the door with an understanding and reassuring smile despite his inner turmoil. His one insistence on the arrangement had been that Cate had to check in with him each night at around eight o'clock, via any means, telephone call, or text message—even an email would do if she somehow lost her phone.

If Harry didn't hear from her within another twelve hours, they'd agreed he would take Lottie and run, just in case. He'd given Cate his word that he would hide her away, forever if that were what it took to keep her safe, and she believed him.

Cate didn't know what the future would hold for the child, a half-breed mix of both good and evil. Perhaps she would have no choice which path she went down, or maybe she could choose her own way. Cate could never be sure until that day eventually came, but she hoped that against all odds Lottie would thrive and ultimately be free to choose for herself.

She dreamed that she might even be able to join her in the darkness, much preferring the unholy fate to her being an outcast of Heaven. Lottie would no-doubt be shunned by the elitist angels who sat on their thrones in the astral plains above, yet she'd be expected to follow whatever path the High Council of Angels set out for her.

The only setback in her wishful hopes for Lottie's future was Lucifer. She knew he'd never allow her into their home. No pillow talk or alluring persuasion would ever win him over on that subject, she was absolutely sure. Regardless, Cate knew she had no choice but to hide her on Earth, for as long as it took to figure out where their lives might end up. Lottie would be safe there, and she was glad that Lucifer would never be able to read Cate's thoughts to find out about her. So, provided the light beings didn't find her either, she figured Lottie might actually be able to live a somewhat normal, happy life.

Cate arrived at the flat later that afternoon, with some shopping and DVDs at the ready for her couple of days away from normality. She'd intended to hide away during her short visits to the flat, and that's just what she did. She locked the doors and lay in bed watching movies and eating junk food all day. Cate tried not to let her mind wander too much, but the quiet solace of her time alone allowed her more painful thoughts to creep up on her. She couldn't help but think of Dylan. Cate missed her terribly and while she was glad her best friend was with the twins in her absence, she still wished she were there with her. She knew Dylan would understand and be able to help her get through all of this, just like she'd before.

She wondered what the dark witch was getting up to in Hell without her. Cate hoped she was with the children, teaching them, and playing games together as she'd always done before. She spent hours fantasising what Blake and Luna might look like now, and how their little personalities and characters may have developed in her absence. The bittersweet wonderings bought her both smiles and tears, and Cate curled up under the covers in the small bed, kicking herself for being so damn emotional. She grabbed her headphones and plugged in her MP3 player, opting for a diversion via heavy metal music. Cate dried her eyes and lay back on the pillow, Berith's deep, soulful voice singing in her ears. It didn't matter that he'd annoyed the hell out of her the last time, the familiarity of his voice brought her comfort, and worked to help distract Cate from her depression.

When the moon began to wane again, she grabbed her things and quickly tidied up the flat, feeling eager to leave. She returned to Avebury later that afternoon, and was glad to be back home with her small family at last. She was eternally thankful to walk through the doorway and back into Harry's loving arms, and kissed him fervently to let him know it.

CHAPTER THIRTY-EIGHT

Cate and Harry were incredibly happy together, and as the years passed by she couldn't help but fall in love with him more and more. He'd captured her heart forever, despite her dark vows to her King. He was the perfect friend and lover, and was the most wonderful father she could've hoped for. Harry was firm but kind in a way she'd never known Lucifer be to the twins, and she saw how Lottie loved and respected him for it.

They eventually moved out of the flat into a two-bedroom house closer to his practice where Lottie could have her own room, and they made it their own. The trio were always together, thanks to the careful and necessary paranoia the pair of them shared when it came to their precious child's protection. They never let anyone babysit her, and chose instead to spend their evenings together in front of the television rather than going out with their friends, regardless of their taunts that the pair of them were boring.

When she turned four years old, Lottie was enrolled at the local primary school, and Cate couldn't help but worry about her while she was away from her protective gaze. She quickly decided that she needed to get a job at the school so she could be close by during Lottie's days there. After a simple interview with the headmaster, a grey haired man in his fifties named Bill who was immediately captivated by her, Cate got herself a position working as the school librarian. It was quiet, secluded, and perfect. She could use the quiet time to check on Lottie regularly, as well as reading and researching as much as possible while things were slow.

One day, after having the idea to run various searches on the Internet for medical miracles and unusual patient stories, Cate happened across a strange story of a young man in Rio de Janeiro.

It was reported that the patient, suffering from amnesia, had developed quite a following from his hospital bed. He was written to have apparently healed a fellow patient's sprained ankle with just touch of his hand, and magically cured another of his migraines thanks to a head massage. Such small miracles were enough to get the local journalists intrigued, but evidently weren't big enough to get the story into the national newspapers so all she'd found was a small piece on him. A quick skim through it revealed nothing of too much interest, however the picture of the patient at the bottom made her heart lurch. It was Uriel. His image on the screen was as clear as day. He was the strange miracle patient they were reporting on, a patient with apparently complete amnesia.

She couldn't take her eyes off the photograph. Uriel looked no different to the last time she'd seen him on the astral plain, right before the fight had started on the beach with Lucifer. His amnesia seemed, in her opinion, the only thing stopping him from realising who he truly was and coming to find both her and Lottie. She shuddered at the thought of what could happen when he eventually regained his memory, and vowed to strengthen the charms and protective talismans she'd placed all around their house when she got home.

She then thought about his condition some more. Uriel was obviously weakened, even still, from his fight with Lucifer. She wondered if her husband might be somewhere close by to where Uriel had fallen as well, or if perhaps he might even be in the same hospital as the injured angel. Another glance over the faces of the other patients that accompanied him in the picture didn't reveal his face, and she couldn't help the little bit of relief that washed over her as she stared into the faces of the small following Uriel now had in Rio. None of the friendly faces around him even had a clue just who they were associating with, and she hoped it would stay that way for as long as possible.

***

Cate and Harry did their very best to maintain a seemingly normal life with their daughter as a few more years passed. There was still no word of Lucifer, while Uriel reportedly continued to reside in the care home she'd found him in via the newspaper article back in the school's library. She didn't dare go to Rio to try and visit him, just in case seeing her face again bought his memory back somehow, and instead kept an eye on the local newspapers. She checked regularly to see if he was featured again, but thankfully there'd been no further reports on the so-called 'miracle patient.'

    The still loved-up pair carried on as usual, and enjoyed their quiet life just them and their precious child. They eventually decided to raise Lottie as strict atheists, and instructed her school not to involve her in any prayers or religious studies of any sort. Cate was worried that her thoughts and schoolwork on the subject, or involvement during mass, might end up being heard by some of the other angels, or maybe even Uriel one day. It wasn't unusual to choose a non-religious path anyway. Many humans practiced different religions, both celestial and demonic, and there were always going to be those who didn't find any comfort in faith at all, so wanted to live their lives away from the binds of religion. Harry and Cate chose to steer clear of either side of the powerful balance, despite them knowing the truth about their existence. Atheists usually got quite a shock when they passed on and ended up in purgatory. Cate knew from experience that they normally found their souls becoming the demonic playthings for the dark creatures in Hell because of their sins in life—sins they didn't believe they'd been committing the entire time. Business had been booming thanks to their non-repentant lives.

    However, Cate knew that Harry was still a good man. She had no doubt that when his time came his soul would go up to Heaven and she would never see him again. It was an insight that brought her both comfort and pain, but one she never shared with him. He had to remain pure when she left him, rather than be tempted into the darkness in the hope of finding her in the abyss.

    As the time had gone by, Cate had needed to start trying to look older. She still looked like a twenty year old thanks to her lack of powers again, when to keep in sync with Harry and their supposed age gap she should actually be closer to forty. She'd decided to wear older styles of clothing, and dressed like their friends of the same age. She also chose more grown-up hairstyles and makeup to make herself naturally look older, and thankfully it seemed to be working.

Human Harry had naturally grown older the last few years, but Cate always thought he looked more and more handsome as he aged. The more pronounced grey flecks in his brown hair just made him look more distinguished, yet he didn't actually look all that much older in the face. His boyish good looks and charming nature still managed to attract him a lot of attention, even though he hated it. The women he worked with and the other mums at Lottie's school would flirt openly with him, but Harry only ever had eyes for Cate. Whether friends or strangers, everyone around them could see it. She didn't even get jealous of the lonely women who would swoon over him, knowing he'd always been hers, and always would be.

***

Five more years passed by in a flash for Cate, Harry, and Lottie, and the three of them continued to live happily together in Avebury as a family. Their small unit were still secretive and private, and Cate and Harry were immensely protective of their young daughter. They'd also slowly learned to trust Lottie's instincts over the years, and had quickly realised she had an intuitive, clever prowess all of her own. Cate had sensed a curious strength within her from a young age, and was sure now that she would always find her own way in any of the three worlds she might eventually end up in. Regardless of the lack of magical power she possessed, Cate was stronger than ever thanks to Harry's unending love and support, and she cleverly put more plans in place to ensure his and Lottie's safety.

She'd gone to visit the witches many times over the years, always without any further news, but she periodically stopped by the deteriorating church anyway, especially during her full-moon visits to her flat. Cate delivered food and blankets to the refugees there each time, and worked hard at cementing her alibi for her time on Earth while she was at it. She told them fake stories of the countries she'd supposedly visited looking for others of their kind and seeking out news of Lucifer. They all believed her cleverly thought out tales, and never questioned Cate whenever she went on her way again. She continued to stay in her small flat during the full days of the moon's phases, but thankfully without any sign of her husband, so she'd returned home safely to Harry and their daughter each time.

On a sunny Sunday morning when Lottie was nine years old, Cate and Harry lay relaxing in bed together. They were wrapped tightly in each other's arms while they listened as Lottie got up and went downstairs to the kitchen to prepare herself some breakfast.

"Coffee?" Harry offered with smile as he gazed into his lover's eyes and planted a light kiss on the tip of Cate's nose. She smiled, groaning as he pulled away, grabbing some tracksuit trousers to wear as he climbed up out of bed.

"Oh, yes," she answered after stretching her arms and legs sleepily, grinning as she fluttered her eyelashes at up him. "But after another five minutes of sleep, okay?" she asked.

Harry just smiled back down at her, rolling his eyes in mock frustration. He then kissed her cheek softly before heading out to see what tasty breakfast Lottie had dreamed up downstairs. She'd developed a particular flair with food, putting together strange combinations that somehow worked brilliantly though, such as her herby flapjacks and banana butter biscuits.

Cate snuggled into Harry's pillow, breathing in his scent as she dozed for a few extra minutes, her mind wandering as she relaxed. She suddenly found herself thinking of Lucifer, his face coming to the forefront of her mind out of the blue, but then she quickly realised it wasn't just that she was thinking of him—she could actually sense him somehow. It was only a tiny feeling, deep inside of her. More of a suggestion of his presence somewhere far away than a strong beacon like it usually would've been. But sure enough, and to Cate's utter dismay, it was there.

She jumped up out of bed, dressed quickly and then ran downstairs to find Harry, her eyes wide and her need for sleep completely replaced by a fearful, ominous feeling.

***

In Moscow, the unnamed patient that'd been in a coma for ten years finally opened his deep blue eyes. He looked around, needing a few minutes to figure out his strange surroundings, and took in the brightly lit room and the wilting flowers that were in a crystal vase next to the hospital bed. Lucifer was stiff, weak, and powerless, but he was glad to finally be awake after so long. He tried calling to his power, willing it to return to his battered body. Nothing. He cursed his feeble body, but hoped it was only a matter of time until he could go home. For the time being, he had to figure out what was going on, where he was, and how he was going to get back to Hell.

A nurse came wandering into his room, and she jumped at the sight of her patient awake in the bed. She shrieked and dropped the vase of newly picked flowers she'd been carrying on the hard floor, but didn't care when it shattered at her feet and the water inside spilled across the tiles. She spoke to him in Russian, asking if he knew his name, or where he'd come from. Lucifer understood the language, but replied in English. His mind was too foggy to respond in her native tongue.

"Luke," he managed to say, and his dry, gruff voice was almost a whisper after such a long time without use. He started to sit up, but felt his weak muscles strain feebly in response as he did so. Yelena ran to his side, quickly pulling an extra pillow out from under the bed and sliding it beneath his shoulders to help prop him up some more. She stared at him in shock for a few moments longer before filling a glass with water, popping in a straw, and holding it for him to take a sip. He gulped it all down, eager for the nourishment, and then looked over at her from the bed.

Lucifer felt as though he'd been in a stifling haze for years, lost in his own thoughts, and unable to sense any of his family or followers during his imprisonment inside his own body. He was grateful not to have ended up in purgatory after he'd fallen from the astral plain, but couldn't help but feel anxious that it'd been so long. He also didn't understand why he was still so weak and it worried the Dark King that the moon's usual power over his dark force wasn't affecting him, nor had it seemed to do during his comatose state. "How long have I been unconscious?" he asked the nurse, looking into her brown eyes as he spoke.

"Ten years," she replied with an awkward smile, seeming nervous under his intense gaze. Her thick Russian accent made Lucifer hope for a moment he'd misheard her, but he knew, or rather felt, that her words were true. His face dropped and paled.

"Has anyone ever been here to visit me?" he asked, hoping Cate might've found her way to him during all that time.

"No, never," she replied, staring into his handsome face.

He nodded in understanding, not sure whether that meant she too was powerless and couldn't find him, or if she'd already returned to Hell. He hoped with every ounce of positive thought he had that she'd not purposely chosen to stay away. Her words from the beach had haunted his dreams the entire time he'd been unconscious, as had his own foolish taunts he knew had hurt her deeply. He didn't want to dwell on the details though, and instead decided to focus his efforts on getting stronger. Then, he would travel home, hopefully finding her and the twins there safe once he did.

***

An hour had passed since Cate had felt the strange pull, but the far away beacon that was her husband's power still lingered within her consciousness, consuming her thoughts entirely.

"You need to go," Harry told her, trying his best to stay calm as he held her close, but she could feel him trembling. "For Lottie's sake," he said, reminding her of her solemn promise to her child and to herself. Cate was packing up some things, getting ready to travel to the flat, while Lottie was playing computer games in her room when he'd appeared with supplies and encircled her in his strong arms. She knew Harry was right, but now that the time of reckoning was finally upon them, she couldn't bear to go.

"I know," she said, her stomach churning at the prospect of leaving the pair of them for good. "But," Cate started to say, desperate to find some loophole in her own careful plan.

"No buts," he interjected, being the strong one, and she needed him to be. Harry took her phone out of her bag and slipped it into his pocket. They'd agreed she would leave it with him in case anyone found it and used it to find him and Lottie. In imposter could easily send a text message pretending to be her, using his weakness for the Queen to find and trap both him and her illegitimate child. The gesture also meant that the time really was up for their little family. It was a symbolic moment that saddened Cate to her very core, but she stifled the sobs that threatened to explode out of her, knowing she had to stay strong.

Cate went into the other bedroom and hugged Lottie goodbye, having decided against putting either of them through the ordeal of a big farewell. She just pretended to be going away for a few days like she normally would, and then she left their home without another word to her darling daughter. Cate stopped for a few seconds to kiss and hug Harry goodbye before tearing herself from his arms and gazing up at him, seeing her pain reflected in his eyes.

"Don't go looking for me," she told him, knowing he knew not to anyway. "I'll come back for you when, or if, I can."

He nodded, tears welling up in his own eyes as she started to walk away.

"I love you, Cate," he called after her. "I'll keep her safe."

"I know you will. Thank you for everything, Harry. I love you, too," she told her paramour, forcing herself to walk away. Her body was trembling, and she struggled to breathe as her grief hit her like a hammer to the heart. Tears streamed down her red face, sobs forcing themselves out of her uncontrollably as she drove away. Her world had ended, and she felt empty. Pain consumed her, and it was unyielding and uncaring. Regardless of her hardships in the past, Cate had never felt anything like it in all her life, and cursed everyone and everything. It was no comfort at all knowing she was doing the right thing, she simply felt dead inside when she knew she should feel strong.

When Cate finally reached the flat in Brixton, she curled up in the cold, empty bed and cried herself to sleep.

CHAPTER THIRTY-NINE.

The next day after an overwrought night's sleep, Cate went to the church, and found it fuller than ever with refugees. None of the dark beings she spoke with, however, had sensed any change. She quickly decided not to tell anyone what she'd felt the day before. Cate wasn't sure how or why she was the only one to have sensed the shift in the air, which was still just an awareness of their leader rather than a strong urge, but she was sure there had to be a reason for it. Either way, she was determined to act on it alone.

Cate caught up with the witches, warlocks, and demons there for a little while, acting as normally as she could. She then gave some money to Bea and bought them food and water before heading out again, doing her best to give nothing away. Berith was there, and he caught her eye as she left the church. She nodded and smiled at the demon, who bowed respectfully over to her, but didn't come over to chat, and she was glad. Their relationship had been much less familiar since her stern talk with him when he'd followed her after that first visit, and although she hated being estranged from her old friend, she knew it'd been a necessary step in ensuring Lottie's safety.

Cate returned to the flat, and waited, unsure what else to do. Two more weeks passed by, and apart from the small presence she still felt, nothing else had changed. After another day of angry solace, she lay in bed and checked the clock on her nightstand. It was nearly midnight, so she turned out the lights, and quickly slipped into that strange place between being awake and asleep.

She was awoken again within just a few minutes as the clock turned to zero, not having realised that it signified the start of Halloween on Earth. The lightning bolt that surged through her out of nowhere quickly made Cate aware that the darkly powerful day had begun, though, and the deluge of power coursed through her entire body in seconds. Her arms and legs grew heavy, while her fingers and toes prickled with a static-like shock. She levitated off the bed by about a foot, unable to move as the power seeped into her and coursed through every muscle—a demonic-like possession occurring as she somehow reclaimed her strong, dark force once again.

Within a few seconds, it was over, and she knew instantly that her powers had fully returned. Cate could feel her physical strength heighten incredibly within seconds, while the full extent of her powerful gifts were at her command again at last. Most importantly, she could now completely sense the presence of her husband on Earth. She saw him in her mind's eye, lying in a hospital bed far away—fast asleep and incredibly frail.

A second later, Cate was by his side, having teleported straight to him. She looked down in surprise at the feeble man as he slept. She'd never seen Lucifer sleep. He was taking small, shallow breaths and resting peacefully as she looked on for a few moments, shocked to see him in such a bad way. Cate reached out and laid a hand on his shoulder, rousing him instantly with a start.

"Cate?" he asked, his voice just a whisper.

"Yes, Lucifer. I'm here," she told him, sitting down on the edge of the bed as she took in his skinny frame and the exhausted look in his eyes. "It's All Hallow's Eve, my love. My powers have returned to me at long last," she told him, reaching down to stroke his face.

She looked down at him questioningly from her perched seat, but Lucifer just shook his head in response, indicating he hadn't been blessed with the same gift of his power. She shrugged, and climbed on the bed with him, sliding herself onto her husband's lap. Despite her sadness at having left Harry and Lottie behind, Cate couldn't deny there was a part of her that felt pleased to see her husband at long last.

She felt she needed to show him she still loved him, perhaps to prove it to herself as well as to him, but it felt awkward. She could sense that he was still weak, but lifted his chin with her hand, leaning down to place her mouth on his. He responded, of course, having missed her too. Lucifer kissed her lips as passionately as he was able, his hands going around her waist as he held her tightly.

The pair of them let their mouths linger on one another's for a few minutes, relishing in their mildly re-kindled romance. Cate ran her hands down to his pyjama shirt and began unbuttoning it, finding herself eager to prove her allegiance.

"No," he said, pulling his head back and taking her hands in his. He looked up into her face, almost hidden in the dark light.

"No?" she asked, watching him in bemusement.

"No," Lucifer said again, sterner this time. He stared up into her eyes and Cate could see the dark circles underneath his usually mesmerising irises, and understood just how weak he must really be. She nodded, lying down on the bed beside him instead, and she then rested her head in the ridge between his chin and shoulder. It was the spot that'd once been her most favourite place in the world to rest, but now felt like the wrong fit.

"It's okay. It's all going to be okay," she said, snuggling into him before they each fell into a deep sleep.

Cate woke the next morning to the sound of a woman frantically screaming and trying to pull her off the bed. She was talking in Russian, but Cate could understand every word.

"What are you doing, how did you get in here?" the woman demanded, still grabbing at her jacket.

Cate climbed up from the bed, and was furious. She felt powerful and commanding, and looked down at the small woman with a scowl. The nurse cowered slightly as Cate gazed down the foot or so of height difference between them.

"This man is my husband," she replied, speaking in perfect Russian, and using her body to block the nurse from seeing to Lucifer. She could see the woman's nametag and addressed her directly. "It's time he was discharged, Yelena," she ordered her, turning to him before she began to pull the covers away from Lucifer to get him ready. The foolish nurse grabbed Cate's arm again, attempting once more to yank her away from him. As she did, she made contact with her skin and Cate got a flash of a memory in her mind's eye—Yelena's memory.

She was in love with Lucifer after all his years spent in her care, despite not even knowing him. Her dark urges had overcome her as she'd watched over the unknown man, and she'd begun fantasising about a life she hoped to have with him when he awoke. Cate could see that Yelena had not only curled up in the bed to be close to him over the years, but she'd also touched him sexually, and tried in vain to make him hard for her as he'd lay comatose in the bed some time ago. She'd put his hands on her naked body too, cupping her breasts with his palms and even thrusting his fingers inside her cleft when her urges had taken over completely.

Yelena's memory was as clear to Cate as if she were watching it in a television screen, both surprising and disgusting her all at once.

The Dark Queen's face went dark, and her eyes speckled with black flecks. Yelena pulled her hand away from her arm, fear flashing across her face instantly. "So, you think you have a chance with him? Shall I tell my husband just how *personal* the care is in this hospital?" she asked the nurse in a whisper so Lucifer couldn't hear her, raising a knowing eyebrow as she did so. Yelena stepped back, obviously alarmed. She was shaking her head quickly, not being able to comprehend how Cate might know her guilty secrets, and she took a stride forward, closing the gap between her and the nurse with ease. She pushed Yelena against the brightly coloured brickwork behind her, staring down at her as she spoke.

"No, please..." she mumbled.

"We'll see each other again, but not anywhere you might expect," Cate told her, knowing she would end up in Hell once her time came. Then the deviant nurse would then know the Queen's wrath, and she would enjoy every moment of it.

She then reached down and pulled up the right arm of the shaken woman, where she traced an inverted cross onto the inside of Yelena's right wrist with her index finger. The mark burned black for just a moment before disappearing again, and she gasped and tried to pull her arm away, but it was no use. Just before Cate released her, she couldn't resist threatening the disgusting woman some more. "For now though, you'd better get the fuck out of my way," she added menacingly, and Yelena ran for the door without so much as a backwards glance. Lucifer laughed gruffly from behind Cate, and she turned to see him rising slowly and cautiously from the bed.

"Jealous much?" he then asked, a satisfied smile on his lips. She didn't know if he was aware of what'd gone on with Yelena during his long sleep, but knew it wasn't the right time to reveal all. Cate just smiled back across at him, shrugging nonchalantly before she wandered over and helped Lucifer get himself changed.

Less than half an hour later, Cate teleported the pair of them to the flat. She didn't want him to be bombarded quite so soon by all the eagerly awaiting beings in the church so she put off a visit for the time being. He absolutely wasn't strong enough to face the masses. Lucifer leaned on her for support and Cate helped him over to the black leather sofa, where he rested while she made him something to eat. When she came back, he devoured four slices of jam-covered toast in seconds. She'd never seen him so hungry before, but urged him to eat as many as he wanted.

"Where have you been, Cate?" he asked her at last, finally full after another two slices. He watched as she slipped down on the opposite end of the couch, curling her legs underneath her as she settled down, and casually pulling his feet onto her lap.

"Back and forth between here and the church mostly," she replied. Cate didn't want to go into too much detail, but she knew he'd need more to curb his suspicious nature. "I searched around for you for a long time, but I had no powers myself until midnight last night, so I couldn't find you. I'm sorry, my love. I had no idea where you'd landed."

"And, what about, *him?*" he then asked. She could sense his distrust in her, knowing she must obviously be holding something back, and she tried to appease him as much as she could, not hesitating with her answer.

"The same as you, injured badly. I believe him to be in Brazil, suffering with amnesia rather than in a coma like you were. As far as I know he hasn't yet recovered," Cate told him and Lucifer nodded, but continued to look at her expectantly, urging her to continue. "I haven't been to see him if that's what you're wondering? I never want to be near him ever again. I found an article on the Internet of a miracle man who had amnesia in Rio. He was somehow healing fellow patients of small ailments. It was him—his photo was in the article, but I would never go to him, please trust me when I say that," she told him insistently, eager to explain herself. Lucifer stared across at his wife, feeling far from close to her. He was confused and felt vulnerable and frail as he lay before her, his weakness bringing him nothing but suspicion and distrust. He could see that there was pain behind her eyes, but couldn't read her to know what was hurting her so much. He wanted Cate to tell him everything she'd gone through and how she felt, but for some reason she was holding back. There was also a tremendous amount of desperation in him to regain their once so easy connection, and to know she hadn't meant the cold words she'd said to him and Uriel that day on the astral plain.

She looked different to him somehow, although physically she was the same as always. Cate had a different energy to her, and a strange newness he couldn't comprehend. It wasn't the lightness he'd sensed in her last time, but a closed-off indifference she was trying too hard to mask.

They took each other in, and an awkward silence passed between the two of them for a moment, before Cate finally broke it. "I've missed you so much," she told her master as earnestly as she could, and Lucifer hoped he'd been wrong to doubt her—suspicion clouding his judgement. He wondered if the emotion he was sensing hidden behind her eyes was all for him, or for the time together they'd lost while he was unconscious. He wanted to believe her. "I haven't been able to go home since the fight," Cate added, looking down at her hands forlornly. He realised then that she must've been missing the children terribly, and that would explain her pained look.

Lucifer calmed his fraught mind, trying his hardest to let go of his own pain, desperate to learn to trust her again. "None of us have been able to travel back to Hell. The witches and demons have had no powers either," she continued. "Vast amounts have been living in the churches awaiting your return. I found them there after I fell from the plain."

"I remember now, were you injured?" he asked, thinking back to the moment on the beach when she'd been thrown backwards into the water. He hadn't been afforded the opportunity to follow her, thanks to the barrage of blows that'd then rained down on him from Uriel's fists, but vividly remembered watching her disappear from sight.

"Yes. I was out cold for a few days, and then I needed a couple of weeks to heal. After that I was fine physically, apart from the lack of my powers. But like I said, I soon found out that it was all of us who no longer had any, not just me," Cate told him, taking his hand in hers. "It must've been a terrible fight?" she asked, looking into his eyes with a sincere, warm smile.

"Yes," he said, thinking for a moment before going any further. "I was so enraged. I couldn't and wouldn't stop. I wanted him dead. Knowing that he'd been with you again was torturing the hell out of me. It still does. And, after he'd taken the children and used them to force you into his bed again, I was completely consumed with rage and my need for revenge. I didn't care if I died, as long as I took him with me," Lucifer added.

He took a deep breath, lulling the anger that threatened to bubble up inside him at the thought of it all again, and guessed it was time to tell her how he'd found them. "Alma had put a plan in place years before for if you were ever taken again. She'd placed a secret charm on Angelica so she could always find her, and we tracked her down within minutes of her return to Earth—she had no idea. The fool was such a bitch when we caught up with her, and she even tried to fight me, but she eventually did as she was told and took me up to that astral plain where you were. I promised I'd spare her life in exchange for her taking me to you, but I couldn't help but beat her to a pulp once she had, relishing in taking her life. I didn't care, all I wanted was you back."

Cate was shocked, but lifted his hand, kissing the palm and placing it on her cheek, leaning into his touch as he continued his dark version of events. "After the lightening began, I knew you'd fallen, but that there wasn't anything I could do to stop it. I couldn't feel your presence once you'd gone over the edge either, so had no idea what'd even happened to you. Uriel and I fought for days, neither of us giving up or giving in. I think we both needed it after all our history, but each blow was deafening, and so very powerful. Eventually, we felt the floor beneath us start to crack, and it shattered like glass. We each went plummeting downwards, but I lost sight of Uriel before I hit Earth. I lost consciousness instantly, and other than some hazy dreams, the next thing I remember is waking up in that hospital bed a few weeks ago," he told her, tailing off. Lucifer seemed exhausted from his storytelling, and Cate urged him rest for a while, leaning over and curling up on the sofa next to him as he drifted off. His story added up, and while she hated that they were so estranged, she was glad they'd cleared the air a little.

CHAPTER FORTY

Lucifer slept deeply for hours, but Cate was wide-awake and struggled to rest. As she lay on the sofa curled up next to him, she watched the sunset through the window and couldn't help but think of Harry and Lottie. She got up from her spot and looked down at him, taking in the frail sight of her usually so strong and powerful husband before her. She watched him for a moment, with emotions that were so mixed and fraught she wondered how on Earth she might overcome them. Cate still cared for him and knew she could be happy by his side like before, but knew she didn't love him the way she once had. She also knew that it'd take a very long time for her to get over the deep and terrible void she currently felt for Harry, but that she would never get over the loss of her beautiful daughter.

She headed into the kitchen to busy herself and stop her mind from wandering beyond the point of no return. The scars were still far too fresh for her to hide them from Lucifer if he questioned her further, and she couldn't bear to let herself dwell too much on the two people she missed so terribly.

After tidying the small kitchen, she sat at the dining table and played around on her laptop for a while, listening quietly to some music as she tried to curb her boredom. Cate then slept alone in her bed that night, having decided against joining Lucifer on the sofa again, and then didn't rush to wake him the next day. In fact, he remained fast asleep until well after midday.

Earlier that morning as she'd lain in bed, Cate had made the decision to bypass the church reunion entirely. Lucifer was still too weak, and she knew she needed to take him home as soon as possible, opting for a return straight to Hell instead. He devoured half a loaf of bread's worth of toast again when he awoke, and was famished but seemingly stronger. After he'd finished, he chatted to

Cate at the kitchen table, and both of them felt far more relaxed than they'd been the night before.

"How have you managed to survive here alone, Cate?" he asked her, smiling at his wife warmly over his hot cup of tea before taking a big sip, finally understanding what all the fuss was about. She peered back at him, laughing at his messy blond hair, but relishing in his relaxed and happy look. She too let go of her guilt and pain, welcoming the time to talk.

"I had to beg and borrow to get money at first," she told him. "But eventually I found work here and there for cash, bar work mostly. I couldn't bring myself to live in the dirty church. It was awful there. After one night I quickly realised that I am not the kind of girl who does well with sleeping rough," she added, and Lucifer laughed.

"Well, I could've easily guessed that," he replied with a cheeky grin, teasing her. "I wouldn't want to hear of it anyway," he then added, his expression serious again. "You should never have to suffer like that. It's not right for the Queen to have to live that way, no matter what was happening. I hope Berith took good care of you?" he then asked, angered somewhat that she'd been seemingly left to fend for herself while also being expected to provide for the refugees at the church. Cate just nodded, unsure how to respond or explain her now estranged relationship with the demon he was so close with.

"Shall we try and go home?" she then asked, eager to get back to their family and friends, and to move the conversation along. Lucifer nodded and took her hand, but she was the one who needed to do the teleporting this time around. Cate focussed all of her efforts on home and pulled the still weak King down with all her strength. It worked, and within seconds they arrived at the dark gates of Hell, where the familiar change in pressures and heat hit them both instantly. Lucifer coughed and fell to his knees, choking on his human-like gasps while his body seemingly struggled to cope with it. He regained his composure after a short while, but Cate was gobsmacked as she watched his body's reaction to having come home. She'd never seen him struggle before, not even for a second.

Cate, however, didn't even react to the changes. She stood tall as she took in the familiar sight of home with a wide smile, and had to bite her tongue when she almost asked him if he needed her assistance. It went without saying he didn't want her to draw attention to his weakness. The dark castle was towering over the dark city ahead, and she couldn't wait to get inside and see her family. Cate focussed on the presence she'd felt almost instantly of Blake and Luna somewhere deep inside herself. She called to her children telepathically, somehow finding a power within to summon them to her, and she marvelled at how wondrous it was having her powers back again. In the blink of an eye, the twins appeared before the pair of them, both wide-eyed as they took in the sight of their parents.

"Mum, Dad!" Luna shrieked, running over to them and throwing her arms around Cate's neck, while Blake went to Lucifer and offered him an arm to lean on. They looked so different since the last time she'd seen them, and Cate did a double take. Now fifteen years old, they were both as tall as their mother, although Blake was actually a good foot taller than her, and looked like young adults already. Luna hugged her tightly before pulling back, her green eyes searching Cate's face, taking her in.

"You look exactly as I remember you," she said, smiling warmly. Luna had her long, dark brown curls pinned up in a high ponytail that reminded Cate of how she used to wear her own hair as a teenager, and she had to smile at their likeness. She drank in the sight of her beautiful daughter and stroked her cheek with her index finger.

"Well I can safely say you don't look the same at all," she told her in reply, laughing as she took in the young girl who could've easily been mistaken for her sister rather than her daughter. "I've missed you both so much. I'm so sorry we couldn't come back sooner," Cate added, giving Luna a kiss on the cheek before pulling back to look over at Blake with a smile.

He caught her eye, allowing himself a moment to bask in her warm gaze before dropping his eyes to the floor, guilt overshadowing his joy. She wanted to go to him, but instinctually knew he didn't want her to, and she sensed a closed-off vibe from him. Cate didn't know why Blake resisted her affections, but she was sure they just needed time to get to know each other again. She knew they'd soon figure out the best way to get him to open up about their sad past, and to help him deal with his dark emotions. Their incredible bond could be strained, but never broken, Cate was absolutely sure of it.

The four of them then teleported into the main entrance of the castle, where they were instantly welcomed with applause and cheers from the dark witches and demons who were inside. Alma appeared within seconds and hurried over, pulling Cate into a tight hug as a crowd began to form around them, everyone eager to speak the with King and Queen.

"Welcome back, your majesty," Alma said, tears welling in her eyes as she gazed up at her. Cate smiled back at the witch, feeling genuinely happy to be home, but she got straight to business, and was careful to speak quietly when she asked Alma to help.

"I need you to take the King away and try anything you can to help. Do whatever it takes to get him his strength back," she commanded, and Alma took her first proper look at her master. She could see instantly that Lucifer wasn't well, and nodded to Cate. She then hurried him away to the witches' dungeons, while Cate made excuses for his disappearance and then chatted animatedly with the beings that still crowded around her.

Dylan then came hurtling through the welcoming committee and threw her arms around the Queen. She gripped her as tight as possible and sobbed in her embrace, much to the annoyance of some of the upper level demons around them. Neither of them cared about the disgruntled elitists, though. Both women held firmly to their long-lost friend, and their circle was impervious to anything other than the love and warmth they each felt for one another.

"I've missed you so much," Cate whispered in her ear, holding back her own tears. "Please tell me you haven't turned my children into raving lunatics in my absence, Dylan?" she then asked as she pulled away, mocking her friend's naturally fun nature. Her motherly worry showed, despite Cate having trusted Dylan completely all these years.

"Well, Luna is a raving lesbian, and Blake's into bestiality, does that count?" Dylan answered, joking with Cate in response, and she relished in the loud laugh she got as reply.

CHAPTER FORTY-ONE

"Don't let your guilt get in the way of your happiness, Blake," Luna said, chastising her brother later that evening. He'd remained quiet and grumpy the whole afternoon, while the rest of the kingdom had openly celebrated the return of their parents—his twin included. Luna knew he was just happier playing the dark and broody teenager rather than address his real feelings, but wished he'd give it up for at least one afternoon. Their mother had tried to speak with him a few times, to tell him that everything was fine and not to dwell on the past, but he just hadn't given her the chance to get beneath his icy exterior, and Luna wanted to scream at him for refusing to let her in.

Cate watched them, and she truly hated that she felt like a stranger to her beautiful children. She had a lot to make up for, and hoped that time would help her heal those wounds.

"That boy is a troubled soul, your majesty," her witch and old friend Sara told her when she caught the hurt look in Cate's eyes as she attended her. "But it's all his own doing. He's happy in his misery, content even, and has been for many years. Blake believes he deserves it after his actions resulted in the loss of both of his parents following that terrible night outside the church. He's blamed himself ever since and won't listen to reason. But now you've both returned at long last, and perhaps together you can help him find his own forgiveness," Sara added, and then she smiled and hugged Cate tightly, happy to have her friend and mistress home again at last.

Devin and Serena had hoped to throw a proper party for her and Lucifer to celebrate their homecoming, but Cate insisted they put it off until Satan was back to his full strength again, assuring them that it wouldn't be long, even though she had no idea if what she'd promised was true. They agreed, and instead presented their three children to her later on that evening, much to her surprise. She'd had no idea that the pair of them even had one child, let alone three, and was eager to meet the new additions to their brood. Despite the absent years that'd passed them all by, she still felt close to Devin and Serena, bound together by the blood of their ruler, and they seemed to feel the same way. The love she and Devin had once known was so long gone it didn't cause any animosity between any of them, and in fact it was getting easier to forget the times that'd changed so drastically for them all.

The trio of children were a perfect mixture of their parents. Their eldest, Braeden, was nine years old, looked very much like Devin. He had his father's dark blond hair, light blue eyes and tall frame, yet he had the quiet nature of his mother. Braeden introduced himself politely and then hugged Cate before bowing to her, evidently knowing to address her formally as his Queen.

The middle child, and the couple's only daughter by the name of Leyla, was seven years old. She was very much like Serena with her red hair and blue eyes, yet she had a fiery nature to her and a strong will that Cate could sense as she gazed into the young girl's eyes. She also had to laugh at her body language, noticing Leyla's stance and the way she poked at her youngest brother with her elbow as they stood before her. He didn't react to her attempts at a fight, obviously used to her irritating taunts already, despite being so young.

He was just a small boy, and seemed somewhat shy towards Cate as he gazed up at her. His name was Corey, and he was just five years old. Corey had blond hair that had a few red flecks growing through it, and deep blue eyes like Devin's. He seemed gentle, and sweet, but his eyes seemed to burn with a desire for knowledge and power. There was either great potential or dire penalties destined for his future, Cate couldn't tell which, but she hoped he would choose to go for the path of greatness.

Cate looked up at their parents after the introductions were over with a big smile. She congratulated the pair of them, pulling Serena into a tight hug before giving Devin a kiss on the cheek. She forced away all pain of the past and felt genuinely happy to be in the midst of her dark family again at last. It was wonderful to have discovered that their small family had expanded so much in the few years since she'd last been with them, and Cate spent the rest of the evening laughing and playing as they cemented their relationship.

***

Only the royal family, upper level demons, and Lucifer's coven were later told the truth about his frailty, and they were all understandably concerned for his health. However much they tried, no one knew how to help him, and so the King hid himself away. He was angry and dismayed that he could possibly be so weak, and Cate found it impossible to connect with him. Her husband seemed furious that she'd gotten her powers back but he hadn't, and he didn't seem bothered enough to hide it. To say they were estranged was an understatement, but she kept up her doting façade in the hopes that someday things might change.

Cate couldn't deny, she was also surprised by her influx of power. Somehow, she felt stronger than ever, although she didn't dare tell Lucifer the truth about how strong she'd suddenly become. Cate used her power to reopen the portals between the worlds again, welcoming back the dark beings that'd been awaiting their master's return in the churches on Earth. Dylan and Sara helped them when they arrived back in Hell, dispensing potions to heal their ailments or replenish lost nourishment. The Dark Queen also rewarded their loyal underlings with lavish gifts and slave souls for them to torture, abuse, or simply enjoy to their hearts' contents. Their celebrations would last for weeks, Cate was sure, and she didn't begrudge them all letting off some steam.

Cate went to visit Lucifer in the witches' chambers when she could get away the following afternoon, finding him lying in the disturbingly familiar tub of black goo. She'd needed that treatment all those years before, thanks to her time spent in the pits and dungeons at the behest of the powerful man who'd eventually won her heart. The sight of the thick, black liquid, and the strong, musty smell brought back many memories of the years of torture she'd suffered, and Cate couldn't fight the surge of anger the reminder of those times stirred up in her. She peered down at him as she stood beside the bath, and Lucifer just laid still. His eyes were closed, and he was seemingly unaware that she'd even come in. Alma then approached and bowed, giving Cate's hand a squeeze, and she gave her an update on her husband's health.

"He is in a bad way, your majesty. There's death in every inch of him, and his powers are not returning remotely as quickly as they ought to be. I don't know what else to do, except give him time," she said, looking down at the hand that still held on to Cate's tightly.

"Then we shall give him time, and hope to see a change in him soon, Alma," Cate replied, offering the witch a warm smile. She was disappointed that there was nothing more Alma could do for him, but knew there was no use in adding to the witch's already guilty conscience.

Cate teleported away, returning to her chambers where she climbed up on the huge bed and tried to make sense of everything that'd happened. She concentrated on her power, feeling her own strength growing inside of her as she called to it, harnessed and controlled it. It gave her vibrancy and a malevolent prowess from somewhere deep within—a seemingly never ending vat of incredulous power that was hers to command. Cate felt amazing, but she still couldn't understand why she'd been blessed with the return of her dark force, while her almighty King was still frail and powerless. The situation made her think back to her previous musings about the possible presence of a higher power. Her mind was alive, considering the need for balance to the forces of good and evil and she couldn't help but wonder if it was some kind of sign. Cate thought that their malaise could even be a kind of punishment for Lucifer and Uriel's abuse of their own almighty powers, whereas she'd followed the path set out for her faithfully, never asking for more, but gaining it anyway.

***

Cate spent the entire night working out what she wanted to do next. Dylan joined her in her chambers for most of it, having felt the Queen summon her like a bolt of lightning to her spine. It'd shocked the witch, but she'd teleported to her friend's side in an instant regardless.

"Hey, how did you?" she began, never having felt her

summon her so forcefully before, but then she saw Cate's determined expression and decided against asking questions. She perched on the bed, ready to hear what her mistress had to say, and gave her a much needed ear. Dylan stayed quiet while Cate had run through the possible options with her, asking for her friend's advice here and there on how best to proceed, but fundamentally she knew what had to be done.

"The realm needs you Cate, you already know what has to happen," Dylan eventually told her, curling up next to the powerful Queen on the bed, giving her the reassurance she needed. There was nothing else that could be done, and they'd both known it.

Cate convened the dark high council in the private meeting chamber the next morning, and they came to the meeting room as soon as they were summoned, however the demons were shocked to find only Cate at the head of the table as they entered. They'd assumed their orders had come from Satan himself, and were all eager to see and hear from their master in the privacy of the council meeting at last. None could hide their disappointment upon realising he still wasn't well, but Cate didn't care enough to nurse their egos. She stood, peering down at them with a stern look as they took their seats.

"Thank you all for coming. It brings me great sadness to inform you that your King isn't well enough to rule our realm at the moment, or for the foreseeable future," she told them honestly, their faces growing solemn at her words. "I will take control of Hell in his stead, but only until he's better, of course," she added modestly.

"And does the King agree to this?" asked Lilith from her chair, her face thunderous as she glared up at Cate. She'd been in control of the realm while both the King and Queen were in exile, and had hoped to continue doing so for as long as she could even though they'd returned. Cate couldn't be angry at her desire to remain in charge. She'd heard from Dylan just how much the demon had enjoyed her role of interim leader, and that she'd been a worthy choice in Lucifer's absence. But, they'd returned, and Cate was going to take what was rightfully hers. Lilith clearly didn't believe that Cate was strong enough to lead the entire underworld, and she didn't bother to mask her displeasure at being pushed aside by the inexperienced Dark Queen.

"Yes, of course," Cate replied angrily, staring Lilith down. "And you'd better learn not to question me, otherwise I can see us falling out." Her eyes turned black, and she felt the familiar buzz of dark power course through her stronger than ever. Her heightened force stirred from within, and she suddenly yearned for ultimate control in a way she'd never felt before. The powerful demon backed off immediately, sensing the change in Cate, and she then stayed quiet for the remainder of their meeting.

***

As the days, months and eventually years passed by, Lucifer remained too weak to lead his dark kingdom. Cate, however, flourished and grew stronger every day. Dylan was by her side, encouraging her and helping the powerful Dark Queen make informed decisions and issue her orders, as well as still being her best friend and most loyal servant. She gave her mistress updates on the King regularly, but there was never much to tell. Cate barely saw him as she was so busy, and the times she did go to sit with him in his chambers, Lucifer only seemed slightly better. He'd hid himself away and was vast becoming a recluse as he was ashamed of his fragile form, but she couldn't blame him, especially given her impressive transformation. After three years, he was finally able to teleport, but only short distances, and his body was still skinny and weak, which only angered him further.

The royal couple hadn't made love to each other at all since before the ordeal with Uriel, and Cate wasn't sure if it was his body or his mind that resisted her love whenever she attempted to rekindle their romance, but she was glad of their lack of sexual connection—it no longer felt right anyway. She also couldn't fight the guilt that rose up as she thought of her infidelity with Harry, stirring her fraught emotions. She wondered if Lucifer might somehow know she'd been unfaithful with someone other than Uriel, but if he did, he never said a word.

Before too long, she gave up on trying to win back his affections. Whenever she was horny, Cate wouldn't bother to demand satisfaction from her husband like she would've done years before. Her thoughts went instead to her secret lover during her moments of self-gratification, and imagining Harry's hands, lips and body against hers always satisfied her need for release. She was embarrassed that she would think of Harry instead of Lucifer, but didn't bother to stop herself as she enjoyed her memories of him time and again in the privacy of her bedchambers. Safe in the knowledge that no-one could read her thoughts, she was glad, otherwise she knew she'd be in trouble for more than just her adulterous revelations.

CHAPTER FORTY-TWO

Cate slowly grew close with the twins after her return, but worked hard to revive their relationship. Even Blake allowed her love and forgiveness to eventually break through the dark walls he'd built so high, and their bond soon flourished. His stubborn and dominative nature had developed into a hard armour, but she'd soon gotten around it. Cate managed to soften those rough edges, and encouraged that kind side of him to thrive again in her company, much to the delight of both her and his twin sister. Blake was still very closed-off emotionally, but she hoped that in time he would open up and let his feelings back in. She guessed only time would tell.

Luna accepted the temporary change in leadership with ease. She relished in Cate's love and warmth, and all the while she ruled Hell with such strength and wisdom that ensured they all thrived. Even Lucifer seemed better for having such a resilient Queen taking the reins. Her relationship with Luna effortlessly grew and blossomed over the years, and Cate often found herself staring thoughtfully at her eldest daughter. She would think of Lottie, and hated knowing she was fast growing up without her on Earth. Cate wondered if she still resembled Luna, just as she'd always done before. Her heart pined for her, but she threw all of that passion into nurturing the twins and showing them all the love they too had missed while she'd been gone. Cate would never claim to have been the perfect mother, but she was trying her hardest to ensure they knew how much she adored them.

When they turned eighteen she threw the twins a huge party, and the entire kingdom joined in with the celebrations. Lucifer managed to come and sit with his children to enjoy the celebrations, he and watched with a smile while the pair received their presents. They celebrated with their friends and family and participated in a special coming of age ceremony their parents had put together for them. They were then given their own covens, and each seemed shocked but delighted by their wondrous gift. It was a surprise that Cate had commissioned for them with the help of Alma, who'd handpicked their magical followers to create the perfect coven each. Cate knew it was time they were taught how to command their own forces, and even the cool and closed-off Blake had one of his rare smiles when he was presented with his new group of cohorts.

Later that night once the celebrations were over, Luna and Blake sat with the witches and warlocks on the sofas in their royal chambers of the castle. They spent time getting to know their new friends in private, and each began deciding on their roles right away. They each knew that time would be the most important lesson, but that together they would learn how best to lead their magical assistants, and the experienced witches and warlocks were tasked with helping them every step of the way. Cate thought the twins looked powerful and strong surrounded by their covens, and both she and Lucifer were already extremely proud. They were both on their way to becoming leaders, and had already shown it by effectively asserting their command over the four members of each new coven.

Over a year after their return, Lucifer called Cate to him in the council chamber. She felt a subtle pull, more like a request than an order, but she was glad he could finally send for her. It was a new development in the strengthening of his power, albeit slowly, but was an improvement nonetheless. She entered the dim chamber, where Lucifer sat at the large table, looking up at her expectantly. He had some pictures in front of him on the dark wood, but had covered them with his hands so she couldn't see what they were.

Berith stood to his right, glaring at Cate. A smirk seemed as if it was threatening to show on his lips, and the vibe was far from right in the room. It all made her instantly uncomfortable.

"Tell me again where you were while I was in Moscow, Hecate," Lucifer said, getting straight to the point, and there was no emotion in his voice as he addressed his wife—not that she expected it anymore. The pair of them had still remained estranged and they barely spent any time alone with one another. A part of her still loved her husband, and knew she always would, but Cate couldn't find her way back to him. Their once strong connection seemed stretched too thin to be mended, and she guessed she'd gotten used to being in a loveless relationship.

"Searching for answers, and for you. I've told you this many times," she replied, in an equally emotionless tone as she stood opposite him.

"Don't fucking lie to me!" Lucifer bellowed, taking the top photograph and thrusting it across the table, his eyes black as he glared at her. She looked down, and gasped. The photo was of Harry. He was much older than when she'd last seen him, and by his side was a teenage girl. She had long, dark-brown curly hair and deep green eyes—the very image of Cate. She knew instantly it was Lottie, and suspected the picture couldn't be more than a few weeks old, or maybe even just a few days.

"I see," she said, aiming for a nonchalant tone as she tried to plan her next move.

"You see?" Lucifer demanded, slamming his palms down onto the dark wood angrily, and shaking the table beneath him. "What do you see? You see the face of your human, piece of shit, lover? Do you see the child you had with him while I was badly injured from trying to save your goddamn life?" he shouted at her, and the spite in his voice was clear as he questioned Cate further. His face was contorted with rage, while his usually blue eyes still burned black thanks to his wrath.

She had to stifle a gasp at his words, trembling as she took in her scary, masterful husband. He thought Lottie was Harry's child. Cate hoped it might help matters slightly if she kept up the pretence, not sure if it might just be a better alternative to the reality. She searched Lucifer's face, hoping to find compassion or mercy there for her child, but she found neither.

"She was an accident, nothing more," Cate told him quietly, holding his dark gaze. "I left them, and came home with you as soon as I found you again, as you well know."

"So, they mean nothing to you?" he asked, an eyebrow cocked as he tried to read her.

"They're of no importance," she replied, feigning disinterest.

"That's not the same thing, Cate," Lucifer growled as he climbed up from his seat. Despite the years that'd gone by and his still weak self, he could still stir fear in her, and she knew it was making him stronger. She grabbed the back of the chair in front of her, tightly gripping the wood with her strong hands to hide her trembling, and she desperately tried to think what move to make next.

He lifted the next photo in the pile, staring at Cate's illegitimate child thoughtfully for a few seconds. Suddenly, realisation began to show on Lucifer's face as he took in the girl's features properly, and he sighed. "She's Uriel's child," he said quietly and then looked over to Cate for her reaction. "Isn't she?" he bellowed across the table at her. Cate didn't respond verbally, afraid her voice would falter, but she shook her head.

Lucifer's eyes somehow turned an even deeper shade of black—a vortex of nothingness—and he regarded her with pure disgust. She knew then and there how there was no love between them anymore. They could never find their way back to one another after this, and she feared for both hers and her children's safety.

Cate tried to move, she wanted to go around the table to him, beg his forgiveness, but was rooted to the spot in fear. She was unable to even speak to try and calm him or reason with the powerful Devil before her. "Berith," he said, commanding the demon that Cate had almost forgotten was even there. He stepped towards the Dark King in response, bowing to him. "Do you know where to find them?" Lucifer asked him, not once breaking his eye contact with Cate.

"Yes, your majesty," the demon replied, consternation clear in his voice.

"Then go," he ordered him. "And kill them both."

CHAPTER FORTY-THREE

"No!" Cate roared from across the table, her heart pounding in her ears as he spoke the terrible command. Her entire body burned as the fear within turned to rage, and she truly hated for Lucifer for giving the order. She summoned all the strength, anger, power, and darkness she could muster, calling to it with every ounce of commanding prowess she could find. Cate felt the ancient power come to her, following her command willingly. It began seeping into her pores from all around the underworld, filling her very soul with pure darkness, before she harnessed and channelled it further into herself. She could feel her soul opening up and fully accepting the wonderful, dark gift, and suddenly felt empowered beyond her wildest imaginings.

Cate then felt a silent command burst out of her like a wave. Her rage drove the blast and shattered the table between her and Lucifer into a million tiny pieces. He was sent flying back into the wall behind, his strength waning after her forceful blow.

Berith watched Cate intently, fear crossing his demonic face as he tried to make sense of the scene before him. "You stay right there, Berith," she commanded, and he found himself routed to the spot, unable to move, somehow having to follow her order. She grinned. It felt good to finally be in full command.

Cate then walked across the scattered debris that was once the huge table. She watched as Lucifer tried to steady himself, and grabbed his frail arms with her strong hands, pulling him up to face her. As she stared into his still darkly speckled eyes, his thoughts washed over her uncontrollably. His memories flooded though her in their wake, and then even some of his most hidden feelings started pouring in, too.

Cate gasped as they bombarded her senses, but opened herself to them, and she laughed maniacally as Lucifer tried to prevent them from escaping him. He couldn't stop it, and as his mind opened up further, she realised that not only his, but the entire kingdom's thoughts were hers to listen in on. Not a single thought was safe from her immense new telepathic power.

She could hear Berith's as well, and she heard him wrestling with the commandment she'd just given him. He couldn't understand why he was forced to follow her order, and she smiled again.

The Dark Queen could even make out Blake's thoughts as he toyed with his witch, Lena's affections in his bedroom. She could also hear Alma in her dungeon as she pondered the best approach to inflict a dark plague on some poor soul that'd annoyed her. Nothing was sacred, nothing was secret. No one's thoughts were safe from her reach, and it took her a moment to focus back on the matter at hand.

"Touché," Lucifer whispered, looking up at Cate, and her attention snapped back to them and her intimidating embrace. Even he could sense her increased strength, and it sent him into an internal frenzy of fear and worry. He did his best not to show it on his face thanks to the years of practice, but his thoughts gave him away. Cate could also sense a small amount of pride and respect for her that he couldn't hide. He'd underestimated his wife profoundly, and was oddly impressed. Lucifer peered up at her, his eyes blue again as he succumbed to her immense power at last. It took a few seconds for the realisation of what'd just happened to sink in, but Cate understood at last. She was in total control, and Lucifer was the one at her command.

"Indeed," was all she said, a wry smile curling at her red lips.

"All hail the new Devil," he said, in a mocking tone. He was trying to anger her, yet his thoughts gave away his admiration of the woman she'd become while his back was turned. "So, now that you've stolen my power from me, what do you intend to do with it? You aren't strong enough to rule, Cate. Everybody knows it," he added, taunting her. She smiled at him, and knew with every fibre of her being that he was wrong.

"I didn't steal anything, Lucifer. It chose to come to me. I should've realised it when my powers returned to me all those years ago, and yet you remained weak, powerless, and pathetic," she told him, spite clear in her tone as he wilted before her. Cate continued to smile down at him, sensing Lucifer's fear. It did nothing but strengthen her even more. "You asked me, no, forced me to love you. I did. I really believed we were meant for each other, but you still continued to push me. Well, I guess you didn't count on my love for my children being stronger than my love for you, did you?" she replied. "Arrogant until the end, my darling."

A snap of Cate's fingers set alight the photographs which now lay strewn on the floor with the shards of wood that were once the great table. They were gone within seconds. She then reached up and placed her hands on her King's cheeks, taking him in for a moment before deciding his fate. She knew exactly what she had to do in order to keep Lottie and Harry safe, and grinned at the sweet irony.

Cate teleported Lucifer with her to a fiery pit, despite his attempts to pull back. She then stood with him in the flames for a few minutes, watching with a sinister smile. The intense heat didn't hurt or even make a mark on her skin, but they burnt away at Lucifer's clothes and singed his skin instantly. He cried out, grabbing Cate's arm when she stepped away from him and leaned against the red-hot wall that had no effect on her at all.

"Don't leave me here," he pleaded, but she knew his remorse was fake.

"My child will be free to choose her own path," she said. "We're over," Cate added, and pulled the black diamond ring from her finger. She tossed it to the ground in front of him, an evil grin on her face as she relished in her freedom at last. "And you will stay here until I can be sure you are of no threat. Maybe you'll stay here for eternity. We shall just have to wait and see," Cate told him with an even wider smile.

She then teleported away, leaving Lucifer alone and burning in the pit with no hope for escape. He called to her with his thoughts and screamed her name as the flames licked his skin, but she ignored his telepathic pleas for mercy. The powerful Dark Queen understood at last that it was both a blessing and a burden being in ultimate control, but she was willing to bear them if it meant her family were safe.

CHAPTER FORTY-FOUR

All of Hell soon knew they had a new mistress. Lucifer was no more, and Hecate had taken complete control of the realm. Berith was thrown into a torture dungeon after Cate had him whipped and beaten for his insolence. His treacherous tongue was cut out, and his lips were sealed with magic thread so he could never tell another soul her secret.

Cate went to him following his incarceration, a cruel smile on her face as she took in the broken sight of one of her ex-husband's most loyal subjects. His thoughts called out for her mercy, and told her just how awful the ordeal had been for him, but she didn't care. He silently begged for forgiveness, promising never to speak of Harry or Lottie again, but Cate just laughed darkly at his promise, knowing he wouldn't have a choice whether to speak of them.

"I'll lift your punishment in due time, Berith," she told him calmly and evenly, and without a shred of guilt. "When I decide you can be trusted again. This is, for the most part, to do with Harry and the girl. I will keep them safe from now on, make no doubt about it," she promised, and then stepped closer. She read him, and relished in his fear—absorbing it.

Cate understood then how it made her stronger, and she lapped it up. "Your punishment is also for your betrayal, to me and to my realm. Despite my every effort to protect our kind on Earth and then to rule fairly back here in my Lucifer's absence, you continued to be distrusting. In doing so, you turned my husband against me. He's rotting away in exile now too, and it's all thanks to you." She then left him to his thoughts, imprisoned in his dungeon until further notice.

Cate's mind raced as she headed back to her chambers, and she knew she needed to have a plan. Her youngest daughter would eventually be found, and she wanted to be the one in control of how things would go when that day finally came. She decided to wait, to hold back until Lottie came of age before she went to her. It was the only time she could effectively act, and she was determined to bring her straight home. Cate was sure that if she made contact before then it'd be foolish. She even wondered whether a trip to Earth might set off a new war between the powers of light and darkness, and if perhaps the High Council of Angels might sense her presence again. Cate didn't even know whether or not Uriel had regained his memory, or when he might find out that she'd taken the throne. If she could hold off, even for just a little while, she would happily do so, even though that meant not seeing Lottie for even longer.

Cate also wondered if Uriel would try to take her away again if he found her, or if he'd give into his dark urges and simply kill her. She could never really know for sure how he'd react to her betrayal, so remained patient. She waited for the day to come when she and her secret family could be together again, regardless of her gut-wrenching desire to be with them.

In the meantime, she busied herself with her new role alone atop Hell's throne, and revelled in her new almighty strength. Cate welcomed the immense power with ease, and made a commitment to always respect the sacred gift that'd somehow found its way to her. She'd already started to enjoy the control she had over the dark dominion, and finally felt as though she had control over herself and her destiny at long last.

***

A few more years passed by, and Cate ruled Hell with natural strength and skills that no one had ever thought possible in one so young. The stronger, darker power had possessed her entirely, and even she continued to be surprised by her extra strengths and abilities. Dylan was her chief adviser and kept her grounded, remaining her best friend and protector even after her transition. She was by her side day and night, and never blocked her thoughts to the Dark Queen. Dylan was always honest whenever Cate would ask for her opinion or help, brutally so at times, but it was exactly what she needed.

Cate knew she could trust her with the revelation about Lottie's existence, and when the day came that she felt her daughter come of age on Earth, she knew the next full moon would be the right time to finally visit them. She and Dylan would go together, and Cate was sure Lottie would return with them. Her child belonged in Hell with her family, and Cate hoped she wouldn't need much persuasion when the time came.

Lottie's beacon called to her strongly through the divide between their worlds, and she knew it was time to act at long last. She refused to believe in anything other than a future in which she and her three children would be together.

"I need to speak to you," Cate said quietly to Dylan when she sat at the top of the new council table. "In private," she added, and stared into her hazel eyes as she read her friend's quizzical thoughts.

"Of course, your majesty," the witch replied, bowing her head respectfully as she addressed the Dark Queen. Dylan was always sure to show the highest regard to her mistress in the company of others, but had always been allowed to speak freely when they were alone. Cate had wanted a true friend around to talk things through with, and Dylan was the only one she could be sure would never betray that trust.

The pair stood, and Cate said her goodbyes to the demons and witches she'd summoned to discuss the possible espousal of her twins to the two youngest children of Devin and Serena. However, Cate didn't like the idea of forcing them into a relationship like her master had done with her and Devin so many years before. She wanted them to choose for themselves, and while the pairings made sense, she'd commanded that it would ultimately be their own decision who they decided to marry. Her vote was the only one that mattered, and she was glad the decision had been made. There would never be betrothals like that again during her reign.

Luna could be a good match with Corey, even the Queen could see that, but she stood by her verdict. It was also argued that Blake could be perfectly matched with their fiery daughter, Leyla. The pair of them possessed strong wills and powerful natures, and although it was thought by some that perhaps the pairing might prove too destructive, Cate disagreed. She'd already seen them together and heard their thoughts, and knew there was already a strong kinship between them. With the right encouragement, she guessed Blake and Leyla might be the perfect balance for one another, and that they could bring out each other's best qualities.

That just left Braeden, their eldest son. He was a free spirit who, while a quiet boy, had hopes and dreams beyond the imagination of anyone else around him in their dark world. He daydreamed constantly, and Cate would often listen in, enjoying his creative vision and open mind. She couldn't help but wonder if he and Lottie might be the perfect fit for one another in the future, but knew that topic would come up in due course. But first, there were much more pressing matters to figure out.

"I have an issue with my daughter," Cate told Dylan once they were alone in her chambers.

"With Luna?" Dylan asked, looking up at her with a puzzled expression.

"No. My *other* daughter," Cate clarified, reaching over to place a hand on her friend's shoulder as she spoke. Dylan's mouth dropped open slightly as she took in what the Queen had just said. Cate smiled back at her friend, listening in on her thoughts as she tried to work out how, when and where. "She lives on Earth," Cate said, replying automatically to Dylan's thoughts. "With Harry," she added with a wide grin.

"Oh really?" Dylan finally managed to say in response, her lip curling at the edges. Cate listened in on her wondering if Harry was the father, but she didn't dare ask.

Her eyes darkened, but not in anger. A combination of fear and panic flooded her core, but she knew she had to reveal all. It was important that Dylan knew the whole truth in order for her to understand the complexities of the situation, and to properly be able to help in bringing her child home safely.

She pointed her index finger skywards, shaking her head, but didn't dare say the words aloud. "Oh really?" repeated Dylan, her voice a quiet whisper.

The playfulness was gone, and the enigmatic witch's face paled as she quickly came to the realisation of the girl's heritage. It suddenly hit home. Cate's words was true, and after all her years of secrecy, she was finally able to tell her most trusted friend the truth about her time spent exiled on Earth.

She spent a while explaining how everything had happened, and how she and Harry had spend those few blissful years together. It felt good to reveal all, like a heavy burden had finally been lifted from her shoulders. Cate was ready to face the truth, and couldn't wait to see them both again.

CHAPTER FORTY-FIVE

As the next full moon rose on Earth, Cate, Dylan, and a now up-to-speed Alma landed silently at the end of a short garden path. It led to a small house in the old British town of Winchcombe. The town was situated directly on the ley lines, and just as Cate had told Harry to many years ago, he'd continued to live in the towns along the ancient powerful lines during his time without her.

Harry had harnessed the ley lines' energy and combined it with the knowledge she'd given him of runes and ancient wards to keep the child of both light and darkness safe from discovery. She'd purposely given him wards and talismans that kept all light beings away, yet only the dark beings that sought to harm the child would be kept out by their magical barriers. Those from the darkness who knew of her existence and wished her no harm could easily sense Lottie's little flame. That clever detail had only been for Cate to know, and use to her advantage when the time came— and it was finally that time. She didn't need it, though. It was Cate's strong link to Lottie that'd helped them find her so easily.

And so, there she stood, staring out into the dark night, and she could sense her daughter inside the house that stood just metres away. Lottie was so close, and yet there was a part of Cate that was afraid to go to her. She was convinced that Lottie would be angry at her, hurt or maybe even ashamed of her mother for having left her without a word when she was just a small child. She would explain all in due time, but she still feared that Lottie might not give her the chance to try, and knew she deserved it after leaving her without a mother all those important years. She was also very aware they had only the two days the moon would allow her to be on Earth. There wasn't much time in which to convince Lottie to return home with them, but she had to. Only then would they truly be safe from the angels' reach. Cate gave herself a mental kick up the backside, and stepped forwards.

Dylan and Alma followed her lead and walked slowly behind their Queen as she moved towards the small townhouse. After a sharp knock on the door from Cate, it was quickly opened, and she expected to see her daughter on the other side. Instead, a middle-aged woman answered, her head peering around the door expectantly. She eyed the trio cautiously, struggling to see them properly in the dim light. Her grey-blonde hair was in rollers pinned to her scalp, and she wore a long nightdress that reminded Cate of the ones her grandmother used to wear when she would visit her as a child.

The woman pulled her fleecy robe tighter around her, as though a cold draft suddenly caught her by surprise, and a shiver ran down her spine as she continued to look at them expectantly.

The three women hadn't aged themselves, so were much younger looking than the woman staring at them from the doorway, when in fact Cate guessed she was probably double her age. She'd opted to look just as she had the last time Lottie had seen her though, despite knowing it would confuse her somewhat at first, but how it was necessary in ensuring she listened to the stranger aspects of her heritage.

"Can I help you?" the woman eventually asked, looking out at the women who were shrouded in darkness on the front step, and Cate could tell that she felt uncomfortable. She tried to read the woman's thoughts, and wanted to figure her out before she spoke, but was having trouble. She knew her fraught emotions had to be playing havoc with her powers, and that she needed physical contact in order to make a better connection, but didn't want to scare the woman by trying to touch her.

She concentrated harder and heard a name, *Lola*, as it flittered across her consciousness. Cate guessed that might be the new name Lottie was going by there, but couldn't be sure. She decided to give the friendly approach a try, and failing that she was willing to just barge in if she needed to—nothing was going to come between her and her child.

"We're looking for Lola, please," Cate said, hoping she was right about the name.

"It's late, she's up in her room," the woman replied curtly. "We've got a busy day tomorrow, maybe you should come by another time," she added, and went to close the door, but was stopped when a young woman's voice called to her from an upstairs room of the house.

"Who is it, Jenny?" the voice asked, and Cate could hear soft footsteps approaching the front door. Her heart fluttered as she heard the voice's owner approaching, and knew it was Lottie. The light above the three dark beings then flicked on, illuminating the porch at last. The woman still blocking the door—presumably Jenny—gasped when she looked properly at Cate, and stepped back, clearly shocked and surprised.

Lola, who was quite clearly Lottie, then arrived at the hallway and pulled the door open fully, taking in the sight before her. She gasped and her hand went to her mouth in shock as she stared into the face of her long lost mother.

Dylan and Alma both jumped as they saw her and stifled their own mutters of amazement upon seeing Cate's double as she stood there before them. She was clearly the child that neither had known about until just a couple of days before, yet was unmistakably their Queen's daughter.

"Mum?" Lottie asked quietly, and she had tears in her green eyes as she reached out and pulled her into a tight hug. "Are you really here?" she asked, her voice a muffled sound from within their embrace. Cate read her thoughts, sensing that Lottie was wondering if she might be imagining her mother's return at long last, and she knew she had to put her mind at ease before saying anything else.

"I'm really here, my darling," was all she could reply, hugging her back tightly. She took in her daughter's memories as she held on to the contact with her, smiling as the pictures of Lottie and Harry's life together flooded her mind. She was happy, healthy and had been well looked after by her father over the years, just as Cate had always trusted he would.

"I think this means we can come in now, don't you?" Dylan asked the still bewildered Jenny as she stepped forward. "Where's her father?" she added, cocking her eyebrow as she took in the woman before her. Jenny took a step back and went into the hallway, ignoring Dylan's last question as she headed back into the house, seemingly bewildered by the sight before her.

The enraptured mother and daughter pulled away from their

embrace at last, and then Cate followed Lottie into the living room. She sat next to her on the brown leather sofa, and the pair took each other in silently as they gazed into each other's identical emerald eyes.

Dylan followed them and sat on the couch opposite, drinking in the wonderful sight before her with a wide smile, while Alma ushered the still bemused Jenny into the kitchen. She silently promised Cate via her thoughts that she'd work her magic on the human woman while they were alone, and the Dark Queen knew her high priestess had come prepared with sleeping potions and memory cleansers in case of such events, so let her get straight to it.

"Dad's at the hotel," Lottie told Dylan after a few quiet moments, but the witch's confused expression spurred the girl to tell her more. "Urm...he and Jenny are getting married there tomorrow," she added, not looking at her mother as she spoke. "He went there to get everything ready, and then he's staying the night so he doesn't see the bride before the ceremony. You know, in case of bad luck," Lottie added, an awkward look on her still happy face.

Dylan snorted, and then did her best to compose herself when she saw the forlorn look on Cate's face, a look she'd tried to hide, but Dylan knew her far too well.

"Which hotel? Where is it?" she then asked, and Lottie told her, giving the witch directions to the Manor House Hotel on the outskirts of the small town. Dylan was then careful to pretend she was going out to her car to head off to the hotel, but instead teleported away as soon as she was outside.

"Where have you been, Mum?" Lottie asked Cate when they were alone, a serious look on her beautiful face, and she took her hand. There was a strange power that seemed to come from her mother's touch, and she knew that something unusual was going on, but was eager to hear her story at long last. Lottie could tell right away that her mother hadn't aged at all since she'd last seen her nearly nine years before, and she could sense the darkness she'd brought with her into their home, too. It was as if a shadow had descended, but she didn't fear it. In fact, she was drawn to it. Lottie didn't know how she felt all those things, but she somehow knew them all to be very real.

"I had to go back to my home for a while," Cate answered her, choosing her words carefully. "I had no other choice."

"And, where is your home? You can tell me," Lottie said, looking into her eyes as she silently pleaded for answers. Cate knew she was already a curious and intuitive young woman, and already felt both her presence and power deep within her. Lottie's untapped strength and dark force reminded her of her own at the same age, and Cate knew she had to be honest.

"Hell," she said, keeping her eyes on Lottie's to let her know she wasn't kidding. "I had to return there in order to keep you safe. You had to be hidden from both my kind and from others who may wish to hurt you, or use you for their own selfish means. Harry and I loved each other once, and he promised to keep you safe for me." Cate's cheeks blushed slightly as she thought of him, and she looked down at her hands. She hated that he'd somehow managed to move on without her, and part of her wanted to storm into that kitchen and rip Jenny's throat out for daring touch what belonged to her.

"Why? Who would want to hurt me?" Lottie asked, seemingly unfazed by Cate's revelation, and her question pulled her out of her sad reverie.

"Well, the latter is unfortunately a conversation that'll need to wait for another time, my darling," Cate told her, reaching up and stroking Lottie's dark, curly hair with her hand before she continued. "But the other one is a slightly easier question to answer. My husband at the time of your conception was Lucifer, the Devil. He's not your father though Lottie, and I knew he would kill you if he ever knew you existed. He and I are no longer together, so I can finally come back to you without worrying about your safety," she told her honestly. Lottie's eyes grew wide, a hundred questions filling her mind following Cate's explanation.

"How do you know that I'll be safe now?" she finally asked, her voice trembling slightly as she feared the repercussions of her mother's betrayal of her ex-husband.

"Because I'm the leader of Hell now, Lottie. I am the Devil. It's only because of this change in leadership that I can come here and be with you today," she told her with a grin before she added. "And I want to bring you back home with me where you belong."

Lottie stared open-mouthed at Cate as her words sunk in. She believed every word though, having suspected for a while that she was no ordinary girl. The change of name and new home every few years had been enough of a clue, but there had been more. She'd found the runes and warding symbols her father had used on their home a while ago, and had been researching their meanings in secret ever since. Harry completely refused to answer her questions, so had avoided the subject whenever Lottie had tried to bring it up, advising her to drop it and forget all about them. But she hadn't been able to.

Cate eavesdropped on her thoughts, and marvelled at her intuitiveness. Lottie also wondered about Hell, and what it'd be like to go and live there with her mother. She was scared, but knew that she wanted to be with her. She wanted know the real story of her life and learn the truth about her long lost family. Lottie could feel the powerful buzz that came from her mother's touch, and felt it course through her as she deliberated.

She also knew she wanted more. She wanted to know what that power might mean for her, too, and let her mind wander, thinking of the power she might already have inside of her and hoping that it might be utilised and controlled. "Yes, of course," Cate said, replying to her daughter's thoughts without even thinking. "You have your own powers already, and can be taught to harness them. You'll thrive in Hell, and then we can spend eternity together where it's safe."

"Whoa," Lottie replied in a breathy whisper, astounded at both the prospect of having powers of her own, and the realisation that her mother had just read her mind.

***

Dylan reached the Manor House Hotel in seconds and went straight inside. She found the event hall immediately, and burst through the doors with a powerful shove that sent them flying open.

"I object!" she shouted, laughing at her own joke as she made her strange entrance, while everyone inside stopped what they were doing and stared at her in annoyance.

Harry was stood over by the makeshift altar, talking and

laughing with another tall man as they drank a beer together. He turned to look at the rude intruder, and nearly dropped the pint glass in his hand when he realised who stood before him in the doorway. He put the drink down onto a nearby table and spilled the amber fluid across the wood, apologising profusely, but left the mess behind him as he made his way over to Dylan. The shock on his face at seeing her again after such a long time was utterly clear as he approached, and he blinked as though gazing upon an apparition, rather than the woman he knew was actually an immortal witch.

"What are you doing here, Dylan?" Harry asked, remembering her true name from Cate's long talks of her and their relationship all those years before. She didn't look any different than she had back when he knew her, and it was strange seeing her after such a long time.

"I came to get you. Duh," she answered, making him smile. She was still the same fun natured free spirit she'd always been, and Harry shook his head jokingly, the glimmer of hope igniting in his chest at what her presence might mean. "Wow, you got old," she added, giving him a cheeky smile before she wrapped her arms around her old friend and hugged him tightly.

Harry hugged her back, feeling confused and surprised to see her, but he hoped it might mean her best friend was finally on her way as well.

"Where's Cate?" he asked when they pulled back from their embrace, looking down into her eyes with a shy smile.

"She's at your house, with Lottie," she told him, raising a dark eyebrow at him.

"You know about Lottie?" he asked, jumping when she spoke his daughter's real name.

"I do now. She's here to take her home, Harry," Dylan replied, and his face dropped. His expression turned somewhat fearful as the prospect of losing his daughter hit him like a hot poker to the chest. "Come with me?" she then asked him, a warm, gentle smile on her lips as she took in his sad face. "She'll explain everything."

Dylan and Harry arrived back at the house a few minutes later, finding his fiancée Jenny asleep at the kitchen table thanks to Alma's strong potions. Lottie sat curled up with her mother on the sofa, with the powerful Dark Queen's arms wrapped around her child as she cradled her in her lap. They were talking quietly, Cate eager to hear all about Lottie's school, love life, dreams and hopes.

She climbed up from the chair, sensing Harry immediately as he and Dylan came in the house. Cate greeted him with a huge smile when he walked into the living room; taking in the face she'd dreamed about for years before saying or doing anything.

He was much older, and seemed to have aged so much more since she'd last seen him. His hair was almost completely grey, and Harry had kept his good looks and fresh-faced charm, but had much more of a distinguished look to him now.

The air between them was thick, and neither spoke as they moved forward to greet each other. Harry had a smile on soft lips as he gazed lovingly at her, and neither seemed to know what to say. A moment of awkwardness hung threateningly in the air, but Cate pushed it away and stepped forward again. She moved to within inches of his face, and then immediately took his mouth in hers.

She pushed Harry back against the wall behind and he responded to her without hesitation. He kissed her back with a deep longing, and finally allowed the love to come pouring out that he'd tried so hard to suppress since she'd left. He'd never stopped loving her, but had forced his broken heart to try, and in that moment, it all came rushing back.

"Let's give them a minute, shall we?" Dylan said to a shell-shocked Lottie before leading her out into the kitchen, and the young girl nodded.

Cate continued to pin Harry to the wall with her strong body, their kisses deepening and becoming more passionate. She could sense how much he'd missed her, and read his thoughts as they kissed. His memories and thoughts of her came flooding back through his mind, and his desperate desire for her took control of him all over again. Harry still loved her with all his heart, Cate knew for sure, and he'd been lonely without her. He'd missed her terribly, despite having had her doppelgänger there to keep him company. If anything, she now knew that'd made it harder. She pulled back, staring into his deep blue eyes for a moment. They were the eyes she'd dreamed about for years, that she'd fantasised about countless times while they'd been forced apart.

"Well, hello to you too," Harry said in a whispered voice that faltered with excitement, and a coy smile curled at his lips as he took in the dark goddess standing before him.

Cate couldn't help but smile back. A giggle escaped her red lips as she thought how their greeting must've looked to Lottie and Dylan.

"So, you're getting married tomorrow?" Cate then asked Harry with a serious edge to her tone as she gazed up at him. Her powerful body was still pinned against his, and she didn't want to let him go, despite knowing they needed to talk.

"Well, recent events *might* have affected that decision somewhat," he replied. Harry watched with a grin as she backed away a few steps and sat down on the sofa. He stepped forward, looking down into her sad face, and needed her to understand, even if it meant hurting her. "I was so lonely without you, Cate. Then Jenny came along, and she made me smile for the first time in years. She's a good woman and, besides—I'm an old man now. I can't have a twenty year old on my arm anymore," A dry laugh escaped his lips, but there was no smile in his eyes.

"I know," she replied, reading his thoughts. She really did, and he was telling her the truth about Jenny. No matter how much she wanted to hate her, she seemed to have been good for both him and Lottie the past couple of years. "I can't stay here anyway, Harry," Cate told him, peering up at him from the couch. "I'm bound by the full moon now."

He looked down at her, clearly confused by the moon's restrictions on her.

"But I thought you could stay as long as you wanted? The moon thing's just for him, isn't it?" he asked, a hint of jealousy in his voice when he spoke of Lucifer, and she had to smile. Harry then moved toward the sofa to join her.

"That was before. I've changed. I'm not the same woman I once was," she said, staring at her hands.

"Well, what are you then? Where's your husband?" he demanded, needing answers.

"Ex-husband. He's gone, I'm the Devil now," Cate told him calmly, and Harry flopped down next to her on the couch with a thud. He was grateful to have had a seat close by when she'd dropped that little bombshell. "Lucifer isn't in control anymore. I took the throne from him," she added, looking across at Harry with a smile. "I'm finally free." Tears welled in her eyes. It was the first time she'd admitted it to anyone, but in all honesty she was glad he'd forced her hand.

"You control the entire underworld?" he asked her incredulously, smiling back at her. She read his mind and knew that he was in shock, but also in awe of her. He was impressed by the strength and power she'd encompassed, but wasn't surprised. He'd always known she could do it.

"Yes, but as well as that, I control every other dark being. I'm their ruler now, and what I say goes," she told him, her smile widening.

"Oh, so will Lottie be safe in Hell now?" Harry asked, suspecting that although their reunion had been wonderful, Lottie was Cate's real reason for returning.

"Yes, she can now take her place at my side with Blake and Luna," she replied, watching Harry as he swallowed hard at the prospect of being left alone. After dedicating his life to raising the beautiful child he'd sworn to protect—the child he loved with all his heart—he couldn't imagine being without her. Harry could already feel his grief for Lottie creeping in, threatening to drag him down into a dark despair. The heartache for Cate he'd pushed aside for years rose up in him too, and he struggled to force it back down, suddenly feeling overwhelmed.

"I wish you could come with us, Harry. We'll have to wait until your time comes, if you know what I mean?" she asked, and he nodded, knowing that Cate was talking about his death. "I can claim your soul, mark it now as belonging to me, and then when you pass on from this world it will automatically go to Hell?" Cate offered weakly. "But, I cannot guarantee anything. You would just be another human soul, technically nothing more than a toy for the demons, witches, and warlocks to play with. You'd need to prove yourself worthy and then climb the ranks."

Harry couldn't hide his foreboding fear at the sheer thought of that future coming true. He shook his head. Every inch of him felt defeated and lost.

"Just take her and go," he replied, slumping back in the chair and not daring to look at Cate as the tears welled in his own eyes.

CHAPTER FORTY-SIX

"I have an idea, your highness," Alma's voice filtered into Harry's living room. She poked her head around the corner and took in the sight of her all-powerful Queen looking into the face of the human man beside her. He was her soulmate, and the man she truly loved with all her heart, Alma could see it so clearly now. She'd always wondered why Cate and Lucifer had been so distant when they'd returned from their exile on Earth. There was no disguising that he'd been disgusted with her for letting Uriel seduce her again, and he'd confided in Alma that he couldn't get over her betrayal a second time, despite knowing she'd been forced. Alma had always assumed that Cate had felt ashamed for her part in the seduction, and she'd never even considered that the Dark Queen might've fallen in love with someone else during their time of separation and powerless existence.

"Let's hear it, Alma," Cate said, desperate to hear any ideas the powerful witch might have.

"A demon could sire him, my Queen," she offered, sending her thoughts to Cate about an ancient ritual in which a demon would participate in a blood-sharing ceremony with a human. They would share their dark essence with them, effectively killing the human and turning them into a new demon. They'd bypass the centuries of torture human souls normally had to endure before they reached the same position—effectively jumping the queue. Lucifer had outlawed the ritual many years before, mostly because he hadn't wanted demons to be created so easily. Part of what he considered their essential makeup had been the pain and suffering they'd endured at the hands of their peers since death. It made them hateful, and far more susceptible to become puppets for his dark whims. He also preferred to choose worthy souls himself for the honour of a place in the demonic hierarchy rather, than to allow human candidates to cross over into the dark ranks.

Cate took it all in for a moment, and jumped up from the sofa, understanding immediately.

"Yes!" she cried, excitement bubbling up inside of her at the sheer thought of Harry completing the transition and becoming a demon. "We'd need to find a willing demon to donate their blood for the ritual, and of course they'd be responsible for him from then onwards. But this way he could come home with us and stay in Hell forever," she said to Alma, who nodded in agreement and smiled.

Cate peered down at the still forlorn man before her, hoping he would give her one more yes. She wanted him to choose to share a dark and terrible existence with her over a human life with Jenny. It might be selfish to want it, but she didn't care. "If you do this, you could be by my side for eternity," Cate offered, looking to Harry for his understanding.

His thoughts told her that he was willing; that he'd do anything it took to be with her and Lottie, and she carried on. "We'll have to turn you into a demon. You would then join my demonic ranks and serve me along with the other demons, but in private we could be together. It might have to be in secret at first, but eventually you'll climb higher, and then we can make our union public." She blushed as she contemplated a long and happy life with her soulmate by her side at last, a life she'd never thought was possible until Alma had jogged her memory.

The demonic rituals had been forbidden for many years, but Cate knew she could finally change that. She had the throne, and therefore the power to alter the rules for her benefit.

"And, I just so happen to know of a demon who owes you big-time, my Queen," interjected Alma one more time. "Perhaps this is the perfect way in which Berith might compensate for his past misdemeanours?" she asked, bowing when her mistress gave her an approving nod, and then leaving her and Harry to talk some more.

Cate climbed down onto her knees and perched before where he still sat on the sofa. He'd stayed quiet, his head bowed as he thought about all that she'd said, trying to make some sense of her offer. She reached up and put her hands on his knees, drawing his attention back to her. Harry gazed into her beautiful eyes intently, mesmerised by the powerful woman he still loved so very much.

"I love you, Harry," she told him with a warm, shy smile. He smiled back at her and laid his own hands over hers while she still knelt before him.

"I love you too, Cate. I always have, and I always will," he replied, caressing her hands in his before stroking them up her arms to her face, holding it in his palms. "I cannot ever imagine a time or place in which I won't love you. I'm willing to do whatever it takes," he promised, kissing her red lips softly. Cate deepened the kiss, grabbing Harry and she thrust her hands into his hair and pulled him closer. She was ready to let herself open up again, and finally felt as though her future might not be quite so lonely as she'd once thought.

"This is the only way we can be together. It isn't easy, and you'll no longer be human afterwards," she told him again, making sure he understood the repercussions of what they were about to do. "You'll be a demon, but it'll mean we can be together, forever. You'll be able to alter your age, be young again. Be with me?"

"Yes, I had already made up my mind, of course it's a yes," Harry added to his earlier promises, but it was all she needed to hear. He knew, remembering well the stories she'd once told him about free will. Harry remembered how object of the powerful being's affections had to give themselves over to them willingly, and say the words aloud. He had done it without hesitation, and meant every word. He was ready to do whatever it took to be with Cate. Having lived without her the past nine years had been torturous and had proven to him how he didn't want to be without her ever again.

A quick click of Cate's fingers bought a beaten and bedraggled man into the living room with her and Harry. He was bowing low, concealing his face, but the man eagerly stood to greet his Queen after a few moments. Harry couldn't hide his disgust at seeing Berith bound, beaten and silenced so horrifically. He was far removed from how he'd been that day he'd met him at the music festival.

With a flick of her index finger, Cate removed the magical thread that sealed the demon's mouth shut and healed his tongue with an effortless, silent commandment. Berith brought his hands up, touching his face gently to check on his healed lips before eventually speaking. He fell to his knees and bowed before her, looking up at Cate adoringly as he spoke.

"My Queen, I am shocked and awed by your mercy. How might I serve you?" he asked, looking at Harry briefly, but focussing his every ounce of attention and admiration on Cate.

"I need you to sire a new demon for me, Berith," she told him calmly, and he remained on his knees before her. He couldn't help but glance again at Harry, knowing immediately what she wanted from him. The ancient demon nodded and raised his arms, offering her the demonic blood in his veins before lowering his head in submission.

"Of course, your majesty. Anything for you," he said.

"That's the right answer, well done," she told him with a smile.

Alma returned from the kitchen with a dagger and metal bowl at the ready. She slit the demon's wrists, one at a time, allowing each to gush black-red blood into the awaiting vessel. When enough had been gathered, Berith slumped back against the wall and cradled his arms to his body while the wounds magically healed.

Harry was horrified, and his mouth hung open as he took in the gory scene around him. Alma said nothing, but gathered up her things and went back in to the kitchen with the blood, in search of Dylan with whom she'd combine their knowledge and magic to put together a spell inciting the ritual's ancient power.

Cate stood in the centre of the small living room, still standing there from when she'd summoned Berith to Earth. She regarded the pale demon with no mercy in her stare, or a hint of regret for almost bleeding him dry, but Harry felt terribly for him, and wondered just what Berith had done to deserve her wrath.

"This fucking rat," she suddenly shouted, pointing to Berith, and making Harry jump in his seat. "He's the one who told Lucifer all about you and Lottie. He was ready to kill you both for the love of his old master. I took the throne thanks to him, my hand being forced by his betrayal. Do not pity him for even a second longer," she bellowed, and the walls seemed to shake with the sound. Her eyes then turned black as she peered down at him.

Cate sat down next to Harry on the sofa and put her head in her hands, her anger vibrating the air around her as she sat and tried to compose herself. Berith stayed silent, having curled up in a ball as she spoke, as though shielding himself from her. The fear in him showed on his face as he continued to stare at her feet, while Harry looked at them both in shock. He wondered how she'd thwarted Lucifer, and how much she'd had to change in order to take his ancient power from him. The Cate he knew would never have hurt another unnecessarily, and Harry trusted that she was still the same now that she'd come out the other side. He believed in her, and told her so via his thoughts.

Cate calmed down, and she ignored the weak demon in the corner as she peered into the warm eyes of her lover apologetically. She reached up, taking Harry's cheek in her hand, and then planted a kiss on his lips. He kissed her back, giving in to his need for her again. Harry wasn't afraid of her, and she was glad, having been worried her outburst might've scared him.

"We need to tell Lottie the truth first," Harry said when they broke away, and Cate knew he was right. She nodded and kissed him again, relishing in the feel of his mouth on hers for a few moments longer.

"Yuk, you two at it again?" Lottie said, joking with them as she came back in from the kitchen with a broad smile. She looked over at Berith in the corner, but quickly turned away. She realised that he must be where the blood had come from she'd just seen the witches working with in the kitchen, but didn't want to enquire as to how or why. Cate bound him again in an instant, an unspoken order demanding that the demon to stay silent and still until she released him again. He didn't even try to fight her command, and she was glad to see he was making progress at last.

"We need to talk," she said as she climbed up from the couch, Harry's hand firmly in her own. Lottie could tell it was important, and nodded, silently letting her mother know to lead the way.

The three of them headed out into the back garden, and having Harry's hand in hers bought Cate a great deal of comfort, as if she felt at home in his presence. "There's more to our story, Lottie. You need to know the full truth before you can truly decide which path you want to go down. We both need you to know," Cate said, looking to Harry as she spoke. The three of them sat down in the chairs by the small wooden garden table and stared at each other for a moment. Harry wanted to be the one to tell her, Cate could read it in his thoughts, so she stayed quiet and let him take the lead.

"Lottie," he said, looking at her intensely through the darkness. "I've taken care of you since the day you were born, and I'll always be here for you, as whatever you want me to be. However..." He hesitated, but took a deep breath and forced himself to continue. "I'm not your real father." He held his breath as he waited for her response.

"I know," Lottie replied. She reached forward to take Harry's hand in her own. "I think I've always known."

"How?" Cate asked, both confused and worried how she could've possibly known.

"I don't know, I just feel it. I always have," Lottie said, her thoughts turning to her friend Claudia and the times she'd spent at her house after school and on the weekends. Claudia's parents were devout Christians. They'd once told the girls about the terrible battles that'd raged between Heaven and Hell. Lottie had been scared stiff, never having heard much about God and the Devil before because Harry had continued to raise her as a strict atheist. Claudia had assured her there was nothing to worry about. She'd said it was all old tales and scripture that people like her parents used to scare their children onto the straight and narrow path of righteousness.

Lottie couldn't help but wonder though, and the stories had played on her mind. She'd then decided to look into it all further and had used her free time at school to do some research on the different religions and prophecies, as well as the historical evidence behind their claims.

Cate could sense that Lottie was well educated on both the good and evil sides of the story, and she'd somehow suspected for a while that she was more than just a normal human girl. She'd eventually found an old book in the library, a supposedly fictional story telling of a child born out of half darkness and half light, and who was doomed to hide their true nature for all time and wander the Earth alone and in fear. The novel was just an elaborately fictionalised version of the Christian bible, and Cate realised that Lottie had almost figured out her own story all by herself. She'd even felt a strong kinship with the last child of Heaven, and the only other of her kind—Jesus.

"I would never let that happen to you, Lottie. Harry wouldn't either," Cate assured her, and Lottie nodded, knowing her mother had read her thoughts again.

"I know, and that's why I waited. I always trusted Harry, knowing that you'd never have left me with him unless you knew I was safe. I never told anyone about my suspicions. In all honesty, I thought they'd throw me in the nuthouse for thinking up something so crazy, so I just ignored my fears and pushed it all away."

"So, do you suspect you know who your father is then?" Harry asked, not knowing what psychic exchange the two women had just shared, but he was desperate to finish off their tough conversation.

"Yes," Lottie answered, looking skywards, and Cate gasped. A quiet sob then escaped her uncontrollably.

"Has he ever come to you?" she asked, scared to know the answer, but needing to ask the question just in case.

"No, Mum. Never," Lottie assured her, smiling warmly. "And even if he did, I would always choose you," she added, calming her worried mother at last.

Cate smiled back at her and she sensed herself opening up to Lottie. Her *expression* started coming through uncontrollably, and it gave her daughter a deeper sense of her love and emotion through the strange and silent connection.

Lottie gazed back at Cate, staring into her face as she basked in the warmth that flowed into her with a broad, loving smile. "And anyway, I don't need another father, because I already have the perfect one right here," she added, making Harry smile for the first time since before they'd come out into the garden.

Alma and Dylan then joined the small family on the dimly lit patio area.

"Everything's ready, your majesty," Alma told Cate, bowing as she addressed her mistress.

"Sorry Harry, but we kinda had to mess up your living room," Dylan added, shrugging her shoulders, but there wasn't even a hint of an apology in her playful tone.

"How very dare you?" he cried in response, throwing his hands up in mock disgust and making them all laugh. They each stood and went back inside, ready to begin the dark and scary ritual. Dylan patted Harry on the back as she wandered in behind him, thinking that it was going to be fun having him around again.

Inside, a giant pentagram had been drawn on the wooden floor in black paint, and the furniture had been discarded in readiness for the rite of passage Harry would have to take in order to make the transition.

"You don't need to stay, Lottie. You can go and wait with Jenny if you'd like? Don't wake her up, though. Alma has wiped her memory, so she won't know who you are," Cate told her, unsure if Lottie would be scared for Harry's safety, but she shook her head and stood firm.

"I'm not going anywhere," she replied, making her father smile. Cate understood, and held onto her hand as they took their places in the corner of the living room. She just had to let the witches and Berith do their magic, overseeing the ritual rather than being part of it. Cate released the demon from his invisible restraints, and he crawled over to the pentagram where he took a seat inside of it. Berith instinctually knew what was expected of him, and was she was pleased he was ready to serve his Queen however she saw fit. His days of going against Cate were well and truly over now, and she read his thoughts with a satisfied smile.

Harry joined him, kneeling inside the pentagram tentatively. Berith sat opposite him inside the ancient symbol, and the demon's drawn blood sat in a large glass between the two of them.

"Are you ready?" Alma asked Harry, standing before them outside the pentagram.

"Yes," he answered, and despite his fear he knew he'd never been surer of anything in his life.

Alma reached down and grabbed his right wrist, slicing it open with a quick swipe of a dagger she held firmly in her hand, and then she fed his blood directly to Berith. The demon drank it down eagerly, holding onto Harry's arm as he sucked on his open vein. Alma looked up at Cate before she carried on, who nodded, urging her to continue.

"Before the almighty Dark Queen, and in the presence of demons and witches. Do you renounce all other allegiances and pledge your soul to your Mistress, Her Infernal Majesty, Hecate?"

"Yes, I do," Harry replied, woozy from the blood-loss, but still clear and level-headed. Alma then reached back down and took his arm away from the demons mouth, and wrapped his wound quickly in a bandage she'd held at the ready, before lifting the blood-filled cup to his mouth.

"Then drink of your demon, share his blood and become his progeny," she ordered him, and Harry did as she asked. He gulped down the thick liquid as quickly as he could, not stopping to let himself think what was now filling his stomach and coursing through his veins as Alma and Dylan stood over him.

"So mote it be, hail to the Dark Queen," Alma finished the ritual, and then they all repeated the last line, Cate and Lottie included.

Within seconds, Harry started to feel his bones grow heavy and his muscles begin to tighten. He slumped down onto the floor, joined by Berith who grabbed both of his wrists and held them tightly in place. It was essential neither of them left the pentagram during the rest of the ritual, and was glad Berith was doing his job to ensure the ritual worked correctly. A strange and ominous black mist then came up as though out of nowhere and shrouded the pair of them, as if they were inside a dark snow globe that'd just been shaken.

It made it hard to watch them, and difficult to notice the transition, but Cate could see clearly through the haze while Lottie and the witches seemed to be having trouble.

The darkness enveloped Harry. It clung to him and then disappeared as though seeping into his skin. He called out, an incoherent shout, but it wasn't from pain. His cries were from the overwhelming power that surged into him so quickly and forcefully. It engulfed his senses while giving him no respite from the flow of power. It was all or nothing, but he let it infiltrate his body without a fight. The dark power was drawn to him at the behest of the Dark Queen and her witch's focussed ritual, and Cate thought it beautiful as she watched him transform.

Every part of the ritual had its purpose, and worked to alter her soulmate before her very eyes. The demonic blood that now coursed through him was a gift from the higher power, and a symbol of Harry's worthiness. Cate smiled to herself as she saw those dark gifts empower her lover and immortalise him, and she silently promised never to take that power, or him, for granted.

CHAPTER FORTY-SEVEN

A few moments later, the strange dark mist settled, and Harry and Berith stood up inside the pentagram. Cate could sense them, both of them. She felt Berith's usual demonic presence inside her mind, and felt too the manifestation of a new entity, a dark flame emanating from deep within Harry's soul.

The ritual had worked. He was a demon. He'd have to be taught about the demonic world, as well as all about his powers and responsibilities in the coming months. Harry would also need to complete the various initiations to climb the levels of demonic hierarchy and reach the top, but it was Berith's job to prepare him for them. As his demonic master he was expected to teach him and ensure that Harry excelled. Any neglect or bad teaching from his part was punishable by death, if their mistress saw fit. Berith knew he had an epic task ahead of him, but he welcomed the opportunity to win back Cate's affections.

Both demons bowed to her respectfully as she approached. She could already feel Harry growing stronger by the second, the darkness empowering him. She also knew they had no time to waste, and he needed to go to Hell right away and continue his transition.

"Berith," she said, and he looked up at her respectfully.

"Yes, mistress," he replied.

"Take your demon progeny to our realm. I will see you both there in due course," she ordered, and Harry looked up at her too, scared to leave without her and Lottie safely beside him. Cate stepped closer and touched his face gently. He could feel her immense power course through him, and her omnipotence overwhelmed his senses, but he lapped it up. His body savoured her powerful touch. He could see her true form too, and while her usual human-looking self was still there, he could make out the extra-dark matter that seemed to surround her formidable body as Cate stood before him. She was even more beautiful than ever.

Harry's love for her was tenfold following his demonic rebirth, and he wanted nothing more than to serve her, please her, and love her—forever. A true disciple already, Cate had to smile at his instinctual admiration. She stared into his eyes, reading his thoughts as she spoke quietly to her lover.

"This is how it has to be, but just for now. Lottie and I will see you soon, my love. We can truly be together now, Harry, and it will be forever," she told him with a broad smile, laying a soft kiss on his still bloody lips. Lottie joined them in the pentagram, leaning up to give her father a kiss on his cheek. She was proud of him as well, and wanted him to know.

With a click of her fingers, Cate then sent the two demons away but she knew they'd be fine. Despite his previous incarceration, Berith was still a level one demon in the hierarchy of Hell, the highest and most prestigious classification in her dark ranks. She knew it might be a long time before Harry could join his demonic master at the top level, but she would wait for as long as it took, and then she would make him her immortal husband at last.

Harry's initiation would require many tests and challenges before they were complete, but she would do everything in her infinite power to ensure he progressed quickly, and knew that Berith would be an excellent teacher and mentor for him.

Cate also knew that she could depend on and call upon each of them at any time, as well as her other loyal demons such as Leviathan and Beelzebub. They'd fast become some of her most trusted demonic companions, and she knew they would take Harry under their proverbial wings when she asked it of them.

She adored hew strongly she could sense Harry, like a presence deep inside of herself, and a beacon. His was a consciousness she could call to at will, just like any other member of her dark service, however their connection was more potent than any other outside the dark royal family. She could sense that he was already safely in their dominion, his new home, and could even hear his thoughts from afar as Berith began his teachings. Cate felt his soul join her dark ranks, albeit at the bottom of the demonic levels, but it was better than the alternative.

"Mum, is it time for us to go too?" Lottie asked, pulling Cate from her thoughts.

"Yes, if you're ready?" she replied, wanting to check her daughter's wellbeing before doing anything else. Lottie had just witnessed a strange and ominous ritual only minutes after finding out a lot of information about herself and her family. Yet, she seemed absolutely unfazed by it all. Cate read her daughter's mind, and her thoughts were of her new home, the possibilities for her future, and her hopes for what it might be like in Hell, exactly as Cate had desperately hoped they would be. She looked up into her mother's eyes with a knowing smile, aware that she was reading her.

"Yes," Lottie told her decisively, and Cate smiled.

"It'll feel strange at first, as though you can't breathe. The heat and pressure down there are something you'll have to become accustomed to, so don't worry if it feels weird at first. Calm your breathing and stop it. You don't need to breathe there, does that make sense?" she asked, her thoughts immediately turning to when Lucifer had given her the same speech so many years before. How funny that times had changed so dramatically.

"Urm, I think so. I suppose I'll just have to give it a try," Lottie replied, and took her mother's outstretched hand.

Cate held her tight and pulled her daughter away, teleporting them both downwards towards their true home. When they arrived, Lottie gripped her hand tightly. She managed to stay standing as she slowed her panting breath, caught it, and quickly steadied it. Cate was immensely proud of her, and by the time Dylan and Alma teleported to their side, Lottie stood tall and proud. Cate watched as her youngest child looked out at her new home with an excited flutter in her belly. She couldn't wait to start her new life there, the darkness no longer hiding secrets from her. Lottie gazed up at her mother and absorbed her *expression* as she opened it up to her again.

"Welcome home. I suppose I'd better show you around your kingdom, oh and I need to introduce you to your big brother and sister," she told her with a smile, and Lottie grinned back excitedly at her Queen. She held her hand tight again as they headed off towards the dark castle, and knew she'd never look back.

***

Warm sunshine streamed in through the open window. The gentle rays hit the man's cheek as he stirred and started to wake. An extra bright ray of light, invisible to the human eye, came shining in through the opening along with the regular dawn light, and it shone brightly onto the man's bare chest. It filled him, bursting through the bloody layers of skin, muscle and bone, and emanating deep inside. He could feel the light making him stronger, and making him more powerful again.

Uriel sat up in the hospital bed, grateful for the slight return of his powers, but most importantly for his recollection at long last. His memories came back to him like a sharp detonation that'd gone off inside his mind. He groaned, the thoughts of Cate and Lucifer both angering and paining him as they flooded his mind.

The angel then sensed a dark change, a shift of power both in this world and in the other realms he and the angelic council had created so very long ago. It was a perverse altering of the very balance of light and dark powers that he could not control, much to his utter distaste.

"Oh Lottie, what has she done," Uriel sighed, whispering sadly as the awareness hit him of his daughter's existence, and the terrible realisation that he didn't have the power to go to Hell and be with her, or bring her back from her mother's evil realm.

He then began to vanish, rising skywards and teleporting home at last, defeated and alone. He would have his revenge, but first, he was determined to do whatever it took to get back the child who had been so cunningly stolen from him.

The end of book one in the Black Rose series.

About the author

Laura started her writing career putting together short stories and fan fiction, usually involving her favourite movie characters caught up in steamy situations, and wrote her first full length novel in 2013. A self-confessed computer geek, Laura enjoys both the writing and editing side of her journey, and regularly seeks out the next big gadget on her wish list.

She spends her days looking after her two young children and their cocker spaniel Milo, as well as making the most of her free time by going to concerts with her friends, or else listening to rock music at home while writing (a trend many readers may have picked up on in her stories.)

Laura also loves hearing from her fans, and you can connect with her via the following:

www.facebook.com/lauramorganauthor
www.twitter.com/lauram241

If you enjoyed this book, please take a moment to share your thoughts by leaving a review to help promote Laura's work.

Laura Morgan's novels include:

The Black Rose series:
Embracing the Darkness: book #1 in the Black Rose series
A Slave to the Darkness: book #2 in the Black Rose series
Forever Darkness: book #3 in the Black Rose series
Destined for Darkness: book #4 in the Black Rose series
A Light in the Darkness: book #5 in the Black Rose series

And her contemporary romance novels:
Forever Lost
Forever Loved

Laura also writes YA Science Fiction under the alias LC Morgans, with her new novels:
Humankind: Book 1 in the Invasion Days series
Autonomy: Book 2 in the Invasion Day series

Made in the USA
Middletown, DE
11 September 2017